Advance Praise for
Upon This Rock

"Perry has written an elegant, twisty thriller in which a gay couple investigates a mysterious suicide in a scenic Italian hill town. It's not hard to imagine that this book could do for Orvieto what *Midnight in the Garden of Good and Evil* did for Savannah."
—**Armistead Maupin**, author of the internationally acclaimed *Tales of the City*

"*Upon This Rock* is for those readers who love Italy and who love crime fiction. David Perry evokes the spirit of the ancient Italian town of Orvieto, in a 21st-century thriller that takes in several centuries of history."
—**Lucinda Hawksley**. author of *Dickens's Artistic Daughter, Katey*

"The gay *DaVinci Code*, but a lot better."
—Fenton Johnson, Guggenheim Fellow and award-winning author of *The Man Who Loved Birds*; *Scissors, Paper, Rock*; and *At the Center of All Beauty: Solitude and the Creative Life*

"You will not be able to put this book down. It is page-turner from the first sentence until the unexpected twist ending. *Upon This Rock* by David Eugene Perry has everything you could possibly want: intrigue, suspense, history and characters so real they almost jump off the page. If you like mystery, suspense and intrigue, drenched in local Italian history, this is the book for you."
—**Lynn Ruth Miller**, author of *Getting the Last Laugh* and the oldest stand-up comedienne in the world

"This is a wild read. David Perry's ability to build suspense is impressive and the denouement of this thriller will not just surprise you, but literally stun."
—**Erika Atkinson**, author of *Ode to the Castro* and *Miles of Memories*

"You will not find a more exquisite, captivating, well-written first novel than David Eugene Perry's *Upon This Rock*. I was literally hooked from the first chapter. A wonderfully addictive and engrossing story with brilliant characters and an ending that will have you perusing your favorite bookstore looking for Perry's next novel."
—**Dennis Koller**, author of *The Rhythm of Evil*

Upon This Rock

Upon This Rock

A Novel
by David Eugene Perry

Pace Press
Fresno, California

Published by Pace Press
An imprint of Linden Publishing
2006 South Mary Street, Fresno, California 93721
(559) 233-6633 / (800) 345-4447
PacePress.com

Pace Press and Colophon are trademarks of
Linden Publishing, Inc.

cover design by Tanja Prokop, www.bookcoverworld.com
frontispiece image courtesy of Diego Tolomelli
book design by Andrea Reider

The cover image (courtesy Shutterstock) for *Upon This Rock* is a detail from Luca Signorelli's masterpiece, *Last Judgment* (1499–1503) in the Duomo of Orvieto. It is believed that Michelangelo traveled to Orvieto to study these frescoes as inspiration for the famous *The Last Judgment* in the Sistine Chapel in Rome. In this section, the Devil is whispering in the ear of a man who appears to be Jesus, but is in point of fact the Antichrist, a warning to all to not be deceived as Evil can sometimes mask itself as Goodness.

ISBN 978-0-941936-06-4

135798642

Printed in the United States of America
on acid-free paper.

Library of Congress Cataloging-in-Publication Data on file.

DEDICATIONS

For my grandmother who taught me to read...

For my mother: Ego amo te...

For Aunt Helen for lessons in gratitude and patience...

For Aunt Blanche whose smile echoed beauty and music...

For Aunt Margaret for days spun with "Camelot" and "The Sound of Music"—you set my feet on the decks of many ships...

For our friend Tom whose life gave us a new life...

For Felipe and Otis and Anthony...you know

In gratitude for C.S. Lewis (November 29, 1898–November 23, 1963) and The Baroness P.D. James of Holland Park (August 3, 1920–November 27, 2014)

To the Orvietani: friends and friends yet to meet.

And most especially, as with all things, for Alfredo. I love you.

In Memoriam:

Luca Seidita
1981–2010

Prologue

He stood on the cliff and prayed.

Useless, he thought, to turn my mind to God.

Behind him, the evening lights of Orvieto reflected in a million icy crystals. Snow had come early this year. It wasn't yet December.

Below, the road would be deserted. He wondered who would find him. Someone would, of course, and for that he was sorry. What a horrible thing to discover: the body of a reprobate, crushed against the rock and never to see forgiveness. Never to see the face of God. Never to see another sunrise.

It should be beautiful, and he smiled. He had often come here to sit near the altar and wait for the dawn. Tomorrow, its rays would reach out to warm the city across a quilt of virginal frost. He had seen it before, prisms of color in the ice. Like a miracle, it had seemed to him as a child.

No more. No more dawns, no more rainbows, no more miracles.

"Don't!"

He heard the scream, but too late. He had already stepped off the cliff, arms outspread like a cross, and dived for the tombs below.

Part I

CHAPTER I

Death Takes
a Sabbatical

Saturday, November 30, 2013, midday, Orvieto, Italy

"Signora Peg is..."

Marco paused, with juggling hands and bobbing head, seeming to weigh his half hour familiarity with Lee and Adriano.

"...a little eccentric?" Adriano offered.

"Si," Marco exhaled. "Very, very nice but a little *eccentrica*, si."

Lee silently nodded—*Marco, you're a little eccentric too, I think*—smiling in melancholy recollection of one of Brian's favorite anecdotes: "I can imagine what he says about me, because I know what he says about *you!*"

Member of the club? Lee wondered. Couldn't tell yet. The ever-smiling and ruthlessly cheerful Marco certainly threw off the gay vibe: thirty-ish, short-ish, cute-ish, and stylish. But, *prego*, this was Italy. Everyone was always kissing everyone and seemed—even when a bit rumpled, as was Marco—slightly gayish. He had just finished giving them the overview of what would be their home for the next two months, a fifteenth-century-built-but-1980s-renovated apartment building.

"It used to be one huge palazzo for a Renaissance merchant," Marco explained. "But now, it's been divided into three units. The one downstairs is owned by a businessman in Rome, but he's out of the country. The one just upstairs from you has an enormous balcony with an incredible view of *Il Duomo,* the cathedral, but it's...it's ah...empty. But, your place is-a very nice, very nice. Beautiful! So, no neighbors to bother you! You have the whole place to yourself. It's very quiet. Ciao!"

With that, Marco dropped two sets of keys in Adriano's hands. He seemed in a hurry to leave the pair and get back to other beckonings. He also gave them three carefully typewritten pages with instructions on everything from where to shop, where to eat, and when to put out the garbage for pickup (the last being the most complex of all).

"And don't forget, come and check out my restaurant, Café Marco! It's just off the Corso, near Piazza del Popolo. You meet my nonna! Welcome to Orvieto! I love Americans! USA! USA! Ciao! Ciao!"

A concert of ciaos exchanged, Lee and Adriano stood in front of the massive wooden double front doors, regarding their new home as Marco disappeared quickly out of sight down a tortuously curved cobblestoned street. With the exception of a weather-worn plaque above and to the left of the doorway memorializing seven WWII-era partisans from Orvieto, their new home could have been the backdrop for a Renaissance tableau. One expected a Medici banker to pop out at any moment. Lee loved it. He could smell the past lives of the place. A perfect moment. They were alone—well, almost. An elegant gray cat paraded in front of them, purring rather grandly, before stopping to regard them with feline ennui. Then, with a flick of its tail, it continued on toward the center of town.

"Well, here we go," Adriano sighed with a smile. "As Brian used to say, 'Be careful what you wish for.' And here we are!"

"Indeed, here we are."

"Happy birthday, honey. Welcome to your thirties."

"Thanks, stud husband. You'll be here in two years, so don't get cocky. But, right now, you're all the present I want." Lee kissed his husband on the nose, briefly fogging up Adriano's glasses.

"That, and a sabbatical in Italy."

"Exactly, Signor Llata de Miranda," Lee said, loving the sound of his husband's melodically endless names, of which these were only the first two. "You do the honors. It's your continent."

Adriano put the key in the door. With an audible click, the tumbler turned and they were in. "Let's go up."

~

Their residence for the next two months was just off the Piazza della Repubblica and a block from the medieval church of Sant'Andrea—buzzing with activity this afternoon since today was the feast day for the saint, who was perhaps best known for the earthquake fault bearing his name in Adriano and Lee's hometown, San Francisco. Later there would be a special Mass that Lee didn't want to miss. He had once visited the Catholic martyr's tomb in Patras, Greece, when he worked aboard ship during his pre-Adriano days. Plus, Lee always went to church on his birthday. It was a hard tradition to break for someone who once considered the priesthood.

"I think you're a closet priest," Adriano said, as they climbed the marble stairs to their top-floor flat, a repeatedly teasing remark over their ten years together.

Lee, slightly out of breath as they approached step number thirty and leaning against the wall for a moment's rest, replied as he always did: "I'm not a closeted *anything*, as you well know. But once an altar boy, always an altar boy. You should know as a Spaniard. Plus, I love anything ancient, and puzzles. Don't forget puzzles."

Burdened with a name like Lee Fontaine Maury, it was difficult to escape a fondness for tales of times long gone. His history-philia had aided his other hobby, crosswords, an obsession he had shared with Brian. During Lee's youth, no Virginia historical marker had been left unstopped at, no Civil War battlefield or Colonial pilgrimage missed by his mother and grandmother. In point of fact, he was named for two of his father's best friends: Lee (crooked, rich lawyer) and Fontaine (honest, poor lawyer). Maury was his by birth, and to believe his pop (a speculative endeavor at best), he was the direct descendant of renowned oceanographer and Confederate naval officer Matthew Fontaine Maury—a complex and disquieting legacy not uncommon in the South. Armed with the children's book *Pathfinder of the Seas* about his supposed ancestor, Lee had developed a joint fascination with all things nautical and historical, eventually leading him to two years working aboard ship during his late teens after his parents' and grandmother's deaths, events only somewhat anesthetized by a circumnavigation of the globe, but never far below the surface of memory or emotion. There weren't enough waves on earth to wash away such bloody sands.

His first name, he loved; its namesake, he detested. His middle name, he loathed; that uncle, he respected. He never used Fontaine, except on legal documents, and had only heard it uttered during childhood by his mother yelling from the porch when he was late for dinner, had forgotten some household chore or both. "Lee Fon-TAINE Maury!" Of course, now, all of his family was dead. And Brian was dead. Adriano Llata de Miranda was all the family he had left—or needed. He continued climbing, following his husband's more athletic form.

"Appartamento numero sette," Adriano motioned theatrically. "Siamo arrivati."

"How many steps was that?" Lee asked.

"Sessanta-quattro."

Lee gave him a look.

"Sorry, sixty-four. We have arrived."

"I got that much."

The apartment was dark—and chilly—and it took them a while to find the lights. Adriano, more familiar with European electrics, and as usual hungry to figure out anything technical, was the first to succeed.

"Ta-da!"

Like a stage set suddenly brought to life, their refuge presented itself.

"I love it!" Lee almost squealed. Ancient stone walls and sleek Euro-mod furnishings, all chrome and burnished wood. He felt like Goldilocks, just right. A simple but elegantly appointed living room spilled into a dining room. He could just make out the bedroom, with a wooden beamed and vaulted ceiling behind. Good, contemporary art dotted the walls with a smattering of titles in English and Italian competing for space on a large bookcase that took up one complete wall. "It's so, so *Italian.*"

"Watch your head in the kitchen. I almost knocked myself out," Adriano called from the other room. "Let's drop our things and get to the store or we won't have coffee in the morning. Small towns like this shut down quickly, especially in winter."

"OK, just let me do one thing."

Carefully unzipping his backpack, Lee took out a small wooden box, carefully wrapped in the British royal standard.

"Brian." Adriano put his hand on Lee's shoulder.

"Brian," Lee said, kissing his husband's hand. "You're almost home, dear friend." With that, Lee carefully put his mentor's ashes on an empty bookcase shelf next to the sofa. For a moment, he said nothing. "OK, let's go. Just leave the bags inside the door." A few seconds later, they were back on the street. Dusk was rapidly crowding out the day.

"Can't wait to meet the great Peg," said Adriano, pulling up his jacket collar.

"Me neither," agreed Lee, now pondering Marco's reaction to their announced meeting later today with "Lady Peg," the self-styled American expert on Orvieto and a semi-famous writer. Perhaps he was just picking up on local jealousy, now that Marco might be replaced as their go-to contact during Adriano and Lee's stay here in the fortresslike hilltop town of Orvieto. Maybe that's why Marco beat so speedy a retreat after leaving the pair with their keys and apartment instructions. No reason to take it personally, Lee reminded himself (another bit of Brian advice). Marco had just been doing his job. He wasn't supposed to be the temporary expats' new best friend, nor, frankly, did Lee want such newly volunteered entanglements. He wanted to be alone, with Adriano, for two months, to relax, recoup, and rejuvenate after a very hard year. Well, almost alone.

Halfway through their sojourn, Magda was to join them for a well-deserved vacation of her own. She was the one who had found Orvieto for them in the first place. To make sure Lee and Adriano were situated, Magda, with her usual ruthless efficiency, had arranged for the rental company to provide Marco and Peg as first-day greeters to ensure that the couple got settled in. That was their only function. As usual, Magda was pulling international strings from her political perch back at San Francisco City Hall.

"Perhaps Peg's not eccentric," Adriano offered. "Maybe she's just *American*."

Lee laughed. "That could be it. To you Europeans, we Americans are just that, eccentric."

The couple chuckled together as they made their way slowly to the local market in search of supplies. They had briefly flirted with the idea of renting a car for their time in Orvieto, but had voted to be as "off the grid" as possible. Now that they were getting their first real look at Orvieto, their decision was reinforced. Although a few cars did make their way into town, driving about on the summit and parking there were not for the fainthearted. It was a long way down and the streets were, well, *medieval.* For Lee and Adriano, these two months living on the Rock were to be primarily a pedestrian experience.

~

Lee loved watching Adriano's stylish creativity.

"It's pretty PFC, you have to admit," said Adriano, pirouetting with his iPhone camera on panorama mode to get the third such 360-degree vista of the day and using the couple's secret acronym for "pretty effing charming," which seemed to describe everything thus far about Orvieto.

Orvieto was indeed PFC, a picture-postcard-perfect history lesson, perched a few hundred feet up on a stark and threatening butte of volcanic rock. Lee and Adriano's first sight of it had come while riding the train up from Rome's Fiumicino airport earlier that morning. The Rock had looked like a great airship hovering over the Umbrian plain. Now, an afternoon haze of fog separated the town above the cliffs from the farmland below. It appeared as if Orvieto was suspended, a city in levitation, with seemingly no clear way to the top. Created by cataclysmic eruptions eons ago, Orvieto didn't so much dominate the surrounding countryside as *preside* over it with a stone-hewn patience girded by over three millennia of human habitation.

"Wow—it's got everything," Lee marveled, reading from their guidebook. St. Patrick's Well, a wealth of Etruscan art and antiquity, a legendary Italian Renaissance cathedral, and only four thousand people living on the summit. Not too big. Not too small. Just right. As usual, Magda had made perfect arrangements. Everything Magda did was "perfect" and she commanded the same of everyone else—especially Lee. He was looking forward to and dreading her visit, in equal measure.

"This is about as far from pretentious San Francisco techno stress as you can get," Adriano offered, putting away his iPhone and giving Lee that "Aren't I one lucky nerd?" look that Lee had fallen in love with ten years ago. "I could live here just fine."

"You bet," Lee replied with genuine enthusiasm.

Indeed, Orvieto seemed just the place they had been looking for to make a fresh start after the "year of death" that had preceded this escape from reality. A chill came over Lee, half from the late-autumn, prewinter breeze and half from the memory of their truly annus horribilis. Having carefully, if temporarily, partitioned off their retinue of PR, design and IT clients back in San Francisco, Lee and Adriano had freed themselves from the constrictions of work for two months. Frankly, for the last year, all work had taken a back seat to the needs of a dying man, Brian. It had been a challenge to run a small pop-and-pop business from hospital lobby after hospital lobby, and then, finally, from the foot of a hospice bed. Lee shivered again.

"Yes, we certainly could," he said, shaking off a miasma of memories. "Who knows what we'll find here."

CHAPTER II

Refugee

Saturday, November 30, 2013, somewhere at sea

Maryam didn't want to die this way.

All around her in the darkness, people moaned. The air reeked of sweat and urine and vomit.

Was it day? Night?

Instantly, the world turned upside down, and someone screamed—man, woman, child?—impossible to tell as an inhuman concert of tormented steel and tumbling chains, chairs, and tools slid toward her, burying hundreds of voices beneath the racket. She rolled over on her side in time to escape a huge metal container that had flung itself against the bulkhead. A rat scurried over her filthy, rag-wrapped feet too late. It was crushed. *Praise Allah, we will eat,* she *thought. If I live through this...*

Above on deck, she heard the scrambling thuds of a dozen running feet and the barked commands of a crew desperate to save their ship. Maryam did not recognize the language in which they spoke, but she understood the tone. They were in trouble.

The compartment shuddered and vibrated. In the dark, the moans became sobs and then silence. Slowly, their prison ship righted itself. An even keel—for now—until the next wave. Up on deck, the sound of nervous masculine laughter translated to the bowels below.

The baby kicked in her womb.

CHAPTER III

Of Expats and Paintings

Saturday, November 30, 2013, late afternoon, Orvieto

Peg was very American.

Lordy, Lee thought. And people think I'm a screaming Anglo.

"Always start on the right," she said, offering first one cheek, then the other as she breezed into the Café Volsini with flourishes and waves to the staff, all of whom she clearly knew and who definitely knew her. The central casting doyenne at the cash register gave her a gray-haired look over her wire rims, simultaneously glassy and murderous. "It took me a while to learn that when I first moved here. Almost broke my nose a few times."

Somewhere between sixty-five and Debbie Reynolds, swathed in scarves, gray leather gloves, expensive but not ostentatiously so, unless one considered gloves in and unto themselves ostentatious, Lee thought, Peg was the exemplar expat, a grade C *Tea With Mussolini*.

"White wine, si?" Peg asked, then answered for them to the formidable la donna now waiting at their table with pursed lips and order pad (complete with carbon paper between the sheets). "Tre vini bianchi, per favore. You'll love it, Orvieto Classico. Quite one of the most *fabulous*, and cheap, white wines you'll ever have! I tried to find it when I was back in California visiting my sister last year for the holidays, but they didn't even have it at BevMo! I thought about buying twenty crates and going into the wine import–export business, but my goodness, everything is a *struggle* here to get arranged. And it's a *very* small town—*molto piccola città*. Everyone will know you in three days. But this place is a *find!* Even this close to Rome, people outside of Northern Italy seem not to know about Orvieto, and what a *treasure* it is, an absolute *treasure!*"

Wow. Lee wondered if she had an air tank to fuel such machine-gun-fire delivery. She had to take a breath sometime. God, he wished she would, he thought, as he inwardly rolled his eyes.

All six cheeks bussed, the trio sat down. Peg's skirt, in some sort of voluminous silvery-gray upholstery fabric, swirled around their feet and the legs of the chairs like an incoming crinoline tide.

As Peg nattered breathlessly on about the wonders of their tempo-rary home, Lee looked around their chosen lunch spot. Café Volsini was like something out of the past. Scratch that, it *was* out of the past. All the counters were marble and supported by intricately carved wooden bases entwined with figures from the hands of a mythologically inspired artist. Clear glass cases displayed martially aligned rows of tiny mouthwatering pastries and candies, handmade and stamped *Volsini* as if by wax imprint. There were even chocolate coffee cups—demitasse size—and matching spoons for the offing. Over the register, a procession of antique Italian money from Etruscan and Roman to Mussolini's Nazi puppet state to the late, lamented Italian lira—marched in procession above a bewildering and delicious assortment of liquors unknown to Lee. Above a bottle of something called Aperol a thorn-crowned Jesus rolled his passionate eyes heavenward. Next to a thin, green-tinted bottle of Svinnere Nonna Velia the Virgin Mary contemplated above a flickering electric candle.

Lee watched La Donna signal with a nod and a glance for the bartender to pour the wine. Images of Talia Shire and *The Godfather's* unmistakable theme music played inside his skull. He wondered if there was a gun hidden in the tiny toilette, whose entrance was marked by an antique sign he could just spy between the Virgin Mary statue and her son's beleaguered visage next to the amaretto. The only thing out of period was a large, abstract, and almost brutalist painting, like an Italian version of Picasso's *Guernica*, of seven bodies contorted in pain, and clearly bleeding from gunshot wounds to the head. A small bronze plate was attached to the simple black frame and inscribed with the words *Camorena: I Nostri Sette Martiri*. The artist's name was scrawled in the right-hand corner, as if bleeding off the bottom-most victim's palm. *Volsini*. Perhaps the café doyenne was an artist herself.

"As I was saying…" Peg pierced him with a glance conveying her awareness that for a second her monologue had been interrupted, or worse yet, ignored. Deep in artistic contemplation, Lee had indeed lost the conversation's thread. He scrambled to catch up.

"Oh, sorry," Lee said, as Adriano kicked him under the table in typical married-couple "We're new here, be nice" fashion, and gave his husband a look. "I was just taking this all in. It's like something out of a movie."

"I *know*!" enthused Peg. "And our friend there"—Peg indicated with a whispered tilt of her head—"is *Volsini*—quite the oldest name in Orvieto and possessed, according to the locals, of many secrets and connections, if you know what I mean." Peg let herself drift off with a balletic twirl of the wrist as if dying to have Adriano or Lee offer up the obvious.

"Mafia?" Adriano gasped back in a flash, and Peg absolutely twinkled in pleasure that her hint had been picked up. "Should we be worried?"

"Oh no, she looks too nice," Lee said, nonetheless wondering himself and contemplating the picture behind the bar. *Camorena: I Nostri Sette Martiri* certainly looked like a mafia hit. "Plus, as my grandma used to say, 'Worry is like a rocking chair. It gives you something to do, but it gets you no place.'"

Adriano rolled his eyes.

Lee knew that his down-home philosophizing sometimes annoyed Adriano. Frankly, *his* annoyance annoyed Lee. It wasn't the first time, and likely wouldn't be the last. Lee let it pass. Memories of his grandmother were sacred.

"Seriously, though," Adriano whispered. "You don't think she's mafia?"

"*Depende*," Peg offered quietly with a subtle warning finger to her lips. "Like everything in Orvieto, depende. Don't expect anything to be what it's supposed to be or to operate efficiently. Ask for a plumber to come at eight a.m., he might show up by dusk the next day—depende. Be promised that your dry cleaning will be ready on Tuesday and show up on Thursday to be safe and find it still on the counter where you left it to be picked up. Depende. It drove me *mad* my first six months here, then..."

"What?" Adriano asked.

"I surrendered," Peg said with a toothy smile and a big "Ha!" laugh. "Ah! Here's our wine! Grazie, Signora Volsini! Grazie mille!"

The elderly café owner presented a tray with three enormous goblets of wine and three small dishes of delectable savories and nuts, warm and freshly prepared as evidenced by their enticing aroma and the temperature of the delicate crystal dish, engraved *Volsini*.

"But we didn't order lunch," Lee said quietly after the tray had been placed in front of them.

"This isn't *lunch*," Peg smiled. "This is what you get when you order wine, or any alcohol, in Italy, and especially at *il vecchio* place like this."

As Peg spoke, Signora Volsini slipped a small silver tray with the bill next to them. Four euro fifty. About six dollars.

"That's it, for all this?" Lee was amazed. He had heard that Italy was cheaper than San Francisco (wasn't everything?), but this was quite something.

Peg shrugged her shoulders and smiled as Adriano and Lee lifted their glasses in a toast.

"To Orvieto!" Adriano said as their glasses clinked.

"And to new friends," said Peg as they all three drank.

"And to Café Volsini," Lee proffered, popping a cracker into his mouth—sinfully delicious, cheesy, puffy. He was going to like Italy. As he chewed, he looked up to see La Donna staring at him questioningly from her perch behind the cash register at the door. Cerberus with a calculator. "Mmmmm." He smiled at her with his mouth full as if to say "Delicious!"

Signora Volsini nodded once with a curled lip whose commentary was Volsini clear—"Of course it's delicious"—and went back to her cash drawer. *The Godfather* music started to play again in Lee's head.

"There's another bar on the other side of Piazza del Popolo, Clement's Bar, that's even cheaper, but they only offer chips and crackers," Peg rattled, "and *anything* closer to *Il Duomo* is more expensive since that's where all the tour buses stop."

Lee had already decided. *I think I'll come here.* He had a feeling La Donna of Café Volsini would know in short order that the couple from San Francisco were temporary locals. Lee wouldn't want her to think he was disloyal. She might prove to be the "La Madrina" of the whole town after all.

Between glasses two and three, Peg revealed her status as a retired biotech exec from Northern California turned Italian food writer, a three-time divorcée, and occasional blogger. Ten years ago, she came to Orvieto and stayed. Several of her books had become moderate best sellers, and her blog, *Square Peg on a Round Rock*, was now de rigueur for anyone visiting or researching Orvieto.

"I came, I saw, I bought," she said with glee. "Real estate was dirt cheap then and has only gotten dirtier and cheaper. Heaven, I tell you, Orvieto is *heaven!*"

An hour later, the trio walked out into the late afternoon beginnings of twilight. Somewhere a bell struck the hour, five great clangs.

"Ah yes," said Peg with a theatrically melancholy sigh of recognition and a gloved hand to her bosom. "The Tower of the Moor. It's quite the best alarm clock in town."

Five o'clock. Lee would have to rush if he wanted to make the *Sant'Andrea* service at 5:30 p.m. He might even talk the Catholiphobic Adriano into joining him.

"Now, if you need anything, just give me a call. I live right next to *Il Duomo*," Peg, said, pointing a leather-clad digit down Orvieto's main street and simultaneously waving away a swarthy street peddler hawking home-made CDs to passersby. "Or you can just yell. I'm always walking up and down the Corso. You never know whom you might meet and what might inspire an article or research into a recipe. Ciao!"

With that, and a cheeky sextet of goodbye kisses, she was off, leaving Adriano and Lee to their first night in Italy.

While Adriano did more iPhone documentation, Lee dashed back into the bar and squeezed between Madonna and the Crown of Thorns for a bathroom pit stop. There wouldn't be time to go to the apartment before the service at *Sant'Andrea*. That entailed sixty-four steps up and sixty-four steps down. He had counted. Actually sixty-four and a half. There was a weird half-step to nowhere sticking out of the wall near the top. Plus, they hadn't even had time to begin unpacking and settling in. As he zipped up, he glanced at the old-style water tank, Coppola-like, suspended against the ceiling. He wondered if anyone had ever hidden an assassin's gun there. He wouldn't be surprised. For all its antique whimsy, there was an aura of something hidden—almost dread—although artfully restrained about Café Volsini, and its owner.

As he walked out, La Madrina, as Lee had decided to dub her, looked up, briefly, from her cash register.

"*Buonasera*!" Lee called out cheerfully in his best "I so wanna be a local" tone.

La Madrina just stared. "Ciao," she offered coolly, and returned to her euros.

Well, Lee thought, it was a start. Somehow, he really didn't want to get on her bad side.

CHAPTER IV

Upon This Rock

December 10, 1527 (Julian Calendar), Orvieto

Clement couldn't decide.

"Your Holiness wears our collective grief in a most distinguished fashion," offered the nearby cardinal, bowing low to the cold marble floor of what passed for Orvieto's papal bedchamber.

"Hmmm," grunted the Pope, stroking his beard and contemplating his visage in the mirror. "I don't know." After six months, the whiskers were getting scraggly. Plus, they itched. Also, their advancement across his face revealed a distressing propensity for gray. His privileged Florentine youth was obviously long passed. This job will kill me, thought the Pontiff as he regarded his begrizzled chin. He had spent his forty-ninth birthday as a prisoner of the Holy Roman Emperor and was about to spend Christmas as a refugee in this hilltop hovel. So much for being Pontifex Maximus.

"Being unshaven is against canon law," said the Pope, turning from the glass to find the cardinal still prostrate before him. He motioned impatiently for the Prince of the Church to get up. As a Medici, Clement was accustomed to genuflections, but the last six months, especially, had made him tired of all such gratuitous displays, especially here in this dismal fortress retreat of Orvieto. Orvieto wasn't Rome. That much was certain. Of course, after this past May, Rome wasn't Rome either.

"But *you* write canon law, Your Holiness. *You* are the Church," offered the cardinal, with only slightly less obsequiousness than before. "Plus, there is precedent. Pope Julius II wore a beard, briefly, as a sign over his grief at the fall of Bologna. His portrait by Raphael shows it clearly."

"He did?" Clement perked up. A precedent—that was good. He liked precedents. His was not a papacy to court controversy. Well...that had been the plan. Before Luther and his so-called "Reformation." Before King Francis. Before Emperor Charles. Before the sixty of May. "Where is the portrait now?"

The cardinal blushed and shrugged, with a slight but noticeably sad downcast of his eyes.

Clement had his answer. "The Sack."

"Yes, Your Holiness. The Sack. I believe it was taken from the Vatican in the first wave of looting by Charles's troops." Then, in a lower voice he said, "Evidently it was subject to some minor desecrations, as were the bones of the Blessed Julius himself." The cardinal crossed himself.

The Sack of Rome, Redux. Pope Clement VII shook his head and sighed. His complete and utter failure as temporal and spiritual ruler of the Papal States already had a name. It was an obvious one, a repeat of Rome's earlier dismemberment at the hands of the Huns in 410, over a thousand years previous. But that had been the barbarians—godless savages! What would one expect? Clement's Eternal City had been raped and pillaged by the Catholic troops of The Holy Roman Emperor, Charles V!

Charles. Clement ground his teeth. The very name rankled just to think of it. Some protector of Christ's vicar on earth he had turned out to be. It'll be a cold day in Bologna before I lay my holy hands on his head in coronation, thought Clement, and that seemed to please him. No matter who they were or from what noble line they had coerced a twisted pedigree, they all wanted the Pope's blessing.

"It stays," Clement pronounced, and the cardinal nodded and crossed himself again, instinctively, as if the Pope had just issued a papal bull. Clement was good at bulls. His *Intra Arcana* was a classic, authorizing violence in evangelizing—no pain no gain! He had the voice for it, so when he did finally decide something, always preceded by much cerebral dancing, it rang with authority. Since most of his decisions got re-decided, there had been a lot of authoritative-sounding pronouncements over the four years, thus far, of his papacy. Decisiveness was not a Clementine virtue.

"Yes," he repeated with a final tug on his beard before turning away from his reflection. "It stays."

The beard was the result of the six months Clement had spent hostage in Rome's *Castel Sant'Angelo* without a razor or his regular chamberlain to shave him. With an eye toward legacy, Clement would pick up on the tale of his illustrious predecessor, the "Warrior Pope" of fourteen years previous. Like Julius, Clement had grown a beard as a sign of grief for the loss of Rome and the pain of its populace.

He liked that. Made him sound humble, sincere, wracked with anguish but still tough. Also, as loathed as he had become, there was no way he was going to let anyone near his neck with a razor, not after the year he was still having. Who knows, he thought with a smile and one final look at his whiskers, I might even start a trend.

The second Fall of Rome. He had presided over the second Fall of Rome. His good humor faded. Well, he had hoped that his reign would be memorable, and not just that of a second-rate Medici, overshadowed by the memory of his more illustrious, more legitimate, and more popular cousin, Leo X, née Giovanni de Medici, Pope before last.

Dear Gio, how I miss you. He reminisced about his cousin, mentor, and best—perhaps only—friend. It was hard to believe, just a few weeks ago on December 1, he and his fellow prisoners in Rome's *Castel Sant'Angelo* had offered up a Mass on that the sixth anniversary of the great Pope's death. Yep, the Sack of Rome just might get bigger play than Leo's art-and-sex-filled procession through papal history. Truly, Gio/Leo had been the master Medici—with all deference to his father, *Lorenzo Magnifico*. He *himself*, on the other hand, was fast becoming *Il Medici Mediocrito*. A week after their imprisoned Mass, he and his coterie were on the run, having bribed the guards to let them out. Then, dressed up like two-bit *befanas*, they had made a dash for every pope's favorite escape hatch, Orvieto, seventy-five miles north of Rome.

"The City that has taken the world has herself been taken." Clement remembered the words penned by St. Jerome after the first Sack of Rome.

What a pompous, quote-happy ass he had been. He wondered what penniless penitent destined for beatification was even now sitting in some monastic cell already gleefully penning the obituary of his papacy.

Clement shivered. It was cold here in Orvieto, and every bit of ermine, fox, and bear fur that had hitherto warmed his illustrious body had been left behind in Rome. He had barely escaped with his life, much less the Vatican bed sheets. No, now was not the time for self-recriminations. He would regroup, rethink, and relaunch his papacy here in Orvieto. He'd need help—and money. Charles was certainly out of the question. He shuttered once again at that dreaded, treacherous name.

Francis, King of France, was a possibility. He despised Charles even more than the Pope did. But, then again, he had not been the most loyal guardian of Francis's imperial aspirations, so maybe now wasn't the time to ask for a favor. Though no one had given him credit for it, he had tried to broker peace between the two rival monarchs and the English king early in his papacy, but such diplomatic niceties had now been long forgotten. The Sack was a dirty cloth that wiped away every other previous beneficent effort.

"Fool that I was," he harrumphed to himself. Why would they want to make peace when it was so much more advantageous to do battle in the hopes of taking all of Italy one day, including the Vatican and Papal States? Well, Emperor Charles seemed to have wrapped that up—for the moment at least.

Clement paced around the grim and dilapidated "Papal Palace." His predecessors had spent and built lavishly in the past to make it pontifically ready. Even that hideous Borgia, Alexander VI, had left his mark on Orvieto, had the nerve even to make his son, Cesare, podesta of the town! *At least I'm not a Borgia. Even I am more popular than those blood-soaked papal pretenders.*

Clement let his gaze circle the room full of rot, decay, and freezing breaths of Umbrian wind whistling in through chinks in the masonry. Temporary or not, if this was to be the home of the papacy in exile, some improvements would have to be made. All the faith-induced fruits of papal labor (and the papal purse) had seen better decades. Orvieto was a dump. It had never recovered from the Plague and the intervening centuries hadn't been kind. Now, one day into exile, he paused to look out the ice-glazed window. The monstrous and gaudy hulk of the still unfinished Duomo across the plaza loomed to fill his view. God, it was ugly—big, blocky, and plain. The front was nice, if they ever finished the mosaics, but that seemed unlikely. True, it did house some admirable frescoes by that Goody Two-Shoes, Fra Angelico. More to his liking, he thought, were the wickedly profane works by Luca Signorelli in the Cathedral's side chapel. Cousin Leo would have *loved* those, all those virile, naked, oh-so-male bodies clawing their way out of the earth toward a muscular heaven. Even the morose Michelangelo had made the trip to Orvieto a few years back to admire their naughty and gloriously detailed nudity just across the nave from the body of Orvieto's patron saint and the relics of the "Miracle" of Bolsena—

Henry!

It came to him in a flash: England's Catholic King. He snapped his fingers. "Why didn't I think of that before! He wasn't as rich as Francis, but he did have resources. Plus, Henry's wife, Catherine of Aragon, was Charles's aunt. That might come in handy. "Defender of the Faith," he whispered, remembering the sobriquet that his cousin, Leo X, had bestowed upon the devout English prince, now Henry VIII, King of England.

"What did His Holiness say?"

Clement jerked around to find the forgotten cardinal still shivering by the door. He must've spoken out loud.

"Send me a Switzer," Clement commanded with a clap of his hands, for a second his old pre-Sack Medici self. Nothing invigorated him more than finally coming to a decision, even one as mundane as arriving at an excuse not to shave, much less finding a new source of revenue.

"Right away, Your Holiness," the cardinal said, then bowed and backed out of the room, closing the door behind him, which locked with a loud, echoing bang.

Hadn't Henry even written *Assertio Septem Sacramentorum—Defense of the Seven Sacraments*—a ponderously purple and in-perfect-Latin endorsement of Rome's supremacy over all earthly monarchs? Naturally, Henry was doing his best to suck up and become Holy Roman Emperor.

Wasn't everyone whose blood was blue under God's arc of heaven? Nonetheless, it was appreciated and Rome took notice.

Even his cousin, Leo X, had taken notice. The brief interregnum papacy of Adrian VI (God rest his tired soul, Clement prayed between plotting) had continued the notice. So now it seemed time for him to offer his own signs of appreciation—along with a subtle request for money—to England's Most Catholic King, Henry VIII, a rock of Christian manhood in an age of waning faith.

I will, secretly of course, send one of my guards to Henry's court, he thought. I don't want any official chroniclers preserving this little foray into fundraising. It must seem as if the idea were *Henry's*, not mine, Clement stewed. Henry would want something in return, probably one of the lesser Papal States or a cousin-created cardinal. That would be easy—the worthless Woolsey couldn't live forever—a promise none too soon to be realized if I had my way. If only cousin Gio and I had crossed the English Channel when we were on our Borgia-forced tour of France and the north oh so many years ago, we might have made better, more personal connections with Prince Henry during his youth.

Oh well, no use weeping over spilled claret. We must deal with the moment, the reality in which we find ourselves. Now, we will appeal to Henry, to his generosity, to his mortal soul, to his treasury.

Clement smiled, quite pleased with himself. It was the best he'd felt since before The Sack. Well, I'm not done yet, he thought. I am still pope and Rome still lives, although greatly diminished, to be sure. I will get it back. Perhaps if I can return to Rome in triumph, the people would forget how I lost it and fled in terror. I might even commission that disagreeable Michelangelo to do something in commemoration.

Yes, and here in Orvieto, upon this rock, high and impregnable above the Etruscan plain, I will rebuild my church...and my reputation.

CHAPTER V

A Crooked Cross

Saturday, November 30, 2013, evening, Orvieto

L ee splashed himself with holy water as he entered *Sant'Andrea*, once
the site of an Etruscan temple and even older cave system. Adriano
rolled his eyes and wondered if his husband would genuflect when he hit
the main aisle. *That's what comes from marrying someone who had actively
considered the priesthood.*

Bingo—it's a good thing I didn't bet against that, Adriano thought. *I'd
have lost.* He loved Lee, very much, but for ten years had been perplexed,
and more than occasionally troubled, by his husband's fascination with all
things Catholic. By even Spanish standards, it was a bit much.

"The day that nasty old bishop slapped me across the face during my
confirmation, I was done," Adriano said quietly. He had often repeated the
story throughout their marriage, generally the punctuation to a dinner
with friends. "Thank you very much, but the Church ain't done *me* any
favors."

Adriano looked around for signs of underground entrances and to
his delight found none. His optimism was short-lived. If they were above
an ancient anything, Lee would find it eventually. Anything ancient or
cramped with history, and Lee practically swooned. Not me, Adriano
thought. *Dark, dank spaces are not my favorite things. I've certainly crawled*

through enough of them for him. Let's hope he doesn't find too many here.
Adriano shivered at the thought.

"It won't kill you to be respectful," Lee said with a disapproving glare.
"Plus, I'm curious."

"And I'm an atheist."

It was Lee's turn to roll his eyes.

For all of his protestations, Adriano had an almost disconcerting mysticism not based in any religion. It would have horrified him to think of it as "religion." That was Lee's thing, not his. Not with my parents, Adriano thought. *I've had quite enough of religion, thank you very much.* His presleep hobbies bounced between books like *The Holographic Universe*, with computer games along the lines of *Knights of the Old Republic* thrown in for good measure. The closest he came to anything "churchy" was a book called *Faith Without God.* Adriano knew that Lee found that a "hopeful sign," but he always emphasized to Lee the "without God" part of the title. It was one of the things that had drawn Adriano to his husband, a mutual fascination with figuring things out. But, for Adriano it was an interest. For Lee, it bordered on fetish.

"Soul mate" they called each other, complete with secret names and a personal pantheon of influences that would have shamed a shaman. For all his cynicism, Adriano shared Lee's interest in most things mythological and historical. Brian always used to say, "Hire people smarter than you; they make you look good." Lee had done it one better, often telling Adriano he was glad he had married someone smarter than he was, and a computer whiz to boot.

Many times, Adriano reflected on how Lee's PR skills, added to his own technological prowess, equaled a partnership in life and business. Adriano knew that Lee loathed the term "PR," as public relations was only a hair above carnival barker in most people's minds. "I'm not in public relations," Lee would often huff. "I'm in *communications.* My job is to take the ponderous and make it palpable. To turn mush into messaging." Whatever he called it, Lee had—to Adriano's mind—a skill for figuring stuff out and making the complex comprehensible. It was a gift Adriano sometimes wished he had—and the patience for. Certainly, Adriano thought, patience is not one of my virtues. Plus, Adriano's fluency in several languages made trips such as this one ever so much easier. There were few earthly languages beyond Adriano's gifted tongue.

"Give me a break, you're practically as hippie-dippie as I am," Lee said, offering his best dimpled smile, the one Adriano had first fallen in love with.

"Yes," said Adriano, with a subtle squeeze of his husband's arm, "but I don't need all the trappings of the *Church*."

Adriano hissed the word as if it were synonymous with all that was evil in the world. To someone whose family had suffered through Europe's last and longest-lasting dictator, Spain's very Catholic Francisco Franco, Adriano's suspicion of any and all things religious was deeply embedded. And, of course, given Adriano's family, he had plenty of reasons to despise organized religion. It hurt him sometimes that Lee couldn't see that.

"I don't *need* it." Lee interrupted Adriano's thoughts. "I just find it intriguing the same way I find an ancient Greek temple or an Egyptian tomb interesting."

"You're obsessed." Adriano shook his head. "They don't pass the hat in Grecian ruins or the desert of Cairo and claim religious tax exemptions."

"Shhh," Lee warned. "Here comes the procession."

Adriano kept it to himself. He wasn't going to fight back on their first night. He'd bide his time.

The congregation rose stiffly to their feet, a group of about 150 mainly elderly, mainly female, and almost entirely Italian locals. A smattering of men accompanied wives, mothers, and cousins. Two teenage Chinese tourists, looking completely lost, hovered at the back of the thousand-year-old edifice clutching cameras and folded tour maps. A good-looking twenty-ish young man clad in jeans and a sleek leather jacket stood next to the rear side door, as if not quite sure whether to enter.

"Wow," whispered Adriano. "It's a bishop."

Lee turned his head.

Adriano watched a grand episcopal mitre sailing through the crowd, sticking up above the heads of the assembled faithful.

"For a would-be atheist," Lee said, "you certainly know your Catholic paraphernalia."

Adriano smirked.

The bishop was in full feast day dress, black cassock with red half-drape, bishop's staff—crozier, as Adriano recalled its Latin name—and a retinue of altar boys and fellow priests, likely from Orvieto's ring of other parishes, all here today at *Sant'Andrea* for the church's namesake commemoration. Just then the organ heaved and huffed into a groaning rendition of the familiar hymn.

"My favorite," Lee said.

God, Adriano thought. This was going to be a long night.

The air bloomed with a chorus of Italian voices—"*Santo, Santo, Santo*"—mingling in the cold along with a cloud of incense from the acolyte's swinging brass sensors.

"I used to be really good at that," Lee whispered to Adriano. "I mastered the 'double clink' pattern when waving around the incense that is the hallmark of an expert altar boy."

"What are they doing now?" Adriano was on tiptoes, trying to see over the sea of matrons to his left. "They're stopping."

The clerics gathered at the left side of the church in front of a huge wooden statue of an athletic St. Andrew, depicted, as usual, grasping his crooked cross.

"What's the big X he's holding on to?" Adriano asked.

"St. Andrew's Cross." Lee sighed in mock exasperation. "According to legend, Andrew didn't feel worthy to be crucified like Jesus, so when he was martyred in Greece, he asked to have the crossed turned on its side. You really are a bad Catholic."

"I try." Adriano winked coyly. "And all this time, I thought St. Andrew's Cross was just an S and M thing."

"It is an S and M thing as well as a holy symbol of martyrdom," said Lee. "It's also a perennial crossword clue."

As the bishop and his entourage assembled at the statue, amid swirls of scented smoke and the moaning organ, an octogenarian lady stepped out of the crowd and laid a white rectangle of carnations marked by an X of red roses in front of the pedestal.

"La Madrina," Lee whispered.

Adriano nodded. Sure enough, it was. Café Volsini's doyenne walked right up to the bishop, who bowed stiffly with a slight twitch of his lips, and carefully placed the wreath at the foot of the saint. He made the sign of the cross over her head, but she turned before he was done and headed back to her seat as if she couldn't be bothered.

As the procession got closer to turning down the center aisle, Adriano looked at the prelate as he passed, sixty-ish, six foot, mordantly slim, and ever so slightly sinister in his gait. "Why do they all look like Darth Vader?" he muttered.

Lee said, "I admit that's a bishop I wouldn't want to meet in a dark alley. Certainly, a Prince of the Church, as in Machiavelli."

"This one looks nice though," Adriano offered as a smiling, elderly, elfish priest walked past them, obviously the junior partner, holding the bishop's train. "He looks more like Yoda."

Adriano followed the procession as it made its way to the altar. He noticed the vestments as they swept the well-worn tiles, like embroidered dusters, behind the parade. The incense was nauseating, like everything in every church. Damn, he thought, the things we do to get through a marriage.

Finally, the procession got to the altar and with all the requisite blessings bestowed, the Mass got formally underway. The Chinese tourists stood against the back wall, seemingly at a loss what to do, but now somehow stuck in mid-ceremony and afraid to leave, and even more afraid to snap a photo though they were trying to find the right time to do just that. *Dorothy, we're not in Nanjing anymore!* A young mother walked along the rear nave of the church, patting one baby on the back to keep her quiet while pushing another in a stroller. Nothing unusual there, thought Adriano. Catholics were famous for "watching from the sidelines" during Mass. Hypocrites.

Lee, apparently noticing Adriano's wandering eyes, said, "In the old-fashioned Virginia parish of my youth, people were always walking in mid-service and dashing right after communion to beat the crowd in the parking lot or get a jump on the Sunday football game."

Hypocrites, Adriano thought again.

Lee turned back to his hymnal.

Everyone sat down, except the young man in leather they had spied earlier, standing against the back wall, face hidden in shadow. Slowly, almost casually, as the congregation was seated and the bishop removed his mitre to preside, the youth walked over to stand next to the statue of St. Andrew and look solemnly at the flowers laid there.

"Check out the talent," Adriano whispered to his husband.

Lee looked up.

Having stepped into the glow of candlelight next to St. Andrew, Mr. Leather Jacket revealed quite the form sublime poured into his designer duds, sleekly muscular, blond, and, well, dangerous looking, like someone who should be advertising cigarettes or a Harley.

"Somehow, I don't think that's a priest." Adriano smirked quietly.

Leather Boy stood just to the left of St. Andrew's Cross. Every now and then looking up from the flowers laid there by La Madrina and then staring, fixedly, at the altar, eyes glistening.

Are those tears? Adriano wondered as he followed the line of his stare to the front of the church. No, he wasn't crying, he was *glaring*, and right at the bishop. At first, the cleric seemed not to notice, but as if he could feel it, he looked toward the congregation and directly at the young man. His face went gray and his hands started to shake. The bishop's missal slipped from his grasp with a *smack* against the marble floor. Yoda bent quickly and scooped it up. The bishop grabbed it with a scowl and pointedly turned his gaze to the other side of the congregation, away from Leather Boy. For a second, his eyes fell upon Adriano's. In that moment, Adriano and the bishop looked right at each other as if they both knew they would see each other again. I need to warn Lee, Adriano thought, but he didn't know why he thought that, and soon after it was forgotten. The bishop had turned away.

∼

"Looks like a gay bar," Adriano said in a conspiratorial voice, gently nudging Lee in the ribs. "Love's young leather flame has company."

Just like Adriano, Lee thought, to inject the profane in the midst of something spiritual. He knew Adriano hated that Lee didn't hate the Church, but why did he have to spoil the moment? But, Adriano was right. Something was happening separate from, but clearly connected to, the service going on inside the church. Two plays were taking place simultaneously, one voiced, one in pantomime. A second youth was now approaching the statue of St. Andrew who, while nominally handsome, was not as distractingly so as his predecessor.

The newcomer stood behind the first. He had slicked back hair, black to the point of blue, and was more formally dressed. His tie was slightly askew, as if hastily tightened on the way in, and some sort of name badge peeked out from beneath his jacket. He looked as if he had just come from work. Leather Jacket took no notice until the second man—a doctor, perhaps?—tapped him gently on the shoulder.

It all happened so fast, Lee didn't think many people noticed, especially since now that the hymn before the Gospel reading was in full swing. As the first youth turned to see who had touched him, fisticuffs seemed imminent. The doctor—Lee could now see a stethoscope hanging from his neck beneath his coat—leaned back defensively and in genuine fright, while Leather Boy advanced on him threateningly. With a speed that belied her age, La Madrina dashed from her pew, put her matronly bosom between them, and hissed, *"Basta!"* loud enough for Lee to make out over the music. The doctor backed away from the old woman, like a vampire from garlic, but the first one mouthed, "I've had enough," and dashed out the side door of the church. La Madrina slapped the young physician on the arm with a "What do you think you're doing?" dismissal of her hand, pushed him toward the door, and returned to her seat. The doctor sank into the shadows.

"Wow, what was *that? Quelle* drama," said Adriano.

"Yeah," whispered Lee. "Maybe you were right. There was a little 'gay thing' going on here and La Madrina didn't like it."

La Donna Volsini had retaken her pew as if nothing had happened. She didn't look behind her to see if the doctor had left. Lee felt she wasn't someone who needed to check on whether or not her commands were obeyed. As the congregation sat to listen to the sermon offered by the bishop, Lee watched La Madrina's mouth muttering something slowly, and silently, as she looked to the altar. Those aren't prayers, he thought, seeing the steely glint of her eyes and the firm set of her chin. She was saying something all right, aimed right at the bishop, but it didn't look like prayers. More like a curse.

Lee turned to see what had become of the young doctor. He was kneeling in front of the statue. He kissed the statue's carved feet, got up, and dashed for the door as if to make sure he was gone before the old woman saw him again. As he stood, Lee saw that the young doctor had left something behind, a flickering candle in front of St. Andrew and beside the bloodred floral cross placed by La Donna Volsini.

It wasn't until he was home later, Adriano playing computer games next to him in bed, that Lee had a thought about the boy in the leather jacket. There was something vaguely familiar about him. He had seen him before—he was sure of that—but could not remember where. As he fell asleep, he had another thought. *I'm sure I will see him again.*

CHAPTER VI

A Voice in the Wilderness

Saturday, November 30, 2013, evening, Rome

She didn't expect him to answer.

He couldn't. It wasn't allowed. Not that he would take her call anyway. Why would he want to speak with her after last year?

She put down the receiver.

One year.

Maybe he'll call me?

You foolish woman, he won't call. He was never going to call again. He'd never even speak her name again. It was done. Over. It was over before it started. An abortion of love. A relationship cold, and stillborn.

It was raining in Rome. The Vittorio Emanuele Monument hovered in blurred and watery reflection from her window. As she looked, the lights flickered to life against the colossal memorial.

Time to go. Quickly, she checked herself in the mirror but as always, wished she had not. Stuck in the groove between reflection and frame was the thin piece of paper inscribed with the coordinates that proved the complicity of her life.

(48) Per quelle che patiscono per causa della loro orecchie

(56) Per quei padri e quelle madri che non educano i loro figli.

(13) Per quelle per le quali il Padre desidera che si preghi accio siano liberate da quelle pene

(43) Per quelle che frastornarono gli altri alla devozione

Those four lines bore the proof of her sin, the key to her own private purgatory. She put on her collar with practiced ease. No need for a mirror. She didn't want to see herself anyway.

Opening the door, she walked down to her congregation in the church below.

Heretics.

CHAPTER VII

Magda

Sunday, December 1, 2013, midmorning, Orvieto

"Magda's not coming," Adriano said.

He knew his husband well. They had spent a quiet, romantic dinner at home, just the two of them, a perfect way to begin Lee's thirties.

Lee looked up from his book, *Magnificence and Malfeasance: Medici, Metrodorus, and the Medieval Papacy,* a birthday gift last night from Adriano. "What a surprise."

"Here's the email." Adriano turned the laptop around on the kitchen table so that his husband could read.

> Adriano & Lee,
>
> Sarah has been in hospice for the last few weeks. I have been see-ing her daily. I know you two, more than anyone this last year, know what that's like. She has made it clear to me that she wants me to plan her memorial. In consultation with her palliative care nurse, it would seem that her time of transition is rapidly approaching.
>
> I have decided that I should cancel my trip to Italy. I really appre-ciate the invitation and was looking forward to it.
>
> I am terribly disappointed that I won't be able to see you. At this time, however, the responsibility of fulfilling Sarah's wishes are of par-amount concern to me now.
>
> Regards, Magda

"Well, we knew it would be *something*," Lee said, putting down his book. Adriano nodded his agreement.

With Magda, there was always *something*: press secretary's imminent death (the case here), World Series parade, July Fourth fireworks, Running of the Olympic Torch, a senator's retirement amid scandal to be "dealt with." All of these had been and were the purview of Magda and all had been used as excuses against taking a vacation. Something always came up, and always at the last minute. She could advance a papal visit to California (and had) but couldn't stay away from work for more than a full charge of her three cell phones, one personal, one for the mayor, and one whose number and list of contacts was more secret than NORAD's nuclear codes.

"When was the last time she had a vacation?" Adriano asked, peering over his glasses.

"Bush was president, the first one," Lee offered drolly.

"That was twenty years ago!"

"Twenty-five. If she took all of her accumulated vacation time, the City and County of San Francisco would go bankrupt."

Having survived five mayoral administrations in any city was no mean feat. In San Francisco, where politics was blood sport, it was bordering on miraculous. Over two decades, Magda Carter—a name that always made Lee giggle, but never to Magda's face—had made herself indispensable. Mayors came and went but Magda stayed. Lee was convinced that she knew where Jimmy Hoffa was buried—or maybe not. Adriano called her "the real Mayor of San Francisco." Her title was as shifting as the fog through the cables of the Golden Gate Bridge: permanent, amorphous, and ever-changing. At the moment, her card read "Manager of International Affairs," but that meant nothing. In reality, she was Ambassador Without Portfolio. She was simply "Magda," and her word was law and her justice, implacable. She was teutonica in stilettos.

"She scares me," Lee said.

"Oh?" Adriano pursed his lips and wiggled his finger across the table at his husband. "You just don't know how to handle her. She's a pussycat."

"More like a saber-toothed tiger."

"Has she ever had a boyfriend?" Adriano asked.

Lee put down his book in faux exasperation and pinned his husband with a look. "Who could survive *that*? Don't you remember the Italian ambassador's party at the Consulate in SF?"

"Poor guy." Adriano almost moaned with the memory. "His pants probably fit better after his encounter with Magda. More room."

"Madga is married to her work. You know that. Nuns may be brides of Christ, but Magda is faithful to the Mayor of the City and County of San Francisco—whoever holds the title—period."

"And," said Adriano, finishing the sentence, "woe be it to the person who so thoughtlessly flirts in disregard of that committed relationship."

"Exactly." Lee put a stinger on the conversation.

Many had been the man who had unknowingly wandered into Magda's vixen-ish snare only to come out bruised, battered, and submissive. "Maybe she's a dominatrix," Adriano offered.

Lee laughed.

She'd make a good one, Lee thought, all legs, hair, and gravity-defying bosom, a cross between Cate Blanchett in the last *Indiana Jones* movie and Lucy Liu in *Charlie's Angels*. Naturally, men flirted with Magda—even I get that, he thought, and I'm a complete Kinsey Six. Magda was a stunner, no doubt about it, but it was dangerous to tell her. She was a professional and that was that. She did not broach being noticed for her looks—which, in fairness to heterosexual males, and probably lesbians too—were very hard to disregard. The closest Lee had ever gotten to a compliment was saying "nice shoes" after arranging for a helicopter visit for the Governor's wife to an aircraft carrier during Fleet Week. The FAA and the Navy brass frowned upon such midair PR stunts. Permission had been promptly and officiously denied when Lee had called to secure the permits.

"Gimme the phone," Magda had snarled, and grabbed the receiver from Lee's quivering hand. "Hi, this is Magda Carter. Lee is working for me." Pause. "Thank you, Captain. Zero- nine hundred hours will be fine. I'll let Sacramento know. The flight deck sounds lovely."

Military speak came easy to the fifty-ish uber bureaucrat, as it was rumored that she was an orphaned military brat and had grown up on army bases somewhere in West Germany. However, no one really knew her provenance or age and *no one* was going to ask. Lee had heard—where, he didn't remember—that she had almost died at birth. He could just imagine the attending surgeons, petrified over the nativity they were about to midwife. They needn't have worried. Lee was sure that at the crucial moment, Magda had simply yelled, "Open up!" and like Athena, sprung forth fully formed.

Since the Fleet Week incident—maybe four years ago now?—Lee had started all calls on her behalf by saying, "Hi, this is Lee Fontaine Maury calling for Magda Carter." The conversations usually proceeded more smoothly that way, and thereafter he seldom had any trouble finding preferred VIP parking at official events. She had once even gotten Lee's car through the cross-traffic of a presidential motorcade in San Francisco's financial district. She had been in a hurry, and the police, responding to a call from Magda, had swiftly waved Lee's Subaru across the intersection after a brief and completely understandable inspection by bomb-sniffing German shepherds. Although it was nowhere written down in the terms of their work agreement, under "Other Duties as Assigned" Lee had become, somehow, Magda's chauffeur and amanuensis.

Lee made a good Magda puppet. As he had once quipped for Adriano, mimicking his chief client's voice, "I work best behind the scenes, out of sight, but you're *good with people*." Magda had spoken as if that character trait was to be despised, but nonetheless deemed necessary for her purposes. "And remember, when you work for me, you have one and only one client."

"You?" Lee had offered an octave higher than his usual.

"No!" Lee had remembered her violet eyes flashing. "Like me, you work at the pleasure of the Mayor of the City and County of San Francisco—and don't you forget it!"

Don't hate her because she's beautiful, Lee had often thought. *She scares me.*

"She loves us, you know," Adriano said, interrupting his husband's Magda daydream. "And, the fact that she trusts us speaks volumes."

"Oh yes." Lee laughed. "Agreed. I'd certainly rather be on her good side than her bad."

Adriano nodded his understanding. People on Magda's bad side found their desks at city hall—and sometimes even in Sacramento, Washington, and other cities—quietly emptied and neatly boxed up for them.

"We couldn't have gotten through this last year without her."

Lee looked in through the salon doors at Brian sitting on the shelf in his box, carefully wrapped in the Union Jack and illuminated by a battery-powered candle emblazoned with the face of Padre Pio, Italy's most popular and most-votive-candled stigmatic.

"Did you dust him today?"

"I'll let you do that," Adriano offered quietly, but without malice. "He was your best friend."

"Yes, he was," Lee said, staring at the mortal remains of the Right Rev. Brian Henry Swathmore, first openly gay bishop on planet Earth, "openly" being the operative word. His had been a long life, so it wasn't that cancer was an untimely end, just a messy and undignified one for someone as formal as Brian. Ashes to ashes, dust to dust, Lee thought, and now Brian is on a world tour headed to his final resting place, Ireland's Cliffs of Moher. He hadn't been back to his native Ireland since he had been young. It was Brian's dying wish, and there was no way that Lee wasn't going to honor it. Sometime in February, on their way back from their European hijra, Adriano and Lee would climb the steep path to the sheer rock face on the west coast of Ireland, say a few private words, and thus end Brian's journey, and theirs, before returning home.

"Do you remember the proclamation?"

"And the police escort?"

"And the honor guard?"

The couple smiled at each other, remembering all the ways, sacred and profane, in which Magda helped to make Brian's last months something to be cherished. Lee and Adriano's sabbatical had been her idea, and her connections. She was wonderful at organizing other people's getaways, just not her own.

"He may have been Anglican, but he was as grand as any Catholic."

"Grander," Lee replied with real affection.

As any post-Vatican II Roman Catholic knew, no one did High Church better than the Anglicans. Catholics, at least in the US, may have become more susceptible to folk Masses and guitars, but the Church of England and its American Episcopalian brethren knew how to do ritual. "Bells and smells," Brian had always called it, and as a retired bishop at San Francisco's Grace Cathedral, no one had been bellier or smellier. His funeral had rivaled that of Diana in spectacle and in attendance. Magda had made sure the Mayor and several other city, state, and federal officials were present. The President sent flowers.

Adriano quietly got up, walked over to Lee, and put his arms around his neck. They looked at the urn holding the ashes of the man for whom they had cared, and with whom they had lived, for the last few years, including the last six months of a ravaging cancer. He had introduced them. He had married them. He had loved them very much. He had been their *family*.

"When I go, please just toss me into the surf," Lee said after a bit.

"And put my ashes in the middle of a redwood sapling so that I can become food for a forest."

Lee smiled, knowing his lover's romantic notions of the afterlife.

"We've got a while for that."

"Let's hope," Adriano said, all seriousness. "One never knows."

"No," Lee said. "One never knows. All the more reason to live in the moment. These next couple of months, I'm certainly going to try."

"Do. Or do not. There is no try," Adriano offered in his best, raspy Yoda impersonation.

Lee laughed, kissing the hands Adriano had draped around his shoulders. He closed his book, marking his place with a folded crossword puzzle. "Whatever thy bidding is my master. Let's head out and see what Orvieto has to offer. We promised Peg we'd meet her for a drink. The grand Lady of the Plaza awaits!"

"Café Volsini?"

"Where else?"

CHAPTER VIII

Vescovo

Sunday, December 1, 2013, midmorning, Orvieto

The Bishop of Orvieto lit a cigarette and looked out the closed window of his office toward the cathedral. He wasn't supposed to smoke inside, but who was going to stop him?

Outside, a bus of German tourists was disgorging itself on the plaza in front of the Duomo. Jesus—he was supposed to bless them later. Christ.

A year. It had been a year.

God, these people. What was it with them? Now every age had to have a martyr, and this town was already crawling with them. *Crawling* with them.

He took a long, deep drag and coughed. There was a knock on the door.

"Yes, what?" the cleric snarled, stamping out the butt in a cut-glass cruet, ostensibly reserved for communion wine.

The door opened, and his secretary, one of the diocese's many overly devout, bored, and retired gray-haired battle-axes, poked in her carefully shellacked head.

"Your Eminence. The doctor is downstairs. He said that you called. Are you feeling all right? I didn't know you weren't well. I'd have been happy to send for him if you need—"

"Dear God! I can make my own phone calls," he snapped. "I'm fine."

The woman shrank back against the door frame.

"I'm sorry." The bishop bared his teeth in a semblance of friendliness. *Oh, these people. Everyone is so sensitive.* "Yes, I'm fine. I called him myself." He patted her gently on the shoulder, suddenly wishing he had a Tic Tac to mask the odor of his vice. "I didn't want to worry you. Send him up. It's nothing."

The elderly assistant smiled, appearing somewhat placated, and backed out the door, shutting it quietly.

"Christ." The bishop reached for another cigarette, dropping his grin like an exercise painfully undertaken. *You can't do a fucking thing in this town without everyone knowing.* It was a problem—*had* been a problem. Still was, only a little less so since last year. "Come in," the bishop commanded, hearing his guest approach. He didn't bother hiding the cigarette.

"You sent for me, Reverend Bishop?"

The cleric motioned for his guest to sit. The young doctor took a seat in a simple straight-backed chair facing the desk. The prelate sat down, the cathedral's facade behind him in the window framing his red-capped head.

"*He* was here."

"Yes," the doctor whispered. "I know. I saw him last night in *Sant'Andrea.*"

The bishop leaned back in his chair and took a deep drag of his cigarette. The smoke was bothering the doctor. Good. He blew a mighty puff directly across the desk.

"I thought he was not to be seen again. I asked you to take care of it."

"I-ah...I have no excuses, Your Eminence."

"Indeed, you do not," the senior priest snarled, stamping out the butt with a vengeance. "At least you have not forgotten the prohibition on excuses. Fix it." He hastily made the sign of the cross from across the desk. "Now go."

The young man got up slowly, bowed, and turned for the door.

"Luke? *Dr. Wagner?* Aren't you forgetting something?"

The doctor stopped, pivoted gently, and slowly backtracked across the room. Walking around the desk, he dropped to one knee and took the bishop's right hand in his own. Delicately raising it to his lips, he kissed the episcopal ring.

"Forgive me, Reverend Bishop."

"When we're done, then we'll speak of penance and salvation. Get out of here."

Luke stood up, bowed again, and backed slowly out of the room, crossing himself as he exited and closed the door behind him. The Bishop of Orvieto didn't look up.

CHAPTER IX

Andrea

Sunday, December 1, 2013, early afternoon, Orvieto

"Cari! Ciao!"

Peg was already waiting for them at "her" table at Café Volsini. Kisses exchanged, the trio sat down just as a tray of wine and nibbles descended.

"I took the liberty of ordering for you. Grazie mille, Signora Volsini!"

La Madrina nailed them with a look and slipped the bill underneath the stem of Peg's wineglass.

"I don't think she likes us," Adriano grimaced.

"She doesn't like anyone. She doesn't need to." Peg smiled while popping a *pizzetta* into her mouth. "She just *is*. So, how was your first full day in Orvieto? Isn't it a treasure!"

For the next twenty minutes or so, Adriano and Lee shared their impressions and Peg nodded, smiled, and tacked on recommendations for day trips to each of their revelations and queries.

Somewhere between "You simply *must* do the walk to Bolsena" and "Don't miss the Etruscan necropolis," Lee noticed La Madrina Volsini walking quietly behind the counter of the antique bar to light a small white candle—definitely not electric or battery powered—in front a faded Polaroid photo of what looked to be a young, almost boyish, priest. She said nothing as she did so, but Lee noticed that as she struck the match, the other three bar staffers stopped what they were doing, bowed ever so slightly, and said nothing while the elderly café owner lit the votive. Delicately, she let her wrinkled fingers caress the photo. Crossing herself, she turned abruptly, once again all business. As if momentarily in suspended animation, the café staff quickly returned to life, pretending not to have noticed the almost sacred machinations of their boss.

"Who's that?" Lee asked quietly, nodding toward the mini-memorial behind the bar.

Peg looked to where Signora Volsini had just lit the candle. Her smile cracked, and her face froze. "Oh dear, yes. The Feast of Saint Andrea. It's been a year. Let's go outside. Arrivederci, Signora!" Peg was up and out the door with astonishing speed, as if wanting to be anywhere but inside Café Volsini. Lee didn't know a dress with that many pleats could move so fast or dexterously.

Outside, Peg hustled them down the pavement half a block before she spoke. "Deacon Andrea. Bernardone. She found his body, last year, after he jumped from the cliffs here in Orvieto."

Lee's face went ashen.

"Oh my God," Adriano said, squeezing Lee's hand and looking at him for a reaction. Lee barely felt it and avoided Adriano's eyes, avoided his own thoughts.

Suicide. Adriano squeezed harder. Lee came back to the present.

"Yes. It was quite the scandal, let me tell you! A week before he was to be ordained fully into the priesthood, the bishop got a letter directly from the Vatican in Rome saying that Andrea was 'unfit' or some such excuse. The rumor was that Andrea was gay and that an embarrassing secret was about to bust loose. It was all highly unusual. They told him by fax, if you can believe it. Anyway, poor Andrea just broke down. He jumped from the cliffs right after Mass—on his birthday! Signora Volsini found him the next morning while she was out for her morning walk along the Rupe in front of Floriano's altar."

"The Rupe. What's that?" Lee asked.

"The *Anello della Rupe*—the Ring of the Rock. It's the walking path that circles the entire city at the foot of the cliff. It's quite a drop. Horrible.

His body and face were terribly mangled. Probably died right away. One certainly hopes at least. His body fell right in front of the *Chiesa del Crocifisso.*"

"The Church of the Crucifix," Adriano translated.

"Exactly. Evidently it was one of Andrea's favorite spots. He always helped with the annual Mass in honor of Floriano. So tragic, and ironic, that he should die there."

"I don't recall a St. Floriano," said Lee, searching for historic information, but only as a mask for his own darkening memories.

"He wasn't a saint. He may have been no one at all," said Peg. "His legend is one of Orvieto's most treasured tales. Supposedly, Floriano was a Roman soldier stationed here in the sixth century. Orvieto has always been somewhat rebellious of Roman authority, then and now. Anyway, Floriano, who was Christian, was falsely accused by his fellow soldiers of some horrible crime—murder, theft, adultery, the accounts differ on what was the trumped-up charge. Whatever it was, the stories all have the same ending. Overcome with hopelessness, Floriano threw himself from the cliff before his comrades could do the same."

Lee listened without really hearing. Next door, a ballerina in a mechanical jewelry box popped up while a shop owner finalized a sale to two tourists. Lee's mother had one just like that. He pushed away the thought.

"And the *Chiesa del Crocifisso* is where he was buried," Adriano stated with none of his usual irony when discussing Catholic shrines

"Oh no," said Peg with a dramatic holding up of her palms. "He didn't *die*. As he fell, the story goes, Floriano clutched a crucifix he was wearing around his neck and landed completely uninjured. In gratitude, he immediately carved a cross into the soft tufa, volcanic rock...*with his hands.*" With that Peg put down her arms.

"Is it still there?" Lee asked.

"Yes, if you believe that sort of stuff. I mean, *really*. There's a little chapel there now and every year, around the middle of September as I recall, there's a small service. For the last few years, Andrea was quite in charge of it."

"So," Adriano ventured, "Andrea was popular in Orvieto."

"Popular is the understatement of the decade," said Peg, with none of what Adriano and Lee had already come to expect as her signature theatricality. "Everyone in town just loved him. If there was a good deed to be done, Andrea was doing it, quietly. He didn't call attention to himself. He just moved through the town helping people. It was his birthday the night that he jumped. He killed himself right after Mass at *Sant'Andrea*. His funeral two days later was immense."

That must explain the scuffle during Mass last night, Lee thought. The two young men must have been friends of Andrea, come to pay their respects exactly a year after his death. Was one of the boys Andrea's lover? Both perhaps? Was La Madrina trying to shoo them out of the church because they were gay?

"Wow. Two days after he celebrated his birthday, he was buried from the same altar," Lee stated quietly. Adriano squeezed his hand again. This time he felt it, and was grateful.

"Oh my God, *no*." Peg grabbed her bosom and threw back her head, once again the drama queen holding court. "No. He was buried from *Il Duomo*, the *cathedral*! *Sant'Andrea* isn't big enough to hold all the people that came to Deacon Andrea's funeral, let me tell you. There was even a cardinal who came from Rome. The press was all over, but the bishop refused to let them inside. I, of course, was an exception."

"You went?" Peg didn't strike Lee as the churchgoing type.

"*Everyone* went, the whole town. I did a special blog post all about it," Peg said, releasing her chest and drawing her scarf closer to her neck. "It was the biggest thing to hit Orvieto since the town was liberated from the Germans in World War II—and no, I *wasn't* around for that."

"His name was Andrea and he was born and died on the feast of his namesake," Lee said quietly, more of a statement than a question.

"Hmmm, yes, I hadn't thought of that." Peg frowned a bit and stopped walking. "That would have been a good angle into the story. Can't believe I didn't use it. Oh well, I can always update the blog, but, maybe not. I wouldn't want people to think I was trying to promote myself using Andrea's memory."

I can't imagine that would stop you, Lee thought. Fear of pissing off La Madrina was more like it.

"How old was he?" Adriano asked.

"Twenty-nine when he jumped. Yesterday would have been his thirtieth birthday."

"My age," Lee said. "To the day."

The trio walked on in silence for a few minutes. Then Peg started up again with a list of sights for Adriano and Lee to visit. "....and you simply *must* take in the British war cemetery just outside of town and the site of the Camorena massacre, kind of a locals' WWII fetish if you ask me. And you must not miss Civita di Bagnoregio, like a mini-Orvieto and just a few miles away. It's another one of Umbria's delicious mountaintop villages and practically deserted. Less than a dozen people live there full-time. It's totally isolated from the outside world and only connected by a tiny little pedestrian bridge that looks for anything like an Italian Great Wall of China. No thank you."

The same street vendor they had encountered briefly yesterday afternoon ambled up to them.

"How 'bout you, Signor? CDs. Music for the soul."

"No thanks," said Lee as he turned away.

"It's great music. Why don't you give it a listen, man? Please?"

"I told you no already," snarled Peg with her hand uncurling like a fern in dismissal. "Now leave us alone!"

"You don't have to yell at me." The dark-skinned peddler shuffled away, dejected, like a puppy caught peeing on the rug. The two Chinese kids from Mass the night before turned the corner, and the hawker perked up, in hot pursuit.

"CDs. Music for the soul." The street merchant continued his plaintive and futile query.

"God, he drives me crazy," Peg harrumphed, shoving her gloved hands into her coat. "I never take his crap and *still* he asks. I don't know why the carbinieri let these people roam around like that. It didn't used to be that way. Most of them are just drug dealers, pimps, and hookers from *Africa*. We're getting overrun by *immigrati*!" She spit out the word, then instantly retreated into a practiced serenity. "Ah, here we are. My street. You can drop me here. Ciao!" said Peg, who was gone in a swirl of fabric and arm gestures.

"I guess she doesn't like music," Lee said.

"Yeah, so much for Ms. Nicey-Nice."

As they started to make their way back to their apartment, Lee glanced over his shoulder. Head down, and backpack heavy with his wares, the huckster wandered down the street. It was pretty clear this guy was not Italian, likely illegal, probably from somewhere in North Africa. The papers were full of the exploding refugee crisis. Syria. Morocco. Libya. Every day seemed to bring another story of some ship, hideously crammed, crashing ashore on the southern coast of Italy. Or, worse yet, sinking with hundreds of petrified people aboard.

Lee could hear Brian's voice now: "Everyone's a refugee from somewhere and someone. Remember, our number one job here on earth is to make more love in the world."

Even on his deathbed, Brian had been a priest. Sermonizing to the end. Suddenly Lee missed his best friend very much.

As the peddler wandered out of sight, Lee couldn't help but wonder about the youthful deacon who had jumped to his death last year on the Feast of St. Andrew. November 30—both Lee's and Andrea's birthday. Thirty years ago. That day, two mothers labored to bring a child into the world, one in Italy, one in Virginia. Only one of those children remained. At some point, both had wanted to become priests. A strange coldness came over Lee, one that had nothing to do with the Italian winter.

Everyone's a refugee from somewhere and someone. Remember, our number one job here on earth is to make more love in the world.

"Earth to Lee, come in Lee." Adriano was waving his hands.

"Oh, sorry. My mind was somewhere else. What did you say?"

"I said, we'd better be getting home, or you'll be bartering for black market CDs." Adriano motioned with a nod of his head down the Corso.

The would-be music man was headed their way again, having terrified the Chinese couple into practically running into a nearby gelato stand. Lee didn't want to be rude, but neither did he want to be pinned down for a sale.

"CDs. Music for the soul."

Poor guy, Lee thought, looking at the immigrant as they quickened their pace and headed to their apartment. Must be rough having everyone treat you like a walking radioactive isotope. He certainly didn't look like someone surrounded by a lot of love.

Love. According to Peg, the young deacon Andrea had been surrounded by the love of all of Orvieto, and still that hadn't been enough to keep him from stepping off a cliff. Andrea must have felt terribly alone, terribly rejected, terribly afraid. Lee knew all about that.

"CDs. Music for the soul..."

Hand in hand, they walked homeward, leaving the peddler behind.

CHAPTER X

Fallen Angel

Sunday, December 1, 2013, near midnigh, the outskirts of Rome

The dance floor was packed. A thousand sweaty bodies writhed in a Roman hypnosis of drugs, music, and alcohol. The floors were wet with sex.

His inside chest pocket vibrated with the text. Grigori pulled out his phone.

No Jew. No Co. Uni. Usual. 2

A regular. He recognized the number instantly, and the code: No jewelry. Don't wear cologne. Bring the uniform. Our usual. Two a.m. Well, that would pay the rent this month, actually, a bit more. After his trip to Orvieto for Andrea's anniversary, he needed some distraction. After running into *Herr Doktor,* not to mention that asswipe bishop, he needed a break. He needed money. He needed to fuck. He needed to forget. The drugs would take care of that.

Si, he texted back and slipped the cell phone into his leather jacket, squeezing past a trio of groping dancers to make his way to the exit.

At least this one didn't even want to touch him. Who was he to judge? And, it paid well. Very well, actually. Grigori glanced at his watch, a gift from that very same client. The train from Orvieto had been late last night, and he hadn't gotten much sleep. Tonight was supposed to have been a welcome escape, a few drunken, ecstasy-fueled hours at the club to wipe away the memories of last night—of the last year.

Fucking bishop. Fucking doctor. Andrea.

"Ciao, Grigori." A slinky blonde in a short and diaphanous sheath wrapped a leg around him. "Haven't seen you in a while. How 'bout it?"

"Can't. Gotta go. Duty calls."

The young woman pouted.

"Sometimes, Grigori, I don't think you like girls."

The muscular youth bit her ear gently and licked the back of her neck. "Cara," he said with an indecent grab under her skirt. "You know better than that. I like everything."

Grigori stepped outside into the rain and hailed one of the many taxis waiting outside.

"*Il Vaticano. Presto.*"

CHAPTER XI

The Rupe

Monday, December 2, 2013, Orvieto

Jet lag finally caught up with them. The Tower of the Moor had chimed eleven times before Adriano and Lee managed to pull themselves from bed, make breakfast, ply themselves with strong Italian coffee, and begin their first official tour of Orvieto by foot. Courtesy of the online guide from Lady Peg, they had outlined a complete circuit of town, from top to bottom, literally.

"We'll start at St. Patrick's Well and then down to the Rupe through the Porta Soliana," Lee said. "From there we head left and pass right by the base of the well and then walk over the tunnel that takes the funicular down to the train station. Doing the whole route back to Porta Soliana should take us about two hours, just in time for a peek at the cathedral, then home for crosswords, a cocktail, and dinner."

"You want to see where that young deacon jumped from the cliffs."

"That's a morbid thing to say," Lee said, annoyed at having been so accurately pinned.

"I know you, Poirot," Adriano said, kissing Lee on the neck as they exited the tall wooden doors of their rented palazzo. "You can't ignore a mystery."

Agatha Christie's fussy Belgian detective was one of Adriano's favorite pet names for Lee and also one of Lee's favorite fictional characters.

Lee shrugged, returned the kiss, and wrapped his scarf dramatically around his neck against the cold. "Well fine, then. Let's go, Captain Hastings," he said, the moniker that of Poirot's faithful sidekick. "Lead on."

The path in front of their apartment coiled under the arch of Orvieto's mayor's office and onto the town's main square, Piazza della Repubblica. To their right, the Corso—Orvieto's main commercial street—spread out in the distance, with an ever so slight downward tilt.

"This leads straight to St. Patrick's Well," Lee said, reading from his iPhone. "From there, there's a walking path down to the Rupe."

For the first fifteen minutes, the Corso was all business: a mixture of small family-owned shops, tobacco stands, delicatessens, trattorias, bars, and wine shops, along with the more than occasional European fashion brand. Orvieto may be medieval, but it catered to the vacation trade. Lee was surprised, but grateful, not to see a Starbucks. Everything was Italian here.

"They certainly know how to preserve their culture," Lee said.

"They've been doing it for three thousand years," Adriano replied. "They've become good at it."

About twenty minutes into their stroll, the Corso abandoned its touristy veneer and became more subdued. Instead of stalls selling bottles of Orvieto Classico bunched in packs of three for easy shipping overseas, the side streets gave way to small chapels, neighborhood butcher shops, barbers, florists, small hardware stores, and bars clearly meant for locals. Half an hour after they set out, they were at the end of the Corso and the eastern edge of Orvieto's daunting cliff face. Directly in front of them, punctuating the terminus of the Corso, was a twenty-foot-high iron sculpture of a chalice, crowned with a huge oval host radiating a halo of golden rays, the official monument to the Eucharistic Miracle of Bolsena in 1263.

"No question about this being a Catholic town," Adriano said, shaking his head. "You can't miss that."

To the left of the artistic religious statement was Orvieto's connection to the outside world, a funicular built in the late 1800s. Originally powered by water and gravity, it had been converted to electricity and now whisked people up and down the side of the mountain in less than five minutes, right to the front of the train station. It had been their ceremonial entry vehicle into Orvieto a few days ago. To the right of the funicular, overlooking their entrance to the Rupe and Porta Soliana, was the first stop of their tour, St. Patrick's Well.

"It has nothing to do with St. Patrick," Lee explained as they walked toward what, if the guidebooks were accurate, was one of medieval Europe's architectural wonders and one of Orvieto's chief tourist attractions. As if to prove the point, a small van of seniors and a dozen or so middle school students were standing in line for a ticket. "It was named this because it reminded people of St. Patrick's cave in Ireland, supposedly the entrance to purgatory. It really should be called Pope Clement's Well. He's the one who built it, actually basically replumbed all of Orvieto in the late 1520s after he escaped from the Vatican following the Sack of Rome. He was petrified of being cut off from food and fresh water again like he had been when he escaped Charles the Fifth."

"Spain's Charles the Fifth?" Adriano perked up. "What did he have to do with Orvieto?"

"He was the Holy Roman Emperor who looted the Vatican and forced Pope Clement to escape here to Orvieto in 1527. Orvieto was the papacy in exile for almost a year. Actually, a bunch of popes lived here over the centuries."

"You learn something new every day," Adriano said, drawing close the lip of the well, then drawing back. "Yikes, that's not for me."

Lee stepped forward and peered down. The well spiraled down for over 170 feet, surrounded by a unique staircase, constructed in a double helix—DNA in stone. It had been considered a miracle of design in the Middle Ages. Now, it just seemed vast, dark, and claustrophobic.

"Is there a door at the bottom?" Adriano asked, half pleading.

Lee shook his head, knowing his husband's fear of subterranean spaces. "No, it's a long, dark walk down, then a long walk back up. It's not recommended for seniors or people with heart conditions."

"Or people who don't like rats or basements," said Adriano, adding, "It will be a cold day in hell before I go down there."

"We can skip it," Lee said, to Adriano's obvious relief.

Leaving behind the senior and student tourists, Adriano and Lee walked along the fortified wall that formed the border of the well and one of Orvieto's medieval gates, now semi-abandoned. The worn and chipped masonry looked down now only on the occasional hiker, stray dog, or curious San Franciscan.

"The Rupe," Adriano announced with a flourish. "The Ring of the Rock."

"Perfect for me," said Lee, giving Adriano's butt a playful squeeze. "Even I can't get lost."

"You are terrible at directions," Adriano said, shielding his glasses from the sun. "How did you make it around the world by ship?"

"I wasn't driving." Lee wiped a gnat away from his eyes. "I was editing the newspaper for the passengers."

"Good thing. Let's go." They began their descent down the steep, uneven, and stone-pocked path and through the Porta Soliana. For the first time, the pair got a real sense of Orvieto's scale and strategic importance. Looking up from the walking path, the volcanic walls of Orvieto presented an unforgiving edifice several hundred feet straight up. "Yep, that would do it," Adriano said, as if answering Lee's thoughts. "A jump from there would not be something you'd live to repeat."

"No," Lee answered quietly. "No."

They walked on for over an hour without encountering anyone. To their right was a dense tangle of bushes, trees, and the occasional rugged fence denoting a private olive grove, garden, or vineyard spreading down the rest of the mount's more gentle slope. To their left was the relentless verticality of Orvieto's impregnable natural defense, the Rock.

For about half an hour the route was paved, albeit roughly. Soon thereafter, however, the path sloped downward before heading up into a thicket of brambles, bamboo, and ancient ivy-dripping foliage. A huge tree, recently fallen, to gauge by the wetness of its roots and ripped-up moss, blocked the path.

"Now what?" Lee frowned.

"This way." Adriano pointed to a stone plinth painted with two stripes, white on top, then red. "This is the sign for footpath."

"Well, aren't you the Eagle Scout?"

"You're not the only one who can google." Adriano smiled, stepping over the obstacle and offering Lee his hand. "Onward!"

"It's like being on a big 'splore with Winnie the Pooh!"

"Let's go, Christopher Robin."

About fifteen minutes later, the path veered sharply upward to cross the road, revealing the first cars they had seen in over an hour. Now against the rock face, they found themselves below a complex of buildings considerably newer than medieval.

"Those are the abandoned WWII barracks," said Lee. "I was reading about them last night. Mussolini built them. They're next to the old Augustinian church near Porta Vivaria, the gate that Pope Clement restored after he fled here following the Sack of Rome."

After a leafy bend in the path, the view opened up to a stunning vista of huge moss-covered stone structures, about three hundred yards to the right, and slightly downhill from the Rupe. It looked like pictures of Mayan temples from the *National Geographic* of Lee's youth.

"That must be the Etruscan necropolis," Lee said flipping through his iPhone for the Wikipedia page he had found last night. "In ancient times, Orvieto—then known as Velzna—was the capital of the Etruscan nation. Once a year, all the other Etruscan cities would send representatives here for a huge congress. The city was considered the most important city on the Italian peninsula."

"Before Rome."

"Yes, and even after," Lee scrolled through his device. "Wow—listen to this. The Etruscan citadel of Velzna, or Volsini—"

"Volsini," Adriano interrupted. "That's the **café owner's** name, right?"

"Hmmm." Lee pursed his lips. "You're right. Maybe she is Etruscan. God knows she's old enough."

"Keep reading."

"Velzna/Volsini, now known as Orvieto, was one of the most powerful cities of Etruria with great wealth, luxury, and art. According to old accounts, their great wealth and power made the citizens of Volsini so indolent that they at length suffered the management of their commonwealth to be usurped by slaves. Fearful of losing everything, the aristocratic families of Volsini sent a clandestine embassy to Rome in 265 BC asking for military assistance against their former slaves."

"I am Spartacus!" Adriano said with mock dramatics.

"You're a ham, but I love you," Lee said. "Can I finish?"

Adriano nodded.

"Shortly thereafter, a Roman army arrived to lay siege to Orvieto. The subsequent conflict was intense. The Roman consul and commanding general, Quintus Fabius Gurges, was a casualty. A year later his successor, Marcus Fulvius Flaccus, receiving the surrender of Orvieto through its starvation, razed it and executed the leaders of the plebeian party. The first display of gladiators at Rome in 264 BC is believed to have featured now captive freedmen from Orvieto/Volsinii. The Romans rescued and restored the remaining Etruscans of Volsinii, but decided it was necessary to remove them from that location to a less easily defended town on the shores of the nearby Lake Bolsena, from which the new town, gets its name. Bolsena, an adulteration over the years of 'Volsinii,' had none of the natural defenses of the mountain Volsinii and was in no way sovereign. Whereas Volsinii/Orvieto was proudly free from the yoke of Rome, Bolsena was entirely a subjugated colony."

"There's a point coming, yes?" Adriano pushed his glasses up. The sun was intense and making him sweat.

"Almost done," Lee said. "The portable wealth from the Etruscan citadel of Velzna/Orvieto was carried off for the pleasure of Rome and the Romans."

"Now that's cool," Adriano said, once again all geek. "Kind of *Laura Croft: Tomb Raider* meets *Raiders of the Lost Ark*."

"Wait, there's more. This is interesting."

"Oh boy. Here we go."

Lee ignored him. "The great Roman historian, Pliny the Elder, tells a story, taken from the Greek writer Metrodorus of Scepsis, that the objective of the Romans in capturing the Etruscan capital city was to make themselves masters of two thousand rare and spectacular statues that it contained. The two thousand statues—which some consider to be a myth—disappeared with the Roman legions, never to be seen again. Although, over the years, many tales of this hidden cache have surfaced. What is known, is that the ancient city of Orvieto produced the most spectacular examples of high Etruscan sculpture, including the world-famous *Mars of Todi*, which some believe to have been one of these two thousand statues. To this day, archaeologists and black marketers dig in the soft *tufo* of Orvieto for priceless Etruscan artifacts, both on the summit of Orvieto, where many residents are rumored to have basements full of uncatalogued Etruscan masterpieces, and within the valley housing the Etruscan necropolis—a City of the Dead."

"Ooooooh, spooky," Adriano said, mimicking a Halloween ghoul, then stopped. "If you don't think there will be rats."

Lee smiled. "No, unless we come at night and coat ourselves with peanut butter, I think we'll be fine."

Next to the entrance of the necropolis, a small food kiosk had been set up; "Igloo German Beer Garden" an incongruous placard pronounced. Although there were no walls or gates to prevent entry, a ticket booth guarded access to the historic site, three euros each to enter. Adriano ponied up from his pocket with surprising alacrity and paid the politely bored teenaged girl ticket taker.

"I thought you'd kvetch about paying," said a clearly surprised Lee.

"I told you, it sounds like something out of one of my video games— *SimCity* goes ancient. Let's go!"

The necropolis was a two- or three-acre excavation, a mossy Pompeii. Several dozen tombs spread across the flats directly beneath the cliff, most of them open for inspection, with weatherworn inscriptions in the lost Etruscan language carved in the lentils above. Lee and Adriano were the only visitors.

Inside, the tomb was completely dark and musty.

"Spooky," said Lee, repeating Adriano's earlier apt description. "Not a place I'd like to get trapped in at night, but no rats. Come on down."

Adriano ventured in, holding his iPhone on flashlight mode in front of him like a low-rent Indiana Jones. "Don't push me. You know I don't like tight spaces."

"I know, dear."

Inside, the abandoned tomb was just that—abandoned. It smelled of wet earth and moist leaves, but not unpleasantly so. A stone bench was carved against the wall and covered with moss, except for a worn spot in the middle.

"What's this?" Lee motioned for Adriano to shine his iPhone.

The flashlight beam revealed a pile of wax, as if from a long-burning candle.

"When I was a teenager, it was the back of a car," said Lee. "I guess in Orvieto, the Etruscan tombs are where one escapes for a bit of hormone therapy with your significant other."

"Yuck," said Adriano. "I can't imagine a less sexy place for romance than this. Let's go. Wait, what's this?"

Just next to the exit, on the wall next to a display of Etruscan artifacts dug up at the site, was a bronze plaque, faded and patina-covered. It read:

Ministero per i Beni e le Attivita
Soprintendenza per i beni Archeologici dell' Umbria
PERUGIA

Necropoli di Crocifisso Del Tufo
CENTRO VISITA
DOCUMENTAZIONE
Nicolo Volsini
1914–1969

"Volsini. La Donna's husband?"

"Hmm," Lee said. "Possibly."

Leaving the necropolis behind, they continued on with Lee in front. A few minutes later, the path led upward in a gentler slope than the path from where they started. Up ahead, they could see the turn to the largest of Orvieto's four gates, Porta Maggiore.

"This is it."

Lee stopped in his tracks in front of a small door cut into the rock face, secured by an iron gate and rusty padlock. Flanking the door were two bar-covered windows with stone sills, one adorned with a bottle of water from Lourdes, the other with a plastic vase of freshly cut flowers. Above the door was a stone overhang paved with tiles, several of which were chipped and broken in the front, jagged teeth in a stony smile.

"*Il Chiesa del Crocefisso del Tufo,*" Adriano said simply. "This is where Deacon Andrea jumped."

"Where he landed, at least." Lee was already standing up on tiptoe to see inside the darkened cave through the tiny aperture of an iron-barred window. There was no light except for a single glass-enclosed votive candle on a simple stone altar against the back wall of the grotto. Lee could just make out a cross carved into the back wall.

"It looks deserted."

"Except for that candle and these fresh flowers," Adriano said. "Peg did say that once a year there was a ceremony."

"You're right, but that's not a Padre Pio battery-powered job. That's one of your wax seventy-two-hour long-burning specials. Someone has been here to light that candle recently, not to mention the bouquet."

"In memory of Andrea, no doubt," said Adriano, gently putting his hands on his husband's shoulders.

"Or not," Lee said flatly. "They light candles for everything. They're *Catholic.*"

Lee shaded his eyes from the late afternoon sun and peered up the near-vertical rock face. There was nothing on the cliff above them except a solitary olive tree, its aged and gnarled branches clinging to the summit over a hundred feet above.

"What's this?" Adriano pointed.

Turning back to look, Lee's eyes caught sight of a line of squiggled white lettering, painted onto a stone next to the path in front of the chapel.

أنردي: اراك الله فيكم

"Looks vaguely Arabic," Adriano said.

"It's still a bit wet," Lee said, touching the letters. "Maybe the same person who lit the candle?"

"Oh yeah," said Adriano in his most faux ironic tone. "Muslims are always leaving inscriptions at shrines to sixth-century Christians."

"Maybe it's not for Floriano," Lee said. "Maybe it *is* for Deacon Andrea after all."

Adriano nodded. "But why in Arabic?" He pulled out his iPhone to take a photo. "I'll check it out later."

They trudged on, past Porta Magiorre, and then fifteen uphill minutes later walked past Orvieto's main vehicular entrance, the Porta Romana.

"Remember that picture I showed you the other night?" said Lee. "Porta Romana is the one where the Allied tanks entered during World War II to liberate Orvieto from the Germans. Orvieto should have been leveled by the Allies, who were fighting their way up the Italian peninsula, like Monte Cassino was. But there was a German colonel who spared the town."

"I thought you said the Allies would have bombed it? How did the Nazis save it?"

"Orvieto was occupied by the Germans," Lee explained. "After the Allies landed on the Italian mainland, Mussolini was still *officially* in charge, but the real power lay with Hitler's forces. The German commander overseeing Orvieto was a devout Catholic. He didn't speak Italian, and a young local priest didn't speak German, so they communicated in Latin. The colonel knew he couldn't stop the Allies, but he also knew that *der Führer* would expect the Germans to fight to the last man, so he coordinated with the priest and sent a message to the advancing British troops proposing to declare Orvieto an open city."

"Like Rome," said Adriano.

"Exactly. In fact, Orvieto was only the second such open city, after Rome. So, to escape the bombing and inevitable destruction of the city, they agreed to spare Orvieto and its priceless cathedral and medieval buildings and moved the battle. The Germans and the Brits slugged it out, with many casualties, about twenty kilometers away."

"I have to admit," said Adriano, "this town has had more than its share of history. What happened to the Nazi?"

"No one knows," said Lee, "or to the priest. They both kind of disappeared after the war. The article I found was an interview with the British officer who accepted the German's terms. He survived the war and became quite the hero. He's actually been back to Orvieto a few times—received like a conquering hero, you know. According to him though, it really was the mystery German who should get the credit."

For the final forty-five minutes, their walking path was again vehicular free. They were alone with their thoughts and the occasional gecko scurrying for cover among the tufo. To their right, other, smaller hilltop towns encircled Orvieto like a charm bracelet with glittering highlights: a medieval abbey now turned into a Euro-swank B and B; the ruins of Pope Clement's restored aqueduct; some prehistoric fossilized trees; and, cradled in an especially scenic notch, a Cappuchin monastery whose sequestered monks must have a truly spectacular view of Orvieto across the valley. A little more than twenty minutes later they were back at their starting point, Porta Soliano.

"Look!" Lee was practically jumping up and down. "There over the gate! I can't believe we didn't see it when we left this morning! If we'd just turned around and looked up, we would have seen it. The Medici crest! The city must have put it there in gratitude to Giulio de Medici—Pope Clement VII—to thank him for building St. Patrick's Well!"

"More like, Clement put it there himself to remind people."

"St. Patrick's Well wasn't finished by the time Clement left, cynic," said Lee, snapping a photo of the iconic shield with six round balls. "Come on. There's only one more stop on today's grand tour."

"I'm actually quite tired," said Adriano, citing one of their favorite lines from *Erin Brockovich*. Is it much farther? There's an Orvieto Classico with my name on it waiting for me at home."

"Not much farther," said Lee, leading them down the Corso and onto the Via del Duomo.

"This better be worth it." Adriano raised his eyebrows. "I know you. You make it sound like Chartres or the Sagrada Familia. How famous can it be if I haven't heard of it?"

Lee made shooshing motions with his hand and pulled up Peg's breath-lessly hyperbolic blog on his iPhone. He read as they walked.

Considered the ultimate expression of Italian Renaissance archi-tecture, the Cathedral of Orvieto is at the pinnacle of ecclesiastical design. No trip to 'The Rock' is complete without a visit. Located next to the Papal Palace—now a museum of the Renaissance and Etruscan archaeology—the cathedral and its environs have been a safe haven for more than one pope during times of political duress. The Borgia, the Medici, several others, all have decamped to Orvieto's castle-like slopes when danger threatened. Started in 1290 by Pope Nicholas IV and completed over three centuries later, Orvieto's cathedral, *Il Duomo*, was built specifically to house the relics from the Miracle of Bolsena. It also contains the bones of Orvieto's patron saint, famously murdered by a band of Cathar heretics, and priceless art-works by the renowned Fra Angelico and Signorelli. Quite simply, *Il Duomo* is considered one of earth's great masterpieces, and the most complete and unaltered example of Italian High Middle Ages art, culture, design, and spirituality given form. *Il Duomo de Orvieto*—man's aspirations for the afterlife and his devotion to God set in marble, tile, and paint.

"Peg never met an adjective she didn't like." Lee frowned.

Like a giant jack-in-the-box, *Il Duomo* popped into view around the last corner of the street leading to it.

"Sweet Jesus. That is the most gorgeous church I have ever seen," Adri-ano said, with none of his usual edge.

"Wow," was all Lee could manage.

Even in the gathering twilight, the cathedral fairly glowed, as if lit by an independent power source, its four delicate towers and entire facade clad in a golden skin of mosaic tiles with Biblical themes. The four evangelists, as represented by their winged symbols, St. Matthew's angel; St. Mark's lion; St. Luke's ox; and the eagle of "the beloved dis-ciple," St. John, crowned pilasters above the doors. Over the two-story bronze great doors was perched a pietà, Mary holding the body of her dead son, Jesus.

Peg, it seemed, hadn't been overstating.

"It's locked." Adriano pulled harder on the handles marked "Tourist Entrance" in four different languages.

"Let's check around the back. Catholic cathedrals almost always have a small side door where the faithful enter."

"How do you know this stuff?"

Lee shrugged.

Sure enough, to the left and rear of the cathedral was a smaller, almost hidden entrance, two simple wooden doors and a sign.

"Ingresso riservato al culto. Entrance reserved for religious worship," Adriano read aloud. "You were right. Let's go!"

"So suddenly you're devout?"

"For this, I'm a member of the faithful. Plus, praying is free. The tourist entrance costs four euros." Adriano had already taken off his hat and was entering, a practical if not practicing Catholic. Lee followed.

The cathedral's interior was vast, and surprisingly stark in its simplicity.

"It's huge," Lee whispered, crossing himself with holy water from the font to the right of the entrance. A few yards away, an elderly security guard walked back and forth.

"Let's check it out," said Adriano as he crossed himself with holy water. Seeing Lee's raised eyebrow, he replied, "If I don't bless myself, he'll think I'm just a heathen tourist trying to sneak in without paying."

"Aren't you?"

"Let's go see the relics."

Except for the guard, they were alone. Their steps echoed in the cavernous space, as unadorned as the exterior was spectacularly over-the-top. The glittering exception to the nave's echoing two-tone gray-and-white marble was the high altar, behind which the walls were completely covered in frescoes depicting scenes from the life of the Virgin. Framing the altar, like nearly identical bookends, were two side chapels.

"That will be the Chapel of the Madonna," Lee said as quietly as possible, motioning to the right. "It's the one with frescoes by Fra Angelico. I read about it on the plane. It also has the priceless works by Signorelli, including the *Preaching of the Antichrist* and the *Resurrection of the Flesh*. Quite racy actually, the 'flesh' being resurrected is generally beefy and male."

"I'll drink to that." Adriano leered.

"Apostate." Lee smiled.

"It's closed."

"What?" Lee was downcast, but his husband was correct. The chapel was locked up tight with the lights off. Lee peered through the bars and could just make out the muscled thigh of a naked man clawing his way out of the earth with Jesus beckoning overhead.

"Of course, it's closed. This is the *Church*. Praying comes for free but viewing priceless fifteenth-century masterpieces..." Adriano rubbed in fingers together in the universal sign for "pay me."

"The Chapel of the Corporal is open, on the other side."

"Corporal who?"

"Jesus, you really *are* a bad Catholic. The 'corporal' as in the 'corpus.' The body of Christ. Come on. I'll show you."

Almost a mirror image of its sister sanctuary, the Chapel of the Corporal was indeed open, and empty save for a white-habited nun sitting at the very front, clutching a rosary and staring fixedly at an enormous and elaborately adorned silver-and-gilt reliquary, the Miracle of Bolsena.

"Luther was right," Adriano huffed. "The cost of that alone would have fed a lot more than the five thousand. Grotesque."

The couple walked quietly to a rear pew and sat down to look at the grandiose sanctuary, crawling with gold leaf and ringed with various papal coats of arms and religious iconography. Just visible inside a two-foot-by-two-foot locked glass door was an ancient piece of cloth, marked by two dark stains. A dozen candles flickered and danced in reflection.

"According to legend," Lee whispered, "a priest who was doubting his faith, specifically the presence of the body and blood of Christ during communion, was in the town of Bolsena—"

"Volsini? The town that the Romans built to relocate the Etruscans they had defeated here in Orvieto?" Adriano interrupted.

"Exactly. It's very close. Peg mentioned it too, the other night. Anyway, while he was saying Mass, right at the moment of transubstantiation—"

"The moment that Jesus miraculously pops down from heaven and enters the Holy Communion Twinkie."

Lee ignored him and continued. "Yes, *that* moment when, according to Catholic teaching, the sacred host actually *becomes* the incarnate body of Christ, and the wine, his blood. At that very moment, the host began to actually bleed onto the altar and onto the corporal, the cloth under the chalice. *That* up there above the altar in that orgy of gold, silver, and precious stones, behind the glass, is the actual cloth with the bloodstains."

"The bloodstains of Jesus Christ?"

"If you believe."

"Let's go, I'm done." Adriano got up to leave.

Lee made the sign of the cross, habitually, and followed, leaving the nun to her vigil.

Outside, darkness had fallen and the Duomo's facade was bathed in carefully focused spotlights. The effect was breathtaking.

"Well, I'll give it to the Church," said Adriano. "They do know how to build gorgeous buildings. Gaudy, obscenely expensive, and a testament to the hypocrisy innate in its nature. But impressive."

Lee didn't say anything.

"You don't actually *believe* that stuff, do you? I mean, the blood of Jesus, the stain, yada yada yada."

"What I *believe* is that for over eight hundred years, people have been coming here to see it," said Lee. "The *history* is what I believe in. It's fascinating."

"It's troubling."

"Apostate."

The couple walked on, stopping several times for Adriano to get pictures ("I don't have to believe to believe that it's fabulous"). A few minutes later and they were back in the apartment.

"I'm going to cook dinner now, Your Holiness. Want a drink?"

"Yes," Lee answered. "I promise not to bless it."

"It's Orvieto Classico, anyway. I don't think the Miracle of Bolsena bled white."

While Adriano started dinner, Lee settled in on the couch with an especially challenging acrostic crossword puzzle themed "Medici, Borgia, and the Renaissance." Right up his alley. On the coffee table lay a new book titled *41.43 N; 49.56 W*, indicating the coordinates of Lee's other obsession, the *Titanic*. It was a present from Magda that had arrived in the morning post. Ah, a perfect moment, glass of wine, a cryptogram to untangle, a new book for bedtime reading, and his talented husband cooking dinner. Lee surveyed their sabbatical surroundings: small, even cramped, but tastefully laid out. Ikea for the Dark Ages. Phillip the Fair meets Philippe Starck. All the furniture was sleek, simple, and small. And, even though you hit your head on a stone arch if you weren't careful after its use, the bathroom had a bidet. *You gotta love Europe.*

"Suicide is a mortal sin."

Lee looked up from his cocoon on the sofa.

"What?"

Adriano stood in the entrance between the kitchen and living room, his hands coated in flour, the sound and aroma of sizzling olive oil in the background. "Peg said that young deacon killed himself by jumping off the cliff, right?"

"Yeah, so?"

Now it was Adriano's turn to pierce his lover with an "I thought you were a good Catholic" glare. "Disgraced gay deacons who kill themselves don't have elaborate funerals in the Catholic Church, presided over by a bishop, much less in *the* biggest church in town and the depository of a supposed miracle. Suicide is a mortal sin."

Lee put down his book and thought about it. Adriano shrugged and disappeared into the tiny kitchen.

Adriano is right. That is strange.

The Anglicans might get by with that, or maybe even a remote Catholic church in the hinterlands, but here in Italy, less than an hour from Rome in one of Europe's prime pilgrimage sites? Plus, Peg said that the funeral was packed, so it wasn't like the deacon who jumped to his death was given a private, small-time send-off. And a cardinal. Peg said that a cardinal came from Rome for the funeral. That would seem an odd choice, given that the Vatican had so summarily put the kibosh on Andrea's vocation—by fax no less. Was the cardinal there out of guilt, to observe, or something else?

"Oh, I almost forgot," Adriano said, popping his head out of the kitchen. "I checked that Arabic script we found next to Floriano's chapel."

"What did it say?" Lee propped himself up on the couch.

Adriano brought the laptop and turned the screen toward his husband. Lee looked up and met Adriano's gaze.

"Google Translate doesn't lie."

أندريا: بارك الله فيكم. Andrea: May Allah Bless You.

Adriano closed the laptop and returned to cooking. Lee tried to steer his interest back to his puzzle. No such luck. Why would a Catholic deacon be eulogized in Arabic? Suddenly, acrostics and the reigns of Medici Popes Leo X and Clement VII seemed much less intriguing than the suicide of Deacon Andrea Bernardone, the young man from Orvieto who shared his birthday.

CHAPTER XII

The Swiss Guard

December 10, 1527 (Julian Calendar), later that evening, Orvieto

"Enter and be blessed," Clement said upon hearing the secret knock—six sharp evenly spaced raps on the door frame (one for each ball of the Medici coat of arms) and three staccato taps (one for each Person of the Holy Trinity) on the door itself—that bespoke one of his guardians. Cousin Giovanni had devised the code to identify his boyish lovers for discreet admittance to his Vatican apartments after he became Pope Leo X.

Dear cousin, Clement thought, you got by with murder, figuratively speaking, and the people loved you for it! *I had to sneak out of Rome dressed as a peasant and they're burning my effigy in the streets! Life was so unfair.* Clement unlocked the door, then seated himself in the unsuccessful semblance of a throne in this godforsaken burg.

"Your Holiness."

A young man entered and fell to one knee, head bowed.

"Arise, my son. Speak."

The Swiss Guard stood, revealing the already classic colors of his uniform, the blue and gold of the late Pope Julius's della Rovere family crest, on top of which Pope Leo had added a dash of Medici red. The effect was formal but rumpled after six months without a wash and a muddy flight from Rome.

"I am your servant, Holy Father."

The youth rose. Cousin Gio would have liked this one, Clement pondered in that corner of his mind where resided his most secular and distracted thoughts. If he had a sister Clement might be interested, but she couldn't be any prettier than this. Oh well. Sodomy and consensual debauchery weren't unique to Cousin Gio, before or after his ascent to the Throne of Peter. *Yes, dear cousin, you would certainly have found pleasure in the handsome physique of this one, worthy of one of Raphael's models, I dare say.* Poor Raphael. Clement was sure every fresco in which a Medici or one of their lovely consorts had artfully cavorted had been marked by the vandal's torch after The Sack. He did hope the rabble at least didn't desecrate Raphael's tomb in the Pantheon the way they did to the burial chamber of Pope Julius. A mental shudder. Defacing the tomb of a pope he could live with, but the Divine Raphael was another thing, he—

The Switzer coughed.

"Ah yes." Clement smiled, snapping out of his reverie. "I have a job for you."

"Yes, Your Holiness." The strapping soldier started to genuflect again.

"Oh stop, please," admonished Clement, and waved him up. "You'll be doing that all night at this rate." He chuckled while he said it.

The guard smiled back.

My God, even his teeth are straight, such a novelty in 1527. Ah, youth. "How old are you?"

"Seventeen, Your Holiness."

Clement sighed. *Seventeen...* At seventeen Clement was gallivanting around France and the Netherlands with Cousin Gio—sorry, Su Eminenca Cardinal de Medici di Firenze—waiting out the reign of that wretched Borgia, Pope Alexander VI. Oh well, as forced exiles went, that one had been pretty good. Gio/Leo had had his fill of willing French boys, and a plethora of Dutch girls had seemed pleased with Clement's largesse, as well. The Emperor Maximilian and his son had been divine hosts, certainly better than this new Holy Roman Imbecile, Charles. *Ah, where was I?*

"We must secure ourselves from future troubles. I need a discreet messenger to our Most Catholic Prince, Henry VIII of England. Will you undertake such a charge?"

"Your Holiness," gasped the young man. "Your wish—"

"Yes, yes, I know. My wish is your command. Would that his most vaunted and pernicious Excellency the Holy Roman Emperor had felt the same and we'd both still be in Rome inside the Vatican wall. Charles, the Borgias, nothing good has come out of Spain since the time of Hadrian."

"His Majesty, the Holy Roman Emperor Charles was born in Flanders, Your Holiness."

"What?" Clement didn't know whether to be more shocked by the impudence of this teenaged correction or the fact that he had made a mistake.

"Your Holiness"—the guard once again sank to his knees—"I beg your forgiveness, I was merely—"

"Sacred Heart of Christ, please think nothing of it. You are quite correct. The King of Spain he may also be, along with seemingly everything else under heaven including this 'New World' at the end of creation in whose thrall Portugal and Spain seem so bewitched. But you are correct. Born in Flanders was 'Our Protector,' Holy Roman Emperor Charles V née Charles I of Spain. You are forgiven." Clement laughed, waving the lad to his feet yet again during this suddenly most casual and unusual of audiences. Most people trembled in front of a pope, especially a Medici one. This one seemed, well, uniquely self-assured.

The guard smiled.

Those teeth again, and that dimple. Where had that been hiding? "Do you have a sister?"

"I beg your pardon, Holiness?"

"Nothing, I-ah...You were with me in Rome...on the steps when Charles's troops stormed St. Peters?"

"Yes, Your Holiness." The smile disappeared from his gloriously dented chin. And then, quite quietly he said, "We all were."

Silence.

"One hundred forty-six?"

"One hundred forty-seven, Your Holiness. My best...One of our comrades died as we fled en route to *Castel Sant'Angelo*."

One hundred forty-seven out of one hundred eighty-seven Swiss Guards, dead on the steps of Christendom's holiest of holies, yards away from the bones of St. Peter himself, the very Rock on which Christ's Church had been built. They had died so that Clement might live. They had fought, almost to the last man, just to give Clement and his ragtag curia time to escape Charles's troops as they scaled the Vatican walls to begin a debauch of rape and pillage. And Clement had let it happen. He should have seen it coming. How could he have been so foolish as to think that mere religion would prevent thousands of mercenaries from looting the world's richest city when they hadn't been paid or properly fed in months? They were hungry, they were poor, and they were constantly fighting to defend a corrupt and bloated aristocracy of faith. Perhaps Luther had been right after all.

"Why does the pope, whose wealth today is greater than the wealth of the richest Crassus, build the basilica of Saint Peter with the money of poor believers rather than with his own money?"

Oh, how the Medici have fallen.

"I am sorry." Clement heaved a great, groaning breath, escaping in a chilly haze in the frigid air of Orvieto's Papal Palace. He was sorry for so, so many things. "I, too, have lost my best friend." Would that Gio, Pope Leo, still be alive. He would have known what to do.

"Your Holiness did everything that he could," the guard offered quietly, starting to step closer to his pontifical sovereign, but then stepping away.

"Maybe. Maybe not. It is in God's hands now."

"You are God's hands."

The Pope looked up to find the teenager's face streaked with tears. More to his surprise, so was his own. "My son." He reached out to the young man, who knelt and kissed the Pontiff's ring.

They stayed that way for a while, a minute, maybe five, saying nothing in the cold winter evening of Orvieto. Outside, the Tower of the Moor clock chimed five times. Finally, Clement patted the young man on the head and then reached under his chin to pull his face up to look at him.

"You know, my son is about your age." The Pope looked directly in the eyes of the young man at his feet.

The guard pulled his chin from the Pope's hands and turned away, his jaws working in silent consternation as if desperately searching for something to say, before finally offering, "Your cousin, you mean, *Il Moro*, the Noble Alessandro, the son of your nephew, Lorenzo the younger—"

"My dear boy, enough lies. We all know whose son he is, don't we?" The Pope knew that honesty, not often the realm of conversations between Pope and subject, hung unconfessed in the air.

"Yes, Your Holiness," the young Swiss Guard finally whispered. And then, a bit louder with a cheeky grin. "Who am I to contradict the Vicar of Christ?"

"Ha!" Clement let loose with a great guffaw of such not heard since before the horrors of the previous year. Before The Sack. "For such impertinence I will take away any indulgences hitherto granted to you or your kin."

"Mea culpa, mea culpa, mea maxima culpa," said the guard, bowing with exaggerated mock reverence tainted with a natal affection.

The Pope laughed and the boy followed.

"What is your name?"

"Giovanni, Your Holiness."

Clement gasped. "My dear Gio, you share the name of our late, great cousin, the ablest Pope of the Age, Leo X."

"Yes, Your Holiness."

"Very well, Giovanni..."

"My friends call me Gio."

"And so shall it be. Let us be friends. Arise, young Gio. I hereby confer on you the Knighthood of the Golden Spur."

"Holy Father, I am not—"

"You are worthy, by action and by my authority." The Pope stood imperiously, grabbed his crozier, and laid it gently across each of the young guard's shoulders. "So shall it be written, so shall it be done." Clement loved that phrase.

"I offer my life to your service, to the point of death."

"Let us have no more talk of death. There has been enough of that this year. But, ride you must. In truth, you will earn your 'spurs.' Ready a horse and send for that wretched cardinal secretary of mine. The Pope still has friends between here and God's outer most reaches of Britain's realm, nay, to Hadrian's Wall along Scotia. His Eminence will give you what you need as far as contacts and my letters of request to the Tudor Court and our 'Defender of the Faith,' King Henry VIII. Let's see if he is willing to help his pope during this most urgent hour of *our* need."

With that, the Pope opened a drawer in his desk and pulled out a tightly rolled parchment, leather-bound and wax-sealed, with the imprint of his pontifical hand, the Ring of the Fisherman.

"I will not fail you, Your Holiness." With a bow the newly minted Knight of the Golden Spurs turned to leave, grasping the document firmly in his hand.

"And Gio?"

"Yes, Your Holiness."

"Let this be just between us."

"It will be our secret."

"Go with God."

Clement stood, making the sign of the cross while the young knight backed out the portal, and listened as the door locked into place. Only then did the Pope look out over Orvieto, surprised to see that during their conversation a heavy snow had begun to fall. The city seemed to glow, briefly, made clean by the weather's sudden transformation. Even the cathedral looked better with its frosty mantle.

"Alessandro." He whispered his son's name. "I wonder where you are tonight. Please forgive me. You, too, are now an exile. Because of my failures, how many mothers' sons are exiles this night?"

And now, thought the Pope, we wait. He sat down in the wooden chair, hitherto reserved for Orvieto's bishop, but like so many things in this desolate hilltop fortress in the Etruscan wastes north of Rome, hastily requisitioned for the Papal Court in Exile. Clement leaned back and suddenly a potent *crack* echoed across the chamber as the throne's rotten frame collapsed beneath his weight. Before he knew it, his papal bum was splayed out on the cold stone floor in a most undignified manner.

Despite himself, the Pope laughed, picked himself up, dusted himself off, and started all over to contemplate the future, this time settling on the stone casement of the window overlooking Orvieto's vast, imperfect cathedral. That seemed solid enough. Lit obscurely from behind by the frozen illumination of the snow, he stared at and through his sanctified reflection.

He was Giulio de Medici. By birth son of the murdered Giuliani and nephew of his brother, the Magnificent Lorenzo, by law his heir. Cousin and confidant of Giovanni, by Grace of God and Apostolic Succession, Pope Leo X, by whose hand Clement was elevated to the purple and by cardinal election four winters ago, now Supreme Pontiff, Bishop of Rome and Lord of the Papal States, His Holiness and Holy Father, Clement Septicemic.

Indeed, it had been a bad year, but Christmas was coming and the decision had been made. Yes, the decision had been made. Next year, things would be better. The year 1528 would certainly bring him news from Henry VIII, news that would change everything. He just knew it.

CHAPTER XIII

Fall from Grace

Tuesday, December 3, 2013, breakfast, Orvieto

It didn't take long to find the story. Adriano .googled "Deacon Suicide Orvieto" and his laptop lit up.

"Lee, listen to this."

Adriano read.

Orvieto, Saturday, 1 December 2012. AKI. A twenty-nine-year-old man committed suicide by throwing himself from the city walls in the medieval central Italian city of Orvieto, apparently because the Vatican refused to ordain him as a priest. In a printed suicide note found in his room, typed on his computer, Andrea Bernardone said he killed himself because the Vatican had blocked his ordination that was to have taken place a week from today, next Saturday, December 8, the first anniversary of his having become a deacon.

"I wanted to be a priest, and dedicated my whole life to this goal, but it was denied me," typed Bernardone, who had been born in Bagnoregio. The note continued. "I am fragile and I ask for forgiveness."

Adriano looked up to see his husband's ashen face, a blank and distant look to his usually clear and cheerful blue eyes. "Shall I go on?"

"What?"

Lee seems far away, Adriano thought. *This whole story is beginning to give me the creeps. Worse, I'm sure, for Lee.* Adriano waited and shrugged.

"Yeah, yes, go on," Lee said. "I need to hear it all."

"Need?" Adriano pushed back, but only a bit. These were seas he'd rather not swim in, and certainly hadn't expected here. Orvieto was supposed to be an *escape* from death, not a reminder of so much they had both already seen—especially Lee.

"Read," Lee said simply. An order.

Adriano continued.

Bernardone took his own life late last night by throwing himself from the walls of Orvieto after the Holy See intervened directly to stop his ordination from going ahead.

The body was found by an elderly Orvieto resident during her early morning walk. His body showed injuries consistent with having fallen thirty meters, but with no signs of foul play. Magistrates were due to decide today on whether to order an autopsy.

"Wait," Lee said, grabbing his husband's arm. "An autopsy. You usually only order autopsies for suspicious deaths."

"Lee." Adriano gave his husband a quizzical look over his nerdy-chic glasses. "You're reading too much into this."

"And you need to keep reading. Humor me."

Adriano sighed. *Some vacation.* He didn't like where this was going. Lee's obsessions always became work, social work, for him. He continued to read.

The Vatican on Friday, November 30, informed Bernardone that his ordination had been stopped "due to the direct intervention of the Holy See."

"The reasons for this will soon be subject to clarification," the Right Rev. Giovanni Sancarlo, bishop of Orvieto–Todi, had commented shortly after receiving the news from Rome. "We—I—pray that don Andrea may soon recover from this great test.

Bernardone had been Bishop Sancarlo's deacon for one year and was in charge of the diocesan offices as well as overseeing the day-to-day operations of the Bishop's residence in Orvieto.

Local media reported there had been "murmurings" that Andrea might be gay, but Orvieto Bishop Sancarlo refused to comment or speculate.

"There were only some issues about a friend—ah, friends—of his," said Bishop Sancarlo in an emotional interview. He then added, "For me, he was ready to be a priest, but the Vatican said he wasn't 'mature' enough."

The bishop related his last conversation with his deacon, just before what would prove to be his final service on the altar of *Sant'Andrea*, a service that coincidentally was the deacon's twenty-ninth birthday. "Over and over again he kept asking me, 'Bishop, what have I done, tell me what I've done.'"

With that, the Bishop ended the interview, clearly moved. His closing words to the press were "May God forgive all of us."

"There's a picture too, with a caption." Adriano turned the laptop around for Lee.

"Bishop Sancarlo?"

"No, some young cardinal. Not bad looking, actually, for a Vatican apologist."

Lee looked at the photo, black-and-white, of an exceedingly handsome fifty-ish cardinal standing in front of an office desk piled high with books, a computer screen, and a fax machine.

"It's Gorgeous George!" Lee gasped.

"Who?"

"The Vatican's PR guy, Giorgio Maltoni. That's his nickname—Gorgeous George. He was Pope Benedict's right hand and is evidently still ensconced at St. Peter's working for the new Pope, Francis, although I can't understand why."

"I thought working in the Vatican was like a job with the DMV," Adriano said between sips of coffee. "Employment for life."

"Normally, that's the case," said Lee. "But Giorgio was very much the former Pope's man. When Benedict resigned and Francis was elected, G. G. wasn't shy in his opinions. He even said that Francis wouldn't have been his choice and was shocked at his elevation to the papacy. I remember he said something to the effect of 'Francis is the darling of the media at the moment, but that won't last. He's not everyone's darling.' Personally, if I'd been Francis, I'd have sacked him right away for insubordination."

"Sounds like a spurned lover. Maybe he and Papa Ben were more than just friends."

"Don't think so, although gay priest gossip goes with the territory," said Lee. "Cardinal Maltoni appears to be quite straight. Used to be a professional soldier and athlete and evidently quite the ladies' man before he was ordained, kinda the Curia's JFK. Had some sort of sudden conversion, a real Paul-on-the-Road-to-Damascus moment. Actually, not much is known about his pre-Church life. He was an orphan supposedly, raised by Italian nuns somewhere around here in Umbria as I recall. When he was eighteen, he did a stint as a mercenary in Africa before he found God. Anyway, something happened to him, and before you know it he was on the fast-track to Vatican VIP. He's supposed to be the kinder, gentler face of the papacy. He's always quoted in the Catholic News Service."

"Guess I have to renew my subscription." Adriano looked over Lee's shoulder at the photo. "Hmmm. I didn't know clericals came in Gucci. What does the caption say?"

Lee read the caption. "Vatican Spokesman Giorgio Maltoni speaks to the press about Deacon Andrea Bernardone: 'The Vatican does not intend to comment on this affair. Nor does it intend to state why it blocked his ordination. We are talking about one of the sacraments and the Holy See cannot provide any explanations. We will have no further comment.'"

"Typical." Adriano shook his head while he poured coffee and set out some Italian meat and cheese for breakfast. "Con La Eglesia, hemos topado, amigo Sancho."

"Beg pardon?"

"It's from *Don Quixote*. Roughly translated, 'Sancho, we have met the Church.' How typical. The Vatican is nothing but a nest of vipers."

"This new pope, Francis, seems better."

"Better is a relative term." Adriano huffed, slapping some prosciutto onto Lee's plate. "He's still the pope and he represents a corrupt and morally bankrupt theocracy governed by fear, bigotry, and pseudo-religious perversity."

"Tell me how you really feel."

"Perhaps your friend," Adriano said, pointing to the image of Cardinal Giorgio, "has some dirt on both the popes. That could explain his job security."

"Hmm," Lee said in contemplation. "Possible."

For the next hour, between bouts of salami and strong Italian coffee, Lee would urge Adriano to find out more about Deacon Andrea and his mysterious suicide. Adriano wasn't happy about it—for all kinds of reasons. It stank of the Church, in his opinion quite rotten enough to smell quite ripe. Also, he knew that Lee was feeding an old hunger—a dangerous one—with this mystery. Like that old *Star Wars* cliché they both loved, Adriano had a bad feeling about this. Nonetheless, to keep the peace, for now, he continued. But, other than the few articles they had already uncovered and the mention of a refugee's unclaimed body the day before Andrea's jump, there was little else to be found online and most of that was almost word-for-word copy and pastes of the original article.

"It's like the Vatican sent out a press release and everyone just picked it up, verbatim, and ran the story as is," Lee said.

Actually, Adriano had to admit, it was *exactly* like that.

Besides the write-ups, someone named Dawud had posted a tribute video on YouTube, complete with spacey music and quotes about love fading in and out, with pictures of Andrea, a young, slim-but-not-overly-so Italian youth with tousled brown hair on a boat somewhere (in a modest T-shirt and shorts); Andrea with friends outside the Church of Sant'Andrea (Andrea in clericals here); Andrea eating brunch at what looked to be Cafe Marco. Adriano thought the shoulder in the upper left of the video belonged to La Donna Volsini, but he couldn't be sure. The video montage had garnered an impressive 533 thumbs-up responses all from December of last year, right after his funeral. It looked like the sort of thing that had been put together for a memorial and then lost to the mists of the internet. Working his online magic, Adriano was able to tell that they were the first people to have looked at the video since last year. Hmmm, that's interesting, thought Adriano. A lot of likes but no comments. Digging further, he saw that Dawud, whoever he was, had made the video so that no one could leave a note. Maybe he was afraid of online homophobes trolling the poor kid. Of course, 533 likes was nothing to sneeze at. Seems like someone would have wanted to leave a more personal commemoration. Oh well, that was life. One day you were alive, the next you were dead and the subject of a kitschy online tribute. After that, you were nothing but a digitized memory. "Wow! Check this out."

Lee looked up from his coffee. "Whatcha got, honey?"

"The article on Andrea's funeral."

Lee motioned for Adriano to read aloud.

Orvieto, Sunday, 2 December 2012. In the Cathedral of Orvieto this afternoon was celebrated the funeral of Andrea Bernardone, the young deacon who committed suicide late Friday night/early Saturday morning.

"That was a year ago yesterday," Lee interjected.

"Yeah, no wonder Orvieto is on edge. It all happened exactly a year ago this week."

"Go on."

Deacon Andrea's ordination had been scheduled for this coming Saturday, December 8. However, in a dramatic and unexpected turn of events, Bernardone and his bishop received a fax from the Vatican saying that the young deacon's ordination had been "suspended and postponed" by a direct and almost unprecedented intervention of the Holy See.

"Poor guy," said Lee, shaking his head. "I only started to think about going into the priesthood when I was in my early teens, and the sheer volume of work and study required made my head explode. After all that, to have it yanked away at the last minute, by fax no less. No wonder he cracked."

"That's your Holy Roman Catholic Church for you," Adriano said with a sneer. "Evil and cowardly. What do you expect?"

"Keep reading."

Along with Andrea's mother were over a thousand people, including many priests from the surrounding area and towns such as Narni and Civita di Bagnoregio. Reportedly, over forty people rode up on the early train from Rome including a cardinal whose identity was not immediately available. The light wood coffin, unadorned except for a single red rose on the lid, was placed before the altar, in line with the sacred relics from the Miracle of Bolsena in whose honor the cathedral was constructed over six hundred years previous.

"Today we are not here for a funeral, but our beloved Andrea has not really left us," said Monsignor Giovanni Sancarlo, the Bishop of Orvieto. in his homily. "Let us make this a party—a party like we were going to have next Saturday at Andrea's ordination."

Later, Bishop Sancarlo, voice shaking with emotion and with tears in his eyes, spoke directly to the young deacon's family. "Especially to Andrea's dear mother, please let me offer not only my undying love, but also, let me ask for your forgiveness. Andrea was a son to me. I was unable to prevent his being taken away from us so suddenly and tragically."

In closing, the Bishop said, "Andrea will meet Christ—who is like a rock, our salvation."

After the funeral, Andrea's coffin was carried into the crypt of the cathedral attended by only Bishop Sancarlo, don Andrea's mother and the Rev. Vicky Lewis, and three young local men.

The article was accompanied by two photos, one of Andrea's coffin, a simple pine box on the cathedral floor with its lonely rosette. The other image was another view of Gorgeous George, a close-up this time, sitting behind his desk. Behind him was a Superman poster. In front of him, a bank of microphones and a sign under the fax reading "ufficio media Vaticano." Even Lee could translate that: Vatican Press Office.

"No picture of Andrea, but Cardinal Giorgio has managed to get his foxy puss in front of the cameras again," Adriano harrumphed.

"Look!" Lee gasped and pointed at the bookcase behind George's photogenic image. *"How much do you want to bet that's the fax machine that sent the 'You're fired' letter to Andrea? And how much do you wanna bet that Gorgeous George was the unnamed cardinal who came to Andrea's funeral?"*

"According to you, everyone knows that face," said Adriano. "He's the Vatican's flack. There's no way the press wouldn't mention his being here. That doesn't make sense."

"Of course it does," Lee said. "Young, clearly beloved, gay deacon commits suicide. The Church wants to control the story, so they send the Vatican flack up to Orvieto, quietly, to deal with any press that might want to dig more into the story."

"Is this your publicist gene taking over, or the coulda-been-a-priest one?" Adriano was teasing, but he also knew that Lee's entire being had been infected by the story of Andrea, with all its admitted parallels to Lee's own experience. It was like the incubus from the movie Alien, hibernating in Lee's gut just waiting to be born in messy fashion. He had to find a way to talk Lee off this psychic ledge. But carefully.

"You're a conspiracy theorist," Adriano said, wagging a finger.

"Isn't that what we're talking about here?" Lee shot back with some heat.

Adriano opened his mouth to speak but decided against it.

～

For the rest of breakfast, Lee retreated to the couch while Adriano cleaned up in the kitchen. He knew that Adriano wasn't happy about his latest obsession. He didn't care. Adriano didn't understand, and even after ten years together, didn't want to. To Adriano, everything about the Church was bad, or at the very least, questionable. Of course, from what he knew about Adriano's ultra-orthodox parents, he couldn't blame him for feeling that way. He looked over at Brian's ashes, the only ordained person Adriano had tolerated. Of course, he was Anglican, not Catholic. More to the point, he was Brian.

"Hey, listen to this." Adriano had come back in, iPhone in hand. "I found something new about Andrea, kinda a sidebar to the article I missed before."

Lee took the phone from his husband's hands and kissed him on the nose. How sweet. He knows I'm an addict, but he's humoring me. On the screen was a black-and-white photo of the Vatican's publicist, Gorgeous George, and a small caption:

Reached by phone immediately after Deacon Andrea's funeral, when asked for further clarification on the matter, Vatican spokesman Giorgio Maltoni tersely replied before hanging up on this reporter, "I told you yesterday. We will have no further comment. Roma locuta; causa finita est."

"That's some famous Latin phrase, right?"Adriano asked.

"Yes. Probably, the only language I know better than you," Lee said simply with a strange feeling in the pit of his gut as he stared at Giorgio and his fax machine. "Latin is still after almost two thousand years the official language of the Vatican and used for all official pronouncements."

"What does it mean?"

"Rome has spoken: the matter is finished."

Why don't I believe that, Lee thought, peering again at the fax machine in the photo, one of the original types with rolls of paper instead of individual sheets. When a message came through, an embedded blade sliced it off. It reminded him of a guillotine, its roll.

Rome has spoken: the matter is finished.

Somehow, Lee didn't think it was finished at all.

CHAPTER XIV

Imprisoned

Tuesday, December 3, 2013, late morning, Convento dei Cappuccini

His cell was cold. Outside, an evening fog wrapped around the tower in a misty vise.

He wasn't going anywhere. Hadn't gone anywhere, for almost a year. He'd likely die here, alone with his thoughts. Better that way. He didn't want to see anyone, and he was sure there was no one interested in seeing him. Well, there was at least one person who didn't want to see him, or hear from him.

He had sanctioned enough perversity in her life—in their lives. His was a voluntary purgatory, but a living penance nonetheless. Only the living can know that death is not a punishment.

With nothing else to do, he prayed, playing out his sentence on the map of his mind:

(48) For those who suffer for because of their ears
(56) For those fathers and mothers who did not educate their children
(13) For those whom the Father wants freed of their pain
(43) For those who bewildered others with devotion

Guilty as charged, my Lord God.

As he had done for a year, Bishop Sancarlo looked out his window and stared toward the cliff.

CHAPTER XV

De Perfundis

"Ciao! Ciao! Hello USA!"

Adriano and Lee waved back to Marco as he swept toward them, wiping his hands on the front of his chef's whites. The couple had almost forgotten their lunch date with the pleasantly pesky Marco, so absorbed had they been in their online research about Deacon Andrea.

"Come in! So glad you came to my-a place. Sit, sit down. Nonna! Miei amici Americani sono qui!" he cried out toward the kitchen, hidden somewhere in the bowels of the tiny and bustling restaurant squeezed into an alley in the shadow of the Tower of the Moor. Marco was bubbling with his usual enthusiasm. If his cooking was as upbeat as his mood, they were in for a treat. "What you like to eat? I bring everything. My great mother started this place right after the war. She come later. I introduce you. Nonna!"

For the next hour, a seemingly inexhaustible array of Umbrian delicacies came out of Marco's pantry, half of them unordered. Marco was putting on the dog for the visiting *stranieri*.

After they had finished and were lingering over coffee and waiting for a tray of Italian liquors that Marco had pressed on them—"My gift, no money. For you. Welcome to Orvieto! I love America! USA!"—Adriano pulled out a folded sheet of computer printer paper and handed it to Lee.

"What's this?"

"Take a look. I translated it special for you. Took a while."

Lee opened the page and began to read.

Deacon's Mother To Pope: "Why"?

Orvieto, Saturday, 8 December, 2012 (AKI). "Why?" is the heart-breaking cry of the mother of deacon Andrea Bernardone in a letter to His Holiness, Pope Benedict XVI, leaked to AKI from unnamed sources. Bernardone, whose body was found a week ago at the foot of a cliff in Orvieto, 120 kilometers north of Rome, was to have been ordained a priest today, December 8, the one-year anniversary of his having become a deacon. Informed by Vatican fax that his ordination had been canceled, Bernardone apparently despaired and committed suicide following Mass on his 29th birthday in the historic Church of Sant'Andrea in the medieval Umbrian town. Though pressed for a response, the Vatican has so far refused comment via their press office.

"Wow." Lee looked up, mouth agape. Memories of Brian flooded in. "Poor woman."

"Keep reading. It gets better. This woman knows how to turn a screw into the papal backside. I translated it this morning."

Lee bent back to the letter.

Holy Father. I am the mother of Deacon Andrea Bernardone. I write to you today as a devoted mother and as a devout Catholic. I have just returned home from Orvieto, a city wounded from the death of my son and the betrayal of its beloved bishop.

Since the loss of my son, every day I have tried to find refuge in the Gospel, but for the first time in my life, I find none. Instead of comfort, I have found nothing but torment, such as is described in Luke, Chapter 8, verses 27-38:

They sailed to the region of the Gerasenes, which is across the lake from Galilee. When Jesus stepped ashore, he was met by a demon-possessed man from the town. For a long time, this man had not worn clothes or lived in a house but had lived in the tombs. When he saw Jesus, he cried out and fell at his feet, shouting at the top of his voice, "What do you want with me, Jesus, Son of the Most High God? I beg you, don't torture me!" For Jesus had commanded the impure spirit to come out of the man. Many times, it had seized him, and though he was chained hand and foot and kept under guard, he had broken his chains and had been driven by the demon into solitary places.

Jesus asked him, "What is your name?"

"Legion, for we are many," he replied, because many demons had gone into him. And they begged Jesus repeatedly not to order them to go into the Abyss.

A large herd of pigs was feeding there on the hillside. The demons begged Jesus to let them go into the pigs, and he gave them permission. When the demons came out of the man, they went into the pigs, and the herd rushed to the cliff and threw themselves off into the lake below and were drowned.

Holy Father, what demons live in each of our hearts is known only to us and to our God. But, in my son there were no demons, no malice. His was a pure, if naïve heart. The only demons doing torment to him seem to be those from Rome: demons of bureaucracy, fear, and legalese, driven into my son at the hour of his greatest tenderness, in the hour of anticipation of his greatest joy—to become a priest in service to God—in service to his beloved bishop, and to you Holy Father.

Why?

I have heard rumors. People who for their own reasons, their own sins, wanted to block my son's elevation to the priesthood. I do not listen to rumors, for nothing can bring back my dear son. But there are other rumors, Holy Father, about sins of the flesh or lusts of the mind that may have tormented my son. Is death a just sentence for one who has thought impure thoughts? If so, Holy Father, there will be no priests left in Rome, no cardinals in the Curia, and I dare say, an asterisk beside every pontiff on the throne of Peter. As Jesus said, "Let he who is without sin cast the first stone."

Forgive me Holy Father, for I write as a woman torn by grief and plagued with doubt. In his youth, my husband, a brave carabinieri, was taken from me by criminals. Doing his job, he was gunned down by the mafia he had sworn to defeat. His son, born on the Feast of Andrea, never knew him. And now, that same son has been killed— yes, I say killed—by the fear and hypocrisy of people within the Church that he loved, the Church that he longed so to serve. His patron and guide, the great, loving, and tender Bishop of Orvieto, loved my son like a father, like the father he never had. He tended to him like Jesus the Good Shepherd tended to his sheep. I understand that this good man is now terrorized himself by the Holy See.

Holy Father, in you I place my trust, my final hope. You sit at the pinnacle of your Church, our bond between our Savior Jesus Christ and His people. But, look to those who bear you up, to those who kiss your ring and shine the pilasters of your altars. Beneath the Dome of St. Peter's there is rust and decay and rot. Its smell has carried all the way to Orvieto. Its stench has circled the globe like a pestilence. Its latest victim is my son, but there have been more, unjustly accused to cover the odor of putrefaction coming from Rome. Please, dear Holy Father, prevent such a fate for others.

I am heartbroken and have no more tears. As that other beloved youth, David, pleaded to his Master in Psalm 130: "Out of the depths I cry to You, O Lord; Lord, hear my voice. Let your ears be attentive to my voice in supplication."

Holy Father, be attentive to my supplication. Hear the impudent words of a poor widow and grieving mother. Forgive me my impertinence but look to the sins of your own Church. Here in Orvieto, home of the Eucharistic Sacrament made manifest by the Miracle of Bolsena, there is nothing but grief, and darkness and lies.

—Clarissa Bernardone

"Ahh!" Lee almost jumped out of his chair as Marco leaned over his shoulder, placing a glass of limoncillo in front of him. "You startled me."

"No problem. I sorry. Prego!" Marco beamed, then looked down at the paper in Lee's hands. His face went white and his voice became dark. "Dio mio! Per favore! Put that away! Presto, before mia nonna sees it. Ah, Nonna, there you are!"

Perplexed by Marco's sudden transformation but nonetheless instinctively trusting it, Lee hurriedly folded up the paper and slipped it into his pocket. Turning around he came face-to-face with—"Nonna! Incontrare i miei amici Americani, Adriano e Lee."—La Madrina.

Donna Volsini, pursed her lips and stared. "Ciao."

CHAPTER XVI

Schism

Early March, 1528 (Julian Calendar), Orvieto

"A divorce!" Clement screamed, loud enough for all Orvieto to hear. "After twenty-four years of marriage, King Henry VIII wants a *divorce!*"

"Not a divorce, Your Holiness, an annulment."

The Pope howled.

The English knight looked down at the floor while his associate, a young priest from London, continued to bite his fingernails. A small pyramid of cuticles was fast accumulating at his feet.

"So, I have three choices, according to your arguments presented here," Clement counted, pacing around his chamber. "One, I can declare that Henry's marriage to Queen Catherine was never legal, and therefore the last quarter century of their relationship is null and void, thus making Henry a de facto bachelor and available to marry anyone he wishes. Oh yes, that leaves aside the issue of his daughter by Catherine, Princess Mary, who by this course would be made illegitimate. Messy, very messy. Two, I can declare that the marriage, while hitherto consummated, is now spiritually 'dead,' thus making King Henry a widower, Or three, I can—and I love this one—grant a petition for Henry to take Anne...Anne...what was her name?"

"Boleyn, Your Holiness."

"Yes, I can grant a petition legalizing bigamy and allowing Henry to take this Anne Boleyn as his second wife!"

"Abraham, Jacob, King David, all had more than one wife," the English ambassador offered.

"Solomon had seven hundred," the young priest suggested cheerfully.

"You dare bring biblical witness to the *Pope!*" Clement thundered, bringing down his fist on the desk with such force that quill pens and ink wells went tumbling. "Who does Henry think he is? A *Borgia*? Leave me!"

The representatives from England beat a hasty retreat, almost tripping on themselves as they bolted, backward, from the papal presence. Before they could close the door themselves, Clement slammed it shut upon them.

"Ouch!"

Good, Clement thought, I hope I broke one of their noses.

Dear God, the man had more balls than the Medici coat of arms. If that didn't take the cake for standing and leaping gall. An annulment, Henry VIII, Kind of England, Roman Catholicism's "Defender of the Faith"—what a laugh that was"—wanted the Pope to say that his twenty-four-year union with Catherine of Aragon was in point of fact never really a marriage to start with.

Hadn't Pope Julius given Henry a special dispensation to *marry* Catherine in the first place? That was something most specifically forbidden by Church law since Catherine was the widow of Henry's older brother, Arthur. Brothers couldn't marry their brothers' wives. The sacredness of marriage was one of the pillars of the Church.

Clement sighed and slouched into his chair, jumping up as if burnt before settling down again somewhat more gingerly. Fixed. At least his throne had been repaired in the last few weeks since his retreat to Orvieto. His Church was in shambles, and the man he had looked to for financial salvation was now about to start a religious civil war. Even a pope couldn't "unmarry" someone.

Clement sat, stewing, for a few minutes.

Who am I kidding, he thought. Popes could undo *anything* and had been doing so with alarming, profitable regularity. I'm a prime example. Dear cousin Gio was so hot to stack the deck in his favor that he made me a cardinal, even though I was the bastard son of his father's brother. No worries. By papal dispensation, Leo X "declared" that I was "legitimate" and thus made me a cardinal. That was a pretty neat trick, and done in such haste that he didn't even realize I wasn't yet a priest. No matter, he promptly had me ordained—the first time in history it was done in reverse—first a cardinal, then a bishop, then a priest. Oh yes, papal dispensations were the cure for what ailed you.

Clement looked down at the floor where the parchment from King Henry's messengers had rolled after his outburst. He stooped down stiffly and picked up the scroll. He scanned down the page. Ah yes, this was his favorite part:

> Dearest Holy Father, as your most faithful Defender of the Faith, I humbly beg your forgiveness for the rashness of my youth. I see now the error and sin was mine in asking His Holiness, Pope Julius II, for a dispensation to wed Princess Catherine, a woman previously married to my brother, the sometime Prince of Wales, and would he still be alive, England's rightful King. For in such case, I would be truly what I am meant to be, a servant to King, Country, and through your grace, Holy Father Clement, to God. I have sinned. For does it not say in Leviticus 20:21 "If a man takes his brother's wife, it is impurity; he has uncovered his brother's nakedness; they shall be childless."

Fantastic, Clement thought. My God, Henry has a flare for the creative that Erasmus would envy. "Childless" he now claimed his marriage to Catherine to have been. No, not childless, *sonless*. And that was exactly the point. To keep England in Tudor hands, Henry needed a legitimate male heir. There was the bastard, Henry FitzRoy, by one of Henry's many mistresses, but of course, that didn't count. Bastards couldn't become king. But, of course, look at me, they *can* become Pope.

What a world in which we live, so obsessed with the sex of our rulers, all meanings intended. One day, a queen might just make as good a "king" as any man. Henry should think on that. Even the Vatican, if one believed the legend, had once been ruled by a woman pope who had passed herself off as a man. That had taken "balls" too. Clement moaned at the heretical badness of his own joke.

"Dear God." Clement sighed and sat down heavily in his newly restored throne. *I'll never get the money now.*

There was a knock at the door, six evenly space knocks to be precise, followed by three short ones in succession.

The Pope threw open the door.

"Dear boy, come in. You're the first pleasant thing I've seen since Christmas."

"Your Holiness."

The Pope stopped the young Swiss Guard in mid-genuflection and pulled him to his chest in an affectionate and paternal hug. "My son. Welcome back. I was worried about you."

"I have failed you, Holy Father."

"No." The Pope held Gio at arm's length and fixed him with his gaze. "*You* have not failed me at all. The King of England has managed to throw a sabot into the gears of my plan, but because of you, I have learned of it sooner than I would have otherwise."

"He is anxious to marry Queen Catherine's young courtier, the Lady Anne Boleyn."

Clement poured a glass of mulled wine for the guard and beckoned him to sit. "So, you know of His Majesty's wishes?"

"Your Holiness, the Tudor court talks of nothing else."

"Hmmm." The Pope took a deep draught from his cup. He imagined it was the talk of every inn and roadside refugio between here and Calais. "We'll see about that. Yea gods, suddenly King Henry has discovered scruples. As if any noble had to be married to have children by his mistress. We Medici—*I*—should know."

The young guard laughed, and wine dribbled from his chin. "A thousand pardons, Holiness."

Clement laughed too.

"Perhaps there is something to be gained from the English King's 'problem,' Holy Father. It seems that you both want something that the other has."

"A bribe, you mean," Clement stated flatly.

The Swiss Guard shrugged.

"Yes, I had thought of that, King Henry gets his divorce and I get five hundred thousand ducats. Quid pro quo, as Caesar would have said."

"It's an idea."

"No." Clement stood up angrily. "No! The papacy and God have been for sale for too long."

He remembered the already infamous words of his cousin, Pope Leo: "Since we have been given the papacy, let us now enjoy it." Well, Leo had enjoyed it, to a fault, and left behind a legacy of culture and sexual exploits paid for with the sale of indulgences, a tawdry practice. In fairness, Pope Julius had come up with the idea first as a way to fund his constant wars to retain the Papal States, but no matter. It stops with me. "No. We will find another way."

The two friends sat quietly for a bit.

"Holiness?"

"Yes, dear boy."

"Are you acquainted with Hassan de Wazzan?"

"The Moor?" Clement put down his cup and leaned back. "The Andalusian who translates for Cardinal Endigo from Viterbo?"

"The very man, Holiness. He is from a rich and powerful family and has many well connected friends."

Yes, Clement did remember de Wazzan. Cousin Gio had taken quite a shine to the handsome, ebony-skinned traveler and effected his "conversion," as it were. To great splendor, de Wazzan had been baptized in St. Peter's by Pope Leo himself and taken a baptismal name to honor his patron, Joannes Leo de Medici. He had been extremely kind and solicitous of Clement's secret son, Alessandro, as well, two black faces amid the pallor of the Roman court. Clement had been touched by it.

"Leo Africanus, isn't that what everyone calls him behind his back?"

"Yes, Your Holiness, but he prefers to be called by his birth name of Hassan."

"I see. He has returned to the faith of his fathers, then?"

The young guard lowered his voice. "His is a proud and ancient name. I believe that his conversion was more a matter of convenience than an epiphany of the spirit."

"You seem to know a great deal about this Moor."

The guard smiled and started to speak, but shut his mouth. "I should not say, Holiness."

"Speak, my son. Supposedly I hold the keys to heaven and to earth. I can keep a secret."

Gio took a long sip from his cup. "I have met him through a friend. She is—"

"*She?*" Clement said with a naughty tone. "I see that we have been busy since your return from the English court."

Gio blushed. "She is a pure and lovely girl, Holiness."

"I'm sure she is, Gio. Go on. What is her name?"

"Sofia, Holiness. She introduced me to the Moor."

"He is here in Orvieto?"

"Yes, Holiness. He managed to escape Rome soon after the Sack."

"With whom are they staying?" A Muslim—or one who looked liked one—no matter how nobly born, would not have entered Orvieto without help, or some high-placed connection. Even Alessandro was safely away for the moment. His heart ached with the memory of his son.

"Moses de Blanis."

"The Jewish banker?" Clement asked.

"Yes, Holiness. Sofia is the daughter of de Blanis. She runs his household. The mother is long dead."

Clement emptied his cup and rose deliberately from his seat. He walked over to Gio, bent down, and kissed him on the forehead, followed by a gentle stroke to his hair.

"Well done, my Knight of the Golden Spur. Yours is a fearless curiosity. We will meet with de Blanis and de Wazzan, and with your Sofia if you like." Clement looked around his gloomy apartments. Not quite up to the standards for a party set by the Medici. "Perhaps, they will invite *us* to dine with them one evening."

"Holiness! That would be impossible! A pope cannot enter the home of a Jew!"

"Or a Moor?" Clement smiled. "My uncle, Lorenzo the Magnificent, entertained Cathars, whores, saints, sodomites, and pagans at his table and because of it, Florence is endowed with artistic greatness. When next you see your Sofia, tell her that His Holiness—no, tell her that Giulio de Medici would be honored by an invitation. We will accept."

"As you wish, Holy Father."

Yes, Clement thought, pouring them both another drink. I know a thing or two about the diversity of God's creation. Judaism, Islam, Christianity, a Holy Trinity of faiths, and all from the font of *Genesis*. The Magi had knelt before our Lord Jesus Christ with humility, and he was a Jew. This pope, this Medici, would not be too proud to do the same.

CHAPTER XVII

nonna

Wednesday, December 4, 2013, early afternoon, Orvieto

"La Donna Volsini is your grandmother?" Adriano asked, giving his husband a sideways glance. *I wonder if Lee was right and we've dropped into a friendly clan of culinary mafia.*

"Si, si, naturalmente." Marco's hand shook as he lit a cigarette. The match sputtered and went out. Adriano obliged with a lighter, knowing that Lee would later ask where he'd been hiding that. "I need drinks—no, not Volsini, let's go to Clement's Bar."

Marco puffed nervously as they made their way under the arches of Via del Moro and into the least touristy of Orvieto's public squares, Piazza del Popolo.

"Clement's is over there. It's running by friends of mine."

Even though it was chilly, the trio sat down at a table outside next to an ancient fountain, now dry, so that Marco could finish his smoke. A weather-wracked coat of arms graced the lips of the denuded stone pool, now a perch for Orvieto's after-school teens.

"Tre whiskey, per favore," Marco called out to the waiter, endowed with the trendy hipster haircut that was this year's fashion rage among European youth. As the door opened, Madonna's "Like a Virgin" blared on the widescreen TV above the bar. A scroll on the screen denoted "Italian MTV" and today's feature, "Retrospectivo '80s." Michael Jackson's "Thriller" was promised next. Marco offered them cigarettes. Out of politeness, and to keep Marco talking, Adriano accepted; Lee too, but not as readily. I'll pay for this later, Adriano thought, ignoring Lee's scowl. It's Europe, not California. They smoked silently until the drinks came.

"Grazie." Marco downed the drink in a gulp and motioned for another round. Adriano and Lee followed his lead.

"Marco, I'm so sorry," said Adriano, remembering Andrea's private memorial on the shelf at Café Volsini. "I had no idea that we'd see La Donna Volsini at your restaurant, or that she was your grandmother. I'd never have taken the article to your restaurant if I'd known."

"Don't worry." Marco waved his hand at them. "No problem. It just that when I saw the paper it bring back many sad memories. I no want mia nonna to see it. She had, how do you say, a soft part in her heart for him."

"And you?" Lee asked. Adriano knew that Lee was angling for an answer to the question of whose team Marco played on. His foot tapped Lee's beneath the table. Too late, the question had been asked.

"I loved him," Marco said quietly. "Andrea was like a brother to me. I miss him very much. Molto."

They sat quietly for a few moments. Adriano kept his foot poised over his husband's shoe.

The fresh drinks arrived, accompanied by small bite-sized crostinis and tiny plates of pasta. The waiter returned inside and Marco lowered his voice. "Poor Andrea, everyone loved him. My nonna, my great mother, has never been the same."

"Since she found his body," Adriano stated simply.

"Si." Marco took a deep drag. "It happened on his birthday. That's why his mother named him Andrea. He was born on the Feast of Sant'Andrea, November thirtieth. We were going to have a surprise lunch for him at the restaurant. A sort of *buon compleanno*, how do you say—happy birthday and congratulations on becoming a priest celebration the next day. Mia nonna had make a special cake. Andrea's mother, she was a-coming and also the lady priest from the English church and the bishop."

"Your grandmother invited the bishop to lunch?" Adriano asked.

"Si, of course, molto. My grandmother loves him very much. Such a good man."

"You could have fooled me," Lee said taking a sip. "Didn't look that way the other night at *Sant'Andrea*."

"Not *that* bishop, *Arnaud*"—Marco spat out the name—"he is the new bishop. No. Bishop Sancarlo. The one before. The one that was going to ordain Andrea. Everyone loved Sancarlo. And Andrea. Now, they both are gone."

"What happened to him?"

"Sancarlo? Forced out by Rome. Right after Andrea...ah...oh..."

"Because of Andrea's suicide," Adriano helped him out. "People blamed him for it?"

"No. No one blamed Don Sancarlo. He *loved* Andrea. He made him deacon. No, Arnaud had been waiting for a reason to get rid of Sancarlo for a very long time. Arnaud had—has—many powerful friends in the Vatican, the most powerful."

"The Pope?" Lee offered.

"Him too." Marco smiled slyly. "We are Catholic country. You would no understand."

"I am Catholic," Lee said. "We both are."

"*Were* Catholic," Adriano corrected.

"It is different," Marco said. "Catholic, ex-Catholic—you are not Italian. You no understand. What the Vatican wants, they get, and Arnaud is very powerful in the Vatican."

"But why would the bad bishop... What's his name?"

"Arnaud," Marco answered.

"Why would Arnaud want to get rid of...?"

"...Sancarlo."

"Yeah, I thought the brotherhood of bishops was quite clubby," said Adriano, enjoying the gossipy Church bashing.

Marco lit up again.

Adriano accepted. Lee demurred..

"There are bishops and there are bishops," Marco said. "Depende. Bishop Sancarlo was—*is*—one kind of bishop. Gentle. Sweet. How do you say, *molto progressivo*."

"Very liberal," Lee stated.

"Si," Marco said with emphasis. "Molto liberale. Sancarlo is who started helping the refugees here in Orvieto. He—" Suddenly Marco stopped mid-sentence, as he if had offered too much. "Molto gentle. Very kind. Molto," he added quickly in summation.

"And Arnaud is not?"

Marco hunched his shoulders and looked around like a character in some Cold War spy thriller. He whispered, "Arnaud is Opus Dei."

"The Work of God," Lee intoned, the Latin translation.

"That explains his sermon," said Adriano.

"What?" Lee looked puzzled.

"The other night during the service at *Sant'Andrea*. His sermon was nothing but empty platitudes and calls for a rebirth of Catholic tradition. It was big on obedience and finding God in everyday life. Blah, blah, blah. Men as backbones of the Church. Women as servants of God—meaning as servants of *men*. Boilerplate Opus Dei." The words stung in his mouth. He could see his parents' pamphlets now, scattered on the coffee table of his childhood.

"I didn't think you kept up on ecclesiastical institutions," Lee said.

"It was a Spaniard who founded the sect, Josemaria Escriva. Every Spaniard knows Opus Dei. It's the Church's SS squad, answerable directly to and only to the Pope. J2P2 even made that hideous creature, Escriva, a saint." Adriano almost spat.

"J2 what?" Marco looked puzzled.

"J2P2," Lee explained. "It's Adriano's little nickname for his favorite pope, the late John Paul II."

"Not!" Adriano huffed. "What a reactionary piece of"—Lee's foot dug into *his* shoe this time—"work." Adriano gulped. "Sorry, Marco. I know you are Catholic."

"It's OK. I no practice," he smiled. "It's Italy. *Everyone* is a little Catholic." He polished off his second drink and motioned for another round.

For a while they discussed the weather, Italian food, and Orvieto's upcoming Presepe, the Living Nativity that was the culmination of the holiday season.

"So, what about the rumors," Lee ventured, nursing his drink.

"What rumors?"

"You know," Lee said. Adriano shot him a warning glance and poised his shoe. "The gossip that Andrea was gay. That the reason the Vatican stopped his ordination was because he was homosexual."

Marco stopped smiling. You've gone too far, Adriano thought.

"Gay. Straight. Virgin. Who knows?" Marco leaned back in his chair. "He was simply Andrea."

"Lee," Adriano said, stepping on Lee's foot so hard the shoe leather was creasing. "Let's not bother Marco anymore. He doesn't want to talk about it."

"No." Marco twirled the ice in his glass. "It doesn't bother me. I just have no talked about it in a long time. No, it doesn't bother me. It's nice to remember Andrea."

"What about the bishop?"

"Arnaud?" Marco blew out smoke as if choking on the name.

"No, Sancarlo," Lee asked. "The 'good bishop.' You said he was 'molto

progressivo.' Very liberal. Was Sancarlo gay?"

"Ha!" Marco let out an enormous guffaw, almost upsetting his glass as he waved his arms. "Bishop Sancarlo, gay? No, no. He was no a gay. That's a-funny. No offense, I mean, be gay is no problema, it's..."

"No offense taken," Lee replied.

"You mean he wasn't celibate?" Adriano jumped in, his own curiosity now aroused.

"Celibate? Ah, *celibe*. You mean, did he have a woman here in Orvieto?" Adriano shrugged.

"No," Marco said with sudden force. "No. Vescovo Sancarlo was a good man. He loved his Church. He wanted to make it better, more modern, that is all. He believed in his vows, he was celibe. Even if he wanted to, he would never break his vows, not now. Above all, he loved his Church."

"You said Rome, Bishop Arnaud, wanted him gone," Adriano said. "Where did he go?"

"A monastery. He retired. Andrea's death was too much for him. A month after, he left and Arnaud become the new bishop. The people here, they hate Arnaud. Arnaud is not *Orvietano.* He does not belong here. Rome put him here."

"So, Bishop Sancarlo was from Orvieto?" Lee asked.

"Si, si, naturalmente. An old family, molto vecchia."

"Like your grandmother," Adriano said.

"Si, like my grandmother." Marco paused, his face morphing into a huge grin, something between goodwill and a friendly-if-warning tease. "Si, like mia nonna. Mia nonna is many things. You'd be surprised!"

They clinked their glasses and Adriano thought to himself, I wouldn't be surprised at all.

CHAPTER XVIII

At Sea

Wednesday, December 4, 2013, late afternoon, the Mediterranean Sea

The steel hatch slammed open. A young man pushed past Maryam and the huddled refugees. Heman scrambled up the ladder and into the light. Several hundred faces turned skyward for an answer. Where were they?

"ماذا ترى؟"

The youth waved for his fellow prisoners to follow, then rushed away in further exploration.

The sun hurt Maryam's eyes as she crawled out onto the deck. For a week, there had been nothing but darkness. She hadn't bathed in many days, not since long before she was put upon the ship. Her thin burka, long since torn and with its face cover discarded to make breathing a bit more possible, stuck to her thin, quivering frame in sweat-blotched sheets. But now the air—fresh air! She filled her lungs. They were free.

"أين هي الطاقم؟"

An elderly woman called from below. Her lips were cracked from thirst. One arm was strapped in a bloody sling.

Minutes passed. The scout, eyes wide in panic, returned. Over and over he screamed, "نحن وحدها! نحن وحدها! لقد تخلوا عنا !"

Abandoned. They were alone.

Slowly at first, then faster, the crowd poured out of the stinking hold and onto the deck. The storm had ended, for now. All around, the Mediterranean spread in deadly calm. The ship sat low in the water. Too low. Somewhere there was a leak. The bulkheads had been much farther up from the water when they had sailed—what, a week ago?

"ولت قوارب النجاة!"

She looked to where a man was pointing. All gone. The lifeboats were all gone. A girl next to her clutched her mother's skirt and began softly to cry.

On the horizon, a single cloud loomed gray. Like a match sparking to life, a small flash of lightning lit it from behind. Another storm.

"Oh," she cried out in pain. The baby pushed against her organs. Please, she thought, please, do not come. Please do not let me live to see you drown. If you die, die in my womb. Please, Allah, spare me from witnessing the death of my child.

The wind picked up. A single wave broke over the bow. Everything tilted, and it started again, the groaning creak of steel under stress. People scurried for the cargo compartment.

No. I will not die in the dark. Not again. Not like the basement blackness she hid in during the war. She closed her eyes to the memory. "Ohhh!" she cried out, clutching her gut. The pain in her womb was intense. She could barely stand. She pushed against the swarm retreating back into the bowels of the vessel. She continued onward. If she were going to die, she would face it outside. She would confront it head-on. She had not come this far to drown in darkness. No. She would live and once she got to land she would start her life again. The men who had put her on the ship had promised her a job when she came ashore. A real job, in Europe, safe from the battlefields of home. A job so she could help her brother and pay off this passage.

She hoped it was working in a beauty salon, or a restaurant, but she didn't care. She'd clean toilets if she had to, as long as she was away from the explosions and the bullets. And now, she had a reason to live, her child. The father... The father had taken her virginity as the deposit for this passage, a forceful and painful payment that had raped both her body and her soul of innocence. But no matter, the child must live. All children were a gift from Allah.

Ahead above the pitching plates she could make out the bridge, the highest place on the ship. That would be the last place to go under. Fighting against the agony in her gut mixed with the nausea of seasickness, she pulled herself along the rail and struggled upward to the gangway.

To make sure it had not come unstitched, she clutched the receipt to her salvation, sewn into the lining of her coat. The man who had put her aboard the ship had shown it to her, only once, and told her, "Do not lose this. It is the ticket to your new life. When you arrive, friends will greet you. Remember to tell them this: 'Purgatory is the key.'"

Just before the last stitch was made, she had looked at what was written on the two thin pieces of cardboard, a few lines scrawled in ink, now hidden in the folds of her clothing:

طقف هللا اوبحن نيذلا هذه يف كئلوأل ةبسنلاب ةايحلا
باذعلا يف سوفنلا عيمجل
نآلا نكنأو ،ملاعلا اذه يف مكتدعاس نيذلا كئلوأل ةبسنلاب
ركذتن نأ نكمي ال
.مهربص دافن ببسب نوناعي نيذلا كئلوأل ةبسنلاب

On the back, another message:

طقف هللا اوبحن نيذلا هذه يف كئلوأل ةايحلا ةبسنلاب
كئادعأ ءالؤه نم سوفنلا لكلتل
ةسدقملا ايرام ،ةديسل ءاعزألا كئلوأل ةبسنلاب
باذعلا يف فعضت ال يتلا ةلئاعلا هذه حاورأل

It meant nothing to her, these Arabic phrases—like prayers, but not ones known to her. No matter. She did not need to understand. She only needed to deliver the message and get to Italy. There she would be free. But first, she'd have to live through the voyage.

"Caro fratello. Ti amo!" She spoke to herself in the only Italian she knew, carefully practiced over the phone between blackouts and riots.

Dear brother. I love you. I am coming.

CHAPTER XIX

Reunion

Wednesday, December 4, 2013, late afternoon, Civita di Bagnoregio

Civita di Bagnoregio: the town that dies.

Grigori looked up at the nearly deserted village and started the long climb to the summit. An apt description, he thought, as he walked along the thousand-foot pedestrian bridge that was Civita's only connection to the outside world. His steps were heavy, like his heart. Not like the first time he had come here. That first time—with Andrea. Then, the town was full of life, like Andrea, like both of them. Now, the town, winter-deserted and buffeted by Grigori's windy grief, earned every bit of its name. For Grigori, hope, love, and a new life had both been born and died here.

Civita di Bagnoregio: the town that dies

What a beautiful death it was. Separated from the world yet in the middle of it. Dangling from an eternal rope, hung from heaven as if awaiting execution, shimmering against the clouds in reflected glory. One day, the chord, worn thin by millennia of rain and earthquake and eruption, would come unstrung. Someday, the entire hamlet would plunge into the valley hundreds of feet below. Already, several homes dripped from the hill, half-ruined walls and crumbling stone cornices teasing gravity and defying their fate——for now. Yes, Bagnoregio would die, but not yet. Not today. It had been dying for eons.

But not the church. Grigori knew that was in the middle of the tiny central piazza. It would be the last to go, this delicate and humble church with its lonely single bell tower and sun-bleached salmon plaster facade. A century from now, or two, or five, or maybe ten, when a truly devastating tremor occurred, or if the center of Italy again erupted en masse, the final edifice to tumble into the abyss would be the Church San Donato.

Andrea's church. He closed his eyes and recited without speaking:

(17) Per quelle che sono tormentate per i loro disordinati amori desideri
(18) Per quelle che per i loro occhi troppo licenziosi patiscono
(20) Per quelle che sono castigate per i loro disordinate amori e desideri
(41) Per quelle che in questa vita poco amarono Dio

He was sure the prayer board was still there, a medieval construct in the midst of a modernity in limbo. Of course, not much modernity had an impact on Bagnoregio. Grigori doubted very much whether anyone still prayed for the souls in purgatory, besides him.

Besides Andrea.

(17) Per quelle che sono tormentate per i loro disordinati amori desideri
(18) Per quelle che per i loro occhi troppo licenziosi patiscono
(20) Per quelle che sono castigate per i loro disordinate amori e desideri
(41) Per quelle che in questa vita poco amarono Dio

Grigori would never forget the words. They were carved on his psyche more indelibly than the carefully written text he knew was still there, haunting him, inside the church just ahead.

The wind whipped at his face. He trudged on.

There were ninety levels of purgatory, according to the antique wooden petition pegboard inside the Church of San Donato. Ninety reasons for people to pay and pray to free the souls of the dearly departed. The first time that Andrea had shown it to him, Grigori had laughed, and derisively at that. He knew all about paying the Church, and what the Church expected in return. No one went to heaven free of charge.

"Grigori, you should be ashamed of yourself," Andrea had lashed out at him. "It is the only reason we are here on earth, to help others, the living and the dead."

It was the first and only time he had ever seen Andrea angry. He didn't risk it again. Andrea's compassionate smile had turned dangerously dark.

He remembered Andrea telling him the story of Saint Donato and the Emperor Julian. Andrea had brought Grigori home to Bagnoregio to meet his mother, one of the last eight people to still live on the spectacularly desolate volcanic stump. At night, it was like being on another planet, completely separated from the rest of earth by the surrounding volcanic canyons.

"The Saint and the Emperor grew up together, the best of friends," Andrea had explained as they roamed through the ancient sanctuary in the middle of the gloriously decrepit town. A smattering of Roman tourists were browsing the tourist stalls, brought outside onto the square that day of their first summer, *their* last summer. "Both of them actually became deacons in the Church. But, when Julian became emperor he rejected Christianity and tried to return Rome to paganism while Donato became a leader in the Church, a bishop in fact. Of course, that's the *official* version of the story. Since after Julian's death, Rome again became officially Christian. Many people believe that, in point of fact, Julian was actually quite enlightened, and that he didn't want to suppress Christianity. Rather, he wanted to acknowledge all beliefs as equally valid."

Grigori and Andrea had stopped for gelato. Andrea, in his deaconal collar, was sweating from the humid August sun. Grigori reached inside his designer shorts and paid.

"Zeus equal to Yahwey, and Venus equal to Mary, you mean?" Grigori offered Andrea a taste of his cone and angled for one from his companion. *Nocciola.* He had never liked that flavor, but it was Andrea's favorite. There were a lot of things he was learning to like.

"Something like that," Andrea had smiled, a crooked dimple of facial expression poised between seduction and sanctity. "So, you see, Julian and Donato were a lot like us, the closest of friends, one a believer, the other not."

"Are you calling me a heathen?" It was Grigori's turn to tease.

"Of course not," Andrea had smiled again.

It was a flash of white that seemed to swallow Grigori's breath in a way he had never experienced with anyone, man or woman.

"I would never so impugn the reputation of a decorated soldier and a guard to the Pope!" Andrea offered another lick from his cone. Grigori accepted, leaving behind a hazelnut mustache. Andrea wiped it away with a wink. Grigori wondered if anyone noticed. He didn't care.

That had been, what, two years ago now? Grigori thought. A lifetime.

He kept walking toward San Donato, Andrea's church, and its abacus of salvation, the top ninety sins and the prayers (plus two euros) guaranteed to help free those tormented in purgatory but living in hope of the Resurrection. He had his numbers—nineteen, twenty, thirty-three—and a pocket full of euros. Even if he didn't believe, Grigori was quite sure what his sins were. And, of course, the clue that he and Andrea had uncovered echoed in his brain:

"Purgatory is the key."

A loud bang and Grigori threw himself against the rusty railing, his only hope between the tiny bridge and the stony valley below. He looked behind him in terror. His heart strained against his chest. They have found me, he thought.

"Grigori! Ragazzo!" The three-wheeled Ghia rolled to a stop, back-firing with another loud retort as it strained against the steep grade of the viaduct. Andrea's mother was behind the wheel. "It is a long walk, dear boy. Get in. I will drive you the rest of the way to the gate. Nothing with a motor is allowed in the town, but we can walk the rest of the way to San Donato from there."

Grigori smiled in relief. "You startled me, Signora." His hands shook and he lowered them from his straining form. "Yes, thanks."

"Thank *you* for coming, for Andrea." Signora Bernardone patted Grigori's knee. "Thank you for remembering."

(17) For those who are tormented by the perversity of their desires

(18) For those who suffer for the licentiousness of their eyes

(20) For those who are punished for their disordered love

(41) For those in this life who just loved God

Of course, he remembered. How could Grigori forget. Perhaps when I die, then I will forget, he thought. Until then, he lived in a painful hope for death.

The tiny dilapidated scooter labored against the incline, bearing its pilgrims to the peak as Grigori remembered Andrea's words—words that were becoming clearer every day.

"Purgatory is the key."

CHAPTER XX

Puzzle

Wednesday, December 4, 2013, evening, Orvieto

Lee was peeling a grape and doing a crossword. "What's an eight-letter word for 'adobe abode'?"

"Beg pardon?"

"An eight-letter word for 'house.' Today's theme is South of the Border," said Lee. "You know, Spanish words that have entered the English vernacular. It's Wednesday, an easy day, but my brain isn't exactly firing on all thrusters."

"That is so offensive," huffed Adriano. "'South of the Border,' as if only Spanish speakers were struggling to swim the Rio Grande. Nothing against South and Central America..."

"Naturally, since you were born in Venezuela after your family fled Franco."

"But," Adriano continued, on a roll, "The language is *Spanish*, not Mexican."

"It is the *New York Times* crossword, dear one, not *El Pais*."

"Even so," Adriano frowned. "Hacienda."

"Duh, even I should have gotten that. Perfect! It fits. You get a prize." Lee tossed a grape into his lover's open mouth. "What about a 'lady priest'?"

"Is this a crossword clue?"

"No, silly, what Marco was saying at drinks earlier today."

"Great minds think alike." Adriano was typing furiously on this laptop, sitting cross-legged next to his husband on the couch. "Already found it. Check this out, courtesy of everyone's favorite overwrought blogger, Signora Peg."

Lee motioned for Adriano to read. He loved the sound of his husband's voice.

Luther Who? Henry the What?
All Forgiven on All Souls Day in Orvieto.

On the November second, Feast of All Souls, it is very cold—molto freddo—in the twelfth-century Church of Sant'Andrea. So cold in fact, that portable patio heaters have been brought in to warm the ecumenical bodies—Anglican and Roman Catholic—packed in for the first-of-its-kind religious lovefest to broach this medieval town's storied tufo.

Before construction of the fabulous Duomo was begun in 1290, *Sant'Andrea* was Orvieto's most important church—

"She used the word 'fabulous' to describe the Cathedral of Orvieto?" Lee shook his head. "I'm gay, but please, I'd never even consider the word 'fabulous' outside of a press release for *Ab Fab*. She needs to be stopped."

"May I continue?"

"Si, continuare."

"I'm impressed. Not bad Italian for a gringo."

"I'm not a total Luddite," Lee said as he tossed another grape at Adriano, who caught it in his mouth. Although a whiz at remembering numbers and dates, Lee was somewhat sensitive about his nonpropensity for language. He had signed up for an Orvieto library card this afternoon and had to be saved by Adriano when he hadn't understood a field marked "ESEMPIO: GIO BONETTI."

"'Esempio' means example," Adriano had patiently pointed out. "It's where you write your name." Lee had smiled, signed his name, and tried not to look like an American.

His husband's voice pulled him back to the present.

Originally the site of an Etruscan road, the location later played host to a sixth-century church before construction of the present *Sant'Andrea* around the year 1100. In 1281, *Sant'Andrea* saw the coronation of Pope Martin IV—since he had been forbidden from entering Rome—complete with attendance by Charles of Anjou. Perhaps most famously, it was here at the Church of Sant'Andrea in 1209 that Pope Innocent III called for the Fourth Crusade—the so-called Albigensien Crusade—to eradicate the heathen heresy of Catharism that had perverted the Catholic faith and was rife, itself, here in Orvieto.

"Oh yeah, those evil vegetarian, equality-of-the-sexes Cathars." It was Adriano's turn for editorial comment as he stopped reading. "They had the right idea, screw the Church and defy the Pope—"

"And get slaughtered as a result in 1244 at Montsegur Castle in France. Hmmm, I didn't know about the Cathar connection to Orvieto. That's interesting. You learn something new every day. Go on. This is fascinating. But what does this have to do with the woman priest?" Lee asked.

"I'm getting there, or should I say, Peg is finally getting there."

A mélange of US, South American, and African Anglicans from all over the Italian boot (including some who have traveled over an hour from The Eternal City herself to be here) have hoofed it up to Orvieto for a history-making occurrence: a woman on the altar (and I'm not talking nuns offering communion as lay ministers to overburdened padres). The Rev. Victoria "Vicky" Lewis—like an American actress in a collar—wears well her ebony cassock and virginal surplice. There's a lot going on with Rev. Vicky. Like Churchill, she is half Brit, half Yank: American mother and British father. But, whatever her lineage, tonight she is most assuredly in charge. A smattering of local Catholics have snuck in as well (trying desperately to suppress genuflections and other overtly Roman gestures) to see if it's true. A female priest on a Roman altar. And we ain't talking Hestia or Vestal Virgins here.

Little old Italian ladies gasp in amazement as "Gio" Sancarlo, the much loved, almost idolized some would say, Catholic bishop of Orvieto and Todi rushes in following an afternoon service at the Duomo. He is warmly welcomed with a kiss on each cheek by Vicar Vicky, as she is commonly known. "Una donna sull'altare!," is heard to murmur as shock shivers across the congregation. And, not just any woman, but a female Episcopal priest, the American branch of Anglicanism, which shocked the Christian world by electing an openly gay bishop and even elevating a woman as its primate.

"I wonder if Brian knew Vicar Vicky," Lee interrupted, looking at his friend's ashes on the bookcase behind the sofa. "That name sounds so familiar."

"Silly question, my love. As you well know, Brian knew *everyone* in the Anglican Church. He called it the Pansy Mafia, remember?"

"Hmmm, go on."

Officially, the Pope and the Archbishop of Canterbury get along in an "imperfect communion" as fellow Christians. Of course, things were perfect until Henry VIII asked Pope Clement VII for a divorce—another local footnote as Pope Clement was living here in Orvieto at the time—but since the Reformation-heavy days of the late 1520s, well, things have never been quite the same between Roman Catholicism and its copycat Romano-lite Anglican Church.

But, here in Umbria, Christian love springs eternal as the broad-minded Bishop Sancarlo seems happy to help "a broad," as it were, saying that he is committed to "warm relations" with Vicar Vicky and her tiny flock. Touchy-feely "We're all Christian here" PR aside, the service is controversial. When the All Souls service ends, even Vicar Vicky is stunned, albeit pleasantly so, when Bishop Sancarlo joins her on the altar for a simultaneous benediction of their assembled faithful.

"Our Anglican brothers and sisters," Bishop Gio added with a wink to the congregation and his liturgical lady friend, "are surely our closest siblings. As the prayer of St. Francis says, 'Make me an instrument of your peace. Where there is hatred let me sew love.'"

Afterward, Bishop Gio and Vicar Vicky, as always joined by the lovely-if-somewhat-light-footed deacon Andrea, invite the congregation to cross to the medical center and give blood for use by Orvieto's seemingly unstoppable immigrant population.

As the visibly surprised crowd exited the church, one wondered how strong were the stitches being sewn in this interfaith coat of many collars. And, more to the point, one has to wonder, what does Rome think about this cozy crazy quilt being woven here in Orvieto?

—written by Lady Peg, *A Square Peg on a Round Rock*

"She doesn't think much of Episcopalians, does she, our Peg?" Lee suggested.

"Evidently not. Nor of Andrea either," Adriano said.

"Yeah." Lee frowned. "That was quite the bitchy comment. 'Lovely-if-light-footed Deacon Andrea.' A bit *Tea and Sympathy* with thinly veiled homophobic arsenic. When was that blog from?"

"Last year, November second. Exactly a month before Andrea's suicide."

"Or whatever," Lee said.

"So, you think there's something strange to all this?"

"I don't know, does seem odd." Lee shrugged. "Call it a publicist's intuition. I can tell when a story is being put to bed, as they say. A guy gets a devastating bit of news on Friday morning. Everyone sees him at Mass that night. A few hours later he dies mysteriously. Twenty-four hours later, his funeral draws an enormous crowd and the Vatican Press Office shuts up like a clam. I know a PR campaign when I see one. I've created enough of them in my time."

"You read too many *Hardy Boy* mysteries when you were an unspoiled youth."

"*Nancy Drew*," Lee corrected. "But yes, possibly." Lee chewed his lip. There *was* something here, but just out of range. His brain couldn't quite grab on to it, or let it go. "Do you still have the link to the article about Andrea's funeral?"

Adriano clicked on his keyboard and called up the link. "Here it is."

"I wanted to be a priest, and dedicated my whole life to this goal, but it was denied me," typed Bernardone, who had been born in Civita di Bagnoregio. The note found on his computer continued. "I am fragile and I ask for forgiveness."

"Bagnoregio." Lee's lip was practically doing a hula. "That's where Deacon Andrea was born."

"And, one of the towns Lady Peg was saying we needed to visit."

"She may be right, but not quite yet. There's something else I want to check out. I've heard that name before. Vicky. Keep scrolling."

"Bingo." Adriano read out loud.

After the funeral, Andrea's coffin was carried into the crypt of the cathedral attended by only Bishop Sancarlo, don Andrea's mother, and the Rev. Vicky Lewis, and three young local men.

"How much you wanna bet that two of those local men were the doctor and Leather Boy *from Sant'Andrea's* the other night?"

"And Marco makes three," Adriano added. "You think someone is hiding something about Andrea's death?"

"I don't know. It's just a feeling. The Church getting involved so late in the process of Andrea becoming a priest is strange. Local bishops *always* have the last word when it comes to ordaining priests. If the Vatican wasn't happy about something, they'd have called Andrea's bishop, and long before a week before ordination. It's suspect."

"Well, I suspect everything when it comes to the Church, so I'm with you there," said Adriano.

Lee's lips were twitching like one of those vibrating airport massage chairs, a clear sign of his mind on overdrive.

"Google her name and Brian's name."

Adriano entered the names "Brian Swathmore" and "Vicky Lewis." Even for an Italian modem slightly newer than medieval, the results popped up quickly.

"Thank yee, gods of the internet." Adriano turned the screen around again for Lee.

"EpiscopalianChurch.org." Lee scrolled down the page and clicked on a picture from 1985, then read the caption. "Representatives from the Anglican Communion gather in Cambridge."

Among a group of eight rather staid-looking clerics, two faces stood out instantly: one, a pretty blonde woman, the other—

"It's Brian! They knew each other!" Lee exclaimed, looking to his mentor's flag-wrapped urn.

"Well, they were at least standing next to each other in a picture about twenty-eight years ago."

"Where is Vicar Vicky now?" Lee asked.

Adriano's fingers clicked out a keyboard concerto. "St. Paul's Anglican Church."

"Here in Orvieto?"

"No." Adriano shut his computer lid and opened his mouth for another grape. Lee obliged. "A bit down the road from here."

"Far?"

"No, not far. All roads lead there," Adriano said.

Lee smiled broadly—a road trip to the mother ship. "Rome!"

CHAPTER XXI

Dinner with a Medici

Passover Saturday, April 4, 1528 (Julian Calendar), Orvieto

"Next year in Jerusalem." Clement rose from the table with a smile toward his host.

"Or in Rome," replied Moses de Blanis to the easy laughter of everyone assembled.

The six Passover guests raised their goblets.

"Blessed are You, Lord, for the land..." said Cardinal Egidio de Viterbo.

"...and for the fruit of the vine," Wazzan finished the blessing for his friend.

"Amen to that," said Moses, beckoning his guests to his terrace overlooking Orvieto. "As Prince Kohelet says in the Torah, 'There is a time for every purpose under the heaven,' and now is the time for feasting."

"Feasting?" Gio, the young Swiss guard looked perplexed. "Didn't we just eat?"

"Sofia, what are you doing bringing so ignorant a gentile into our midst?"

Clement listened as her father taunted gently.

"We must teach him the hospitality of the Jews!" Moses walked between his daughter and the handsome Swiss guard, with an arm over each of their shoulders. "That was merely the ceremonial food of Passover. Now, we celebrate with a traditional supper."

Clement watched as Moses pushed back the curtain, revealing a rooftop patio lit with torches against pink and blue streaks of the waning sunset. A few hundred yards away, the Duomo's gilded facade loomed up, reflecting the lights of both. In the distance, a pastiche of village fires punctuated the Umbrian hills. Below, the River Paglio made its way languorously to the sea. Nearby, the mountains gave birth to the Tiber, beginning its patient journey toward Rome. In the center of it all, a table groaned with food of all kinds, surrounded by couches and cushions for a reclining meal.

"Magnificent," Clement whispered, taking in the view. "Your hospitality and your home do us honor. Thank you, Lord de Blanis."

"Moses, please, Holy Father. Call me Moses."

"And you must call me Giulio."

"Dear God," said Cardinal Egidio. "There may yet be hope for mankind when popes and Jews are on a first-name basis."

The laughter continued as the group reclined at the table and two servants, a young man and woman, placed silver platters before each guest.

"Your Holiness...?" Moses said.

Clement raised a friendly eyebrow.

"Giulio," Moses continued. "If it is amenable to Your Hol—To you—after my household staff has served us, I would like to dismiss them so that we may enjoy a more colloquial and private evening."

My God, this is a shrewd and clever man, thought Clement, leaning back against the delicately embroidered pillows. *He knows why I'm there. And, of course, as with all aristocratic Jews, his servants are Catholic.* Clement looked at them, husband and wife. A couple of Orvieto. Undoubtedly, they would be in the cathedral tomorrow for Palm Sunday Mass. *Certainly, they have recognized me by now. Tomorrow, all of Orvieto will know I have dined with a Jewish banker, a woman, a Moorish scholar, a common soldier, and perhaps the most secular cleric since my cousin Pope Leo X, Cardinal Egidio.*

"May I offer them my blessing before they depart?" asked Clement, in as purposefully casual a manner as possible.

It was de Blanis's turn to smile. "You need not ask permission for anything in my house. I am quite sure it will not only be their first papal blessing, but the first for this house. I hope, however, that it will not be the last."

"Call them in, please," said Clement.

The couple walked in from the kitchen with their eyes downcast. They appeared to be in their early twenties.

"Look at me my children," said Clement, and the husband and wife simultaneously fell to their knees in genuflection. "Approach me."

Kneeling before the Pope, first the man and then his wife kissed the papal ring. Clement placed his hands on their heads and spoke in Latin. "May God make you like Ephraim and Menasheh and like Sarah, Rebecca, Rachel, and Leah. May God bless you and guard you. May the light of God shine upon you, and may God be gracious to you. May the presence of God be with you and give you peace."

With furtive and confused looks, they crossed themselves, kissed the Pope's ring a final time, and backed out of the room.

When he heard the inner door close, Moses spoke. "Your knowledge of Hebrew blessings is impressive. However, I rarely hear them offered in the language of Rome."

"My uncle, Lorenzo de Medici, was a great believer in the study of all cultures and languages."

"A wise man," offered Cardinal Egidio, accepting a dish of roast pheasant from de Blanis's daughter. He served himself and passed it on to Clement, immediately to his right, seated at the head of the table. To Clement's right, opposite Egidio, sat Hassan, attired as richly as any sultan. Next to the Moor and opposite Sofia sat Gio the Swiss Guard. Moses de Blanis sat opposite Clement at the table's other end, flanked by the Switzer and his daughter, both of whom seemed oblivious to everyone at the table except each other. "Lorenzo the Magnificent was a student of philosophy. He agreed with the words of Epictetus: 'All religions must be tolerated...for every man must get to heaven in his own way.'"

"Yes," said Clement, wryly passing a salver of roast boar to Hassan. "And as the noble and much abused Seneca the Younger stated, 'Religion is regarded by the common people as true, by the wise as false, and by the rulers as useful.' Unfortunately, his student Nero didn't ascribe to such humanist ideals."

"Wasn't it Seneca who tried to assassinate Nero." Gio spoke up. "He committed suicide after, yes?"

"That was Nero's version of the tale," Wazzan replied, accepting the roast pork from the Pope. "But, of course, the rulers of imperial Rome brooked little dissent."

"And, as has always been the case, history is written by the victors," said Egidio. "The vanquished are usually painted as fools, heretics, or whores—excuse me, dear girl." He bowed to Sofia at his elbow.

"No offense taken, my Lord Cardinal," de Blanis's daughter said demurely, but without shock. "As the great Eastern teacher called Buddha has said, 'The sharpest sword is a word spoken in wrath.' I find no wrath in your words, Your Eminence, only passion, which is easily forgiven."

The Cardinal gently patted his dinner partner's hand while everyone at the table chuckled genially.

"How true, my dear Egidio," said Clement, looking to his young guardian, seated across from Sofia. His eyes were transfixed by her every movement and tone. *My God, she is lovely. How I envy them both.* "Unfortunately, now we have no victors in Italy, only the vanquished and constant war. I shudder to think who will write of these times, and we seated here."

"Don't worry, Your Holiness," said Egidio, filling Clement's cup. "To once again quote the wise Epictetus, 'If anyone tells you that a certain person speaks ill of you, do not make excuses about what is said of you but answer, "He was ignorant of my other faults, else he would not have mentioned these alone."'"

"Cold comfort that, my friend," said Clement, then giving into silent thought. *My faults are legion, and only exceeded by my debts. A pontificate disgraced, Rome devastated, a Church in revolt, and a Catholic king trying to divorce the Holy Roman Emperor's aunt.* "I am sure volumes of prose will be dedicated to my faults, real or imagined, by my successors, or conquerors."

"Your Holiness," said Sofia quietly. "Yours is not a life of mere prose for historians. It is a life and a legacy more attuned to that of a poem. Was it not Plato who said that poetry is nearer to vital truth than history?"

"Too kind, dear child. And, if I may say so, you are unusually well educated for a female," said the Pope, with one eye toward her father. "You have a pearl of great worth in so beautiful and talented a daughter, friend Moses."

"You honor my family, noble Medici. The gratitude, however, should go to your own Prince of Viterbo, Cardinal Egidio. From him has my library grown, and the world view of my daughter, and myself. Your Church is greatly blessed to have such a visionary scholar within its midst."

"I couldn't agree more," said Clement, who was feeling suddenly transported back to the Florence of his youth, the palace of the Medici, when conversations such as this, and freedom of thought, flowed like wine at the table, unsullied by prejudice, prayers, or predilection. "Egidio is that most unique of men, of religion, a Roman; of scholarship, a Moor; of wisdom, seemingly from Solomon's court. He has been a wise and patient teacher to both me and our revered cousin, Pope Leo. Most importantly, he has been our friend."

"My dearest Prince," Egidio said taking Clement's hand in his, "you humble me with your words."

"Indeed." Wazzan jumped in. "It was your sainted cousin, Pope Leo, who brought me into the Christian faith, but Egidio who taught me its most valued lesson."

"Which is?" Moses queried as he poured more wine for his daughter and young Gio.

"God is everywhere," Wazzan said, motioning for everyone to raise their goblets. "Sometimes, he can even be found in church."

At this, the merriment reached its greatest height, with Clement laughing so hard tears ran down his face. "God forgive you. You are a blasphemous and beloved heretic. I see that none of us here are trammeled by convention or dogma," said the Pope, pointing his fork at the already half-consumed platter of pork in the middle of the table. Although, Moses and his daughter had eaten none, the Muslim-born Wazzan had partaken liberally.

"Born to Muhammed I was, but in the land of Andalus. There among the Iberians, the meat of the sow is, unto itself, a kind of religion. So, you see, my conversion was fed at table. I live like the birds, flitting from one country to another, trying everything and trying to harm no one. When I hear Africa derided, I say that I am of Granada. When people speak ill of Granada, then Africa is my home."

"So, you adhere to the maxim of St. Ambrose," prompted Cardinal Egidio. "When in Rome, do as the Romans do."

"Well, then," ventured Gio, grateful for a chance to offer some youthful wit, "I am proud to be a Roman, for I have always believed that one of humanity's greatest moments was the first time a caveman threw a pig upon the fire."

At this everyone laughed and toasted the young guard. Sofia glowed in reply.

"As it also says in the book of Kohelet, or as you gentiles call it, Ecclesiastes," their host said and smiled. "'Every man who eats and drinks and enjoys what is good in all his toil, it is a gift of God.' Your presence, noble son of the Medici and highest prince of your faith, is indeed, a gift from God this night. In your honor, we have served foods to your liking. Since you grace us on the highest of my religion's holy days, I have prepared the finest food in the manner of your court. I hope you are enjoying it."

"My dear friend, Lord Moses de Blanis," said Clement, wiping away the remaining tears of his mirth but finding new ones fueled by the evening's conviviality and wine, "I am, indeed, enjoying it all. Very, very much."

The dinner continued late into the night, flowing from dialogues inclusive of all six, sometimes separating into pairs or triads, but always retreating and progressing naturally, organically, like the tides. Shells of laughter, and occasionally bawdiness, were strewn across the sands of the crumb- and wine-stained table. Finally, driven in by an encroaching fog and the gasping torches, the party retired inside, Sofia to the kitchen to clean up in the servants' absence, Gio at her side. Cardinal Egidio and Wazzan employed themselves, as usual, poring over the rare and leather-bound tomes of the de Blanis library. Clement followed Moses on a tour of the residence, impressed by its size and opulence, in stark contrast to the "Papal Palace." Papal Palace indeed, Clement thought. In words only. There was nothing palatial about it, although like everything, that could be remedied with money. *What a loathsome whore I've become. Worse than a whore, who after all performs a useful, and hopefully mutually appreciated, service. I have less than nothing to offer my host as collateral for my begging.*

"Please, make yourself comfortable," Moses said, leading them through an intricately carved archway at the end of a long, tapestry-hung wall. It was the banker's private study.

"My uncle Lorenzo would have been quite comfortable in your home," said Clement, as Moses gestured for him to sit in a well-upholstered chair by a roaring hearth. Hovering in the glow of a dozen candles, antique sculptures of Etruscan, Greek, and even Oriental heritage crowned the shelves. "I salute your good fortune."

"I take that as a great compliment, coming from not only the Pope, but more importantly from a Medici."

Clement just nodded. They sat for a few moments in silence. Finally, Clement opened his mouth to speak, but he was interrupted before he could start.

"The year 1492," said Moses, looking away from Clement, his face half in shadow, half orange from the cracking fire. "You remember that year?"

"Yes," Clement said evenly. "Until last year, I thought it was the worst year in history. My uncle died that year, Lorenzo the Magnificent."

"You never knew your father, did you?"

"No." Clement sighed, realizing the significance of this year, this coming Easter in just a few weeks. "He was assassinated in the church on Easter Sunday, 1478. Fifty years ago this month. The Pazzi family killed him. I was born a few months after his death, and then my mother died soon thereafter. I was an orphan practically at birth."

"The Pazzi almost killed the great Lorenzo as well."

"Yes," said Clement, staring fixedly at the fire. "But he lived, and took me into his home. Lorenzo raised me as his own son. Giovanni, Lorenzo's son, Pope Leo, was my cousin, but really my brother. Michelangelo came soon thereafter, sent by his father to study under the Medici. It was a lively household."

"I can imagine," said Moses, stoking the fire with his boot. "A glorious time for Florence, and your family as well. That all ended when Lorenzo died in 1492, for a while, at least. Do you know what else happened that year?"

Clement coughed and turned uncomfortably in his seat. *I know where this is going.* "Yes, the wretched Spanish discovered their so-called 'New World.' Now, they pretend to be the masters of the old one. Their King, Charles, has driven me from Rome, and once again caused the Medici and my family to be expelled from Florence."

"As was my family expelled from Spain in 1492 when your uncle died. As was the family of my friend, Hassan de Wazzan, forced to flee as well." Moses kicked the fire again. "Ferdinand and Isabella gave the continent a united Spain, but they didn't want Jews or Muslims to share in it."

"And Girolamo Savonarola drove the Jews from Florence, along with my family, as soon as Lorenzo was entombed."

Moses turned to smile at his guest, the Pope. "We have a lot in common, this Jew and this pope, do we not? Both of us are refugees."

Clement laughed. "It would seem so."

They sat again for a while in silence. Finally, Moses spoke, not looking at his companion. "The Medici have always been fair to we Jews. When your family was in power in Florence, my people were safe. Our businesses thrived. My family had no fear. When we needed help, your family was there. In Rome, when your cousin, Leo, was pope, we were protected. Oh yes, of course, many despised us—despise us still—but your family respected our faith, even though the Church considers us damned, and killers of Christ."

"My church says many things," Clement said quietly but with force. "I am supposedly its head, but my personal beliefs are nothing against the weight of Vatican history and prejudice. I have always been respectful towards and protective of Israel's tribe."

"Yes, yes, please—I am sorry. I didn't mean to imply anything else. Quite the opposite." Moses reached over and laid his hand on Clement's knee. "I know why you are here."

Clement sat rigidly, saying nothing. The moment was arriving.

"The Medici bank was the greatest of its age. It partnered with Jewish banks, it partnered with my family. My family has grown rich—I have grown rich. Thirty-five years ago, Spain was torturing my ancestors if they did not convert or flee. Thirty-five years ago, Savonarola was glorying in the death of Lorenzo de Medici, holding his perverse bonfires of the vanities, and driving the Jews from Florence. And, now, here we both sit in Orvieto."

"In Orvieto."

"A Jew bound for hell according to the frescoes on the walls of the cathedral we can see here from my window, and a pope driven from Rome and his son driven from Florence."

"Alessandro," Clement whispered the name.

Silence again descended upon the pair.

"And so, Your Holiness, Clement VII and Lord Giulio de Medici, I am here if you need."

Clement looked up from his reverie directly into the eyes of Moses de Blanis. "It has been said, dear Moses, that there are only two prayers."

"What are those, my friend?"

"Please and Thank You."

"Indeed," said Moses, slapping the Pope's knee. "Well, we have uttered both tonight. Let us talk no more of this. We need no more words than that. Consider yourself taken care of, as the Medici took care of me and my family oh so many years ago."

"Thank you," said the Pope, and the two men turned back to the fire. Behind them, through the balcony doors, the Cathedral of Orvieto glowed in the moonlight.

Later that night, back in his dismal "palace," Clement crawled into his creaking bed and wondered what future ages would make of such a gathering as tonight. A fallen pope, a Jew, a woman, an infidel, and a scholar gathered together in one room, when in other rooms such groups would be apostasy. If I get out of this, he thought, just before dropping off, I'm going to put Moses's money, his *loan*, to good use. I'll find a way to repay him. To repay all of these people who have taken me in, a refugee. Maybe that was the lesson of Orvieto, and he slept and dreamed of a future Orvieto. In the morning, he did not remember his dreams.

CHAPTER XXII

Strangers on a Train

Thursday, December 5, 2013, early morning, Orvieto, Scalo

The train to Rome was late.

"What are they saying?" Lee's words came out, illustrated in foggy, icy puffs. *I really should work on my Italian.*

Adriano tilted his head and listened to the announcement over the public address system in Orvieto's tiny train station. "Thirty minutes delay."

"Do you think it will stick to that?"

Adriano shrugged. "Depende."

"Let's go inside for a coffee," Lee said, rubbing his hands together. "I'm freezing."

Walking down Orvieto's cobblestone streets at 6:15 a.m. to make sure that they made the 7:30 a.m. train on time ("Depende!"), they had noticed the digital clock/ thermometer on the pharmacy next to San Andrea stating it was four degrees.

They got to the funicular at 6:45 a.m. but found the waiting room closed. At 7:12 a.m., a woman casually drove up in a comically dented and antique red Fiat mini, parked diagonally across two spaces, lit a cigarette, and sauntered over to the ticket office and opened the door, seemingly oblivious to Lee, Adriano, and a group of locals who suddenly appeared the moment the attendant arrived. They knew the drill. So much for arriving early. Lee made a mental note. Amazingly, the tram's 7:15 a.m. departure down the mountainside had been on time. Less than five minutes later, Adriano and Lee were shivering on the platform for Rome at the foot of the slope.

Orvieto hovered somewhere above, hidden in an early morning mist. Only at 7:35 a.m. had the announcement been made that the train would be running late.

Typical Italian operating procedure. Peg warned us, Lee thought. After more than an hour outside, they were frigid indeed. He noted that Adriano seemed annoyed with the inefficiency of it all. He was too. The fifty or so other commuters seemed to take the delay in stride and shuffled inside.

"Uno caffe latte e uno cappuccino, per favore." Adriano rattled off their order to the matronly barista as they saddled up to the small but fully stocked train station bar. I'll never be able to speak this language, and certainly not that fast, Lee thought. Frank Sinatra was singing "My Way," punctuated by steamy gurgles from the Fascist-era espresso machine.

While Adriano waited for their coffees, Lee walked across the station café-cum-newsstand to pay at the separate register counter where a girl in a Madonna T-shirt and earphones counted change. Everything in Italy seemed to require three times as many steps, staff, and patience as in the US. Of course, that was part of the charm. *I wonder if I can take two months of charm. The simplest things take forever. Coffee. I need coffee.*

"Scuse, Signore, you are the Americans, si?"

Lee looked down to find a cheerful, elderly priest, neatly bundled up against the cold. He was so short that the brim of his homburg hat just cleared the counter. Yoda! He was the priest from Sunday night's service at *Sant'Andrea*, the one who had been the Bishop's concelebrant.

"Si, yes, how did you know?"

The cleric shrugged with an almost elfish grin. "It's a small town. Plus, La Donna Volsini told me."

There was that *Godfather* soundtrack again.

"Uno espresso, per favore," the priest said to the girl behind the register while he opened his small, leather change purse, creased with age and bearing the initials "N. M. / D. B."

"Uno caffe latte, uno cappuccino, e uno espresso, per favore," Lee managed with a painfully practiced effort to the young girl at the cash register, motioning for the priest to put away his money.

"Grazie, my son." The priest tipped his hat. "Most kind, and your Italian is excellent."

"No, my Italian is nonexistent, but I won't survive if I can't at least pay for coffee so I'm trying to learn the basics. Your English is much better. Adriano, he's the one with a talent for language."

"Adriano? He is your..."

"Husband."

The priest's eyes fairly twinkled. "I am Father Nicolo Monaldeschi," said the cleric, taking off his glove and offering his hand, "but for some reason everyone calls me Don Bello."

"Well then, we will too, Don Bello. And here comes my husband, Adriano."

Adriano gave Lee a questioning glance as he crossed the room holding two cups of coffee. Adriano offered the usual morning pleasantries, fluidly, in flawless Italian. Don Bello led them across the increasingly crowded room in search of a table. Two conservatively dressed businessmen jumped up from theirs, instantly recognizing the elderly priest, and motioned for the trio to take their places. While Adriano and Don Bello draped their coats over their chairs and settled in, Lee went back for the priest's espresso. Adriano smiled when he returned. The conversation was in full and lively swing.

"Adriano tells me you are a student of history." The priest was positively puckish in his enthusiasm.

Lee sat down.

"You have come to the right place." The priest pushed his chair closer to the table. "Orvieto is rich in history. You must let me give you a tour before you go."

"That would be super, yes please!" Lee almost spilled his coffee in delight. He noticed Adriano rolling his eyes affectionately.

"How long are you here?"

"Two months," Lee answered, taking a sip of his latte. *My god, even train station coffee was delicious here.*

"Wonderful! Plenty of time, then! You'll practically be Orvietani before you leave."

"Oh dear, Don Bello," said Adriano. "You don't know what you've done. Lee will drive you crazy with questions."

"Not at all," he continued gleefully while he delicately imbibed his espresso. "I can show you the catacombs and underground passages at San Andrea. They say that some of the popes used them to hide during difficult times. Borgias, Medici, Jewish refugees from the Nazis, Italian partisans subverting the fascists. Cathar heretics escaping the Crusaders. The occasional pregnant nun on the run. Oh yes, Orvieto has many secrets."

"Your church is beautiful. We were there for its feast day Mass Sunday evening," Lee said, ever the eager, albeit aging, acolyte and would-be priest.

"Oh no, dear boy, *Sant'Andrea* isn't my parish, I just help out there since—since it lost its pastor and its deacon last year." Don Bello's winsome demeanor dimmed a bit, but for just a second. Recovering quickly, he went on, "My parish is *San Giovanale*, right on the cliff. It's the oldest church in Orvieto, even older that *Sant'Andrea*. *San Giovanale* is built over the remains of a Roman altar and an even older Etruscan temple." The cleric offered this last fact with more than a little bit of obvious pride.

They chatted amiably for the next fifteen minutes or so, until the speakers overhead crackled to staticky life. The train was five minutes away.

"Ah, time to go," Don Bello said with a slight frown. "But, we can continue our conversation on the train if you like."

"That would be lovely," Adriano said with genuine enthusiasm, and helped the priest into his coat.

Lee looked on in bemused amazement. It wasn't like Adriano to cozy up to someone so professionally religious, no matter how charming. God knew Adriano and Brian had had their share of arguments over, well, just that. God.

"I'm so sorry to hear about your friend," Don Bello said, patting Lee's shoulder as they walked toward the train. "Adriano told me. Your bishop friend must have been a very special person to have had two such wonderful men to care for him, in life and death."

"He was," Lee replied. "Thank you for that."

"We miss him very much," added Adriano. "Especially Lee."

"He was lucky to have you both, and the Church must have been lucky to have had him," Don Bello said kindly.

"Well," Lee said, remembering the article about Bishop Sancarlo's and Reverend Vicky's ecumenical lovefest and subsequent controversy. "Brian wasn't Catholic. He was a bishop in the Episcopal Church."

"Roman Catholicism. Anglicanism. Two sides of the same religious coin. Episcopalians are just Catholics with half the guilt."

Adriano laughed out loud. "That's terrific. Brian would have loved that. May I use it?"

"Of course, dear boy. Quote me at will. It's not often that I say something memorable."

"I doubt that, Don Bello," Adriano said.

"I won't even charge you residuals, although I am always fundraising. We need money to restore the frescoes in *San Giovanale*. Eleventh century. Quite rare. Unique in Italy, actually in the world."

"Are you hitting us up for money, Don Bello?" Adriano teased. "We've only just arrived in Orvieto."

Don Bello raised his gloved palms upward in mock supplication: "Render to Caesar what is Caesar's and unto God what is God's. Perhaps. The American dollar is strong this year, I believe."

Adriano chuckled again. "I have a feeling you'll meet your fundraising goal."

In ten years of marriage, Lee had never seen Adriano warm up to a priest like this. Well...Brian, of course. But that was different. He was a bishop, not just a priest. More to the point, he was *Brian*. Brian had been Lee's friend, mentor really, for years before he married the young couple, but when Brian got his terminal diagnosis, it was Adriano who had suggested he move in with them. Lee looked lovingly over at Adriano, now quite smitten it would seem with the elderly cleric. *Thank God for Adriano, he keeps me sane. He helps me forget—forget many things.*

The train was full, but as if endowed with a bubble of goodwill and luck, Don Bello secured three seats together for them in a compartment, instantly abandoned, but with conviviality, by its already seated occupants.

Wow, thought Lee. Don Bello knows everyone in town. He's like an Italian version of the leprechaun from the old Lucky Charms commercials of my youth.

"You seem quite popular," Adriano noted genially.

"Well, I wouldn't say that," said the priest, grinning. "Just old."

As the train pulled out of the station and headed south to Rome, an hour distant, Don Bello turned to the couple and asked, "Where are my manners? What is it, after all, that takes you to Rome? Sightseeing? Museums? A papal audience?" He offered this last with a wink at Adriano.

Lee screwed up his courage. Somehow, he had a feeling that Don Bello wouldn't be pleased with the answer, for all his joviality.

"We're going to meet an Anglican priest actually, a colleague of our friend Brian's, we think. It's a bit of a gamble. We've never met and she doesn't know that we're coming."

"Who would that be?"

"The Reverend Victoria Lewis."

Don Bello inhaled quickly and a slight twitch ran across his face, like a computer screen processing a new bit of data or a just introduced connection. In a flash, it was gone and the priest's florid good humor rebloomed.

"At St. Paul's Inside the Walls." Don Bello smiled. "What a coincidence. That's where I'm going today. Reverend Vicky and I are having dinner. Perhaps you can join us?"

Before Lee could answer, Adriano jumped in. "We'd love to," he said. "But wouldn't it be an imposition?"

Lightning will strike next, Lee thought. Adriano chumming it up with one priest and about to break bread with another.

"No imposition at all. Vicky is an old friend. She'll be delighted to meet you, especially if you find that she knew your friend, Bishop...?"

"Swathmore. Brian Swathmore."

"It wouldn't surprise me at all. Vicky knows everyone in the Church."

"The Anglican Church, you mean," said Adriano.

"Canterbury. Rome. Jerusalem. Mecca. Vicky has been everywhere and met everyone. She is one of the greatest woman scholars—that's not fair. She is one of the greatest religious scholars alive today."

"She sounds like quite the woman," Lee said.

"Quite the person," Adriano corrected gently.

"She is both," agreed Don Bello. "I miss her. She is a dear friend. Orvieto misses her."

Adriano and Lee remained silent. Finally, Lee said. "We heard that she once had a congregation here in Orvieto, until last year."

"Yes, she did. Until, yes, until last year."

There it was again, that brief dermal glitch across Don Bello's face. If lasted only a second, then was gone. But Lee had caught it. He wondered if Adriano had too.

"Well, my, my. What a small world. Imagine that, both going to the very same spot in Rome on the exact same day on the exact same train! Quite the coincidence indeed." Don Bello took in a deep breath.

Lee said nothing. He leaned back while Umbria gave way to Lazio outside the speeding windows of the train, accompanied by the soothing hum of the rails and the occasional punctuation of the locomotive's horn.

Somehow, Lee thought, grasping his husband's hand, I don't think it's a coincidence at all.

CHAPTER XXIII

A Conspiracy of Shadows

Thursday, December 5, 2013, midmorning, the Archbishop's office, Orvieto

Revelation was burning.

"Jesus Christ!" Archbishop Arnaud swept the glowing ember off the page of the open Bible on the desk in front of him and onto the carpet. He stomped it out, but the damage had been done already. The phone had startled him.

"Saba⊠u Al-khair," the voice on the phone said in clearly native Arabic, then followed in an English that bespoke North African origins, "Salvation to Your Grace."

"E-rev Tov. Adonai Eloheinu, melekh ha'olam," offered a second speaker before switching to English with a strong Israeli pronunciation. "Good evening."

"My apostolic blessings upon you both," answered Arnaud.

"Amen," the phone-connected trinity answered as one.

"The Surahs of the Holy Quaran show our peaceful path," said the first.

"Shalom," added the Israeli, emphasizing the second word in tone and with a pregnant pause. "Indeed, these are the sum of our joy."

"Amen," they again repeated.

"From the birthplace of Paul to where the Star of David, the Crescent of Allah, and the Cross of Christ unite in sands of everlasting peace, may the Great Work continue," said the Arabic speaker.

"Peace to us all," intoned the Israeli.

For the next few minutes the trio exchanged small talk, sports scores, and various minor headlines of the day—all with a listless and practiced nonchalance, actors in a play just now realizing that rehearsals were over and the curtain was threatening to lift. After fifteen minutes or so, the first speaker sighed.

"Well, I must sign off. I have to get my children ready for school." He laughed. Then, without humor he said, almost robotically, "The sleepers have awoken."

"Oh!" the Bishop gasped. Hands shaking, he lit another cigarette and inhaled deeply. "Give them my best." Idiot. What was there now to say? How long? he wondered.

"In the month of Tevet, we all give thanks to God."

"Tev—" the Bishop almost squealed before biting his tongue into silence, slicing the cigarette from his lips like a guillotine and sending it tumbling onto the sacred texts of the triumvirate.

Ignoring the outburst, the Israeli spoke first, in flawless Italian. "Per quelle che confidate nella misericordia di Dio, facilmente peccarono."

The Arab followed suit in smoothly practiced English. "For those that trusted in God's mercy, easily have they sinned."

"Per quelle alle quali particolarmente sei tenuto."

"For those of your particular prayerful intentions."

The Bishop grabbed a file card from the drawer and starting writing furiously, checking the words of his compatriots against a folded piece of paper on his desk. Nervously, he knocked it onto the floor and didn't hear the last bit of the conversation.

"I'm so sorry, my, ah, my connection is bad." The Archbishop lied to cover his clumsiness. "Please repeat the third, ah, petition to our Heavenly Father."

The first speaker sighed with more than a note of impatience but complied. "Per quelle che sono tormentate per i loro disordinati amori desideri."

"Yes, yes, of course," said the Bishop. "For those who are tormented by their disorderly love desires."

"Per tutti le anime del purgatorio."

"For all of the souls in purgatory."

"Per quelle che—"

"Another line?" Arnaud interrupted.

"Yes!" The first speaker's irritation was evident. Then, somewhat gentler, a thin glove over an even thinner blade, he said, "Our prayers are almost at an end. Tu ad esse a te o ad altri hanno dato occasione di peccare."

"For those that you and others have given an occasion to sin," mumbled the Bishop glancing south from his window. South.

"Amen," said the Jew.

"Amen," intoned the Arab.

"Amen," said the Bishop, but the line was already dead.

And soon, Arnaud thought staring at the phone, I likely will be too.

CHAPTER XXIV

The Eternal City

Thursday, December 5, 2013, noon, Rome

"Welcome to the Hotel Byron. A l'il bit of London in the heart of Rome. My name is Cedric. Here you go, gents, room number seven, with a lovely view of the wedding cake."

To judge from his accent, the perky young desk clerk could have just arrived from Piccadilly, or a gay pub nearby.

"Thanks," Adriano said, "but what's the wedding cake?"

"That's what we locals call it," Cedric chimed in, shamelessly assessing Adriano's jet-black top and swimmer's trained bottom. "The King Vittorio Emmanuel monument. It's bloody over the top, all drippy with statues and sculptured gewgaw, just like a big bridal pastry. You can't miss it. It's right up the street from here. You simply *must* take a gander at it."

"Thanks," Lee answered, making sure his wedding ring was visible as he signed the guest register. "*We* will."

True to Cedric's description, the hotel was a bastion of Empire in the midst of Rome's urban chaos, an exactingly restored antique edifice crammed with Georgian furnishings and a seemingly inexhaustible collection of prints featuring Lord Nelson, Wellington, and, of course, Byron. Tea was served at 4:00 p.m., Pimms cups at 6:00, all in the tweedy bar off the lobby dominated by a bust of Queen Victoria. The royal yacht *Britannia* sailed across the walls over the urinals in the reception level bathroom.

More importantly, they served a full English breakfast and were immediately adjacent to St. Paul's Anglican Church, Reverend Vicky's parish. Perfect for two nights in Rome.

"This will do, pig," said Adriano, throwing open the double doors of their tiny but nonetheless spectacularly situated balcony overlooking the city. "That's got to be the gayest monument I've ever seen in my life."

Lee joined his husband. Flirtatious or not, Cedric had been right. The view was to die. The grotesquely ornate tribute to Italy's last king loomed up like a gaudy marble cake about to explode in the oven from over-yeasting.

"Rome, the eternal city." Lee sighed, remembering his first time here when he was a junior officer aboard the *Ithaka*. "I do love this place. There's more history here per square foot than anywhere on earth. I escorted a group of cruise ship passengers from Boca Raton, but only for the day. Didn't get to see much."

"Well, let's make the most of our visit, then. Beside nosing into other people's business." Adriano gave Lee a look.

"I'm not nosing, I'm just curious," said Lee, picking up the hotel brochure on the nightstand. "Oh look, this hotel used to be the palace of one of the Orsinis. That was the family that married into the Medici. Lorenzo the Magnificent's wife was an Orsini. I do want to try and find the Medici palace where Leo the Tenth and Clement the Seventh entertained during the Renaissance. I think it's used as the Roman senate now."

"Don't change the subject. You know what I mean."

Lee put down the brochure and grabbed his lover's hands. "Listen, I just feel some sort of connection, you know. Andrea was my age, for Christ's sake. We share the same birthday. The same year, even. Thank goodness I wasn't named Andrew. That would be really creepy."

Actually, Lee already felt it was more than creepy. He hadn't said anything to Adriano yet, avoiding a fight as long as possible, but he knew this from his own experience: No one destined for the priesthood, a true believer, would ever commit suicide unless he had truly lost his faith— or been pushed. How he wished he could speak to Archbishop Sancarlo, Andrea's mentor—Andrea's own Brian Swathmore, as it were. As for the new bishop, Arnaud, Lee didn't want to run into him if at all possible. He had seen how he looked at Adriano that night at *Sant'Andrea*. Plus, Opus Dei was nothing to take lightly, nor was the power of the Vatican. He remembered Cardinal Maltoni's cryptic answer from the newspaper article following Andrea's death.

"Roma locuta; causa finita est."

Rome has spoken; the matter is finished.

"Andrea reminds you of you, and, well—you know." Adriano's voice trailed off.

"Yes," Lee answered, somewhat absently. "Exactly. That must be it. I don't know. I just know that I'm curious. It's an interesting story." I'm lying, Lee thought, and Adriano knows I am. He won't let this go, damn him.

Adriano pushed back and regarded his husband. "Is that all?"

"Yes, of course," Lee said, giving him a kiss. "Besides, you know I love a good puzzle, and this one's got everything. Sex, death, Vatican intrigue."

"OK, Miss Marple." Adriano wagged his finger somewhat playfully. "Just don't embarrass us. Don Bello said he'd meet us in the lobby bar for a drink and then take us over to meet Reverend Vicky."

Whew, Lee thought, Adriano seems to be letting me off easy. Humor I can handle, but I know there's something else here. "By the way," he said, "you seem awfully chummy with Don Bello. Do you think he's gay? He seemed terribly pleased to find out that we were married. Not the expected reaction from an octogenarian Italian priest."

"I think he's a sweet, lonely, and gentle old man," Adriano said quietly. "That's enough for me. He reminds me of my grandfather."

"Ah, I see."

"Yes, well." Adriano picked up his iPhone, fell back on the bed, and started searching for the hotel wireless code. "We have that in common. We both lost our parents at an early age. At least yours are really dead. I don't have that luxury."

The flash of anger came out of nowhere, like an eruption. Then, just as suddenly, the lava cooled and sealed over the wounded vent.

Lee opened his mouth to say something but decided against it. *Some things are better left unsaid. Especially in a marriage.*

~

"Welcome to Rome. Don Bello has told me so much about you." Reverend Vicky swept into the salon, high heels clicking on the parquet floors of the St. Paul's rectory. An antique record player in the corner gushed forth a repertoire of light operatic highlights. Vicky seated herself on the sofa to the aural backdrop of a very young Maria Callas as Butterfly, pining away for Pinkerton in "Un bel di."

"Oh dear, now the boys will think I've been gossiping," Don Bello chuckled as Vicky stood up to embrace him warmly with a hug and a kiss to the top of his balding pate. "My reputation for discretion is shattered and they've barely met me."

"Strangers on the train, eh?" Adriano laughed. "I hope you didn't divulge too many of our secrets."

"Only that you're happily married and spending your sabbatical in Orvieto following a difficult year," said Vicky. She smiled and motioned for them to take their seats. Her voice was sweetly accented with just a touch of her British heritage, but by birth or professional itinerary Lee couldn't tell. It reminded him a bit of Brian's voice, still British after thirty years in the States.

The priest's hair was dark blonde and clearly natural, swept up into a bun and fastened on the left side with an antique tortoise-shell comb. Her clerical dress, light gray and just a touch above the knee, was accented by a simple but carefully tailored matching jacket fastened with a braided fabric frog clasp in an Asian motif. An unadorned pewter pectoral cross hung from her neck on a matching chain. It swayed gently as she walked across the room, revealing an inscription on the back that Lee couldn't make out. Her earrings were simple, miniature black pearl studs. All in all, the thin white collar at the top of her ivory white blouse seemed nothing so much as the perfect accessory to an elegant ensemble.

"I understand that we have friends in common," said Vicky, motioning for Don Bello to play bartender. "I met your friend, Bishop Swathmore, twice, briefly in the eighties at an interfaith gathering in Rome, and in 1998 when he was in England for the Lambeth conference. We were both protesting the Archbishop of Canterbury's anti-gay rhetoric and disinvitation to gay Bishop Gene Robinson. I liked him. He had spunk."

How completely disarming she is, Lee thought. She's managed to steal an arrow from my conversational quiver before I've had a chance to pull it out myself. Don Bello must have given her quite the full report while they were freshening up at the hotel next door.

"I told Lee you'd have known Brian," Adriano said.

"He was a great man. One of first openly gay bishops in the Episcopal Church as I recall."

"The first," Lee said. "Gene Robinson was the first openly gay person to be *elected* as bishop but Brian had already been bishop of California for many years when he came out of the closet. He announced that he was gay in a sermon at Grace Cathedral. Said he couldn't take the hypocrisy anymore. I was there in the congregation when he spoke. I'll never forget his words: 'We must make more love in the world and being gay is part of God's love.'"

"Perfectly said." Vicky leaned into the couch and crossed her legs at the ankle. "The perfect example of what a church—*the* Church—should be. Open, inclusive, inviting."

"Now Vicky," mock-lectured Don Bello as he helped himself to the bar behind the sofa. "You mustn't fault Rome for being—"

"Medieval? Homophobic? Misogynist? Sexist," she offered back, clearly a cordially and oft-practiced verbal tennis match. "Do stop me, dear friend, when I've exhausted accurate descriptives."

"I was going to say, You mustn't fault Rome for being a prisoner of its traditions. Some things take time."

"Yes, well," said Vicky archly, "it's long past time for the Vatican jailer to open those stuffy cells of repression. Does not the Bishop of Rome, our Holy Father, hold the keys to heaven and earth? It's time to loosen up a bit. Francis has been pope for nine months now, the appropriate time to give birth to new ideas, don't you think?"

"I told you boys, our dear Vicky is possessed of a formidable mind and crackling opinions."

"Grazie caro." She pursed her lips and blew Don Bello a kiss. "But right now, I'd like to be possessed of Stoli on the rocks, and don't forget our guests."

"Of course, where are my manners," said Don Bello with a chuckle. "What beverages of the Raj may I offer you?"

"A vodka martini would be fantastic," said Adriano.

"Two, please," Lee seconded the drink order.

"I read about Brian's death in the *Episcopal News Service* online edition," Vicky said, taking her drink from Don Bello and leaning forward on her knees toward Lee. "They sent out the obituary to all of the Anglican churches in Europe. I remember it had a wonderful image of Brian in a 'Silence Equals Death' sweatshirt, along with his official photo in clericals."

"I took that picture, right before Brian performed our wedding ceremony," said Adriano. "Brian loved it."

"As well he should. Both of our churches have gluttoned themselves too long on the plate of silence, and because of it, many have been pronounced spiritually dead. Congratulations," Vicky said, raising her glass in a toast. "I'm so proud to say *our* church honors marriage equality. Your friend Brian, he was ahead of his time."

"As are *you*, dearest Vicky," said Don Bello, rejoining her on the couch. "You open the door so that the rest of us may follow."

"Thank you, Vicky. Yes, Brian was a great man," said Lee quietly. "And a very dear friend."

"I suppose you know we, too, lost a beloved member of our pastoral family this past year as well."

"Yes," Lee said. He took a sip of his martini and looked the priest straight in the eye. My God, he thought, she's appropriating every subject I was going to offer up. Why did she bring that up? Neither Adriano nor Lee had mentioned anything to Don Bello about Deacon Andrea. Unless Marco had said something to him. But, why would he do that? "Adriano and I were reading something about that."

"It was right after last year's Mass of San Andrea, his feast day, and his birthday," Don Bello said quietly, patting Vicky gently on the knee. "We were all on the altar together that last night. Remember, Vicky?"

"Yes," she said quietly, suddenly looking like an actress onstage in a play, caught off guard by her cue. "So much changed in just a month. On All Souls Day on November second, we were all so happy to be together. Andrea, as usual, had arranged everything for the migrant blood drive, even though he was less than fond of needles." Vicky gave a slight smile at the memory. "That blood drive chang..." Her voice drifted off. "Anyway, less than a month later, it was all over when we were on the altar together again. I remember how upset Andrea was. He had just found out about the letter from the Vatican—by fax..." She drifted off for a second time. "He was incredibly distraught. We'd never seen him like that, Gio—Bishop Sancarlo and I."

"You were close to him?" Adriano asked quietly.

"Who?" Vicky looked up sharply, spilling a bit of her drink. She had a strangely quizzical look on her face. "Andrea, you mean. Yes, of course. We all knew him—loved him. He would have made a fine priest, in any church. But, now he's dead. There's really nothing more to say about it. He is gone." She finished off her drink in a violent gulp. "Truly, your friend was right. Silence equals death, in so many ways. Shall we eat?"

Abruptly, Vicky stood up and motioned for them to follow her into the rectory's dining room. Adriano gave Lee a look as if to say, "What was that about?" and quickly polished off his martini as well.

"You must forgive Vicky," Don Bello whispered, putting his arms around Lee and Adriano and leading them into dinner. "It was rough on all of us, but, well, Vicky feels things very strongly. She cares deeply about her family, her church."

The dining room was warmer, cozier, more personal than the salon had been. Photos on a sideboard showed Vicky as a young woman, laughing with two young priests. Long lanyards and plastic name tags hung around their necks, the sort used for conventions. Lee could make out the dome of St. Peter's in the background of the picture. Several awards, engraved vases, a simple oversize coffee cup engraved "You Go Girl!" competed for space with various knickknacks, postcards from around the world, and a beautiful and carefully groomed bonsai tree. A pile of DVDs was topped with one called *Pink Smoke Over the Vatican*. Next to it was a half-burned flare, like the type one used in a lifeboat or next to a roadside flat tire, wrapped in rainbow ribbons. On the wall, a framed bit of calligraphy, a paraphrase from Bobby Kennedy's eulogy: "Some *women* see things as they are and say why. I dream things that never were and say why not."

A quartet of gas wall sconces provided light. A stack of books, files, and assorted papers were stuffed under a credenza on the left, kept in place by a laptop balanced precariously on top. This was the room she spends most of her time in, Lee thought. This is where she lives. This is *her* room. The rest belongs to the Church.

The large, antique wooden dining room table had been converted into a buffet. The four guests circled the room, selecting from various bruschetta, a collation of Italian meats and cheeses, and a large tureen lit by a small gas burner filled with steaming pasta alongside two others warming a meat and a cream sauce.

"Dig in," said Vicky, once again all smiles and charm. "I don't often have guests, so I hope a casual buffet is all right. Serve yourself, and then we'll all go back into the living room with our plates."

As Lee helped himself to a dollop of pasta and several truffle-laden pieces of bread, he glanced at the photos on the sideboard. One caught his attention in particular. He waited until all four of them were back in the dining room, plates balanced on their laps, and laughing at an innocently ribald joke told by Don Bello, before making an excuse that he needed more bruschetta.

Alone for a moment with the food and the flickering light of the gas, Lee walked over to the photo of Vicky and the two clerics he had seen before in passing. Picking it up, two of the trio were immediately identifiable. One was a twenty-something, laughing Vicky, blonde hair slightly askew in a breeze forever frozen on film. On her left, she was framed by a handsome young priest, mouth open in mid-laugh. His right hand could just be seen gently resting on her shoulder. On her right was another, more dour-looking priest, a smile of tight fortitude pulled across his face like a mask. Lee turned over the transparent frame. The photo shop's mark was clearly on the back, "Foto Trestevere: 1-3-83." And next to it, a scrawled inscription written in cursive ink, "The Magi." Of course, now Lee recognized the other man in the photo. Even across two decades of aging it was clearly Bishop Arnaud, the officiant at the *Sant'Andrea* service in Orvieto earlier this week.

Lee quickly put another piece of bruschetta on his plate and rejoined the group in the salon. Before his body finished sitting, Lee was pretty sure he knew the identity of the other man in the frame—he was the beloved former bishop of Orvieto, Giovani "Gio" Sancarlo.

CHAPTER XXV

Doctor, Heal Thyself

Friday, December 6, 2013, morning, Orvieto

A year.

Dr. Luke Wagner stood at the front window of his office in Orvieto's tiny hospital overlooking the plaza in front of the cathedral. It was chilly, actually downright cold. Occasionally an errant snowflake would float down in front of the glass, a promise of even colder, if more atmospheric, weather to come.

A white Christmas would be nice. It had been a long time since he had seen one, and not here. In Germany, at his grandfather's home outside Cologne. They had walked to the cathedral and lit candles in front of the reliquary of the Magi. As a child, Luke had loved visiting there. It was the largest reliquary in Europe, holding the bones of the Three Wise Men who had visited the baby Jesus. They, too, had survived the Allied bombings of May 1942. His grandfather had been on leave and visiting home that night, the night of a thousand bombers, the greatest aerial attack in the history of the world. The skies had rained a vengeful death, and all around the Cathedral Cologne erupted in flames. Hundreds died, and 45,000 homes were destroyed—ninety percent of the city. The death toll would have been higher, but Cologne's bomb shelters were deep. Still, Luke's grandfather had fled not to the shelters, but to the church, to the kneeler in front of the Magi. That night, he had prayed to the three kings of three different faiths, Melchior, Gaspar, and Balthasar, and they had listened. While Cologne was consumed, its cathedral lived.

Now, Luke's grandfather was old, very old, just a few years short of a hundred. And every year, he would repeat the story to Luke, the story of the Three Kings and how they had saved his life. How he wished he was back there now with his grandfather. How he wished he were anywhere but here in Orvieto.

As if in confirmation to his thoughts, Bishop Arnaud walked briskly out of the episcopal residence across the frozen plaza on his way to Mass. Luke quickly pulled the cord on the window shade and the Venetian blind came crashing down with a satisfying clatter, shutting out Arnaud's despised visage.

How I wish you were dead. How I wish I were dead. I've sold my soul to a soulless man, Luke thought, then immediately ground his fingernails into his palm, a practiced strategy to remind him of his vows. *I must obey. I must not question.* Obedience *is what I need.* Obedience *to my master.* He remembered Archbishop Arnaud's teaching. "When the student is ready, the teacher will present himself."

Fuck you, Arnaud, Luke thought, then crossed himself, but without enthusiasm, only by rote

The doctor walked across the room and looked out the far window toward the Franciscan monastery in the hills outside the town. There, another man was seeking absolution, Bishop Sancarlo. *If he begs for forgiveness, a* bishop, *descended from the apostles, what chance do I have?* He closed his eyes and silently mouthed the words of Bishop Arnaud's lesson on repentance:

> I myself want once again to make a very sincere act of contrition, and I would like each one of you to do the same. As we call to mind our infidelities, and so many mistakes, weaknesses, so much cowardice— each one of us has his own experience—let us repeat to Our Lord, from the bottom of our hearts, Peter's cry of contrition: "Domine, tu omnia nosti, tu scis quia amo te!"—"Lord, you know all things, you know that I love you, despite my wretchedness!" And I would even add, "You know that I love you, precisely because of my wretchedness, for it leads me to rely on you who are my strength. Quia tu es, Deus, fortitudo mea." And at that point let us start again.

Wretched. Cowardly. A pit of mistakes and infidelities. How would he ever expect forgiveness? He had given up. Two years ago, he had been ready to die, but someone had stopped him. Someone had pulled him back from the edge.

Andrea.

He had stood on the cliff and prayed.

Useless, he had thought, to turn my thoughts to God.

Behind him, the lights of Orvieto reflected in a million icy crystals. Snow had come early that year. It wasn't yet December.

Below, the road would be deserted. He had wondered who would find him. Someone would, of course, and for that he was sorry. What a horrible thing to see, to discover, the body of a reprobate, crushed against the rock and never to see forgiveness. Never to see the face of God. Never to see tomorrow's sunrise.

It should be beautiful, and he smiled. He had often come here to sit near the altar and watch the dawn. Tomorrow, its rays would reach out to warm the city across a quilt of virginal frost. He had seen it before, prisms of color in the ice. Like a miracle it had seemed to him as a child.

No more. No more dawns, no more rainbows, no more miracles.

"Don't!"

He had heard the scream, and had turned around to see—Andrea.

Two years ago, Luke had stood on the cliffs of San Giovanale above the *La Chiesa del Crocifisso del Tufo* with the blood of two people still wet on his hands and started to jump, but at the last moment, Andrea had pulled him back.

Andrea had saved his life, his wretched, cowardly, murderous life.

If only Andrea had let him die, justice would have been done. An eye for an eye, a tooth for a tooth, a life for two lives. Andrea had sat with him until the dawn, alone with Luke's two victims, and they had prayed. Andrea spoke of healing and forgiveness, and the inestimable love of God. He convinced Luke that there had been no sin, that he had done everything he could have for the two people now lying dead on the emergency room table. A week before Christmas, Luke had murdered a mother and child. He thought he could save them both but he had been wrong. He had to make a choice, a split-second choice. He chose to sacrifice the baby and save the mother's life. And, in the end, it had not mattered. Both had died. First the baby and then the mother, with her oozing dead infant in her arms. Spitting up blood, she hurled the words at Luke. "You have killed my baby!"

The child had been his.

Having killed his lover and his child, Luke had walked to the cliff.

"You did the best that you could. You tried to save a life. There is nothing to forgive. God knows what is in your heart." Andrea talked him down from the cliff. Andrea convinced him that a God of love had forgiven him. And, for a year, Luke had believed it. Wanted to believe it, wanted to believe anything that Andrea would tell him.

He had told him, "Suicide is not a sin because you are taking your own life. It is a sin because you are taking away the ability of God to love you in this life. Suicide is not the sin of murder. It is the sin of hopelessness. It is the sin of losing faith in God's love. God is a God of love, not vengeance. The love of God is beyond measure. It is infinite."

Who am I kidding, Luke thought, looking to the cemetery across the valley from Orvieto. Andrea did not jump from that cliff. *I pushed him*. I *pushed* him as much as if I had put my hand to his back. Andrea kept my secret and I betrayed him by revealing his, a secret he didn't even know he had. I delivered Andrea into the hands of Archbishop Arnaud as Judas delivered Jesus over to the Sanhedrin. Andrea, Bishop Sancarlo, Vicky...they walked in to give blood for migrants and left refugees themselves.

He turned solemnly from the window, the silent condemnation of the closed mortuary drawer confirming his complicity in it all. A morgue. The hospital of Orvieto was nothing but that anymore. A morgue.

"Andrea." A single tear ran down Luke's cheek. He would allow himself no more.

But enough, enough of this wallowing in self-pity. I have a job to do. I have yet one more sin to add to my soul. Luke turned from the window. *One more level of purgatory in which to descend. Death can not come too soon for me, but first, I promise, death will come for others, to avenge Andrea.*

CHAPTER XXVI

Parrots, Porn Stars, and Popes

Friday, December 6, 2013, breakfast, Hotel Byron, Rome

It was big news in Rome. The porn star's parrot got blessed by the Pope.

"I hope it didn't bite the hand that blessed it."

Adriano pulled the newspaper down and looked over the fold at Lee. "Even for you, that's a terrible joke."

Lee smiled and returned to his full English breakfast.

"What about a gay parrot and the Pope?"

"The porn star wasn't gay. He was straight," Adriano said, shaking out a crinkle in the newspaper. "I'm not sure about the bird. The Pope was riding around St. Peter's doing his weekly blessing and this parrot suddenly landed on his hand, so he blessed it. Turned out the little critter belonged to an aging Italian porn star. He's actually mayor of some small town now, although according to this there were rumors that he ran a prostitution ring with a heavy curiatorial clientele, if you get my drift. But of course now he's found Christ, so he's the perfect manly Mary Magdalene. A sinner forgiven, complete with dove—ah, sorry—parrot of peace on his wrist."

"Gimme that," Lee said, biting into his English muffin and reaching for the paper to see. "You're right. The papers are full of it this morning."

"Full of it is right," Adriano sneered. "I suppose your friend Giorgio Maltoni at the Vatican Press Office is distributing the photo with a caption

The new Francis blessing the animals or some such crap. Blessing some hooker's pet doesn't equal sexual liberation. You of all people should see it's a PR stunt. I think you're being purposefully naive."

"Cynic," Lee said. "He's cute. I grant you that."

"The bird or the porn star?"

"Both," Lee said. "He looks kind of familiar."

"The bird or the porn star?"

"Very funny. I think he was in one of those low-budget Italian exports from the eighties, you know, history porn, *Gladiator Glutimas Maximus* or something like that. We passed the DVD around when I worked onboard ship. It was hetero porn but you work with what you've got when you're at sea. It was in Italian, but that wasn't an impediment to the action. It was one of the few pieces of pornography that succeeded in being dull. I could never even make it through to the end, so I never actually figured out the plot." Lee held up his hands while saying "plot," miming air quotes. "I think I still have the DVD somewhere in a box back in San Francisco."

"Sorry I missed it," Adriano said with an arched eyebrow.

Lee made a kissy-face and returned to his breakfast.

For the moment, they were the only guests in the Hotel Byron's breakfast-room-cum-lounge. The bar was stacked with a buffet of bangers, eggs, baked tomatoes, and roasted potatoes, just like the Queen Mum would have made, minus the gin and tonic. Perky Cedric had practically flown out from behind the desk to show Adriano to his seat and whip up his cappuccino, and if encouraged, undoubtedly other options. Hotel tramp.

Lee noticed Cedric, now re-ensconced behind reception, checking out an early morning departure, a middle-aged priest, not bad looking from beneath his mantle of sunglasses, scarves, a big fur-trimmed hat with brim and ear flaps pulled far down over his face, and a black woolen cape with a lining delicately trimmed in red. Lee noticed that his skin was quite tan, unusual for an ordinate in wintry Rome, and his shoes were newly shined. Vatican vanity. Also, he seemed in quite the hurry to leave. He brushed by Adriano and Lee's table as he rushed out the lobby door to hail a taxi. A miasma of heavy, cloying cologne preceded and followed his exit. It was slightly redolent of cinnamon. The effect was nauseating in its intensity to Lee.

"What time are we meeting Vicky?" Adriano was waving away the smelly haze with his hand.

"Nine a.m.," Lee answered, checking the clock underneath the bust of Victoria over the bar. It read 8:30 a.m. "Just enough time to finish your bangers."

"Whatever you say, Lord Grantham."

"Is Don Bello joining us?"

"No," said Adriano. "He had some business with the Vatican and then was taking an afternoon train back to Orvieto. He invited us to come by *San Giovanale* when we're back in Orvieto. He wants to show us the frescoes."

"Sounds suspiciously like 'Come up and see my etchings sometime,'" Lee said, popping the last bit of English muffin into his mouth.

"Are you jealous of an old man?" Adriano smiled, finishing off his cappuccino. Lee leaned across the table and wiped off his husband's residual foamy mustache.

"No," Lee said. "Just observant. Don Bello has, what would Marco say, 'a soft part in his heart' for you. It's sweet. Very 'the disciple that Jesus loved' sort of thing. Here, read this. Some more research about our charming hostess from last night, in her own words." Lee handed his iPad across to Adriano.

Adriano looked up. "You're obsessed."

"Read," Lee prompted.

Upon This Rock
2 November, 2012
Story by the Reverend Vicky Lewis

The Church of Sant'Andrea in Orvieto is alive with history: first a pagan temple, then an Etruscan site of worship and for the last thousand years, one of the most historic Roman Catholic churches in the world. Tonight, in a sign of ecumenical peacemaking, that historic church will host an historic service celebrating the Feast of All Souls. After our prayers for all those awaiting the resurrection in purgatory, we'll all go to give blood—another type of soul-infusing hope—for use by the immigrants whom God has washed up here on our shores.

Orvieto is used to such history-making.

Once home to pontiffs on the run, Orvieto is now home to another religious refugee of sorts, a church without a home. Although our congregation is small, every Sunday morning, around twenty people gather for Holy Communion. They are young and old, American and British, a few Italians and a retired schoolteacher from Hong Kong when it was still a royal colony. What they have in common is their religion. These are Anglicans and Episcopalians: A small, often misunderstood faith here in the heart of Roman Catholic Italy. They come every Sunday to worship their God. I am their priest.

When I was eighteen, God called me.

My mother was an American Roman Catholic. My father is a British Anglican. Which path would I choose? After much soul searching, I become a Catholic nun. I joined a Benedictine convent near my home in Belfast where I lived and loved my community for twenty years. Then, I turned forty. My midlife crisis became also a crisis of faith-and gender liberation. I wanted to be a priest, something denied women in the Roman Catholic Church. And so, my life turned again. I moved to the United States to study at the Episcopal Divinity School in Cambridge, Massachusetts. At the age of forty-five, I was ordained a priest in the American Episcopal Church. For about ten years, I led a small parish outside of Boston. Then, on a trip to Italy I saw Orvieto. It was love at first sight.

"That's quite a roundabout journey," Adriano said, looking up. "What's the big deal in wearing a collar? Who cares? I have so little patience for this religious bullshit."

"Are you done?"

"Yeah, OK, I know. Keep reading. You like my voice." Adriano smiled.

"I do."

Adriano continued.

Jesus once said, "Where two or three are gathered, there I am also." Certainly, in the beginning of our little mission church, there were few more Episcopalians in Orvieto than that. However, our Savior was soon to present itself in the person of the Right Reverend Giovanale "Gio" Sancarlo, Roman Catholic Bishop of Orvieto. As he enfolds all he meets in the warm embrace of his ecumenical love, Bishop Sancarlo greeted me at once as a priest: as an equal of liturgical lineage—even if his Church hierarchy did not. A spiritual friendship was born and continues to be fostered. This summer, in Orvieto's historic Roman Catholic Church of *Sant'Andrea*, Bishop Sancarlo and I co-presided at a service of sacred readings taken from the Bible, the Torah, Koran, and selected Buddhist texts. In addition to a mixed crowd of about two hundred Catholics, Anglicans, Episcopals and others, in attendance in the front row were a rabbi, an imam, a visiting guru from India, and even a representative from the Vatican, Archbishop Arnaud. I will never forget Bishop Gio's words at the end of the service.

> "As it says in the Prayer of St. Francis, make us all instruments of God's peace. Where there is hatred, let us sew love. Where there is sadness, let us bring joy. All of us here—Christian, Jew, Buddhist, Muslim, and more—all of us are part of the Golden Thread that binds and connects all human souls."

"This is torture." Adriano looked up in mock pleading.
Lee reached over and took back his iPad. "I'll finish."
"Bless you."
Lee took over.

The Past Is Prologue.
How appropriate it is for words of religious healing to take place here in Orvieto, the nativity of the original schism that broke apart the Catholic and Anglican Churches. For it was here in 1528, that Pope Clement the Seventh received the representatives of England's

King Henry the Eighth requesting divorce from his wife so that he could marry Anne Boleyn. When the Pope refused, King Henry broke away and established the Church of England. For five hundred years, these two sides of the same religious coin have been striving for reconciliation. Would it not be a thing of wonder should that breach be healed by a female priest of the Anglican Communion and a brave and generous Bishop of the Roman Catholic Church—here in Orvieto—upon this rock?

Lee put down the iPad and pinned Adriano with a glance. "So, whaddya think?"

"She does writes beautifully, I have to admit, Adriano said, popping a strawberry into his mouth. Certainly, her descriptions of Orvieto are more authentic and genuine than the dreck scooped up by Lady Peg."

"That's it?" Lee said. "That's all you have to say about that article?"

"What else do you want me to say?"

"Don't you see," Lee said. He knew Adriano was getting irritated with his curiosity, but he didn't care. He *knew* he was onto something. He pushed on. "Vicky and Bishop Sancarlo were stirring things up in Orvieto, religiously I mean. Andrea's suicide was the excuse to get both of them out of town and clamp down on Orvieto's growing apostasy. Bishop Arnaud must have plotted, sitting there with a pew full of heathens, Jews, and Muslims, while Vicky and Bishop Sancarlo made kissy-face up there on the altar of *Sant'Andrea*. I bet you that's the moment he decided to do something about it."

"Oh come on, Lee." Adriano slapped his hands down on the table. "Are you saying that someone killed Deacon Andrea, then made it look like a suicide, just to embarrass Bishop Sancarlo and force him and uber liberal Reverend Vicky to hightail it out of town?"

"No, nothing that drastic," said Lee, although, secretly that and darker thoughts had crossed his mind. "I'm saying that Andrea's suicide was the last straw with a Vatican already burdened by sex scandals, calls for the ordination of women, *and* even recently an effort for the Catholic and Episcopal Churches to reunite."

"You sound as anti-Church as I do," remarked Adriano, with a look equal parts ironic and triumphant.

"Let's go," said Lee, at a loss for a response. "Reverend Vicky is waiting."

Adriano rolled his eyes and stood up, returning a wave from Cedric across the lobby behind the front desk. Lee grinned too—as sweet and poisonous as aspartame—and let his husband lead the way to St. Paul's Church next door. Lee's mind was doing cartwheels as evidenced by his extreme lip chewing, a bad habit only exacerbated by a mystery in need of solving. There was something more behind Deacon Andrea's leap from the walls of Orvieto. More than just disappointment at being denied a Roman collar. And part of it, Lee was convinced, had to do with that picture in Reverend Vicky's dining room. He had a sneaking suspicion that the person taking that old picture of young Vicky and her two clerical escorts in the St. Paul's rectory dining room was none other than the kindly pastor of *San Giovanale*, Don Bello.

~

Cedric answered the phone on the second-and-one-half ring. The management insisted on picking up calls instantly, but Cedric preferred efficiency balanced with a bit of nuance. I've got things *to do* after all, he thought.

"Hotel Byron, this is Cedric. Cheerio! *How* may I be of service?"

"Excuse me, do you have a Lee Maury and an Adriano Llata de Miranda staying at your hotel?" The feminine voice was smooth and even, well trained and deliberate, clearly British, upper-class. Polite, but only because the speaker had been so trained.

"May I ask who's calling?" Cedric was icily flamboyant in his response. Who does she think she's dealing with? He wondered if she could tell he was Cockney. Snotty Brits always acted like they were born at Windsor. "I'm afraid I can't give out personal information about our guests, I mean, *if* they were here, I couldn't tell you even if they were, or weren't."

"Of course, I understand." The voice switched tone, becoming almost apologetic. "I should have identified myself. This is kind of embarrassing. I work for the British Consulate here in Rome. Evidently, Lee and Adriano are friends with the British Consul in San Francisco. They have a Christmas surprise for the lovely boys but it got mis-addressed and, well—as I said, this is *rather* embarrassing. Anyway, the package has ended up here at the Consulate in Rome and I just need to know where to send it. Also, I'm so sorry, I should have identified myself. I'm Pippa."

"Pippa!" Cedric almost squealed. "Like the Duchess of Cambridge's sister?"

"Exactly." The voice laughed. "Didn't she quite steal the show at the wedding? I mean *really*!"

Cedric giggled. "I know, quite, well I mean, Kate *did* look beautiful, but that dress of Pippa's—gasp and swoon! Oh, I do go on. I'm so sorry. What can I do for you, Pippa?"

"Well." The voice giggled, but just enough. "As I said, this *is* embarrassing. Lee and Adriano are friends with Her Majesty's representative back in San Francisco, and he has sent them a Christmas gift. Well, the gift went to San Francisco and then got forwarded here because we *hear* they're staying in Italy."

"Oh yes!" Cedric said, suddenly wondering why he had been so suspicious. "They're both staying here. Would you like to have the gift delivered here?"

"No!" her voice said sharply, then, softer, "No. We don't want to spoil the surprise, and of course, Christmas is still weeks away. We want to deliver it to their *home* here in Italy. We understand they're in the country Italy for several weeks. But, well, as I said, it's so embarrassing. Our records don't show what *town* they're staying in. Did they tell you when they checked in? I called the Italian Consulate who keeps records of visitors arriving, but, well, you *know* the Italians. *Soooo* unhelpful. They wouldn't tell me anything. If I know the town I can have the package delivered to the carbiniere there, and Lee and Adriano can pick it up."

"Well of course," Cedric said. So typical. He felt for her. The Italians *could* be so, so, *Italian.* Let me just check." The young desk clerk flipped through the Hotel Britannia guest register. "Ah, yes, here it is. They're visiting from Orvieto."

"Orvieto," the voice said with a slight intake of breath. "You're *sure*?"

"Oh yes," Cedric said. "Quite sure. They signed in last night."

"Did they leave an address?" The voice was sweet and stiff, like a frozen popsicle.

"No," Cedric said, "just Orvieto. But you said you can leave it with the carbiniere, yes? This should be enough. I mean, Orvieto is *small*. Won't be hard to find two American puftas there, right?" Cedric laughed, and then wondered if he'd gone too far.

"Quite." The woman called Pippa laughed back. "Quite so. I'll have no trouble finding them at all. Now, one thing." And her voice became conspiratorially cozy. "You won't tell Lee and Adriano that I called, will you? I wouldn't want to spoil their surprise. Plus, well, I'd get in a good deal of trouble. Let's just keep this between ourselves, yes?"

"Scout's honor," Cedric said, crossing his heart, even though Pippa couldn't see. "Your secret is safe with me."

"Thanks again, Cedric, and have a Happy Christmas. *So* nice to hear a friendly *English* voice."

"You too, Pippa. Happy Christmas."

As he hung up the phone, Cedric saw the return phone number flash quickly in front of him on the console, then disappear. He just caught the country code, +972, then it was gone.

Funny, he thought, the country code for Italy is +39. Oh well, maybe she was calling on a mobile. Stranger things had happened.

CHAPTER XXVII

Family History

Friday, December 6, 2013, morning, Rome, St Paul's, Inside the Walls

"We're the Yankee Church in Rome," Vicky said, proudly touring Lee and Adriano around St. Paul's. "That's been our nickname since we were built in 1880 after Italy defeated the Vatican States and opened the city to other religions. We're the first Protestant church ever to be built here, the official home for American Episcopalians in Rome. A Romanesque Gothic island of progressivism in a swamp of gooey Catholic tradition."

This morning, Vicky was more simply dressed, just a modest black pants suit set off by the same silver pectoral cross from last night. As she walked through the nave pointing out various works of art and architectural features, it swayed slightly against her tightly buttoned-up bosom. Every few steps, a bit of the inscription that Lee had noticed at dinner would swing tantalizingly into view, but he couldn't make it out. After a while he stopped trying for fear Vicky would think he was looking at her breasts, a silly thought, but nonetheless, gay or not, Lee's Virginia upbringing was hard to avoid. He'd find another way.

"And yet, your best friend is an elderly pre-Vatican II Italian priest," Adriano teased gently as they walked down the main aisle of the elaborate Byzantine-style sanctuary.

"I live in hope of dear Don Bello having a Paul-on-the-road-to-Damascus moment," she purred sweetly. "I await his conversion one day."

"I think it'll be a long wait," Lee ventured. "It's hard to teach an old priest new tricks."

"You'd be amazed," Vicky said, walking toward the front of the church. "Don Bello is surprisingly good at new tricks."

"The church is gorgeous," Adriano said. "You'll forgive me, but it's almost Catholic in style."

"No offense taken." Vicky laughed. "It's a spectacular mishmash of influences. The exterior is high Gothic Revivalist by a British architect, G. E. Street, but the interior is Byzantium meets Boston. The US Episcopalians wanted to make a statement. It's a little bit British and a little bit American."

"Like you," Lee ventured.

"How funny," Vicky said lightly.

Almost too lightly, Lee thought.

"I never thought of it that way," she continued. "Yes, both me and my Church had American mothers and British fathers. My grandfather fought in the Great War, and my father fought in the Second World War, both with the Irish Fusiliers Guards."

"That was Brian Swathmore's unit," Lee exclaimed. "Brian was an Irish Guard. He was at Buckingham Palace as a young man, and later fought in the war. He was part of the effort that liberated Italy. He even fought at Monte Cassino."

"What a small world." Vicky smiled. "I had no idea. We could have had a jolly time talking about our mixed-up heritage if we had known."

"So, your family is Irish, then, not English?" Adriano asked.

Vicky smiled. "How is it they say nowadays?—it's complicated. My family was very, very Irish, but also very, very English. They were from Belfast, Northern Ireland, the part that is still part of the United Kingdom. My grandfather, Victor Lewis, actually worked at the shipyard of Harland and Wolff. He helped build the *Titanic*."

"That's where Brian was from," Lee added. "Well, that's where he was raised, just outside Belfast. He was adopted. He never knew the identity of his birth parents."

"Not an uncommon occurrence during those times," said Vicky. "A great many homes were broken ones between the wars in the British Isles. My grandfather was a Catholic in Northern Ireland. And, like most men during the Great War, he went off to fight."

"He was killed in the war," Adriano stated.

"No, unfortunately not," Vicky said. Seeing the strange looks on Lee and Adriano's faces, she continued. "He came back a broken man when the war ended in November 1918, shell-shocked and destroyed by a year in the trenches. He became a committed pacifist and obsessed with the League of Nations. Evidently read everything he could about it. He was convinced it was the only thing that would prevent another war. He tried to rebuild his life. He would go to speak at local meetings of veterans, urging support for the League. Advocating for nonviolence and opposing anything that smacked of aggression. He was even opposed to Irish Independence because he thought it would lead to Civil War, which it did, eventually of course. The Troubles, as my family always called it. But, for a while, he seemed to revel in his postwar life. He went back to working at Harland and Wolff, but many at the shipyard were suspicious of him."

"Because he was a pacifist?" Adriano asked.

"Oh no." Vicky laughed. "Most everyone was a pacifist after World War I. No, because he was Catholic, not quite kosher in Protestant Northern Ireland, if you'll forgive the mixed religious metaphors. He was Irish and Catholic but working in Protestant Belfast. The pro-Irish rebels didn't trust him, and neither did the pro-British unionists. Also, he became more and more depressed by how plans for the League of Nations were shaping up. He could see that the Great Powers would never allow it to be anything with any real authority. Its provisions were full of loopholes that he was sure would one day lead to another war. Anyway, it was around this time that my grandmother got pregnant, and they had a little boy, my father, Victor Lewis, Jr. on January twentieth, 1919. On little Victor's first birthday, which coincidentally was the day the League of Nations Charter was finally signed, my grandfather took an early morning bus from Belfast, walked to the Cliffs of Moher, and threw himself off. He left a note for my grandmother. All it said was, 'I won't live to see my son go off to war.' My grandmother went completely over the edge and had to be institutional-ized. She died a few years later in an insane asylum."

"Jesus," was all Lee could say.

"Quite." Vicky sighed. "An orphanage took in my father, and by all accounts, he was treated well and was quite smart. When he turned eigh-teen, my father joined the army, the Irish Fusiliers, his father's old unit. Two years later the Second World War started and my father ended up in Italy. He was part of the unit that liberated Orvieto from the Nazis in June of 1944. They were battling their way up the peninsula and as they approached Orvieto, a German soldier drove down waving a white flag."

"The Germans surrendered without firing a shot? That's a first," said Adriano.

"No, the Germans weren't surrendering. It's actually quite a unique story. The German officer came down and approached my dad with a prop-osition. Move the battle."

"That's right," said Lee with a snap of his fingers. "Remember, Adriano. I told you about it. That article I read online about the Nazi colonel and the young priest speaking Latin."

"Yes," said Vicky with a somewhat stilted laugh. "You've heard some-thing about it. Well, it's all true. Evidently the German had quite fallen in love with the beauty of Orvieto and its rich history, specifically the cathe-dral and its priceless art by Fra Angelico and Signorelli, not to mention the relics from the Miracle of Bolsena. Anyway, he suggested to my father that they declare Orvieto an open city so as not to damage it. You say your friend Brian, Bishop Swathmore, fought at Monte Cassino, south of Orvieto?"

"Yes," said Lee. "He was badly injured there, and after the battle evac-uated back to a hospital in Belfast. He didn't like to talk about it much. I gathered that he saw some horrible things during the fighting. I did ask him once if he thought he'd ever killed anyone. 'Yes,' he said. 'I know I've killed someone.' It's one of the reasons he entered the priesthood after the war."

"I don't doubt it," said Vicky. "The Benedictine monastery at Monte Cassino was totally destroyed by the Allies because the Germans had dug into the abbey there. That was two months before the liberation of Orvieto.

Both sides knew that Germany was losing the war, and neither wanted to leave behind an Italian wasteland of destroyed churches if they could help it. Nazism aside, the one thing both German and Italy had in common was Catholicism, especially among the old-guard aristocracy."

"So, the Brits let the Germans leave Orvieto and then just marched in?" asked Adriano.

"No, sadly, nothing quite so bloodless. My father and the German officer just agreed to *move* the battle. Both forces decamped about twenty kilometers away and went at it. The fighting went on for three days. Hundreds were killed, on both sides. It was brutal. The British government maintains a splendid war cemetery just outside Orvieto, on the flatlands at the base of the cliff. My little Anglican flock used to decorate the war graves there every November eleventh on Remembrance Day. Red poppies on everyone's lapel and that sort of thing. Of course, now, someone else does it." Her voice trailed off.

"Your father is buried there," Lee said, more a statement than a question.

"Pops?" Vicky laughed loudly. "Oh goodness, no! I'm not that old! He didn't even meet my mother until well after the war. He's still with us, and quite feisty for a ninety-three-year-old. After the war, he bought a little pub in Liscannor on the west coast of Ireland where he fell in love with my mother, a lovely American girl doing postwar volunteer work, quite a bit younger than my father. It took them a while, but along I came in 1958. My mother died in childbirth. I never knew her."

There seemed nothing to say, so Lee waited for Vicky to continue. It was like an audiobook of *Doctor Zhivago*.

"In a very real sense, it's because of Pops that I ended up in Orvieto. My father came back to Orvieto four years ago in June of 2009 for the sixty-fifth anniversary of Orvieto's liberation. There was a parade and everything. He was hailed as the liberator of the town. It was impossible for him to pay for a drink. I came with him and fell in love with Orvieto. That's when I decided to set up my little Episcopal community there."

"So, 2009—that was your first trip to Italy?" Lee asked, remembering the date near the "Magi" inscription on the photo in Vicky's dining room: January 3, 1983.

Vicky opened her mouth for a second with no sounds coming out. She looked to Lee like a ventriloquist dummy whose puppet master decided to change the dialogue at the last minute, fearful of being caught in an off-color joke or a lie.

"Yes," she stated evenly. "It was."

She chose the lie. Lee knew with utter clarity. The photo in the St. Paul's rectory proved it.

"What about the German officer who came down from the cliffs of Orvieto with the white flag? Whatever happened to him?" said Adriano.

You beat me to the question, Lee thought. He couldn't explain his troubling fascination with the Episcopal web swirling around Orvieto. But, at the moment, he knew that Reverend Vicky, somehow, was at its center. Caught in or spinning those strands, however, Lee was unsure.

"Interesting that you ask," said Vicky. Lee thought she seemed noticeably relieved at the change of subject. "He disappeared. After the war, my father tried to find him, and during the sixty-fifth anniversary commemorations the Mayor of Orvieto and several papers tried to track him down to see if he was still alive, but no luck. After the liberation of Orvieto, he just disappeared. Of course, a lot of people disappear during a war, alive or dead."

"That's some story," said Lee, now more determined than ever to find out the tale behind the photo in the St. Paul's rectory. A young man killed himself and within days both a highly regarded bishop *and* the pastor of a small, unimportant Episcopal congregation are "forced" to leave. Lee remembered that Adriano always called it his Spidey-sense, an inexplicable knack for finding out the story behind the story.

"Yes, well, enough of that," Vicky said with a slight clap of her hands. "Let me show you around my church. The mosaics are quite famous. They're the largest works by Edward Burne-Jones, the noted English artist of the Pre-Raphaelite style. This is my favorite."

The trio stopped in front of the main aisle and looked up at an immense and elaborate semicircular work over the altar. A benevolently triumphant Christ was seated in glory between five luminous men with an empty spot to his right.

"Who's missing?" Adriano asked.

"That would be for Lucifer," Lee jumped in. "It's Christ in the court of the archangels. The empty chair is where Lucifer would have been, before the fall from Grace."

"Correct," Vicky said. "Well done. You do know your Biblical history."

"Just enough to be dangerous," said Lee.

"And he's a killer at crosswords," Adriano summed up.

"It's such a powerful statement I think," said Vicky, looking up at the mosaic. "Lucifer, the greatest of the Heavenly Hosts, the bringer of light, God's greatest spiritual warrior, banished from heaven."

"'And there was war in heaven.'" Lee quoted Revelation.

"Poor Lucifer," Adriano sighed. "That's what you get for betraying the Almighty."

"Yes, but the work isn't a reminder of Satan's betrayal. It's about the promise of redemption."

"I don't get it." Adriano looked puzzled.

"Of course," Lee nodded. "The chair is empty, awaiting Lucifer's return. Like the tale of the prodigal son."

"Yes," Vicky said, quietly staring upward and turning over her cross in her hands distractedly. "Everyone deserves forgiveness, no matter how great the error. Even the Devil can find salvation. With God, everyone can once again come home."

While she spoke, Lee quickly took a look at the cross she was nervously turning over in hand. He was just able to make out the inscription before she dropped it back into place on the front of her blouse: "1-3-83."

The same date on the photo in Reverend Vicky's dining room at the St. Paul's rectory.

I wonder, Lee thought. What happened in Rome on January 3, 1983? What was the meaning of "Magi" and why was Vicky lying about it?

As they exited the church, Lee hung back. Don Bello and Reverend Vicky were conversing in Italian, with Adriano having no trouble keeping up. Lee looked back at the mosaic over the altar and the empty chair for Lucifer. Everything was so perfect, and yet, it was if the entire scene was waiting for evil to return. Lee felt the same way.

CHAPTER XXVIII

Repentance Denied

Friday, December 6, 2013, twilight, Rome

Adriano would never forget. How could he?

"This is the last thing you'll ever get from me."

His father had come into Adriano's bedroom and handed the envelope to his only son with trembling hands. The sharp yellow edges of a check shone through the thin white paper. Adriano took it, tore it up without opening it, dropped it into the trash can next to his desk, and turned back to his computer. Down the hall, his mother sat on her bed, praying among a backdrop of candles, her rosary clicking like worry beads in her hand. Three hours later Adriano was on a plane to Spain to live with his grandfather. Adriano had been eighteen.

Ten years ago, today. Reverend Vicky's words had brought it all back. As if he needed much of a reminder.

"Everyone deserves forgiveness, no matter how great the error. Even the Devil can find salvation. With God, everyone can once again come home."

Easy for a priest to say.

Adriano took in the view of Rome from the rooftop colonnade of the *Castel Sant'Angelo*, Hadrian's Tomb as it had originally been built. Hadrian, one of Rome's Four Wise Emperors. Hadrian, the openly gay lover of the legendary Antinous. Hadrian, his namesake and his grandfather's. When he was a boy, he had drawn pictures of this place on the back of napkins, schoolbook covers, paper tablecloths in seaside cafés near his native Caracas. His parents had always promised to bring him here. Oh well, another promise broken. No matter. Hadrian's body was no longer here. No one even knew where it was. Funny, Adriano thought. My grandparents fled the oppression of a Spanish dictator and started a new life in Venezuela. Decades later, their grandson had done the same in reverse, an immigrant from Catholic homophobia and parental shame. His grandfather had taken him in. Three years later, his grandfather had died. The year after that, Lee had sailed into his life on a cruise ship calling on Barcelona.

Ancient history, or at least Adriano tried to make it so.

His grandfather had fought in the Spanish Civil War for the Republic, against Franco, against the Fascists, against the *Church*. The Republic had lost. His grandfather had lost. A few hours before he died, holding his beloved grandson's hand, he told Adriano, "Your mother, my daughter, she loves you. Your father loves you. One day, you will forgive them."

"They have never asked for my forgiveness," Adriano said.

"They don't know how. They have to forgive themselves, but they can't. Not until you forgive them first."

Adriano had his grandfather buried among the graves of his fallen comrades from the war. He sent a telegram to Venezuela informing his parents. He heard later that they had flown to Spain and put up a memorial plaque. Whatever. Adriano had moved on.

"Barrer debajo de la alfombra" was the phrase in Spanish, a national trait that his family had raised to religious ritual: sweep it under the rug. Franco. Fascism. The Catholic Church's complicity in all of it. A trinity of excuses for his parent's rejection. There wasn't carpet enough in the world to pave over that.

"Adriano, look what I found!"

Lee was running toward his husband like a kid who had just found that the best ride at the carnival was free and had no line. He was so like a little boy in his enthusiasm for anything and curiosity about everything. Adriano smiled. He loved Lee very much. He was his lover, his *compinche*, his friend, his husband. Take that, Catholic Church. Lee was the only family he had left. Adriano reached out his arms and waited for his beloved's discovery.

CHAPTER XXIX

Curious Curia

Saturday, December 7, 2013, Vatican City

"**S**he called."

"What did she say?"

"She wanted to know what they knew." The American seminarian's voice dropped to an even lower whisper as two students passed by.

"They only know that it happened." His companion, an older—much older—Italian monsignor spat *sotto voce.*

"Everyone knows that."

"Yes. But they want to know *more.* That could be a problem."

"Yes."

The two informants looked out over Vatican Square from the promenade of the papal residence. Workmen were busily putting up banners and barricades for the Pope's birthday in ten days. He had mingled with prostitutes, visited a homeless shelter, and washed the feet of a Muslim woman in jail. He had been pope for less than a year and already people were ready to make him a saint. He was a finalist—and shoo-in—for *Time Magazine's* Person of the Year. The power of public relations.

"Does *he* know?" The novice indicated with a nod of his head. To their left, a rigidly handsome Swiss Guard stood outside the new pope's quarters. Three hundred meters away, down several corridors and behind four more doors, another Switzer guarded the new Pontiff's predecessor, the first Pope Emeritus in history. Francis and Benedict: the Roman Odd Couple.

The senior prelate answered the question with a question. "The Holy Father?"

His co-conspirator nodded in the affirmative.

The elderly cleric arched his eyebrow. "Which one?"

Just then, the young man's vestments started to vibrate. He took the phone out of his pocket and turned the screen to his companion. They both crossed themselves.

"Magda."

CHAPTER XXX

Papal Audience

Saturday, December 7, 2013, midday, Rome

"Remember, just dial 39 08 243-3746, by phone or fax! Easy to remember the number! That's country code Italy, city code Rome, and the numbers spell *cheerio*!"

Cedric was finishing up a call but put down the phone and positively twinkled as Lee and Adriano made their way to the counter with their luggage.

"Oh," he said with a faux pout of his seductive lips. "Checking out so soon, Adriano and, and...?"

"Lee."

"Yes." Cedric turned back to Adriano. "Lee, of course, like Bruce Lee."

"Like Robert E." Lee glared, with a smile. "May we leave our luggage here while we do some last-day sightseeing?"

"Well of course." And Cedric dashed from behind the counter and grabbed Adriano's luggage with a wink. "I'll put it right here behind the counter until you're ready to head back to, where was it?"

"Orvieto," said Lee, tossing his overnight bag to Cedric, who caught it nimbly against his chest.

"Of course. Lovely town. I have, ah, *friends* there myself! What a small world! We'll have to get together for drinks...or something when I'm next up there."

Adriano felt like a play toy caught between dueling puppies. "Yes, that would be great."

"Yes," Lee interjected. "*Something.* We'll be back for our bags around seven p.m. Our train is at 8:15 p.m. We're going to play tourists until then."

"Oh, my goodness, I almost forgot!" Cedric started shuffling papers on his desk. "That lovely lady priest from next door dropped this envelope off for the both of you. Said to make *sure* you got it before you left for the day. I almost forgot. I'm just so distracted this morning. I don't know what has gotten into me!"

I know what you'd like to get into you, Adriano thought, opening the envelope and pulling out two gold-embossed pieces of paper that looked for all the world like the golden tickets from *Willie Wonka & the Chocolate Factory.*

"Sweet Jesus. We're going to see the Pope!"

~

"Yowza. You'd think it was a Madonna concert."

"With this many people, you'd think it was *the* Madonna."

Adriano and Lee hopped out of the cab a block away from the Basilica of St. Paul's Outside the Walls. The crowd was already immense, and the service wasn't supposed to start for an hour.

"Jesus Christ," sighed Adriano.

"Not quite," said Lee in a hope for humor to ward off the duel promise of Adriano's Pope-o-phobia and dislike of crowds. "But, close enough."

"Tell me again why we're here," said Adriano through pursed lips. Lee could sense his husband's religious antipathy rising with every breath.

"It's an ecumenical prayer service with the various leaders of Rome's other churches and synagogues. I think there's even a few imams here," Lee said. "Every church in Rome got six tickets. At the last minute, two of Reverend Vicky's congregation said they couldn't go."

"There must be over 5,000 people here!"

Lee shrugged. "Yes, well, do the math. There are more than nine hundred churches in Rome."

Adriano gritted his teeth.

Lee offered his most charming "Sorry, I love you" face and hoped for the best. It was a *Hail Mary*, he knew.

"Well, at least we have tickets." Adriano sighed in resignation and Lee relaxed a bit. That was what ten years of a happy marriage would do for you. One partner dragged his atheist husband to see the Pope and the godless heathen pretended not to mind. Ain't love grand.

"I know you hate this," said Lee.

"Actually, not," said Adriano. "I mean, it's *the Pope.* I'm curious. Plus, think how much fun Don Bello will have teasing me about this when we get back to Orvieto."

"He's a good priest."

"He's a good *person*," corrected Adriano. "I'm turning the other cheek when it comes to his perverse religious affiliations."

Lee rolled his eyes. "Come along, muffin. The line is over there."

In point of fact, the line was everywhere and nowhere. As Adriano and Lee drew closer to the front of the cathedral, they had their first experience of Roman police efficiency. There was none.

"Magda would be *horrified*," said Lee as he and Adriano pushed their way through the sea of nuns, monks, cardinals, and carabinieri. "This is a security nightmare! She'd never allow this. Thank God we have tickets!"

"Lee, honey." Adriano tapped his husband on the shoulder and pointed to a gaggle of Filipino nuns elbowing their way through a phalanx of Nigerian divinity students. "They *all* have tickets."

Lee looked up in despair. Adriano was right. Everyone was waving their Willie Wonkas. Priests, rabbis, and a smattering of orthodox-ordained were all pushing like a football scrum toward the line of Italian police whose perimeter seemed to consist of nothing but a sultry queue of lit cigarettes. Ineffective as a security detail, Italian police were nonetheless hard to top in the looks department. It was like a gay gear party on Halloween in San Francisco. So much for VIP access. This wasn't reserved seating. It was ticketed chaos.

"Quick, over there. Follow that nun!"

Adriano grabbed Lee by the arm and kept pace with a portly Carmelite who would have put an Irish rugby squad to shame. Back and forth she tacked and veered like a galleon under sail, her habit billowing and rosary jingling as she pushed forward through the crowd of papalophiles.

"How are you doing?" Lee yelled to be heard over the cicada-like buzz of singing sisters, chanting monks, and hawking street vendors yelling, "Papa Francesco! Papa Francesco!"

"I'm fine." Adriano smiled wanly, following in the Carmelite's wake. "Just keep moving. Oh, excuse me, Sister."

Finally, they were at the front of the crowd. The congregational mass was getting squeezed two-by-two into a tiny entry funnel guarded by a muscular carabinieri frisking everyone before they entered the sanctuary.

"You touch mi private parts and I'll smack yi all the way to Kilarny," Adriano's nun escort hissed at the handsome policeman reaching for her wimple.

"I wouldn't if I were you," Adriano offered in Italian with a smile to the youthful cop. In a tactical retreat, he let the nun slip through but gave Adriano a not-so-swift once-over.

"Grazie," he said as he leered with a tip of his hat, giving Lee a cursory pat-down and then pushing them both through.

"You get all the luck," Lee said.

Adriano just smiled. "It's a gift."

Once through the security cordon, the crowd took off in a run toward the basilica's massively carved bronze doors. A fleet of selfie sticks were navigating through the mass of religious orders all vying for the best seating. The tickets get you in, but then you are on your own, Lee thought.

"Over here," Adriano motioned. "There are some empty seats near the back and all the ones up front are already taken. The altar's too far away to see the Pope anyway, unless you have binoculars."

Lee frowned, but knew his husband was right. The vast interior of the basilica was quickly filling up. There was no way they'd be close enough to actually share face time with the Pontiff. Also, Lee knew that the closer to the exit—and to air—the better for Adriano. "These are great, honey. Next to the door."

Adriano exhaled in relief and they slipped into a pew two back from the rear and picked up two glossy programs filled with details about tonight's services and various historical factoids. You had to give it to Gorgeous George and the Vatican PR team. They knew how to market. The not-inexpensive book was embossed with the Vatican crest.

"Fancy," Adriano said, flipping through the booklet, always the designer. "They didn't get this printed in China."

For the next few minutes, seminarians and the occasional monsignori squeezed by to get to their seats in the middle. Adriano and Lee held firm to their positions.

"Thank you," Adriano said once they were settled.

"For what?"

"For letting me sit near the exit. I know you wanted to see the Pope, but I can't stand crowds. I'll hyperventilate."

"I know," Lee said, squeezing his husband's thigh. "It's fine. I'm here and that's more than most homosexuals from San Francisco can say. Plus, it will be easier to get out when it's over."

"Wow, check out the ceiling!"

Lee followed Adriano's gaze upward. There ringing the entire perimeter of the vast nave were immense, glittering portraits of the popes in oval frames.

"That's right. I'd forgotten about that," said Lee. "They're all there, all the popes from St. Peter all the way to Benedict. Pope Francis's mosaic is being completed this week, just in time for his birthday. See, there's a blank space for Francis just to the left of Benedict."

"They're running out of room," Adriano said, holding up his iPhone to get a photo. "There's only four spaces left after Francis."

"And when they do, that's it. According to legend, the final spot filled indicates the last pope. The Antichrist will be unleashed on earth and the end of the world will commence."

"As I recall," said Adriano, pocketing his phone, "there are some prophecies that say that the final pope will *be* the Antichrist."

"I'm sure *you* think they're all the Antichrist."

"You said it, not me. Besides the rogues' gallery, what's so special about this church? Except that it's enormous."

"This is St. Paul's Outside the Walls, meaning outside the ancient walls of Rome."

"And Reverend Vicky's church is St. Paul's *inside* the walls?"

"Exactly. This church"—Lee motioned around him—"is one of Rome's four papal basilicas, along with St. Peter's, St. John Lateran, and St. Mary Maggiorre. St. Paul's is the only one not within the actual city limits of Rome and is second in size only to St. Peter's. According to tradition, this church is built on the exact site where St. Paul was beheaded and buried."

"The most homophobic of saints," Adriano said, almost spitting. "I suppose his head is here somewhere in a golden urn."

"No," Lee deadpanned. "Just his body. His head's in St. John Lateran."

Adriano just threw up his hands. "Okay, so officially we're not within Rome at the moment."

"Technically, we're not even in Italy. We're on the land of another sovereign country, Vatican City. That's why you don't see any Italian or Roman police inside the courtyard. They control security, as it were, outside, but inside those guys are in charge. The Swiss Guard. Here, there's a photo in tonight's program. I've seen it before online, bunches of times. Google 'Swiss Guard images' and this is what pops up."

Lee found the page and read the caption under a lineup of Switzers, clearly at Mass.

6 May 2006: His Holiness Pope Benedict XVI offers the Body of Christ to new recruits of the Swiss Guard during a Papal Mass in St. Peter's Basilica to mark the 500th Anniversary of the Swiss Guard. The Pontiff expressed his gratitude to the legion for their service to the Papacy over the centuries.

Adriano and Lee looked around. Sure enough, at every door and in every niche were members of one of the world's most famous military units.

"Go on, I know you're dying to tell me. What's special about the Swiss Guard?"

Lee perked up. "Well, since the late 1400s, the Swiss provided the best and most talented mercenaries in the world. A lot of European royal families used them for security. Switzerland used to be quite a poor county, and of course, geographically because of the mountains, is quite cut off from the rest of Europe. Certainly it was five hundred years ago. Anyway, it was very common for young Swiss boys to hire themselves out as professional soldiers and they gained quite a reputation for bravery. So much so that the Popes started using them for personal security, starting with Julius the Second."

Adriano shook his head. "How do you remember this stuff?"

"I read a lot, and I saw the *Agony and Ecstasy* nine times."

"Continue."

"They were actually just one of several military groups protecting the Papal States until May of 1527. That's when your guy, Charles the Fifth of Spain—"

"Holy Roman Emperor. Yes, we Spaniards know that."

"Well, Charles the Fifth and the Pope ended up on opposite sides of the Italian wars. Pope Clement was hedging his bets, trying to see who would be the most supportive of keeping the Papal States independent. Clement threw in his lot with King Francis of France. Charles got annoyed and his troops sacked Rome, forcing Clement to flee to Orvieto."

"So, the Swiss Guard fought against Charles."

"Kind of. They held back Charles's army until the last moment to give Clement time to escape. Over a hundred Swiss Guards were killed, right on the steps of St. Peter's Rome. Look, here's another picture from that same day. Benedict swearing in the fresh recruits."

They both read from the program.

Thirty-three new members of "The Pope's Army"—The Swiss Guard—take their vows on the steps of St. Peter's Basilica, the same spot where 147 out of 180 Swiss Guards were killed defending Pope Clement VII during the Sack of Rome on 6 May 1527.

"So, what about now? They don't look like an elite fighting force. Those outfits look more like jesters' costumes."

"It's tradition," said Lee. "Although it's probably apocryphal, Michelangelo was supposed to have designed their uniforms. The colors are purposeful too. The blue is from the family crest of Pope Julius's family. The red was chosen by Leo the Tenth, the gay Medici pope, from his coat of arms."

"They're the froofiest uniforms I've ever seen."

"Don't be fooled," said Lee. "Underneath those poofy pants and Renaissance helmets are some of the hardest bodies and best-trained killing machines around. And, you can't volunteer. To this day, to even be considered for membership in the Swiss Guard, you have to be a male Swiss citizen between the ages of nineteen and thirty, have attended a Swiss military school, be at least five feet seven inches tall, and hold a professional degree or high school diploma. Oh, and you have to be single."

"Bet they have fun in the barracks."

"Well, yes, that's the point. The final requirement is that all members of the Swiss Guard possess the highest ethics and impeccable morals."

"I'd never have made it."

"No," Lee said, "citizenship aside. But you do look hot dressed up in a uniform."

"Pervert."

Lee smiled. "Actually, the reputation of the Swiss Guards has suffered a good deal over the last few years. Back in the late nineties, there was a gay love triangle and murder. Quite the scandal. One of the guards shot his commander, supposedly his lover, then the commander's wife, and then turned the gun on himself. Since then, there have been a lot of rumors that there was a gay cabal within the walls of Vatican City. Cardinals and priests setting up sex parties and members of the Swiss Guard hiring themselves out as prostitutes. Actually, the rumor is that Pope Benedict resigned because of the gay Vatileaks revelations."

"Vatileaks... Oh yes. I remember reading about that online. A few months before Pope Benedict resigned his private butler sold a bunch of the Pope's private papers to the press. The stories read like a trashy novel, as I recall."

"Some people think it's ultimately what led to Benedict's unprecedented abdication. Popes have been murdered, but never resigned—well, at least not for over six hundred years. Pope Gregory resigned in the 1400s."

"What flaming hypocrites, all of them," Adriano harrumphed. "I bet you with a little work I could hack into Grindr and find a passel of Vatican sodomites. Now *that* would be worthy use of my technical skills. The Church has done more to perpetrate hatred and violence against gay men and women than any institution in the world, and I do mean *any*."

"Well, yes," said Lee. "I remember when I was thinking about the priesthood, I discovered just how gay was my church. I read a story once that over sixty percent of priests are gay."

"Amazing," said Adriano flatly. "And me from two Catholic countries and somehow I never managed to have sex with a priest."

"I'll wear a collar and you can seduce me sometime." Lee winked.

"Bless me, Father, for I will sin." Adriano leered, reaching his hand under Lee's thigh.

"Be careful," Lee said, letting his husband's hand slip farther under his rump. "The popes are watching."

CHAPTER XXXI

Baked Goods

Sunday, December 8, 2013, an hour before dawn, Orvieto

The Tower of the Moor rang out the hour with four sharp clangs that echoed across the frost-laced tiles of Orvieto's rooftops. The town was still asleep—except her.

A tiny votive candle flickered behind the bar, the room's only illumination. The lines in her storied face reflected the feeble flame, over nine decades of creases folded in shadowed lines and wrinkles. For more than seventy years, she had descended these stairs, at this hour, to do this thing. She didn't need light to see.

This is how it had been done epoch upon epoch. From the time of Velzna when the town was Etruscan. After the rape by Rome. Throughout the Plague and during the reign of frightened popes. Throughout many, many wars. This was a sacred spot of creation, of honor, of escape from the sour tastes of life and the painful pangs of death.

The painting of the Seven Martyrs of Camorena peered down on her work. She didn't look up. She didn't need to see it to remember. It was always there, the tissue-thin skin that contained her life. Beneath the portrait, another image, a photo. Andrea. A year ago today he was to have been ordained. Instead, there was a funeral.

As automatically as breath she opened a huge and ancient cooler, a vintage as old as the war. She pulled out a long tray dotted with four enormous globs of dough. It was heavy, heavier than it used to be. Or just seemed so, more every day. Carefully, quietly, she sat it down on the wax-covered table in the middle of the kitchen. She reached behind her and grabbed a tattered but freshly laundered apron—dried from the night before—and deftly dropped it over her shoulders, tying the strings behind her. Ready for battle, she reached into an earthen jar with her right hand, scattering flour across the table. With her left she grabbed a rolling pin and attacked the mounds in front of her.

Beneath her feet, dusted with a snowfall of sugar and grain, crouched the trap door of her secrets, of Orvieto's secrets. The hidden cache had escaped the pillage of Rome and the greed of dictators. It had already saved many—saved one. As long as she lived—maybe longer—its treasure was safe.

She continued to bake.

Two hours later, Orvieto awoke not to the peeling of bells, but to the bakery of smells that was Café Volsini, macaroons, croissants, pastries, cannoli, and communion wafers.

She took off her apron, put away the sacred dough, and then carefully pulled a tray from the oven. The bread of life. Wrapping the toasty loaf in a linen towel, she then swathed herself against the cold for the short walk across the Piazza del Duomo. The Bishop liked his bread freshly baked.

Velzna Volsini smiled to herself. She wondered if Arnaud remembered today's anniversary. This was a communion he would never forget.

CHAPTER XXXII

Conception

Sunday, December 8, 2013, The Feast of the Immaculate Conception, Orvieto

During Lee and Adriano's two nights' sojourn in Rome, Christmas had come to Orvieto.

Up and down the Corso, tiny living evergreens had been dropped outside of every business and store. Each shop owner was decorating the trees in a manner specific with their specialty. The butcher had sausages draped like garlands around the branches. Marco had made ornaments of wine corks for his, topped with a star made of twisted umbricelli. A constellation of cookies and sweets in the shapes of stars cascaded through the pine needles of the one outside Café Volsini. La Madrina looked up as Lee and Adriano passed. She was humming a gay tune and seemed quite chipper. She offered them a cookie "ornament," and then returned to her decorating.

"Did we just fall into an alternative universe?" Lee whispered, wiping crumbs from Adriano's chin.

"That's the first time I've ever seen her smile."

"And she was singing."

"Maybe she got laid last night."

"What a difference a week makes."

Exhausted from two and a half days of nonstop power tourism, not to mention Lee's relentless and somewhat troubling obsession about anything to do with Deacon Andrea, they had pretty much stayed closed to home last night. Lee was in a positive afterglow about seeing Pope Francis. Adriano chalked it up to the things one does for domestic harmony. He still couldn't believe that he'd actually been to see the Pope. His mother wouldn't have believed it. Frankly, he could hardly believe it himself. He pushed it out his mind, along with his mother's face.

Today, the Feast of the Immaculate Conception, was the traditional Italian beginning of the holiday season. Adriano and Lee ventured out into an Orvieto transformed. A huge Christmas tree had been hauled from the nearby forests and erected in front of *Sant'Andrea* and just below the Mayor's city hall window. Strings of white lights arched over the cobblestones like electric frost.

"Buon Natale, my friends!"

The couple looked up to see Don Bello, weighed down with festively overflowing bags, making his way along the Corso.

The trio embraced.

"So, how was the Pope?" the old priest asked.

"How did you know?" Lee's mouth was agape.

"Well." Don Bello smiled. "I knew something about the tick—"

"The tickets were yours, weren't they?" said Adriano, wagging his finger mockingly as one would to a naughty boy. "They were meant for you and Vicky."

"Perhaps." Don Bello winked. "But, trust me, Vicky and I have seen popes before and we will see popes again. If one lives in Washington, DC, one sees the President drive by. If one lives in Hollywood, I imagine you see movie stars on the street. Here, the Holy Father is always doing something. He's our built-in celebrity. How close did you get?"

Lee looked to Adriano, who smiled indulgently and motioned for him to tell the story.

"He walked right past us!"

"Yes, for once, my antipathy for crowds came in handy," said Adriano. "We sat near the back and after the service we made a dash for the exit—"

"—and that's when Adriano saw the barricades," Lee finished. "Everyone else was packed inside like a sardine and outside there was no one.

So, we just waited. The barricades were right by the main door. I thought they'd spirit Francis out a side, but Adriano told me to stay put."

"Even I, lapsed Catholic that I am, knew that a pope wouldn't exit through the side door. Five minutes after we got to the barricade the doors swung open and out came a battalion of leaders from various faiths, a fleet of cardinals, and then Il Papa."

"An Italian nun tried to push me away, but Adriano kept her at bay."

"Yes," Adriano laughed. "I told her in my politest but most direct Italian that if she wanted, she could peer between our legs, but there was no way we were giving up our front row seats, thank you very much."

Don Bello chuckled and clapped his hands together. "Well done. It is always special being in the presence of the Holy Father. It sounds like even a doubter like you were moved."

"Well, I wouldn't say that," said Adriano. "But I was glad to get close enough for an iPhone video to preserve the moment. Not to change the subject, but to change the subject, how was the Vatican?"

"The Vatican is the Vatican." The elfish Don Bello shrugged good naturedly. "Everyone has an agenda and every agenda is filled out in triplicate. I went begging alms for my church and came back with a thirty-page questionnaire and formal request form from the Vatican bank. If I'd known you were going to be so chummy with His Holiness, I'd have asked for your influence! In time, the money will come. It always does."

"You're a patient man," Lee said, relieving Don Bello of some of his bags. Adriano had already liberated the priest of one enormous box that had been precariously perched on top of his load.

"I am a poor Italian priest in the wastes north of Rome," Don Bello said, smiling by way of answer. He nodded his thanks for the help with his packages. "You are proof of God's providence. I needed help, and you appeared!"

"Your faith is greater than mine," Adriano said gently.

"Ah, but that is the trick, dear Adriano. Whether or not you believe, God is still there. He does not need faith to exist. He simply is! Come, I will show you *San Giovanale*."

He really does sound like Yoda, Lee thought, as they followed Don Bello up and down and round and about through Orvieto's bustling, curving streets. Every few yards, they were stopped by residents who wanted to say a few words of greeting to the elderly priest, tip their hats, and move on. Lee felt like he was in an Italian-dubbed version of *It's a Wonderful Life*.

Five minutes later, Don Bello stopped at the very edge of Orvieto's northwest cliff face, slightly lower than the rest of the town and on an almost geometric point several hundred feet up. "This is *San Giovanale*." As far as vision allowed spread the Umbrian countryside: extinct volcanic buttes, vineyards, forests, farmland, olive groves, and, shimmering a few miles away, the Paglia River. In the distance, several smaller hilltop towns bowed down like beautiful albeit less noble courtiers to the obvious queen of the region, Orvieto. On the very edge of the precipice, its ancient bell tower like a lighthouse warning sailors of the jagged cliff below, sat a small, simple, and obviously very ancient church. "This is the womb of Orvieto."

Don Bello motioned them into the sanctuary through a small side door. Inside, *San Giovanale* was as Spartan and compact as a monastic cell. How close I came to that before I met Adriano, Lee thought. A vaulted ceiling of rough-hewn rock bore witness to several architectural styles and epochs of conquering hordes. The altar was a simple stone slab. The cross, stark and empty of the usually gruesome and bleeding Christ. More like the ones of Protestant churches, this crucifix was not a symbol of death, but rather a statement of resurrection. You will find no body here. The only adornments, which stood out even more because of their monogamy, were the murals, tantalizing and often incomplete dashes of colorful Bible stories scattered around the perimeter of the nave. It didn't take an art historian to see that they were very, very old.

"These are the oldest pieces of Christian art in Orvieto," said Don Bello, walking with Adriano and Lee around the church. "They date back to just before the year 1000. And, before that, this was the site of an Etruscan temple, and even before that, a place where the earliest humans gathered in reverence. From here, Orvieto sprang."

Just then, the side door erupted with the boisterous energy of several teenagers carrying boxes, backpacks, and two guitars. With them was a young nun—obviously their teacher—in a plain gray habit and fluorescent orange running shoes. Their smiles and voices grew louder when they saw Don Bello, greeting him with a chorus of ciaos.

"Ah, the youth choir for tonight's service of the Immaculate Conception." Don Bello beamed and excused himself to go deal with the group. "Go out to the garden. I'll meet you there in a few minutes and continue the tour."

While the priest waded into the army of Catholic adolescence, Lee and Adriano made their way slowly toward the garden of *San Giovanale*.

"You don't see kids that young in churches back home," Adriano remarked as they walked down the side aisle past an especially well-preserved set of frescoes. Next to it was a panel equally as damaged by centuries of neglect. Don Bello would need a lot of money to restore them all. "It's nice to see kids doing something besides graffiti tagging. I just wish their minds weren't being filled with this hocus-pocus. The Immaculate Conception of Jesus. Please. What a crock. As if having sex to bear a child was a sin."

"The Feast of the Immaculate Conception isn't about Jesus," Lee said, looking at an especially delicate wall painting. "It's about Mary being born without sin. God could not be born of anything other than purity and perfection. Not only was Jesus born of a virgin—the Incarnation of Jesus—but she, herself, had to be conceived without original sin. The early Church fathers really wrestled with it, the concept of the *Theotokos*, Greek for Birth Giver of God. It's the one thing that truly separates Catholicism from other Christian faiths, an almost equal worship of Mary—a woman—alongside Jesus."

"So, tonight was the night that St. Anne got knocked up by St. Joakim," Adriano taunted playfully.

"Yes," Lee said, surprised that Adriano actually knew the names of Mary's parents. "If you must put so fine and crass a point on it, this was date night for the BVM's mom and dad."

"The BVM?"

"The Blessed Virgin Mary."

Adriano just looked at Lee in perplexed wonder. "You truly are a font of obscure information."

"It's not that obscure," Lee said, somewhat ruffled. "Over one billion Catholics believe it."

"Well, the Church may worship a woman as a virtual goddess, but they certainly aren't ready to have one on the altar."

"True," Lee said thinking of Vicky and her militant Anglicanism. He was still puzzled by the significance of that date on the back of her cross. January 3, 1983. He looked over at the nun setting up music stands and corralling her flock. "I have wondered sometimes at the devotion of women in the Church, and nuns especially. Why do they put up with being such second-class citizens?"

"Do you believe it?"

"What?"

"In the Immaculate Conception."

"I had an Immaculate Medal. My mother gave it to me for my first communion."

"That's different," Adriano said quietly, knowing he didn't dare delve deeper into that subject.

"You know, my mother was a convert," Lee said. "She was born Southern Baptist but became Catholic to marry my father."

Adriano gestured for Lee to continue. Lee didn't often talk about his parents, unless it followed one of his nightmares, and then, only haltingly.

"My grandmother, Mama's mother, wasn't happy about it," Lee went on. "Catholics were viewed with suspicion in the rural South. Southern Baptists didn't drink, smoke, or gamble."

"And your father did all of the above."

"There were three things my grandmother could never understand about Catholicism: bingo, real wine at communion, and the Roman Catholic obsession with the Virgin Mary."

"So," Adriano pushed, "do you believe it?"

"In the Immaculate Conception?"

Adriano nodded silently.

Lee smiled. "Actually, I do."

"What?" Adriano was truly taken aback. "I know you're kind of hippie-dippie and certainly think there's life after death, but really, Lee, this is too much!"

Lee just grinned beatifically. "Today celebrates the idea that Mary, conceived the good old-fashioned sexual way, was born sinless, immaculate. It's the easiest of church teachings to accept. I believe that all children are born sinless."

Adriano pursed his lips and regarded his husband. "You are one complex piece of work, Lee Fontaine Maury, but I love you. So, in your belief system, everyone is sinless, even a pagan like me."

"Oh no, lover, not you," Lee tweaked as they walked out into the chilly sunshine. "You're a deviant sinner. But you were born blameless."

The entrance to the garden was just to the right of the main door, and down a sloping earthen ramp that wound around the ancient building, ending in a V-shaped plot of land punctuated by a huge stone cave on one end and the foundations of *San Giovanale* on the other. The point of the V was a flat, clearly defined oval of earth rising a hundred feet above the road below. Like a figurehead at the prow of a ship, an ancient but obviously sturdy olive tree stood sentinel, one thick branch overhanging the precipice. Its gnarled branches bore witness to taking the windy blasts of many a winter here at Orvieto's northwestern corner. From here, all of northern Italy and beyond it all of Europe spread out. Behind, Orvieto rose up like a crown.

"This is where he jumped."

Adriano and Lee turned to see Don Bello ambling up behind them.

"Andrea." Don Bello said his name simply. "Here was his last look at Orvieto."

Lee and Adriano stood silently, not knowing what to say. Finally, Lee offered, "I'm so sorry."

Don Bello didn't answer. He just stood and took in the view.

"This is right above Floriano's shrine," Lee said. "The Church of the Crucifix."

"Yes." Don Bello sighed. "Officially, *La Chiesa del Crocifisso del Tufo Orvieto* is part of my parish. It is part of *San Giovanale*."

"So, you put the candle there," Adriano said. Don Bello looked at him sadly. "We saw it a few days ago when we went for a walk around the Rupe."

"Yes," replied the old priest. He nodded and then opened his mouth as if to say something more. Closing it slowly, he only added, "Yes, yes."

"We saw some Arabic lettering there on the rock too," said Lee.

"Of course." Don Bello smiled that indescribable melancholy grin that denoted memories of equal parts pleasure and pain. "Dawud. He loved Andrea too."

"Dawud?" Lee and Adriano both asked.

"The CD peddler. You must have seen him around town. Poor man." Again, Don Bello looked as if he were going to say more but remained silent. After a while he spoke, his voice even but quiet, like a man reciting a prayer. "'And behold, all of this I will give you, if you bow down and worship me.' Do you know that passage?"

"It's when Satan appears to Jesus while he is in the desert fasting," Lee said quietly. "The Devil takes him up onto a high promontory and shows him a view of the earth's riches. He offers it all to Jesus if he will betray his father and worship Satan. Jesus, of course, says no."

"Yes, but that's not the point." Don Bello turned from the view and faced Lee with real fervor in his voice. "He was tempted. He was human."

"Like us," Adriano said simply.

"Exactly, my son," Don Bello said, patting him on the shoulder. "Just like us. No more no less. If Jesus can be tempted by the pleasures of this earth, who among us can pretend to be different? Temptation comes to every man and to every woman and its ways are subtle and many. Sometimes a beautiful gift can hide a poisonous surprise. And sometimes, not every temptation is a sin. Sometimes the sin lies in not giving into temptation."

"I don't understand," Adriano said.

"Oysters are ugly, are they not?" said Don Bello. "On the outside they have nothing to recommend them. Craggy and rough and difficult to open. Many the sailor's hand has been bloodied and scarred by trying to shuck a recalcitrant bivalve." The priest chuckled, but then clasping his hands together tightly suddenly opened them to reveal two foil-wrapped chocolates from Café Volsini. "But when opened, the flesh of the oyster is sweet."

Lee and Adriano lightly applauded Don Bello's sleight of hand and took the chocolates from him.

"And sometimes, there is even a pearl inside, yes?" Adriano was smiling broadly.

"Be careful what you wish for," Don Bello said, motioning for them to unwrap their sweets. Lee looked up, recognizing what had been one of Brian's favorite phrases. "One never knows what La Donna Volsini hides in her creations. Here, let me show you."

Don Bello took back the sweets, and expertly cracked one open along a thin perforation in the chocolate. "Hold out your hand," he said to Lee and out popped a rainbow-hued marble.

"Isn't that dangerous?" Lee said. "You could crack a tooth? What if a child swallowed one?"

Don Bello laughed. "How funny you Americans are. Always worried. A potential lawsuit behind every bush. La Donna Volsini only sells these to kids old enough to know, or to their parents for special occasions. It's an Orvieto tradition."

"It's like the gift in a box of Cracker Jacks," Lee said. "I almost choked on a tiny toy once when I poured an open box into my mouth."

"We have a similar tradition in Spain for Three Kings Day, *Rosca de Reyes*. It's a special cake served on Epiphany, January sixth. A little toy is baked inside, usually a ceramic figurine of Baby Jesus. The child that finds it is 'king' or 'queen' for the day. I always liked the tradition. Life is full of surprises, some of them dangerous, some of them not. Life doesn't come with a guarantee." Adriano expertly cracked open his chocolate and plucked out a one euro coin.

"Bravo, young Adriano." Don Bello grinned. "You are a philosopher indeed."

"Can atheists be philosophers, Don Bello?" Adriano asked, giving the coin to Don Bello. "For your mural project."

"Why of course," Don Bello winked, pocketing the donation. "The Miracle of Bolsena was at the hands of one who questioned his faith."

"What was Andrea's temptation?" Lee ventured quietly. Adriano didn't try and stop him.

Don Bello's playful smile went flat. He suddenly looked very old indeed. "Andrea was never tempted. That was the problem." His gaze was steady as he looked far out over the landscape. "Andrea was almost too good for this earth. I don't believe temptation had found him yet." Then, almost under his breath he said, "The truly innocent are always the ones sacrificed first."

"You miss him," Adriano said. A statement, not a question.

"Yes. We all miss him. But grief is the price of love in this life."

"Don Bello! Don Bello! Come quickly!"

The trio turned suddenly as a young man ran pell-mell down the incline toward them. His white lab coat and stethoscope streamed behind him like a flag whipping in the breeze. It was Luke, the doctor from *Sant'Andrea*.

"Lucca, what's wrong?" Don Bello caught the youthful physician at arm's length. He was panting from his flight.

"The Bishop. He's in the hospital. I don't think he's going to make it. Bring your holy oils. I think he'll need last rites."

The quartet was soon running through Orvieto's tortuous streets across town to the hospital in the cathedral's shadow.

CHAPTER XXXIII

Clement's Fountain

May 1, 1528 (Julian calendar), Orvieto

Clement was pleased. "Like Moses striking the stony earth of the Sinai to bring forth refreshment, let now water gush forth from this rock to quench the thirst of Orvieto."

The Pope hit the pavement with his crozier and up sprang a geyser, raining down in unexpected enthusiasm on the assembled crowd who rushed forward to splash in the quickly filling pool.

"How was that for my first miracle?" Clement whispered to Gio.

"Behold the Lord's mighty hand," the young Swiss Guard replied in the Pope's ear.

The two friends laughed.

"Your Holiness, you have brought life-giving waters to my people—to all of Orvieto—regardless of their faith." Moses de Blanis was beaming.

"Gentiles and Jews all thirst for justice, but first they're just thirsty. This town will no longer have to worry about the safety of its water supply." Take that Emperor Charles, Clement thought somewhat smugly. *While you're tearing down Rome, I'm restoring Roman aqueducts and building new wells for a weary populace. Clement the Water Bearer. I like that. Maybe I could get that bandied about.*

"Orvieto will never forget you for this," said the Jewish physician and banker. "Your legacy is secure."

"That will take more than turning on a fountain." The Pope sighed. "Saving my reputation will be the neatest trick since the Resurrection, but it's a start."

"Every journey of a thousand miles begins with a single step," said Sofia, stepping up between her father and her newly minted fiancé, Gio.

"Is that from the Koran?" Cardinal Egidio asked, joining the group.

"Confucius," Hassan de Wazzan answered, stepping forward and kissing Clement's papal ring. "Wisdom comes in many languages."

"What a day." Clement was genuinely happy. "What a pity Michelangelo isn't here. We could sit for a portrait. How I'd love a way to remember this moment."

"I've thought of that," Moses said with a sly smile. "Good people of Orvieto," he screamed out through cupped hands to be heard over the joyful noise of laughing children and chattering parents. "Orvieto is the heart of our country. A city born of volcanoes and sculpted by the rivers of time. It is a rock upon which much history has been written, nay carved in the rugged plinths of a human record in the language of many peoples and many faiths. But once here, the conversion begins."

"Remind me never to speak in public after your father," Clement whispered to Sofia, whose hand he noticed was clasped tightly in Gio's. "He's a Semite Demosthenese. I don't want to compete with that."

"Shhh, Holy Father." She touched her finger to her lip in friendly rebuke. "He's getting to the best part."

Clement obediently crossed his lips in the sign of silence and continued to listen.

"Once here," Moses continued, "like Paul, visitors are thrown from their horse of previous perception and a conversion takes place. Once here, they drink deep of the societal wine of this miraculous place and all are transformed. Once here, they are no longer pagan, or Cathar, Catholic, Muslim, or Jew. Once here, they are Orvietani. Today, because of our noble newest citizen, His Holiness, Pope Clementius Septimus, Orvieto is once again returning to life, coming out of a deep and frozen sleep. Because of him, business is growing. Inns are reopening. Orvieto is beginning what the French might call a renaissance. A reawakening. My fellow citizens, every day when you have a few more hours to cook your meals, play with your children, or worship your God—a few more hours saved because now you can draw water from this well in the center of town instead of making the treacherous trek down the mountain to pull water from the stream, remember our benefactor. Giulio de Medici, our newest and noblest Orvietani, Pope Clement the Seventh."

With that, Moses stepped aside to reveal a cloth draped over an obvious sculpture placed on the lip of the fountain. With theatrical flourish, he pulled a string and the covering fell away to reveal a majestically carved coat of arms—the papal tiara crowning the Medici crest, Clement's personal seal.

At this, the crowd erupted in cheers and applause while Clement beamed.

"Thank you, my friend," the Pope said to Moses. "It is you who should be having monuments erected in your honor, not me. It is your money that paid for this fountain...is paying for so many things."

Moses waved away the compliment. "My dear friend de Medici. I have given only money. You have used that money here for the good of your people. I doubt a Borgia would have done that."

"True enough," Clement snapped back, but cheerfully. In front of him, the crowd was beginning to disperse, the streets slippery with water spilled from groaning buckets being born away by gleeful families. Cardinal Egidio was playfully splashing Wazzan. Gio and Sofia just sat on the lip of the fountain staring into each other's eyes. "We make quite a team, you and I. the Jewish moneylender and the bastard pope."

Moses chuckled. "Yes, proof that all conceptions are immaculate. Let us go in."

As Moses motioned for Egidio and Wazzan and the young lovers to follow, Clement began to make his way back to the newly restored papal residence—courtesy of de Blanis' munificence. Today, Il Medici would throw a party—upstairs in his rooms overlooking the great Cathedral for the six friends, and outside on the plaza for the people of Orvieto. Pope and people alike would feast on roast lamb and suckling pig. Truffles and the fine wine of Orvieto would flow like water from the new Clementine fountain, the first of several Clement was planning to make sure Orvieto would never again thirst or be strangled by an invader's siege. Already underway was the centerpiece of his papal public works, a vast and spiraling well that went all the way from Orvieto's summit fortress hundreds of feet down into the bedrock itself. St. Patrick's Well they were calling it, because of its resemblance to an Irish cave. He had conceived of it as a fearful pope worried about being trapped. Now, he saw that his fear had given birth to something else, a nascent affection, even love, for this windswept rock in the wilds north of Rome. In five short months, Orvieto had become home, more than Rome or even the beloved Florence of his gilded youth. In both those cities, encrusted with riches and religion, he had been "the Pope" or "a Medici." Here, he was just Clement. Just Giulio.

As he progressed in casual style back toward his home, Clement greeted the people crowding in to kiss his ring, touch the hem of his robes, hold up their children to be blessed, or sometimes just chat. Clement granted all requests.

The celebrations lasted late into the night. Many a besotted partyer laid sprawled, slumbering in deliciously drunken dreams, on the steps of the cathedral. Looking out over the plaza in the hours just before dawn, Clement smiled. Even the massive edifice of the Duomo now seemed prettier than he remembered it. Everything was. As he drifted off to sleep, the Tower of the Moor clock sounded five bells. In the last moments before sleep overtook him on this rarely joyous day, Clement whispered a prayer for his son. "Alessandro." Perhaps, soon, their reunion would make complete his joy. In a month, Clement was set to begin his journey back to Rome, a restoration for which he had schemed but now one not so fervently wished. My God, he thought, in his waning pre-sleep consciousness. *I walked the streets today with no guard, no retinue, with no fear.* The age of miracles, it would appear, was not yet over.

He would miss Orvieto.

CHAPTER XXXIV

Luke

Sunday evening, December 8, 2013, Orvieto

Lee asked, "How is the Bishop?"

He and Adriano jumped up from their chairs in the waiting room of Orvieto's tiny hospital.

"He'll live," Luke said simply, walking toward them through swinging doors. As he walked, he pulled off his plastic medical gloves with a military snap and tossed them into a self-sealing hospital waste bin next to the door. Through the flapping portal, Lee could just spot two sliding morgue shelves—empty and pristine—and a sign marked *EMERGENZA*. "I gave him a sedative. Don Bello is with him now. He wanted to be there when he wakes up, which, based on the dose I gave him, won't be for several hours."

"What happened?" Adriano asked.

"Alimentary mycotoxicosis."

"What's that?" Lee asked.

"Food poisoning. I had to pump his stomach," the young doctor stated evenly, then, with chilly professionalism, thrust forth his hand. "I'm Dr. Luke Schnell. You are the Americans." He stated the obvious, like reading off a medical chart. He spoke in English but with an obvious German accent and cadence, direct, clipped, to the point.

Lee heard the nuances.

They all exchanged handshakes, the first non-cheek-kissing greetings yet received in Italy, Lee realized as he took Luke's palm. The doctor's nails were meticulously trimmed and his hands smooth, and still slightly coated with powder from inside the gloves. His grip was firm but not brutal, manly, but delicate. The handshake of a surgeon, or a watchmaker. A large gold signet of some sort graced the ring finger of his right hand. Lee half expected a salute to follow. Introductions done, Luke pushed both hands back into the pockets of his impeccably white lab coat, seemingly ironed with methodical precision. The harried, panicked man who had dashed into the garden of *San Giovanale* a few hours previous was now fully in command of himself.

"Oh God, that *woman*." Adriano and Lee followed the doctor's gaze to where through the window they could see everyone's favorite blogger, Lady Peg, approaching the emergency room at a rapid jog. "She'll want episcopal gossip for her online rag. Nein. Not from me." Luke took his right hand from his pocket and motioned for Adriano and Lee to follow him. "I know a back way out of here."

Although "Jawohl" would have seemed the appropriate answer, Lee and Adriano joined Luke as he silently led them out the hospital's emergency entrance at the rear of the building and into a small garden. A grove of large walnut trees shaded the tiny parking area next to the door, their branches hanging over the cliff face just twenty yards from where patients were dropped off. Two modern and sleek ambulances sat underneath the nearest tree. Occasionally a husk dropped off one of the branches and pinged against the roof of the compact vehicles, clearly a specific design for Orvieto's medievally narrow streets. Through the dappled light of the trees, an enormous stone building with a Rapunzel-like tower could be seen on the hills about five miles away. The Capuccine Monastery. Lee remembered reading about it.

The trio wound their way along the cliff face behind the medical vans, stooping beneath several nut-laden branches in the effort. The drop down to the Rupe below wasn't as bad as it at seemed closer to the entrance. About twenty feet below the parking area for the ambulances was a well-trod footpath winding down the side of the mount. A sturdy iron gate tucked into the rock just under the ambulance car park, secured with a chain and padlock, prohibited egress from above. Lee noticed that it was topped with sharp, metal tongs. Definitely a private road for the hospital, or some vineyard or olive grove farther down the slope. If you fell from here onto the path, you'd be knocked up pretty badly but probably survive. Of course, if you rolled over from the path, the rest of the descent was a sheer drop over a hundred feet down.

Luke led them onward through light overgrowth for another several yards until he arrived at an impassable façade of bars and vines. With the practiced ease of an expert hand, he reached into the leafy mass and pushed against a gate concealed by a cascade of antique ivy and other vines. "This is where the nurses sneak out to smoke," Luke said with an obvious frown of distaste. The grate squeaked open. Once through, Luke let it drop back into place, which it did with the metallic clang of an automatic locking mechanism. They were now in a small alley. To their right was a three-story wall punctuated by balconies and arches of typically ancient construction. To their left, a sheer drop down to the road encircling the cliff. A short stone wall was the only protection against a fall. The hillside path that Lee had noticed earlier was nowhere in evidence here. Once again taking the lead, Luke walked at a brisk pace down and around to the right along the alley. A few moments later, they exited onto the street, startled by the overpowering façade of the Cathedral directly in front of them.

"You really know your way around," Lee said as he tried to get his bearings—the Duomo in front, the formal Papal Palace to the right, and now behind them the building whose alley served as their secret passage, the Hotel Maitani, proclaimed in raised, marble type over the door of its obviously luxe-but-somewhat-faded-grandeur lobby.

"Making house calls in a medieval city requires a lot of shortcuts," Luke said with a slight smile, the first non-martial response yet exhibited. "Arnaud will sleep for a long time yet and I need a break. I've done everything I can for His Eminence, the Right Reverend Archbishop of Orvieto and Todi." He recited the ecclesiastical list of titles with Germanic precision and correctness but nonetheless, Lee thought, also the slightest edge of a simmering resentment. "Let's go to Michelangelo."

They walked through the receding sunlight of the rapidly approaching winter, each day's light a little quicker to leave the sky, a little colder and dimmer in its seasonal retreat until the solstice in two weeks, the shortest day of the year. The vast plaza in front of the Duomo was almost deserted. Most people were still indoors with late afternoon chores and those stores that did open on Sundays here in this town of Catholic tradition were still shuttered from the typically Italian midday break. Both of Orvieto's clock towers were poised between the final quarter of the hour and the vertical shaft of six o'clock, the time when Orvieto woke from its afternoon naps and the town spilled into the streets to the sound of bells. Like the breath between labor pains, everything was poised on the precipice of Christmas. For a few more moments, it was an almost silent night.

"How did you find Orvieto?"

Luke broke the silence as they walked down the Via del Duomo, away from the cathedral, Hotel Maitani, and the small medical facility toward Orvieto's central artery, the Corso. As they passed, shops along the way flickered into life behind a growing nativity of seasonal window displays. By the time they got to Café Michelangelo, Orvieto's evening life had cracked open.

"A friend arranged it for us," Adriano answered. "I'm not sure how she knew about it."

"Me either." Lee chewed his lip in thought. That was a mystery. Magda, as usual, had made all the arrangements for their sabbatical but had never revealed her connections here. It was typical Magda. Efficient, deliberate, secretive. A lot of confidential numbers spun in the centrifuge of her Rolodex. It would have been lovely to see her, but right now he was glad she had not come. She would have found Lee's obsession with Deacon Andrea's suicide distasteful. "Our friend, Magda, knew someone here." She knows someone everywhere, Lee thought.

"Magda," Luke repeated the name, holding open the door of the café. "Hmmm."

Michelangelo, modern, bright, and bustling with activity, was the antithesis of Café Volsini. It was the only business in Orvieto that appeared never to close. It stayed open on Sundays, holidays, and even for a few hours on Christmas, according to a sign by the register (in the afternoon, with a tenuous nod to respectability). About twenty tables and a reading room with books and newspapers were spread out over two levels around a garden atrium. A long gleaming bar lined with tourists and workers, likely on their ways to and from an orbit of jobs supporting the town, was reflected in a mirrored ladder of shelves sporting liquors, wines, cigarettes, and pastries. A contemporary wooden sculpture of the café's namesake's most famous painting hovered over the inside of the front door: God reaching out to Adam from the Sistine Chapel. Several of the baristas wore Santa hats with bouncy white cotton balls waving from their heads. This joint was jumping.

"Couldn't get away with a mafia hit in here," Adriano whispered to Lee as they squeezed in between the crowded bar and the newspaper racks. "I wonder how La Donna feels about the competition."

Luke expertly led the trio through the crowd to a table at the rear of the café with four chairs, one already possessed by a smoothly combed silver-gray sleeping cat, the same one, evidently, that had greeted them on the day of their arrival. It looked up briefly as they sat down, then went back to its nap.

"We usually go to Café Volsini for coffee," Adriano said, settling in and gently scratching their feline tablemate behind its ears. The cat purred. "This place is quite different."

"Michelangelo is one of the oldest and most successful bars in Italy," Luke said, sitting down. "It is almost as old as Volsini. But, La Donna Volsini prefers to keep things always as they have been. Michelangelo is always changing, always expanding."

Lee was thinking the same thing. If Volsini was old Orvieto, then Michelangelo was new, if not nouveau. Both cafés had clearly been around for a while, but with one looking to the future—Lee noticed the uber-diverse clientele crammed noisily against the bar—and the other, Volsini, solidly anchored in the past.

Luke summed up their thoughts with precision. "La Donna Volsini does not like change." He raised his hand with a sharp salute and a young waitress appeared, pen and Santa bippy poised. Taking charge, Luke secured cappuccinos and cognacs for Adriano and Lee and a double espresso and schnapps for himself. They sat in silence, Luke with hands clasped in his lap, until the waitress returned with their order. When she left, Luke attempted to shoo away the cat. It looked up at him with a stubborn disregard. Luke sighed slightly and shook his head. "It is La Donna Volsini's cat. It has the run of Orvieto. I think it comes here to keep, how do you Americans say, an eye on the competition."

"The owners of Michelangelo don't mind?" Adriano asked.

"It is La Donna Volsini's cat," Luke restated, as if he had not been heard the first time. "Plus, it is a nice, if typically imperious feline. Salut." He raised his schnapps and Adriano and Lee met his toast.

They sat quietly for a while, sipping their drinks and watching the crowd. Lee couldn't help but notice that Luke seemed lost in thought, distracted. Clearly, the doctor wasn't one for idle chitchat. He sat constantly rubbing the engraved surface of his ring.

"You are German?" Lee managed finally.

"My grandfather is German," Luke answered flatly. "I came here after medical school just a few years ago." His tone implied that was as much generational detail as they were going to get. "Why do you ask?" He seemed annoyed at the question.

"Your accent," Adriano jumped in. "I studied German and you sounded a bit like my old teacher."

"You are Spanish," Luke stated.

"You can tell by my accent as well," Adriano said, grasping for amiability.

"Nien," Luke said, sipping his schnapps and slipping into his native tongue. "Don Bello told me."

Adriano translated Luke's comments for Lee.

"My goodness," Lee said with a slightly forced laugh, striving to break what seemed like a burgeoning tension. "I didn't know we were the subject of town gossip."

This time, Luke's smile was genuine. "Gossip is the engine that powers a small town and a young gay American couple arriving in the depths of non-touristy winter with the ashes of their clerical best friend in tow is lively fuel indeed. Excuse me." Luke made a slight bow and went to pay their tab.

"He's an odd duck," Adriano said, stroking La Donna Volsini's feline sentinel. "It's like he's trying to be friendly or ironic but doesn't know how. He reminds me of..."

"Magda." Lee finished his husband's thought and concurred. Both lacked possession of or an interest in social skills. They didn't ask questions. They interrogated.

"Do you think he's gay?" Adriano said.

It was usually Lee whose gaydar was on constant sweep. "He's something, but I don't think it's gay," Lee said, finishing off his coffee. Luke was at the door and motioning—rather, commanding—them to join him. "He's more nervous than a hooker in church, as my grandma used to say."

"Interesting analogy," Adriano said, giving the cat a farewell rub. "Did you see his ring?"

"Some sort of symbol."

"A very specific sort of symbol," Adriano whispered as they pushed through the crowd toward the young German doctor. "Luke is Opus Dei."

"Just like Bishop Arnaud."

Adriano nodded.

Lee thought of a scene from *Star Wars* about the Sith, minions of the Dark Side. "Always two there are, no more, no less. A master and an apprentice."

As they exited, Luke held the door, then led the way back to the hospital, his black greatcoat trailing behind him, not unlike, Lee thought, Darth Vader's cape.

CHAPTER XXXV

Brother and Sister

Sunday, December 8, 2013, late evening, Orvieto

Dawud was worried. There had been no word from his sister for weeks. And, he hadn't sold nearly enough CDs to get the money he needed. The money *she* needed.

"I'll be in Orvieto for Christmas! I don't know what it is, but I hear that Italians love it! I can't wait! We get presents, yes?"

Maryam. That was just like her. Even facing the terrors of war, and starvation and now a journey that would leave behind her entire world, she was smiling. He could hear it over the phone. Then, the line went dead.

What have I done to you, dear sister? My Maryam. She was all the family he had left. It had been his idea for her to join him here—but not yet! He wasn't ready. There was no way for her to pay for her passage. But, she had come anyway. He knew what she had done. She had sold her soul—her body—for the price of freedom. Freedom to be a slave.

And now, he didn't know where she was. Still in Libya? On the train to the port? Somewhere in one of the dusty, duplicitous hideaways of Northern African's smuggling ring? At sea? He had paid his way over a little over a year ago, in full—an obscene amount—and told his sister to wait until he had the money to send for her.

She had not listened. How could he blame her? Even here in Orvieto he heard of the news from Tripoli, from Benghazi. Their home was a bloodstained scar, a country raped and left to give birth to a festering pestilence. She had taken a chance. She could not wait. And now, she would spend the rest of her life paying for the trip, if she lived through the slavery forced upon her. Better never to get off the ship. Dawud knew the sort of "jobs" waiting for young women—girls—smuggled over by ship from Africa's corpse-ridden coast, a plastic chair outside a camper along the back roads frequented by truckers wanting a quick one. And they think we are subhuman, Dawud growled to himself. Better for her never to get off the ship.

No! He would not allow it. He would have to get to her first. He would have to get to the ship and pay for her freedom before her owners took possession first. Dawud would have to find her, but he had no idea where to look, or when.

"CDs, music for the soul," he cried out as he walked along Orvieto's chilly streets. He stood out in a crowd, black, despised, not Italian. He knew he was hated here. How could he not know? But, he was alive. If he had stayed in Libya, he'd be dead by now. They both would be dead, like their parents. He pushed their memory out of his head...for the moment. It always came back in his dreams, staccato nightmares like the machine-gun fire of reality and the smell of burning rubber tires around swollen and blood-bruised faces.

No, there was nothing to do but run, for both of them.

Allah, protect you, my sister Maryam, he prayed every night, laying down his head to the cold, cracked, and filthy linoleum floor of the deserted tenement a few blocks from Orvieto's thriving center. His home, what there was of it, with no windows and slightly but not much more of a roof, used to be a barracks for female soldiers under Mussolini. Now, it was a haven for rats, drug-dealing, illicit sex for teenagers in nearby towns come to Orvieto to escape their parental overlords, and for Dawud. The building was deserted. No one knew he lived here. Actually, no one cared. He had no friends—well, he hadn't for a year now. Andrea. The young deacon had been his friend.

Andrea, the first Christian Dawud had met who didn't want to kill him. The first Christian who didn't think Dawud was a terrorist.

A terrorist. It made Dawud laugh. Nothing could be further from the truth. He had been named for the Quran's great psalmist and singer, David as the Jewish Torah named him. He had grown into the name and became an amateur musician in Tripoli. His parents, and his sister, would come to hear him play. Then, came the war, rebels, loyalists, ISIS, it didn't matter. They all carried guns, and none of them understood God or music. And so, the family fled. Dawud and Maryam were all that was left, and a crate of CDs he had somehow managed to salvage.

He thought again of Andrea. He missed him. He wondered if Andrea would have liked the song he had written for him, the song Dawud wrote in his memory and posted online.

Andrea would never hear it now.

Andrea had spoken to him. Andrea had brought him food. Andrea has visited him, treated him like a human, not like the outcast that everyone considered him to be. Well, not everyone. Andrea's friends—Marco, the lady from Café Volsini, the old priest from *San Giovanale*—they too had been nice to him, because of Andrea, he was sure. But now, if he saw them in the Corso he would turn and hurry down another street. For a year now, he had avoided their gaze. After Andrea's...Well...after last year, Dawud couldn't bear to talk to them. Sometimes, he would find a tray of food at the foot of the stairwell leading to his squalid living quarters, and once saw La Donna Volsini and Don Bello nearby with a basket. He was sure they were doing it, out of respect for Andrea.

He sighed and walked on through Orvieto's chilly, tortuous streets. There was nothing to do now but wait. And pray.

If only he knew where to find his sister when she arrived. If only he knew who to ask. Of course, if he had the money to buy his sister's freedom, someone would present themselves to answer the question. Those who answered the questions always presented themselves. One never asked to meet them first. The answer would have to come first. Then, Dawud would be allowed to ask the question, but only if had the thing he did not have nor knew how to get. Money. He needed money, and a lot of it. Otherwise, his sister would die.

"CDs, music for the soul," Dawud called out into the darkness. No one was buying. No one was listening to the psalmist's plea.

CHAPTER XXXVI

The First Snow

Monday, December 9, 2013, 2:29 a.m., Orvieto

Lee couldn't sleep.

As he popped awake, at first he thought it was morning. The room was so bright. The skylight glowed as if lit by a foggy dawn in San Francisco, light as if seen through a glass darkly.

Snow! The skylight was covered in an inch of newly fallen flakes and the quarter moon was lighting it from above like a celestial scrim.

Lee turned to wake Adriano but thought better of it. His husband loved snow but Adriano was not the happiest of morning people. Being awoken this early would ensure a grumpy day. It was very cold and the snow seemed to be coming down in a steady and even clip. In a few hours, the Tower of the Moor would peal five bells, late enough to wake Adriano and early enough to ensure the snow was still virginal enough for a photo shoot. Adriano would undoubtedly want to document their wintry Italian wonderland.

Had they only arrived a week ago?

Lee turned over and tried to dive back into sleep but by now his mind was awhirl with a cacophony of thoughts and images. Andrea's suicide. His mother's letter to the Pope. The inscription on the back of Reverend Vicky's pectoral cross—"01.03.83"—the same date on the photo in the dining room of St. Paul's Inside the Walls in Rome. And the photo, a young, vibrant, and very pretty Vicky with two young priests, one of whom Lee was sure was the former bishop of Orvieto, Gio, and the other, frowning, clearly the same Bishop Arnaud now resting in hospital following a mysterious bout of food poisoning. Lee fluffed the pillow and renewed his attempt at sleep, but images kept sweeping over his brain. Luke's strange scuffle with the muscly leather boy last week in *Sant'Andrea*. Who was he? Lee knew he had seen him before, somewhere, he was sure of it. It was no use. There would be no more sleep tonight. He peered over at his husband, breathing softly and evenly in the depths of deepest sleep. He was smiling in slumber like a beautiful baby. Lee kissed him gently on the forehead and got quietly out of bed. No need to worry. Adriano could sleep through an earthquake—and had. Nothing short of *Sensurround* could rouse him when he was this far gone.

Lee tiptoed to the front room, carefully avoiding the sloping roof in the hall, no mean feat in the predawn darkness. What he wouldn't have given to have a balcony just now. The view of Orvieto would have been spectacular. According to Marco, just on the other side of this wall was another apartment, empty and with higher, nonconcussion-threatening ceilings, whose views of the city were epic. Oh well, this place was pretty great, and Lee was not one to complain, although, he was one to dream.

The living room skylight repeated the effect of the one from the bedroom. Its frosty pane was punctuated by the faintest sounds of gathering snowflakes against the glass. The red battery flame of Brian's Padre Pio vigil candle flickered against his ashes. Lee blew a kiss toward his friend. The quiet was complete. Everything seemed frozen in time. He wanted to be out in the snow. Quickly, Lee grabbed a sheet of paper on which he'd been working out crossword clues. The back was blank. *2:30 a.m. Walking in the snow. Didn't want to wake you. Back in 30 minutes. Xxxooo, me.* He scribbled the note quickly and taped it to the top of Adriano's laptop. He threw on two pairs of sweatpants, a gray "San Francisco" hoodie, grabbed a scarf and gloves, and headed out into the frigid streets of Orvieto.

The town had become a fairy tale kingdom, even more so than usual. The only sound was the atom by atom plop of each snowflake falling into place on top of each of its confederates, a silent invasion.

"Prrrrrrrrrrrr, prrrrrrrr."

Lee looked down to see a large gray feline, vibrating like an idling Fiat at his feet. La Donna Volsini's cat. It wove its way between Lee's legs several times. Then with a deliberate but otherwise uncaring upward glance trotted away toward the arch into the Plaza de Republica that separated the northern and southern parts of the town. The cat's delicate paw prints were the only adulteration of the landscape, and even those were quickly filling up with falling snow.

Lee followed.

Once through the arch, the Church of Sant'Andrea became visible to the right, its simple medieval grayness now dripping with snowy accents like an oversize gingerbread house. The windows of the mayor's office that straddled the arch on Orvieto's axis—*il sindaco*—were festooned as if in white bunting, ready for an Evita-like greeting by the snow queen and her court. The octagonal bell tower, adorned with centuries' worth of coats of arms, each now with frozen highlights, stood taller and more imposing than usual. Everything looked majestic in the snow, like a stage set or a tiny village whose roofs were adorned with glued-on cotton balls beneath a Christmas tree. Lee suddenly wondered if the handmade holiday villages of his childhood had grown large to envelop him or rather if he, in a kind of Lewisean dream, had somehow grown miraculously small and stumbled accidentally into his own secret Narnia.

La Donna Volsini's cat had disappeared, but the paw prints remained, meandering out of the empty and moonlit plaza toward *San Giovanale*.

Lee followed.

Five minutes later, Lee found himself at the garden beside *San Giovanale*, the spot where Andrea jumped. His feline guide found a dry spot next to the overhang of the ancient bell tower. With a look as if to say, "You're on your own now," the imperious feline curled its tail around itself, fluttered its eyelids twice, and fell asleep to await the dawn.

Lee walked to the edge of the rock.

The snow fell upon his shoulders.

He stood on the cliff and prayed.

Useless, he thought, to turn my thoughts to God.

Behind him, the lights of Orvieto reflected in a million icy crystals. It brought back memories—dark ones.

The water of the Bay would be cold, he had thought. He wondered who would find him. Someone would, of course, and for that he was sorry. What a horrible thing to see, to discover, the body of a reprobate, crushed against the rocks and never to see forgiveness. Never to see the face of God. Never to see tomorrow's sunrise.

It should be beautiful, and he had smiled. He had often walked here, across the famous span, to watch the dawn. Tomorrow, its rays would reach out to warm San Francisco and drive away the forgiving and scar-hiding fog. Like a miracle it had seemed to Lee, from his first day in the city, the finger of fog poking through the Golden Gate and making Mount Tam and the Transamerica Pyramid look like islands awash in a churning tide.

No more. No more dawns, no more rainbows, no more miracles.

He looked over at the Vista Point in the Marin Headlands. A gazillion times over the last few months, Lee had planned the photo he would take there of all them, mother, father, grandmother, and himself. He had biked over one day to find the perfect spot and timed it for the exact moment when San Francisco would be ideally lit by the afternoon sun.

A bicyclist zoomed by. Lee looked up and down the walk. There was no one else around. Good. It would be rude to have someone see him jump. Lee's grandmother had always said that politeness was the most important thing. It was early morning. There were few people on the bridge yet.

Across the Bay, the sun eased its way into the sky above Mount Diablo. Lee looked at his iPhone. It was 6:35 a.m. Dawn. Just a few minutes now. He had timed it perfectly. He would jump at precisely 6:37 a.m. here in San Francisco—the exact moment his family had died. In another city. On another coast. All together, dead in an instant, an instant of horrible, unimaginable terror. They had been en route to him for a three-month visit that would never happen now. Today, they would all have been celebrating Lee's eighteenth birthday, together.

Lee climbed onto the railing. He'd been so tired, and empty. With one step, all the bad dreams would go away. All the pain, all the confusion, all the memories. All the hate. Everything would just stop. That would be nice.

Lee just wanted everything to stop. His brain was a smoldering ruin, like the charred grave in Virginia shared by his parents and his grandmother.

And, now, Lee would join them.

"Don't!"

Lee had stopped, turned, and seen Brian running down the bridge path toward him. Brian had kept him from jumping. Brian had saved his life.

Lee shivered against the cold and the memory and looked out over Umbria, hidden in clouds of snowy mist. It would have looked like this a year ago, Lee thought. This would have been the final thing Andrea would have seen before he died.

Both of us, standing at the abyss. Andrea not able to face a life not dedicated to God. Me, not able to face that I no longer believed in one. The Church had driven Andrea to the cliff. God, or proof that he never existed, had pushed me to the rail.

"*Prrrrrrrrrrr, prrrrrrrr.*"

Lee looked down. La Donna Volsini's cat had returned, rubbing its silken flanks against Lee's calves. Behind him, a snowy but quickly filling path of paw prints led the way back to the center of town; to the apartment; to the bed where his lover awaited. Adriano. Lee had so much to live for.

He knew, however, the feeling of wanting to die. He, too, had stood on a cliff like Andrea. He, too, had just wanted it all to end, to make it all stop. Brian had pulled him back from the edge. Lee would never forget. A month later, Lee had gone to sea. Two years later, he had met Adriano.

Andrea had not been so lucky. No one had pulled him back. Andrea had jumped, and Lee understood the feeling completely.

"Hey, honey."

Lee turned to find Adriano, smiling and holding a snowball.

The couple held hands there on the edge, turning their faces upward to catch the parachuting flakes. After a few silent moments, they kissed, smiled, and turned to walk home hand in hand.

The cat followed, three sets of footprints in the falling snow.

Part II

CHAPTER XXXVII

Excavation

Tuesday, December 17, 2013, Orvieto

By the end of their second week in Orvieto, Adriano and Lee had become locals, or at least liked to think that they had, especially Lee.

They awoke to the bells of the Tower of the Moor and merchants called out their names when they entered markets. La Donna Volsini's cat followed them everywhere. The pert young blonde owner of what passed for a local gym had shown Adriano where she hid the key so he could let himself in. Lee, who thought the idea of paid exercise on sabbatical was defeating the purpose, eschewed such machinations for morning walks along the cliffs between *Il Duomo* and *San Giovanale*. Again and again he walked to the edge of the cliff where Andrea had stood just over a year ago, twins separated by geography but united in spirit. Lee's nightstand had become a groaning board of press clippings about the deacon's suicide, Bishop Sancarlo's forced resignation, and the subsequent exile of Reverend Vicky. Adriano said nothing, but quietly did his own online research, admitting to himself—if not to his husband—a growing fascination with the subject. Lee pretended not to notice.

After their respective morning meanderings, they met up at Café Volsini—usually Lee arriving first—for coffee and a different *dolcini* every day. Lee was determined to sample every one of the delectable bites that spread toward infinity in the glass-and-marble display case. On their third visit, the café's sturdily built doyenne had approached their corner table with a two-day-old copy of the *International Herald Tribune*, folded to the crossword, a pen carefully clipped to the edge.

"Here," she said. "For you."

"Grazie," Lee offered with surprise as she turned away.

Adriano sipped his cappuccino and smiled. "She likes you," he whispered.

Undoubtedly better than the alternative, Lee had thought, watching the elderly owner return to her perch behind the cash register. The photo of Deacon Andrea was still there, but its wax candle sentinel had been replaced with one of the ubiquitous battery-powered Padre Pio flames like the one in front of Brian's ashes.

That had been four days ago. Now, by the time Lee's hand triggered the tiny bell on the café's front door, he could already spy at what he now considered to be "his spot," the intellectual stimulation of an aging but virginal acrostic and a powdered-sugar-dusted plate bearing a pistachio creme cannoli.

The Godfather music again played in Lee's head.

"Buongiorno!" Lee called out with a tip of his Star Fleet Academy baseball hat to tinkling accompaniment, squeezing past the bundled-up local postman, likewise touching the brim of his hat as he headed out on his morning rounds. It was especially cold today. One week until Christmas.

La Donna Volsini looked up—was that the rapid flicker of a smile as Lee entered, or just a twitching lip?—then returned to her pile of receipts. Behind the bar, the morning barista, a delicately pretty girl of about sixteen, looked up with a quietly mouthed "Ciao" as the ancient and elaborate espresso machine whirred into action with Lee's caffeine fix.

From the back room, Lee could hear boxes being moved about and the low-volume music of a transistor radio turned to a Roman pop station. He noticed a small cloud of flour dust hanging, suspended, in the mottled sunlight that curtained the arch between the front and back rooms of the bar.

Lee sat down, taking off his hat, gloves, and scarf and carefully laying them on the chair next to him as the barista placed the coffee in front of him. He started to unwrap the newspaper, but stopped, feeling as if he were being watched. Looking up, he found La Donna Volsini positively staring at him. Putting down the crossword, Lee took a deep breath, and bit into the proffered pastry. La Donna Volsini watched every bite as if through opera glasses.

The flaky sweetness blossomed across Lee's face in an explosion of frothy whipped foam while chopped pistachio crumbs rained onto his newspaper and shirt.

It was the most delicious cannoli in the history of civilization.

"Ol mao *Gawd*!" Lee moaned through cream filled lips. He felt like a human Twinkie. "Delicioso!"

This time, there was no doubt. La Donna Volsini was smiling. With a satisfied nod, she went back to her accounting and left Lee to his morning ritual.

He was well into solving his *Herald Tribune* puzzle when the door chime again rattled with Adriano's crossing of the threshold, preceded by steamy breaths and La Donna Volsini's cat, who instantly jumped onto the chair next to him.

"Buongiorno, Signora Volsini! Come stai questa bella mattina?"

"Ciao, Signor Coráno," La Donna replied with genuine enthusiasm as she pushed herself up from her chair and ambled toward the bar with something approaching enthusiastic rapidity. "Motto bene. Fa freddo, no? Mi permetta di ottenere il vostro caffè e qualcosa di speciale per scaldarsi."

"Grazie mille, Signora."

Lee just stared at his husband in mock scowl.

"Is there any language you don't speak?"

"My Serbio-Croatian is not terrific."

"Show off."

"You have frosting all over your lips and your breakfast is being pilfered by a cat."

Lee looked over quickly to see his pastry-mustached visage in the mirror behind the bar and Madame Volsini's cat carefully licking pistachio crème from a now empty cannoli shell.

"Si, scacciare gatto birichino! Che non è per voi!" La Donna Volsini shooed away the cat but chuckled as she did so. The feline departed with an emphatic flick of her tail, as clear as any middle finger. "She the boss." La Donna Volsini sighed, switching to broken English. "I only live here. She let me feed her and she like my cannoli." Next to Adriano's dry cappuccino she placed two delicate crystal cordial glasses, brimming with a clear liquor. "Drink this with coffee. Good for cold day." And with an efficiently satisfied nod she returned to her station by the door.

"Caffè corretto," Adriano said with a melancholy smile. He held the glass up to his nose for a second, then poured about a third directly into his coffee.

"Sounds like a crossword clue I should know," Lee said, mimicking his partner and taking the aroma into his nose before taking a sip. "Tastes like grappa."

"It is grappa," Adriano said, his grin punctuated by an ever-so-slight glistening of the eye. "Caffè corretto is what Italians call this. Literally, corrected coffee. You can use brandy or saltimbucco, too, but grappa is the most authentic. My grandfather had it every morning until the day he died."

Lee just sat.

"You know, that's how I learned my Italian," Adriano continued.

He didn't speak of his family much. Lee wasn't about to interrupt. "My grandparents on both sides fled Franco after the Spanish Civil War, to Venezuela, although they didn't know each other at the time. It was a pretty common escape route, but expensive. Evidently the ship was some horrible old prewar relic from Greece. Anyway, my mother's father—"

"The caffè corretto guy," Lee prodded.

"Yes. He loved everything about Italy, especially its ancient Etruscan and Roman history, but was fiercely Spanish." Adriano smiled. "He settled in the Italian section of Caracas. I learned to swim at the Italian social club. I practically grew up there. My two grandfathers met there, trading war stories and smoking strong Venezuelan tobacco. I can smell it now. They all played escala cuarenta—a popular card game from Italy. They hung out with a group of Italian expats, anti-Mussolini soldiers who ended up in Spain during the war, also fighting the Fascists. God, the stories they would tell. My parents met there too, as kids. Their wedding was all around the pool."

At the mention of his parents, Adriano's visage changed and his jaw tightened. He finished off the remaining grappa in his cup at a gulp. Case closed.

At voluntary risk, Lee ventured a bit further over the conversational barbed wire into the no-man's-land of his husband's family. "Your parents named you for your paternal granddad, then?"

"Yes, with an extra vowel." A bit of his husband's smile returned. "My grandfather was Adrien—for Hadrian, the Roman emperor born on the Iberian Peninsula. He thought my name was the perfect blending of both the cultures he loved. After my grandmother died, he returned to Spain. He wanted to die in his own land—immigrant to the core. 'One day you will visit Rome and see all the pagan temples that I never got to see,' he told me before he died. 'And, you can spit on the Vatican for me.' At this, Adriano laughed, a dark and mirthless grunt. "He hated the Catholic Church. Franco used it to divide Spain and my parents used it to divide my family. He was horrified at my mother's religiosity. Didn't understand what happened to his daughter at all."

"So your grandfather taught you Italian?"

"Mi abuelo? Not really, although Spaniards and Italians understand each other well enough. The languages are similar. You know that from your Latin. He only spoke Spanish and the language of cards with his buddies. I watched them play and I also listened. I picked up my Italian from a bunch of Italian Communists far away from their homeland. My grandfather only saw two countries in his life, Spain and Venezuela. One he fled to escape the Fascists. The other he fled to escape his children and the Church. I travel for him and learn as many languages as I can for him. Salud, mi abuelo di mi corozan."

At that, Adriano reached over and finished his husband's grappa as well with a tiny tip of the glass.

They sat for a bit in silence: Lee noodling over his crossword, or pretending to, Adriano reading the two-day-old European news wrap of the *Herald Tribune*. Madame Volsini had disappeared into the kitchen, obviously at work on another carbohydrate bomb of delicious decadency.

"Bongiorno!" Don Bello burst in with a simultaneous symphony of bells. Everyone looked up and spoke greetings, even the cat. "Ah, I see La

Donna is warming up to our newest Orvietani." The elderly cleric sat down next to Adriano and Lee as the barista prepared his coffee.

"What do you mean?" Lee asked.

"The crossword," Don Bello said with a sad smile and a bit of a sigh, tapping the newspaper with his finger. "She saved them for Andrea too. He loved to sit here and work them out. We'd do them together. He was a fanatic about figuring out a puzzle. Quite good at it, actually. Shhh, here she comes. Brrrrr. It's a cold one this morning. Grazie, La Donna Volsini, grazie mille!"

Don Bello pulled on a smile, but nonetheless one of genuine affection, as La Donna Volsini placed a cappuccino with a side of grappa next to the Pastor of *San Giovanale*. Over her shoulder, Lee could see a well-formed and muscular arm handing up bags of flour from a hidden hatch in the floor of the kitchen beyond. A culinary miasma of dough and cinnamon wafted heavy in the air as each bag hit the tile with a cloudy announcement. Lee's nose twitched with a memory. That smell was so familiar. Where had he experienced that scent before? It was almost too sweet for cooking, more like... Lee was pulled from his olfactory reverie by Adriano's foot on his shoe, redirecting him to Adriano and Don Bello's conversation.

"I'm sorry," Lee said. "I was distracted. What did you say?"

"The Presepe." Don Bello was positively puckish with enthusiasm. "It's the biggest thing at *San Giovanale* all year. Can I count on your help?"

"Of course," Adriano answered for them both, giving his husband a playful "pay attention" look. "We'd be honored."

"What's a Presepe?"

"A living Nativity," said Adriano, jumping in. "It's almost the same word in Spanish: *presipio*. Remember, Marco mentioned it the other day when we were having drinks."

"Exactly right," said Don Bello. "A real-life reproduction of the Holy Family reenacting the first Christmas, complete with sheep and goats, the Three Kings—"

"We used to do this at my church back in Virginia!" Lee exclaimed. "I was Baby Jesus!"

"Of course, you were." Adriano rolled his eyes.

"The newest baby in the parish got to have their picture taken in the manger on Christmas Eve. I've still got that picture somewhere. Whenever I got a bit full of myself, Mama would say, 'You played the Son of God when you were a month old and you never got over it.'"

"Could explain a lot," Adriano offered drolly.

"So, you want us to play Joseph or one of the Wise Men?" Lee could already envision his costume.

"No, dear boy. Not to disappoint you but we have our cast, as you say. I need help building the stable and the village. We're a little behind this year. Andrea always organized the Presepe and recruited volunteers and oversaw everything, starting around the first of December, but, well, of course—"

"We'd love to help," Adriano jumped in, with Lee nodding enthusiastically.

"Of course. Anything you want."

"Splendid! That's wonderful! Everyone gathers this Thursday in the garden at *San Giovanale*. Make sure to wear old clothes and boots. There will be a lot of lifting and toting as they say. The preparation is almost as fun as the Presepe itself, and we'll have lots of mulled wine for our army of helpers. All the young men in the town turn out to help." Don Bello clapped his hands, looking like an elf who just sent off the first FedEx of Christmas. "Ah, perfect timing! Here's one of our helpers now!"

The trio turned to see a vision of maleness emerging from the hatch door in the kitchen floor. Venus in jeans, lit from behind with a halo of sunlight, the intoxicating youth was bursting out of a work shirt, struggling to contain his almost comically precise musculature.

"Lee. Adriano. This is Grigori."

The leather boy from *Sant'Andrea*. The Swiss Guard from Rome,

"Ciao."

CHAPTER XXXVIII

Brave New World

Wednesday, December 18, 2013, Orvieto

Bishop Arnaud sat at his desk in front of an overflowing bowl of tobacco corpses. Luke had warned him sternly against smoking after he was released from the hospital last week. *Stupid ass. It wasn't smoking that poisoned my bread. Oh yes, I know who my enemies are. There will be a time for you, old woman.* The foundations of Café Volsini may have stood for a millennium, but nothing was eternal. He'd have his vengeance on the crazy bitch. Of course, he had to admire her. She was relentless. If she'd meant to kill him, she would have. She just meant to remind him that she was still there, that she remembered.

She blames me for the loss of her beloved Andrea, he thought, blowing smoke with bored casualness. What else was new?

He viciously lit another cigarette from one still left burning in the tray. Two others had not yet been stamped out completely and were threatening to once again ignite like a toxic thurible of incense. With shaking hands, he dragged the fumes deep into his lungs and put on his reading glasses. If only La Donna Volsini had really killed him, at least this would all be over. This cross was too much for him to bear, not at his age. Not with what he'd already seen. Perhaps, something would change this time. He dared to read the article again.

Mysterious "ghost ship" carrying
900 migrants arrives in Italy

Wednesday, 18 December 2013 (AKI)—Gallipoli, Italy: Almost 900 immigrants landed in Italy yesterday. The 150-foot-long ship *Fatima* had been spotted in international waters during the night. Evidently abandoned by its crew of human traffickers a few days after sailing from an as yet still unidentified port, the vessel was set on autopilot and aimed toward the Italian coast.

"When my men tried to draw alongside they were shocked to see people dangling babies and small children over the side," said Captain Francesco Marconi of the Italian Navy. "They told rescue sailors not to come any closer or they would let go. I have never seen anything like it. They would rather take the chance of their babies being picked up from the waves than having them return to where they came from. They only calmed down and let us on board when we assured them they were in Italian waters and they would not be returned to their departure port."

While many of the refugees were Muslim, themselves fleeing Islamic extremists in Libya, also represented were a number of Christians and Jews escaping the escalating chaos of the Syrian civil war. Italy's long coastline makes it one of the EU's main targets for migrants fleeing unrest in their home countries. The *Fatima*, with over 600 adults and 361 children, was the largest single arrival for nearly five years.

Yes, Arnaud thought, but there's only *one* passenger aboard that ship I'm interested in. He wondered what part of his priestly vows had prepared him for this. Which priestly vows were being *destroyed* because of this. He kept reading.

European border officials believe that such "ghost ships" are part of a new tactic by the trafficking gangs. They buy the boats on the black market and then simply abandon them once they are close to European shores or, in this case, even sooner, by setting the ships on autopilot. Typically, ship owners and crews are contacted in Turkey by human traffickers who post notices on social media (Facebook, Twitter, etc.) offering secret passage to Europe. Each refugee pays between $500–$2000 US for the perilous passage. Fees paid to the ship's captains vary, although typically are in the range of $15,000 US. After they have received their money, the human smugglers lock their passengers in abandoned buildings by the ports, sometimes for days, with only stale bread to eat and questionable water to drink. Under cover of darkness, the pitiful band of migrants are then herded at gunpoint out to the beach and from there onto waiting ships or small boats.

Two months ago, a ship from Libya crammed with more than 500 people sank just off the Italian coast with the loss of 368 lives. A video broadcast widely around the internet shows bodies tangled among the sunken wreckage, including one especially poignant shot of two people clutching each other.

According to reports from the Italian Interior Ministry, though most refugees commonly come from sub-Saharan Africa and the continuing unrest in Libya, this year many are fleeing the Syrian civil war or political turmoil in Egypt and other parts of North Africa. Almost 9,000 migrants reached Italy by boat between July 1 and August 10 of this year, according to Ministry sources. In the 12 months up to August 10, more than 24,000 came, compared with more than 17,000 in the same period a year earlier, and almost 25,000 in the 12 months before that.

"Why do they have to come here," said one unidentified woman watching the refugees debark in Gallipoli. 'These people are full of disease. What if they bring Ebola to Europe? What if they are terrorists? This is the perfect way for al Qaeda or the Islamic State to invade us. I'm sorry their life is hard, but my life is hard too. Send them back or let them drown."

A United Nations report published in June announced that worldwide in 2013, a record number of people—51.2 million, half of them children—had been forcibly displaced by conflict or persecution. The Syrian civil war alone has forced 2.5 million to flee abroad. The majority— 33.3 million—are internally displaced in their own countries. Once they arrive in Europe, they are subject to a shadowy and duplicitous network of modern-day slavers and underworld gangs who coerce them into lives of criminal servitude.

We're all living lives of forced servitude, Arnaud thought. He spat out a piece of tobacco from his cigarette. *Everyone's a slave. Especially me, with many masters.* And now, the ship was *here.* She was *here* and he wasn't yet ready. Who was he kidding? He would never be ready for the mission he had been given. This was a filthy business. Arnaud knew it. The men, they would work—they would survive. But...

...for the women, it is worse: sold into lives of squalid prostitution and forced to work along the roads north of Rome as entertainment for truckers and drug dealers. The forests of Umbria and Lazio are full of their unmarked graves. When they are worn out, their pimps discard them like used toilet paper.

The knock on the door startled Arnaud.

"Shit!" The knock on the door startled Arnaud, and the cigarette tumbled from his mouth onto the open paper. He stamped out the embers with the end of a crucifix paper weight and brushed the butt onto the floor. "Who is it?"

The door swung open to a darkened hall and an even darker face.

"Have you brought the money?"

"Yes, Bishop—"

"Your *Eminence.*"

"Yes, Your Immensus"—the man in the door struggled with the word—"I have it. I had to be—"

"I don't care how you got it. I have another job for you." The Bishop motioned for his guest to hand over what he had brought. Arnaud shoved a small index card across the desk as an envelope bulging with euros passed it along the smooth, polished wood. Quid pro quo. The Bishop didn't open it to count. He knew it would all be there. The prospect of it not being enough was too horrible for his servant to contemplate. The Bishop knew that the man standing in front of him was honest—a heathen—but honest. That, plus his terror, made him the perfect messenger. "Read that and give it back."

Dawud read, then handed back the card.

"You understand, Dawud?" Arnaud's eyes were steely with confirmation.

"Yes, Your Immin, Your immo—yes, Bishop. I understand."

"Good."

Arnaud lit a match, ignited the edge of the paper, watched it burn, then dropped it flaming into his ash tray.

"You may go now."

The immigrant got up to leave.

"Aren't you forgetting something, Dawud?"

Dawud stopped. He turned from the door. He dropped to his knees. He took the Archbishop's ring in his hands and kissed it as he had been taught. His lips had barely touched the gold purple amethyst before Arnaud pulled away as if having touched something disgusting.

"Go. Your sister is waiting."

CHAPTER XXXIX

Time to Say Goodbye

May 27, 1528 (Julian Calendar), Orvieto

"It is time, Your Holiness."

Pope Clement didn't move. He sat at the open window of the Papal Palace overlooking the plaza, where a battalion of artisans and stone cutters were busily at work on the increasingly luminous facade of the Cathedral. In the last six months, all of Orvieto seemed to have returned to employment. The viaduct had been restored, and water once again flowed freely into the city. An even larger well would ensure the city's future for decades, if not longer. The decay that had greeted Clement barely half a year previous had been driven away by papal authority and the munificence of his Jewish banker—his friend—Moses de Blanis.

An unusually warm breeze blew against the Pontiff's cape, dislodging a small piece of peacock feather from the ceremonial collar. It floated briefly in the air and then wafted down onto the table next to a pair of pearl-clasp gloves, scented with lavender from the Umbrian hills. Nearby on a stand rested a newly constructed papal tiara, a gift from Moses to replace the one hocked just after the Sack of Rome when nothing was of value yet everything for sale.

"Holy Father." Gio, the young Swiss guard, called out again.

The Pope did not respond.

Quietly, Gio walked across the room and laid both his hands gently on the Pope's shoulders.

As quickly as a trap snapping shut on its prey, Clement reached back with his right hand to squeeze that of his friend. He turned and looked up into Gio's eyes. "I'm afraid, Gio. I don't want to leave."

Gio walked around to face Clement, then dropped to his knee, kissing the papal ring, by now an act marked more by affection than hierarchy. "You must, Holy Father. The people are waiting for you. *Rome* is waiting for you."

"Ha!" Clement laughed gently and bade his friend to rise and sit next to him. "Rome is only waiting for me to return so they can spit upon me, or worse. They'll have to wait a little longer. First, we join good Cardinal Egidio in Viterbo. A few months there will help us better gauge the mood in Rome, and whether or not it's truly safe to return to the Vatican. Have you decided?"

Gio looked up as if surprised by the question. "My decision was made that day that I took my oath as a Swiss Guard. I serve my pope. I go where he goes."

"And Sofia?"

"She will stay here in the house of de Blanis." Gio paused for a moment. "Until the baby is born. The roads between here and Rome are not safe for an expectant mother. She is better off here with her father. I will return once you are safely re-ensconced in St. Peters."

Clement exhaled deeply, then took Gio's chin in his hands as he did the first night they met. Smiling, he quietly uttered only one word. "No."

"But Holy Father, you—"

"No!" Clement was up in an instant with such rage that Gio again dropped to his knees. "Too many people have died to defend this Church, to defend this pope. One hundred forty-six of your comrades in the Swiss Guard died so that I might live, almost exactly a year ago, including your best friend."

"You are my best friend," Gio said quietly, rising to face Clement.

"My son." Clement fell to his knees in front of the young guard, weeping uncontrollably. "I am not worthy of such friendship. I have lost one son, I cannot bear to lose another."

Gio joined him on the stone floor, holding the heaving shoulders of the man to whom all Europe's monarchs must bow. After a while, the weeping stopped.

Clement wiped his eyes and repeated quietly, "No," then added, "I command it. What God hath joined together let no man put asunder—popes included. I married you and Sofia in the sight of God and his witnesses, Hassan, Cardinal Egidio, and Sofia's father. Yes, you are my friend, my son, and always will be. But now, more importantly, you are a man, a husband, a father. I relieve you, my Knight of the Golden Spur. Go in peace."

Gio rose slowly, helping his Pontiff to his feet as well. Then, with a smile tinged by tears, he said, "So shall it be written; so shall it be done."

"Yes," said Clement, returning the smile. "So shall it be written; so shall it be done." Then he said in a lighter tone, "Go. You can see me off to the turn in the road toward Bolsena, but no more. Then, you will return here to Orvieto, to your family, to *my* family, for never have I felt so welcomed since the days of my Medici youth in Florence."

"As you wish, Holy Father."

The melancholy reverie was interrupted by a knock at the door.

"Enter all who love and serve the Lord," said the Pope, no longer constrained by safety-concerned pass codes. "Moses!" And the Pope embraced his friend.

"Father." Gio smiled. "I will leave you two together. I need to speak with Sofia and tell her that I will be tonight in Bolsena, but, then I will be returning here to Orvieto."

With a slight bow, he embraced both men and exited, quietly pulling the door closed behind him.

"My dear Moses, I didn't expect to see you again today," said Clement, motioning for Orvieto's richest citizen to sit next to him. "We said our farewells at dinner last night, as usual, an epicurean orgy prepared at your home. You do me a double honor but I cannot say I am sad to see you again. I will miss you, dear friend. Without you, my Papacy would already be over, and likely, my life. I have many debts to repay."

"But not to me," said Moses. "Your account is balanced, and your debt paid in full. No, no—" Moses motioned for Clement to be silent. "Your collateral is your life, and more importantly, your legacy. I understand from Wazzan that you have commissioned Cardinal Egidio to write a new book, a book on the meeting of the Jewish Cabala and Catholic mysticism. He tells me it is to be called *Schechina*."

"As usual, not from the Curia nor from his friends, a pope has no secrets." Clement chuckled. "Yes, I have indeed asked Egidio to put to parchment that which his life is so clearly devoted, a love and respect for the study of the divine in *all* faiths."

"He is, then, a true Catholic," replied Moses. "I like the title. Was that your idea?"

"I thought you would. *Schechina*. The divine presence of God and his cosmic glory. Hebrew is a beautiful language."

"As is Latin, Holy Father."

"As beautiful as is ugly, lately, English and German." The Pope sighed, motioning to two large leather satchels poised by the door, ready for the journey. "There, my dear Moses, are pages and pages of the ugliest words of my papacy. One from a king who first begged to be married to his brother's widow and now wants to end said wedlock, the other, the theses of a mad Saxon priest who thinks God has spoken through him. Christ on a stick. Henry the Eighth and Martin Luther will be the death of me. More the point, they will be the death of the Roman Catholic Church."

"Now, now, Giulio, this too will pass."

"No." Clement smiled, suddenly picking up his gloves and buttoning them delicately about his wrists. "No, this divorce petition from the English King so that he can wed Anne Boleyn and this so-called Reformation will not pass. Both issues will grow, flourish, and, I am afraid, merge into one great large protestant movement destined to end the Church as I know it, but...who knows, perhaps something greater will come along. But, thankfully, I will not live to see it."

"You have become philosophical since arriving in Orvieto."

"The Sack of Rome will do that to a man."

At this, they both laughed.

"What will you do now?" Moses queried. "Officially, Henry the Eighth and King Francis of France are allied in warfare against the Emperor

Charles. Perhaps they will prevail. Perhaps you will regain the Papal States, and even increase them."

"I think not, dear friend, but for once, I am not worried about it. I am more interested in finding common ground and common divinity between faiths than in negotiating treaties between earthly princes. War will go on. I cannot end it, no pope can. But I can encourage others to think and to write. As much as it will be Egidio's legacy, I hope this Schechina will be mine. Plus, I hear that Michelangelo might be tempted back to Rome once things are safe on the roads from Florence. Who knows, maybe I'll have him do something to that water-stained wall at the far end of the Sistine Chapel. His ceiling cries out for a suitable frame."

"And your son." Moses spoke quietly. "What of Alessandro?"

"Safe, but safer not with me." Clement sighed. "One day, perhaps, he will take his place as the leader of Florence like the Medici before him. But, for now, Florence wants nothing of the Medici, certainly not my son. I love him too much to bring him to me. He is safer without a father, Holy or otherwise."

"You will be lonely without Alessandro, without Gio."

"When I return to Rome, I will have my young great niece Catherine to keep me company," said Clement. "She's a strange, lonely child, orphaned, abandoned by everyone, forced to flee her home in front of an angry and ignorant mob. We have a lot in common, this little waif Catherine de Medici and I. Lucky for her, she's safely at a convent for the moment. You see, everyone in my family is forced to flee because of the failing of their bastard relative, Giulio de Medici, Pope Clement the Seventh." With that the Pontiff made a theatrical bow.

"Your flare for the dramatic could have led to a life on the stage," offered Moses.

"That's all the Papacy is," retorted Clement, "a stage. But now, enough. You and I both are clearly delaying a goodbye neither of us wants to make, unless I am greatly mistaken. I have come to love Orvieto, and as long as I am here, all Jews are safe, if not beloved, though I wish I could accomplish both. I shudder to think, sometimes, what my Christian brothers and sisters may do to the tribe of Judah without sufficient protection."

"Do not worry, noble Medici," said Moses. "We have survived the plague of rats and Christian princes. I imagine we can survive a few more popes."

"Well, don't rush me to the grave yet. I'll be around for a while. Plus, if anyone, any Catholic enemy, should ever trespass across your threshold in aggression, show them the coat of arms I gave you. Few Catholics, no matter how much they hate Jews or Medici, would desecrate a home bearing the Papal Crest."

"It didn't help you when Charles sacked the Vatican," Moses teased back.

"You have a point, dear friend," said the Pope with a sigh. "An unwelcomed one, but a point nonetheless. Let's hope it works better for you."

"I certainly hope so, Your Holiness," said de Blanis with a mysterious smile. "But, before you return to the Throne of St. Peter at the Vatican, Orvieto has one more surprise for you. I have something to show you."

Clement grabbed his friend strongly, but affectionately by the arm. "Now, you show me a surprise? What, it slipped your mind over the last several months?"

"Wear this," said the physician turned banker, tossing a tattered cape to the Pontiff. "Also, you'll need this," he said and handed him a small torch hanging in a sconce at the side of the door. Then de Blanis motioned for his friend to follow him.

"Where are you going? The entrance to the Duomo is this way," said Clement, stepping into the hall outside his chambers. "This part of the Papal Palace is still abandoned. It's been shut up since the time of Pope Martin the Fourth."

"Longer than that. This is part of the expansion begun by Urban the Fourth. Watch your step." De Blanis continued along the darkened abandoned passage for about a hundred yards until they came to a stone wall covered by a moth-eaten tapestry depicting the crucifixion. Pulling it aside, Moses revealed a large wooden door, old, but clearly well maintained. Reaching into his cloak, de Blanis withdrew two heavy and obviously ancient keys, one gold, one silver. Clement's eyes grew large recognizing the unmistakable duo, each with a locking mechanism in the shape of a cross and embossed with the papal tiara.

"Where did you get those?" His tone was severe.

"I will give you the keys of the kingdom of heaven. Whatever you bind on earth will be bound in heaven, and whatever you loose on earth will be loosed in heaven."

Clement stood with his mouth agape. "You are a man of many secrets, my Lord de Blanis."

The physician shrugged and put the keys in Clement's hands. "I am a Jew. It comes with the territory. Open it. The gold one first. It's a double lock."

The pope pushed the first key into the lock, expecting it to turn with difficulty, but to his surprise, the tumbler fell into place with barely a sound.

"Now the second."

The silver key slid in as easily, and the door stood unlocked.

"After you, Holy Father, and watch your step."

Pope Clement held the torch in front of him, revealing a long and narrow passageway, sloping downward at an angle. The ceiling was low. Clement had to stoop.

"Where are you taking me?"

"You'll see, my friend. You'll see."

The pair continued on for some minutes until the passage became level for a few feet. Suddenly, they were confronted with a wall.

"It's a dead-end," said Clement with a chilling foreboding and sinking of heart. The story of Judas in the Garden of Gethsemane popped into his brain. Could he have been deceived all this time?

"No, my noble de Medici. It is quite the opposite. Give me your keys."

De Blanis held up his own torch to what at first appeared to be a blank stone wall, but in the flickering light was revealed to be a wooden door painted to look like stone. Putting the silver key into a lock disguised by artfully created moss, de Blanis pushed against the door to reveal another passage, dark, damp, and unpaved. The roots of trees grew through the ceiling. "This is the passage to freedom, an escape route to the foot of the cliff beneath San Giovanale, thankfully, that you did not have to use. The last pope to use it was Alexander the Sixth."

"The Borgia!" gasped Clement.

"Yes, as you rightfully noted, he was more unpopular even than you, and perhaps even more misunderstood. He and his son Cesare fled here after the French, briefly, and took Naples in 1495." De Blanis pulled the door shut and locked it back. "*This* door, however, leads to someplace a good deal more pleasant." Slipping the golden key into the lock, de Blanis pushed against a similarly disguised door to the right. Swinging open, it revealed a long stone passage, richly adorned with tapestries and illuminated with intricately carved oil lamps. In the niches along the wall, as far as the eye could see, were statues of exquisite craftsmanship and detail. Etruscan.

"Where are we?" asked Clement.

"Let us say, my dear Giulio de Medici, that my home is a museum, and my museum is a home."

"This is the basement of your palazzo?"

"Below the basement," said de Blanis, nodding. "A good deal below, actually. Closer to purgatory." He chuckled.

Clement walked over to one of the statues—Minerva offering wisdom to two young girls at her feet. A few feet farther down the corridor, Venus rose from a marble surf, a sculpture to shame Botticelli's iconic version. The craftsmanship was superior. The age—he could not tell. They were at once ancient and contemporary, an artistic statement out of time. But who was the artist behind such wonders? Michelangelo would have but blushed. "These are incredible. I have seen nothing to their equal, in Rome or in Florence."

"Indeed," said de Blanis, "no one has for over a thousand years. Orvieto is rich in history and its history is rich. That for which the Romans leveled Volsini and the treasure for which they searched."

"The statues of Pliny and Metrodorus!" Clement gasped. They were *not* a myth. He turned back to scan the secret museum. For a millennia this horde had been whispered about, dreamed about. Written about and sought. His uncle, Leonardo de Medici, would have wept, would never have been able to afford, or even catalog such wonders. No one could. No one had ever seen these before, except— "Moses. Where did you find these?"

The Jewish philanthropist smiled slyly. "Seek and you shall find, as the Good Book says."

Clement stomped his feed in gleeful agitation. "Where!"

"Upon this Rock, my Lord Medici. Upon this Rock."

CHAPTER XL

Dress Rehearsal

Thursday, December 19, 2013, afternoon, Orvieto

In the year 1223, St. Francis organized the first Presepe as a protest against the extravagant excess of the Church for which Christmas was just another way to extort guilt-laden donations or purchases of indulgences from the peasants. Heading into the forest near Assisi, Francis gathered together some poor families, pulled together an impoverished petting zoo, and set up the world's first living Nativity. Since those thirteenth-century origins, towns up and down the Italian peninsula—especially those near Assisi—outdo each other in over-the-top recreations of the first Christmas. Orvieto was no exception, and to watch Don Bello in full CEO mode, Lee and Adriano could be forgiven for thinking that some competitive prize hung in the balance. The clifftop garden of San Giovanale was a circus of activity, with the church's wizened rector carnival barker and ringmaster all rolled into one.

"It's a stable," the old priest directed a young teenage member of the parish who was setting up the manger, "not a hotel. Make it look rustic. Remember, they were poor refugees with a donkey. They didn't take a taxi."

About thirty people, young, old, male and female, were scurrying around, transforming San Giovanale's garden into a Palestinian village circa the year 0. La Donna Volsini was handing out hot mulled wine and pastries, warmly fresh from her oven, to the workers. Her cat was curled up in the manger, as if daring a superior tenant to evict it. All around, local boys were digging fire pits. Others were hammering boards together for temporary stalls. A blacksmith's anvil sat half-uncrated next to the horse cart that had hauled it next to the church. Large copper pots were stacked, wrapped in last year's newspapers, ready for distribution around the site, vying for space with pallets of sandbags, red banners on poles, and rolling racks of costumes for peasants, priests, three kings, noblemen, serving women, and a virgin. It was like being on the movie set for a Renaissance faire documentary, which undoubtedly via Facebook this would become on St. Stephen's Day, December 26, the first of two performances for San Giovanale's Living Nativity. January 6, Three Kings Day, was the second, and closing, performance.

"Can you give me a hand?"

Lee turned to see Grigori, St. Chippendale, standing in sweat-bathed beauty and carrying a baby sheep around his neck. Errant pieces of straw tangled in his dirty blond hair and mud-caked work boots. The left bottom of his work shirt was untucked from his button-fly jeans, and the creamy white hem of his Calvins peaked tantalizingly above his waist. As he lifted the lamb down from his shoulder, a taut sliver of flesh popped into view where his hem had escaped. He had a tiny mole next to his outie navel. The sheep nuzzled Grigori's stomach, then lay down in the grass with an almost post-coital *bahhhhh*.

"Sure," was all Lee could manage, a gay Jimmy Carter, lusting in his heart. *I'm a married man I'm a married man I'm a married man.* He looked over to see his husband on the far end of the lot helping Don Bello and one of his teenage minions with the laptop-controlled sound system. Definitely Adriano's forte. *Help!*

"Great, you can hold this while I hang?"

"I beg your pardon?"

"The ladder." Grigori smiled and mounted the wooden steps. "Hold it while I climb up and hang the star."

"Ah yeah, sure, you bet."

I'll help you hang just about anything you want, Lee thought, biting his tongue against making a joke about well-hung celestials. As he held the collapsible steps while Grigori's trunk-like legs passed by in ascent, there it was again, the smell of cinnamon, like some sticky bun just ready to be licked, which wasn't too far from the truth. Also, there was something familiar about Grigori, as if Lee had seen him somewhere before. Of course, it was possible. We all had dirty dreams, Lee thought, and this one could have starred in one of mine with ease.

"You live here in Orvieto?" Lee asked looking up at, oh, quite a lot.

"Rome," Grigori answered, winching a stubborn Star of Bethlehem into place at the front of the grotto that would house the stable. His biceps rippled with the effort. It was like that old joke about Marilyn Monroe. Grigori had muscles in places where most men don't have places. "I just came up to help Marco's grandmother and Don Bello with some Christmas errands."

"But you're originally from Orvieto?"

"Fluelen. It's just over the border in Switzerland, on Lake Lucerne. Hold on to my calf. I need to balance."

Grigori stood up on tiptoes to wrestle with the LED comet over the manger. "There, almost got it. Lean into my butt so I don't fall."

"Sure." Lee meekly complied, wondering if Adriano was watching the soft-core gay Victoria's Secret scenario from across the garden. "Do you work in construction?"

"Sometimes." Grigori jumped down from the ladder to land right in front of Lee with an almost gymnastic precision. The musk of his perspiration mixed with his unique cologne in a heady cocktail. Lee felt dizzy and a bit wobbly. "I do a lot of things," he said with a smile that promised a diverse résumé.

One lives in hope, Lee thought.

"Oh Christ." Grigori's naughty smile faded. "It's her. Gotta go."

Lee turned to see Orvieto's most relentless blogger standing on the rise above the garden, a lookout scanning for harpoonable prey.

Like a retreating thoroughbred colt, at the first sight of Peg, Grigori bolted across the expanse of San Giovanale's garden and disappeared into a cliffside doorway built into the foundation of the church, half hidden by ivy and other foliage. In a second, the muscular youth had disappeared into the rock face. Robin into the Bat Cave.

"Lee! Mi amico! Ciao!"

Peg sailed down the ramp into the garden, an armada of chintz pushing pleated waves of scattering chickens, goats, and Grigori's sheep in front of her prow-like dress. Scarlett O'Hara would have been hard pressed to have a bigger hoop, Lee thought.

"Where have you been hiding! I haven't seen you for days!" The writer chirped as her flotilla of fabric dropped anchor. She bent over the bulbous bow of her ensemble to kiss Lee on both cheeks. "Was that Grigori I just saw skittering off, typically, into the bushes? Frankly, I'm surprised he had the nerve to show his face here again."

"Why?" Lee suddenly found himself irritated by Peg's practiced coy pond of fishing for a response.

"Deacon Andrea's suicide," she exhaled, slapping the sides of her copious dress as if Lee should see the obvious. "Grigori was the reason the Vatican sent that fax to Andrea." Peg dropped her voice to a conspiratorial whisper. "A lot of people thought they were, well...you know. And, of course, because of the sex scandal at the Vatican." She typed in the air with gloved hands as if googling to heaven. "Look it up. Ah, Don Bello, Adriano! Buon Natale!"

"Buon Natale, Signora Peg." The blogger offered her cheeks, somewhat reticently, Lee thought, for the cleric's cheeky benediction. Adriano motioned that his hands were dirty and just waved.

"What brings you down to our little parish from your writing tower?" Don Bello was smiling, but, as Lee couldn't help but notice, with a copious effort of charm.

"Bambino Jesu, of course," Peg said and tittered, taking out a pad and pen from her lifeboat-sized purse. "Orvieto wants to know, who it's going to be this year in the manger for the living Nativity. It's the highlight of my Christmas-week blog."

Don Bello's face grew ever so slightly dark, and his usual elfish grin took on a decidedly irritated crease. "Now, Peg, you know better than that. The identity of Baby Jesus is never revealed before the Presepe. One baby on St. Stephen's, and a second infant on Three Kings Day, January sixth. You'll just have to come back and file a live report from the scene. Adriano, why don't you show our esteemed journalist what we've been working on today? You don't mind, do you, Adriano? Of course not. Give Peg a tour of our little Bethlehem petting zoo."

Peg frowned, but curtsied slightly in strategic retreat. "Of course, Don Bello. Whatever you say."

Like a pastoral tug boat, the old priest linked Peg and Adriano arm in arm and pushed them toward the stable and its coterie of quadrupeds. "Be careful of the calf next to the stable. There may be cow pies. Ciao."

Adriano looked over his shoulder at Lee in mock surrender as Peg pulled him toward the manger, her voice clear above the mooing of cows and grunting of pigs. Don Bello kept waving until they were at the far side of the garden. Like a guillotine he dropped his hand and turned to Lee in utter seriousness.

"What was she saying to you?"

"She insinuated that Grigori and Deacon Andrea were lovers." Lee opted for frankness and hoped for the same from the priest. Don Bello just sighed.

"I have to go to confession every time I see that gossipy woman. She fills me with violent thoughts."

The question hung in the air. Lee waited.

"They were friends." Don Bello exhaled in surrender. "Very good, dear friends. How friends express their love for each other is no one's business save theirs and God's."

Lee pressed on. "Did the Vatican think they were lovers? Is that why they stopped Andrea's ordination?"

Don Bello stood for a moment looking out at the garden, gazing at the spot where Andrea balanced on his last night in Orvieto. "The Vatican has a reason for everything. They are not in the habit of revealing their secrets to me, or most people. It is a fault, a most grievous fault."

Lee looked at the old man's face and noticed that he was crying and that his hands were clenched in angry fists. "Here." He pulled a paper napkin from Café Volsini out of his pocket and offered it to the priest.

"Thank you, my son." Don Bello smiled slightly and dabbed his eyes. "You and Adriano are good boys...men. You are good men."

"And Grigori?"

Don Bello seemed startled by the question. He paused a second before answering. "Grigori is a kind and generous soul. He's also deeply conflicted, about many things." Then, as if suddenly figuring something out for the first time, he added, "Grigori is a very good man. He just doesn't know it yet."

"Do you think he feels responsible for Andrea's suicide?"

Don Bello started to speak, then stopped. After a second he added in what was clearly meant to be the final word today on the matter. "Grigori would have given his life for Andrea. He still would. Where is he by the way? I thought he was helping you hang the star."

"He was." Lee sighed and cocked his head across the garden to where Adriano and Peg were inspecting the petting zoo. "As soon as he saw her approaching, he dashed inside a door over by the cliff."

"I don't blame him," Don Bello said archly. "Our Lady Peg was most unkind to Grigori before and after Andrea jumped. She said...ah, well. Let's just say her blog is the petty public face of a scurrilous scandal monger. God forgive her and me."

"I've read her blog," Lee said. "I never saw anything about Grigori there."

"I made her take it down," Don said with obvious but distasteful pride. "It was malicious, unfounded, hateful gossip. It wasn't the first time she had written about things that should have remained private, and I got her to issue a retraction. Vicious woman. She even wrote about Bagnoregio—" Suddenly, the old priest clammed up, crossed himself, and kissed his pectoral cross. "Forgive me. I'm giving in to that of which I accuse her. Gossip."

"As our friend Bishop Brian used to say, karma is a bitch. I'm sure she'll get her comeuppance."

"From your mouth to God's ears," Don Bello said.

"Goddamn *it*!"

Lee and Don Bello pivoted at the cursing to see Adriano at the far end of the garden next to the animal lean-to. He was courageously defending a goat from Peggy's wrath. The ram was vigorously devouring her purse. Adriano's efforts were futile. Another goat was beginning to nibble on the hem of Peggy's voluminous dress. The buffet was beginning to draw a cafeteria line of hungry *baahhhhhs*. Like an unhappy Bo Peep, Peggy went screaming up the ramp pursued by the carnivorous cabras.

For a moment, the garden of San Giovanale rang with the crowd's healing laughter, one Lee thought, that had probably been stifled for a year. As Don Bello leaned on his shoulder and they walked up the earthen ramp toward the church, Lee couldn't help but wonder what was in that blog post that Don Bello had successfully pressured Peg into deleting. He wondered who else might have read it. It was time to visit Bagnoregio.

Suddenly, it came to Lee in a flash. He knew where else he had seen Grigori before—and very possibly smelled him.

CHAPTER XLI

Sanctuary

Friday, December 20, 2013, early morning, Orvieto

It wasn't difficult to pick the lock. The apartment had been unoccupied for over a year now and the idea of alarms in Orvieto was just that. An idea. The only danger was being heard by a neighbor, but that too was unlikely. The walls were thick and this was an outside unit. He had waited for over an hour until the lights went out in the building's one occupied residence before he quietly jimmied the lock and accessed the abandoned flat. Well, not abandoned really. Shut-up. Another one of Orvieto's former Renaissance palazzos that had been subdivided and subjugated to the whims of a modern world. Libraries turned into living rooms; grand salons hacked up into closets and bathrooms; bedrooms cut up into a warren of smaller sleeping areas, but all with the occasional sixteenth-century domestic fresco popping into view behind a peeling bit of wallpaper or a carved coat of arms peering out from inside a closet. A TV was mounted over an incongruously intricate marble mantel topping a neutered fireplace of immense proportions, now housing a gas-fed space heater.

Please still be on, Dawud prayed. Heat. That was the main reason for this illegal incursion. And secrecy. No one would think to look here for his sister. Plus, it would be days before they knew that she was missing. But, after that, the men would come looking. He had meant to be long gone by now, on the road deeper into Europe, out of Italy. But that was before he saw his sister. Before he saw her condition.

His sister whimpered, bundled up in the tiny twin bed pushed against the corner. It would not be long now. The baby would come soon. There would be no travel for his sister this night, not for several nights.

He was used to the winter chill of Orvieto by now, but his sister, Maryam, had been through too much to give birth in the frigid squalor of his hovel. The stony streets were slippery with ice, a transparent hazard with none of the romance of snow. The clock on the pharmacy behind *Sant'Andrea* proclaimed this morning's temperature: minus six degrees Celsius.

Dawud reached for the knob that controlled the flow of gas and turned. A quiet hiss escaped. A brief spark exhumed the flat from darkness as he lit a match, the cross on the wall, the draped-over door to the patio overlooking the Duomo, the computer on his desk, and a black cassock still poised on its hanger waiting for the next day's sunrise that never came for its wearer. Dawud touched the flame to the pilot and the heater roared into life.

Praise Allah! It works. They had not cut off the gas. Everything was as it had been left a year ago when its tenant walked out the door for the last time. No one had touched it. No one had dared.

He silently offered a prayer of thanks and asked pardon of the owner for violating his sanctuary. He offered another prayer for what he was about to do. For the price of this sanctuary, and that of his sister. Archbishop Arnaud was a stern man. Evidently, so was the power behind the Archbishop.

Many times over the last year, Dawud had made trips for the Bishop. He had been a courier of prayers. A messenger of spiritual intentions. The Bishop was offering him salvation, was offering him hope, was offering him a home. No one in his home country had done as much. True, this Church of Rome was not the faith of his fathers, but his father, all of his family, were dead. A dead man's religion serves no one. Yes, he had been faithful to Archbishop Arnaud, as he had been faithful to Deacon Andrea and Bishop Sancarlo—both such good men. Neither Andrea nor the kind

bishop who always smiled ever asked anything of Dawud. They just welcomed him. Well, now they were gone, but Dawud had heard their lessons
well. The Bishop represented the Church, and in Orvieto, now, Arnaud
was the Church.

Dawud served Arnaud now.

He reached over and stroked his sister's hair. She was sleeping,
exhausted from her odyssey. The heater glowed softly and Dawud could
feel its warmth reaching out like a comforting hand.

"We must always live in the moment," Andrea had taught him. "For
the moment, we have breath, we have life. We should be grateful in every
moment. God, Allah, asks no more."

For the moment, Dawud and Maryam were safe. For the moment, the
siblings were not running for their lives. For the moment, no one knew
where Maryam was. For the moment, the baby in her womb was safe, but
after that, they would find her.

No. Dawud would not allow it. Maryam would not end up a slave, a
slave on the roads of Umbria. He would not allow the men who had been
waiting for his sister to find her and turn her into... No! Here in this apartment, no one would dare to enter. For now, they were safe. Tonight, they
would rest.

Tomorrow, it might be different.

Tomorrow, he had one final job to do, but not the job he had been
asked to do. Arnaud would not be happy about that.

CHAPTER XLII

Solstice

Saturday, December 21, 2013, the first day of winter, Civita di Bagnoregio

"How many gorgeous hilltop towns *are* there in Italy?" Adriano and Lee stood at the edge of the cliffside town of Lubriano staring across the valley toward their destination, Civita di Bagnoregio, Andrea's hometown. Having successfully helped Don Bello as pinch hitters at the Presepe two days ago, the couple now found themselves at the place of the young deacon's nativity.

"It's like you shrunk Orvieto, put it in a crystal Christmas tree ornament, and hung it from the sky."

"My." Adriano gave polite applause through gloved hands to his husband. "You are waxing poetic today."

"Well," said Lee with a wave of his hand toward the mist-shrouded hamlet a kilometer distant. "Scenery doesn't get more poetic than *that.*"

Like a stage set cued for dramatic effect, the remote and surreal acropolis of Civita di Bagnoregio awaited the sunset. Already the stark canyons surrounding the summit were swathed in shadow, and the few occupied homes inside were beginning to show candlelight. A *Brigadoon*-like mist nibbled at the rocky base of the town.

"Three fifteen p.m." Lee tapped his iPhone. "Solstice sundown is four forty-two p.m. We have just over an hour. We should get to the B and B in time for a drink and a killer view. What a perfect way to celebrate the official start to winter and the shortest day of the year."

"And a shower." Adriano hefted the backpack higher onto his shoulders. "Let's go. According to this map, the path winds down this way, then up to the town."

Always one for ceremony (and organization), Lee had timed their own personal hijra from the front of Floriano's altar, *Chiesa del Crocifisso del Tufo Orvieto*. They had set off at precisely 10:00 a.m. yesterday with the clang of the bell from the Tower of the Moor echoing across the Etruscan Tombs. Adriano, as resident mapper, had laid out a walking tour along the *Via Francigena*—The Franciscan Way--—taken by pilgrims, priests, paupers, and penitents for over a thousand years. Last night, they had arrived in Bolsena, an Italian tourist mecca perched on the shores of a volcanic lake—Europe's largest—of the same name. The hike had been long but unchallenging, except for some minor blisters that only made them feel like they had really accomplished something. They had stopped for drinks and a smoke at a surprisingly welcoming blue-collar bar. Everyone had been gathered around a TV watching coverage of the latest terrorist attack, this time somewhere in Turkey. Same story, different language on the television scroll. Also, an Italian TV station was covering a boatload of refugees washing ashore south of Naples. Both stories competed for space on the bar's tiny wall-mounted TV, two sides of the same painful present currently being inflicted upon the Mediterranean, upon the earth.

After drinks, they had spent a pleasant evening checking out the Basilica of Santa Cristina, site of the Miracle of Bolsena. The altar upon which the doubtful padre Peter of Prague had celebrated Mass in 1263 before the communion host started bleeding was still there, preserved and off-limits to touch. A few years ago, the town had taken the profile of the altar as Bolsena's new tourism logo. It popped up everywhere, including on a sign at the entrance to the town proclaiming "Bolsena—Town of the Eucharistic Miracle." Encased in glass and gold was a piece of marble, supposedly bearing the sanguine-tinged masonry. Take that, Orvieto! You have a bloody cloth, but we have the *floor*! Reliquary tourist traps were requisite and profitable in Italy. As they were leaving the church, Lee had been almost giddy to find out from a brochure in the nave that it had been restored during the fifteenth century by none other than Cardinal Giulio de Medici.

"That was the illegitimate son of Lorenzo Magnifico's brother, Giuliano! Lorenzo adopted him after the Pazzi conspiracy and Giulio went on to become Pope Clement the Seventh, the one who fled to Orvieto after the Sack of Rome!" Lee beamed.

"Fascinating," Adriano smiled, a patient and loving Spock.

"Cynic." Lee made a kissy-face.

As Lee would later recall, the worst was yet to come.

After leaving Bolsena earlier this morning, it had taken them just over five hours to reach their current location, Lubriano, the penultimate stop before the final drive to the summit of Civita di Bagnoregio. On a stone wall next to a field full of sheep, they had stopped en route for a respectfully decadent lunch, the leftovers that La Donna Volsini and Marco had packed for them yesterday morning. As they picnicked on porcheta, hard pecorino cheese, day-old bread, pastries, and a leather flask of Orvieto Classico, Lee's thoughts turned to the mystery of Andrea.

"So, what do you think?"

"About what?" Adriano purposefully wasn't biting as he offered Lee the flask.

"Andrea."

"What about him?"

"Come on, honey. You know it's all very *mysterious*."

"What's mysterious?" Adriano sighed, polishing off the wine in a gulp. "A devout, ideological young man succumbed to the empty promises of the Church. The Church betrayed him. The young man killed himself in useless despair. No mystery there."

Lee didn't answer, but he started biting his lips. He *knew* there was something more than a spontaneous suicide of a brokenhearted seminarian. The inscription on Reverend Vicky's pectoral cross—January 3, 1983—the same date on the photo in the rectory of St. Paul's Inside the Walls. The socially uncomfortable but nonetheless perfectly groomed young doctor, Luke. Hovering in the background, Archbishop Arnaud, La Donna Volsini, and even the kindly but seemingly all-knowing Don Bello. Perhaps on the quietude of a dirt path through the Italian countryside, he could figure out the mysterious miasma surrounding Andrea Bernardone. He could *feel* it. He could *smell* it, actually, for he was convinced that the hunky Grigori and his nauseatingly enticing cinnamon cologne were part of the mystery.

He hadn't yet shared his idea with his husband. Adriano hadn't said anything. He didn't need to. After ten years together, one didn't need words. Lee knew that Adriano thought he was becoming a bit unhealthily obsessed with the puzzle of Andrea Bernardone. His husband's silence spoke tomes. Unsaid, even to himself, Lee agreed.

Adriano heaved the backpack onto this shoulder. Lee was grateful for his partner's duty as Sherpa. His load was heavy enough with thoughts of what they might—or might not—find in Civita.

Having proven an exceptionally pleasant day, they had opted for the slightly longer, more atmospheric route from Bolsena en route to Civita, purposefully eschewing the road more traveled that led directly to the parking lot and modern pedestrian bridge. They were pilgrims, after all!

~

Having now arrived at the rim of the canyon between Lubriano and Civita Bagnoregio, they soon came to regret their decision.

What should have been a straightforward, half-hour hike to the connection linking Civita di Bagnoregio with the rest of the world, quickly collapsed into an hour-long slouching slog. Lee felt like David Niven in *The Guns of Navarone*—everywhere another cliff. Suddenly, everything that was charming from a distance was impossible up close. The vale between Lubriano and Civita offered up improbable challenges of fallen trees, washed-out roadways, and even a small river in flood that threatened hygiene, patience, and safety. There had been no sign at the beginning of the downward berm in Lubriano warning of such obstacles.

"Maybe the passage is closed in winter," said Lee as he pulled up his hood against a sudden assault of sleet from the skies.

"How typically Italian," huffed Adriano, as the chilly, wind-driven rain destroyed all semblance of comfort or desiccation in their clothes. "Even Spain, which isn't the most organized of countries, would have had a warning poster across the entrance to the path. Drowning rats would be less miserable. I told you we should have taken the shorter route."

Lee ignored the comment, knowing this was the beginning of one of Adriano's notorious foul moods. He had noted the "I told you" comment, even though the decision to take the longer route had been reached in concert. Plus, his husband must be grumpy indeed even to mention the word "rat." They forged ahead, wet, tired, and sore from sharing a backpack that seemed heavier with every step. Finally, they found themselves at the base of their decrepitly picturesque destination, Civita di Bagnoregio. They were actually touching the citadel, but the entrance to the foot bridge was at the other end of a rain-washed gully.

"I'm not going back into that valley just to crawl up a hill to cross a bridge," growled Adriano. "This isn't too steep. We can climb straight up."

"You're kidding." Lee was petrified. Where was David Niven when you needed him?

"No, look, it's not too bad." Adriano was already reaching up for handholds. "There used to be some sort of stairway or path here. If we just haul ourselves up, we'll save at least another forty-five minutes."

Lee frowned. A rare clap of winter thunder spurred his decision. "OK, let's go."

Eight minutes later, they hauled themselves over a broken piece of masonry and stood on the summit. Civita di Bagnoregio. Forget the Town That Dies. This was the town that had almost killed them in the attempt.

"We made it!" Lee said, pulling himself over the ultimate obstacle, a wall half connected to the town, half hanging over the abyss.

"Hmmm." Adriano just raised an eyebrow.

"Brian would have loved this. It's like an Italian Camino de Santiago."

"That's exactly what it was," said Adriano, softening his mood. "Even my grandfather, who hated *everything* about the Church, wanted to walk it. One day we'll have to take a month and do it."

"I promise," Lee said, kissing his husband on the cheek, grateful for a reprieve since the expedition had been his idea. "Add it to the bucket list."

"For later." Adriano smiled, good humor fully restored. "Right now, I don't want to plan *any* more hikes."

"Don't forget. We have one more day ahead of us. The return to Orvieto," Lee reminded.

"Yes, I know. But first, I just want to wash off this one. Let's go."

CHAPTER XLIII

The Longest Night

Saturday, December 21, 2013, sunset, Orvieto

Archbishop Arnaud opened the drawer to his desk and took it out.

Outside, earth's tired star was covering itself in blankets of its shortest day. Soon it would be dark, completely dark, and the sun would rest for its longest night, and then, begin again.

Rest. That's what I need, he thought, placing the instrument of his death in front of him. *Rest.*

A thousand years ago, upon this rock, Etruscan clans would have been preparing for the solstice. In Egypt, Horus would be born. The Mesopotamians unleashed the God Marduk to tame the demons of Chaos. The Babylonian feast of Sacaea reversed the order of life for the day—as in heaven so on earth, and slaves became masters, and masters submitted to slaves. Arnaud smirked. That, clearly, was a cult forgotten and not to be born again. *I am a slave forever. We all are.* The emperor Aurelian the Saturnalia's debauchery and the virgin birth of Mithra, the undying Sun God, combined to make way for that greatest of all copycat religions, Christianity. A little bit country, a little bit rock and Rome.

He picked it up and held it close to his face.

Soon, he will come soon, Arnaud thought. He looked hard at the instrument of his death—all of their deaths. It had been thirty years now, waiting, but never forgotten. Oh, he had taken it out before. Every now and then. On anniversaries, birthdays. Drunken nights when he was doubting his faith. No, that was wrong. It was only on nights plied with drink that he didn't doubt his faith. You had to get really drunk to believe that shit. How could anyone who was sober believe in a loving God who granted forgiveness to someone like him?

Like a gun pointed at his heart, it shot him again and again and again, a trinity of bullets preserved forever in the crinkled paper of that photo from three decades ago. He turned it over to see the date—"01.03.83"—and next to it, a scrawled inscription from Gio and Vicky: "Amici per sempre! Su questa roccia e più tardi in Cielo! I Magi."

"Friends forever! Upon this rock, and later in heaven! The Magi!"

Vicky had added a smiley face as the dot beneath the exclamation point.

My God, Arnaud thought, how young we all were. How impossibly young. Yes—impossibly.

He put it back in his desk. He didn't need a picture to remember. He would never forget that day, the happiest day of his life, and the beginning of all the saddest.

Vicky. Gio. Andrea.

I have killed you all.

CHAPTER XLIV

Dead Man Walking

Saturday, December 21, 2013, sunset, Civita di Bagnoregio

In summer, Civita di Bagnoregio was awash in tourists. On a wet, rainy day in December, not so much. Semi-abandoned for decades, and with no easy access until a new walking span had been built in the sixties, the town had languished until an American journalist happened upon it and delivered a manna of televised publicity via a series of unctuous, if upbeat, documentaries. His picture, website, and endless stream of DVD promotions peeked from inside winter-closed shop windows as Adriano and Lee entered the village proper beneath its medieval gate, La Porta Santa Maria. A weatherworn statue of Our Lady peered down in warning. Immediately the attack began.

"Meow! Meow!"

A horde of felines burst forth upon the couple as they topped the final rise at the entrance to the burg. Tippi Hedren stars in Hitchcock's *The Cats*! Lee thought. Like apparitions, dozens of scraggly tabbys emerged from the shadows, perched on columns, crouching in doorways, padding in formation on delicately feral feet. Seeking warmth, one sat right on top of a spotlight embedded in the pavement. Designed to illuminate Bagnoregio's ancient portal, the electric torch now served as an impromptu catcall, à la *Batman*. the furry Bruce Wayne's logo now projected upon the ramparts.

"Excellent," Adriano said with a nod. "An army of pussies means no rats."

"They're not as well groomed as La Donna Volsini's," Lee noted. "They look like street cats."

"What's this?"

Punctuated by the furry "Bat Signal," a bronze plaque peeked out from behind a frame of entangled ivy on the right pillar of the citadel. Adriano translated from Italian and read, "In memory of Andrea Bernardone, a son of Bagnoregio. He gave his life so that others would live."

"A plaque to Andrea?" Lee said, gently pushing Adriano out of the way.

"No. Must have been his father. According to this he was born on June tenth, 1944, and died on March first, 1983."

"Does it say how he died?"

"Wait." Adriano snapped his fingers. "Don't you remember? That letter that Andrea's mother wrote sticking it to the Pope." Adriano stepped under the arch to get out of the rain and started flipping through his iPhone. "Here it is."

Forgive me Holy Father, for I write as a woman torn by grief and plagued with doubt. In his youth, my husband, a brave carabinieri, was taken from me by criminals. Doing his job, he was gunned down by the mafia he had sworn to defeat. His son, born on the Feast of Andrea, never knew him.

"Poor woman." Lee just shook his head and looked back across the slim concrete link between Bagnoregio's handful of residents and the greater world beyond. From here, it certainly looked like the perfect place to escape, a hermitage from grief surrounded by memories. Or, perhaps the opposite, a prison constructed from them.

As if in celestial answer to the cat commissioner's emergency call, as soon as Adriano and Lee were through the arch and had entered Civita di Bagnoregio proper, the rains stopped. For a moment, even, the dying sunset broke through the soggy clouds to send a final salute to the day before slipping behind the hills.

"You see," said Lee, smiling in all his predictable perkiness, "I told you we'd make it before sunset."

"Ti amo, Pooh."

"Me too." Together, they shouldered on.

Civita di Bagnoregio was not so much a town as it was a great stone boat, afloat in a sea of tufo, perched between the mainlands of Umbria and Lazio. Every now and then, a wave of heavy, wet, and overly burdened clay would break over the bow of the village and wash away a door, a window, and soggy Roman arch. Lee did the quick calculations by sight, and realized it would have taken him longer to walk around the entire deck perimeter of the MS *Ithaka,* his shipboard home from ten years previous, than it would to traverse the lido of Bagnoregio.

"Now, *this* is a small town."

Adriano nodded in agreement, and pointed ahead to the town square, a tiny quadrangle of stone fronted by a poetically crumbling church, a small arched building that promised bureaucracy, two small cafés, and a three-story inn with two lit windows.

"*La Torre dei Segriti.* The Tower of Secrets. That sounds ominous. You called ahead, yes?"

Lee nodded in a mock-joking tone. "Yes, and good thing. Otherwise, I doubt there'd be any room at the inn."

"No," Adriano countered politely. "There would have been room, but there would have been no key. In little Italian towns like this during the winter, whole rows of businesses just close for the season, and *La Torre dei Segreti* seems to constitute the entire hospitality row of Civita. I'm pretty sure we won't have much competition for a manger."

"Hmm," grunted Lee in acknowledgment. "Onward."

Once the heavily carved, wooden, but surprisingly squeak-free door of the thirteenth-century *La Torre dei Segreti* was pushed open, the sodden sulkiness of the previous few hours was banished on sight. A roaring fire complete with symphonic crackling logs and the homey aroma of freshly cut branches filled the rustic interior. Six tables checkered with mismatched cutlery, a potpourri of plates, and varying styles of glassware beckoned.

Something delicious drew them like a narcotic toward the kitchen portal where a feminine shadow soon exploded into the room with greeting.

"Buonasera! Si deve esseer Adriano e Lee, si?"

"Si. Buonasera, Signora," Lee said, offering his hand. "We have reserved...ah, *abbiamo prenotazioni.*" He had practiced all day on the hike and wanted to get it right.

"Ees OK." The landlady smiled, a bundle of smiles, pleasantly high-piled graying blonde hair, and a not unpleasantly ample girth cinched in with a carefully patterned dress of homespun. Lee could tell. His grandmother had made all her own clothes, and he knew the look. Lee guessed her age to be somewhere hovering around fifty-seven. "My-a English is-a pretty well, ah, is-a pretty *good.* Sit, sit. You like wine?"

"Si," the couple answered and simultaneously plopped down at the nearest table with communal sighs.

"Oh mio, look at your feets! The rain, is-a horrible and the muds! Give me your foots, your-a shoes. I clean. Tomorrow, all good. Grappa, better than wine. Wait here." And their Rubenesque Angel was gone in a swirl and back in half of one with two miraculously unspilled crystal stems brimming with invigorating grape liquor. Then, sweeping out in a matronly tornado, she left Adriano and Lee gratefully barefoot before the hearth and Lee wondering at it all. On the wall above the mantel, a poster from last Valentine's Day proclaimed, "What Happens in Bagnoregio, Stays in Bagnoregio." Lee was already a believer. Twenty minutes later, they were digging into the special of the night. Cinghiale con polenta. Wild boar never tasted so good. Actually, Lee had never had wild boar.

"I always said it was a great day when the first caveman threw a pig on a fire," said Lee.

"And," added Adriano, "it was probably a Spanish caveman at Altimira."

Lee laughed at. Adriano's usual rejoinder to their practiced banter. As their first forks were raised, the couple were joined by *La Torre dei Segriti's* only other guest of the evening.

"Clemente! Basta! Leava mia guests no lone!" The cheerfully attentive doyenne jogged into the dining room just as an elegantly familiar silver cat pounced upon the table, poised for some feral pork. With a flick of her tail, she gracefully descended to an empty chair between Lee and Adriano, a strategic retreat.

"Nessun problema," Adriano offered. "Ci piaci gatta."

"Bravo!" clapped the hostess in laughing delight, somehow also managing to simultaneously top off their wineglasses. "You-a Italian is-a much-a better than my-a English. Bravo! This is-a Clemente. He-a the cat of my-a friend in Orvieto."

"La Donna Volsini," Lee stated with a hydraulically slow dropping jaw.

"Si!" Clarissa applauded again. "Si! Of-a course. You walk today from Orvieto. You know-a my friend Velzna Volsini."

"How did...?"

"Clemente."

"How did Clemente get here?" Lee didn't think even a cat with such discerning tastes as this one's would hike through the mud for a meal like this. Plus, muddy Clemente was not. He was as impeccably groomed as a Vatican prelate.

"He-a come with me in my little scooter, mia Ape. This-a morning, I go to Orvieto to buy bread and sweet things from-a my friend Velzna. Café Volsini makes i migliori pasticceria in Italia, the best sweet desserts in-a Italy. Clemente, he-a like to travel, especial when I the only one in town. Tonight, all the other peoples be gone. Me the only one person in town."

The cat purred in contented agreement.

"Ah, who are my-a manners. My-a name is Clarissa. Clarissa Bernardone."

Well, Lee thought, that mystery was self-announced. Their hostess was indeed the mother of Deacon Andrea, the author of the Church-ripping letter that Adriano had translated a few days back. Strange, Lee thought, that she presented herself so easily.

~

After dinner and three desserts, the couple plus cat walked outside to take in the town. Their hostess had given them a flashlight and loaner pairs of galoshes while their shoes dried next to the fire.

"Here. You-a go and check-a out the church. *San Donato* is a lovely. Many candles still-a lit, but it dark. You go now. I come later and blow out the candles."

From the front door of *La Torre dei Sigreti* to the ancient portal of *San Donato* was a short commute. About fifteen steps. It was like being on a desert island. The only other sign of human habitation was Clarissa's shadow against the kitchen curtains, washing up the dishes. At least the weather had changed in their favor. The rain had been completely banished and replaced by a spectacular scrim of stars. An almost full but gently waning moon cast a spotlight onto the church. The structure's middle door open, if spookily inviting.

"Do you think there are rats?" Adriano said.

"Only Catholic ones."

Adriano grimaced.

"Just kidding! Besides, we've got Clemente."

The cat meowed and squirmed through Adriano's legs. That seemed to help. He motioned to continue.

The Church of San Donato was old. *Really* old. Sticking to form, Lee had read all about it before their trek. Consecrated in the seventh century, its Christian edifice stood on the frame of an even older Roman temple. At one point, the bones of Bagnoregio's most famous citizen, St. Bonaventura, rested within this sanctuary, until an earthquake in 1695 took down much of the church and town. Since then, its history was a continual crumble. Bonaventura's arm, encased in a golden reliquary, had been removed to the new, less tenuous cathedral on more solid ground across the valley. *San Donato* was left in possession of the mummified corpses of earlier and forgotten saints: Sant'Ildebrando, a ninth-century bishop, and Santa Vittoria, a former vestal virgin whose conversion had earned her martyrdom and a perpetually skeletal grimace in a baroque wedding gown now visible through the glass of the left side altar.

"It's like Byzantine Barbie," said Adriano, shivering as he turned away from the grotesquely preserved body. "What is it with the Church playing deified dress-up?"

Clement meowed in agreement.

"Wait," Lee said. "I want to check out one more thing. Look at this."

Midway up the nave on the right side of the church was a small kneeler in front of a large wooden frame, with carefully handwritten cursive numerals, one through ninety, with short sentences next to each number. To its right was a smaller frame, inscribed with a short prayer in Latin just above an iron donation bin built into the wall. On a marble table in front were three wooden boxes, one with Bingo-like wooden pegs, circular, stamped with red numbers. A second smaller one held blank index cards and a pencil. The final container was stuffed full of text-covered cards from clearly a wide variety of hands, and neatly filed like the card catalog in the library of Lee's youth. His mother had gotten him a summer job there when he was twelve. He quickly pushed down the memory, like stomach bile threatening to erupt. The box was about the same size and shape as the urn holding Brian's ashes back in Orvieto. Lee picked out the first card, marked "ESEMPIO." Lee remembered his earlier lesson at the Orvieto library: *esempio*—example. He looked at the card.

(41) Per quelle che in questa vita poco amarono Dio

(43) Per quelle che frastornarono gli altri alla devozione

(49) Per quelle che perdettero tempo in luchare e ridere

(56) Per quei padri e quelle madri che non educano i loro figli

"What are they voting for? Penitent of the Month?" Adriano snickered.

"No, it's a purgatory board," said Lee, screwing up his lips. "Wow. I've read about them, but never seen one. This is *way* old-school. See, it is kind of like Bingo." Lee reached into the first box. "You pick up a peg like this." He had selected seventy-nine. "Then, you find that number on the board." Lee scrolled down with his finger to seventy-nine. "Here, read this for me. It's in Italian."

Adriano gave him a *duh* look but obliged. "Settantanove. Per quelle dei soldati cattolici. For our Catholic soldiers."

"Fascinating," Lee said, squinting to read the copy in the second smaller frame. "You pick a number assigned to someone who is suffering in purgatory, then you read The De Produndis."

"Oscar Wilde's book?"

"No, silly. This prayer is where Wilde got the title for his tome. His imprisonment for homosexuality in Reading Gaol was his own private purgatory. It's what Catholics offer up for the souls waiting for redemption. Deacon Andrea's mother used part of it in her letter to the Pope after her son jumped from the cliff. It's the classic biblical cry for help."

Lee began to recite from memory.

De Profundis. Out of the depths, I have cried to Thee, O Lord,
    Lord, hear my voice.
Let Thine ears be attentive to the voice of my supplication.
If Thou, O Lord, shalt mark my iniquities, O Lord, who shall
    stand it?
For with Thee there is merciful forgiveness:
and by reason of Thy law I have waited for Thee, O Lord.
My soul hath relied on His word; my soul hath hoped in
    the Lord.
From the morning watch even until night; let Israel hope in
    the Lord.
Because with the Lord there is mercy; and with Him plenteous
    redemption.
And He shall redeem Israel from all its iniquities.
Eternal rest grant unto them, O Lord,
and let perpetual light shine upon them:
May they rest in peace
Amen.

"How did you know that?" Adriano just shook his head.

"I was going to be a priest, remember?" Lee pointed out. "Plus, I was taught by Benedictine monks. I know it in Latin too if you like."

"That's OK. Thanks."

Lee had rifled through his pockets and found what he was looking for. A euro coin. Promptly, he deposited it into the metal slot and then intoned, "Most gentle Heart of Jesus, ever present in the Blessed Sacrament, ever consumed with burning love for the poor souls in purgatory, have mercy on the souls of the Faithful Departed. Be not severe in Thy Judgments, but let some drops of Thy Precious Blood fall upon the devouring flames and do Thou, O merciful Savior, send Thy angels to conduct them to a place of refreshment, light and peace. Amen."

"So, it's not enough to pray for the poor schmucks in hell—"

"Purgatory. It's different. There's no escape from hell. Purgatory is temporary. The prayers of the faithful can get you out faster."

"So, this is like Inferno Monopoly. I'll buy Park Place Limbo and don't pass Go without paying."

"Kinda, yes," said Lee. "This little altar provides a get-out-of-jail-quicker' card. All Catholics are required to pray for the souls in purgatory—especially on All Souls Day, November second. This just helps facilitate the process."

"What about the index card?" Adriano motioned to Lee's hand where the card was still tightly held.

"Oh yeah. Here. Take a look. It's for the priest. You can pray yourself, or you can write down your petitions, put them in this box, and then the pastor will collect them before Mass and offer them up as petitions to God from the whole congregation."

Lee handed the card to his husband for translation.

(41) Per quelle che in questa vita poco amarono Dio
(43) Per quelle che frastornarono gli altri alla devotione
(49) Per quelle che perdettero tempo in burlare e ridere
(56) Per quei padri e quelle madri che non educano i loro figli

"What does it say?"

"Forty-one. For those in this life who just loved God. Forty-three. For those who distracted others from devotion. Forty-nine. For those who wasted time in mockery and laughter. Fifty-six. For those fathers and mothers who did not educate their children."

Those are odd supplications," said Lee, taking back the card. He stared at it with a strange prescience. He had seen this somewhere before, but

260

where? He had never even read Italian before this trip. Next to the stack of cards was a small mimeographed piece of paper listing all ninety sins. Lee took one, folded it up, and stuck it into his pocket. Since he knew most of the prayers in English, it might come in handy as a holy Italian lesson down the road. He plucked out another card from the deck.

Adriano read and translated simultaneously:

"Thirty-eight. Per quelle che penano per pigrizia. For those who are in pain because of laziness.

Eighty-seven. Per quelle che sono comparse a quelche persona non hanno avato soccorso. For those who have cried out for rescue but been denied.

Seventy-seven. Per quelle che invita si raccomandarone a Dio con poco fervor. For those who did not worship God with sufficient fervor.

Five. Per quelle alle quali particolarmente sei tenuto. For those of your particular intentions."

"Oh my God!" Lee grabbed the card from his husband's hands and turned it over. "Look at what's stamped on the back."

"Opus Dei," Adriano said with a softly suppressed grunt of surprise. "It's the seal of Opus Dei."

"The symbol on Luke's ring!"

"So, you think Luke was here praying for the souls in purgatory?" Adriano asked.

"I don't know, but don't you think it's kinda' weird?"

"I think anyone paying one euro to pray for people in a fantasy called purgatory is weird."

"Not all of them have the Opus Dei thingie," said Lee, who was now shuffling through the cards like a champion casino dealer. "Actually, most of them don't. Just a few. Ah, here's another with the seal. Read it for me."

"Forty. Per quelle che confidate nella misericordia di Dio, facilmente peccarono. Forty. Per quelle che confidate nella misericordia di Dio, facilmente peccarono"

"That's strange," Lee screwed up his face. "Why would they repeat the same petition twice?"

"You're asking *me*, Reverend Mother?"

"What's the translation?"

"For those that trusted in God's mercy, easily they sinned."

"Finish it."

"Three. Per le anime di questa famiglia che ancora penanon in purgatorio. For the souls of this family that still languish in purgatory. Six. Per quelle che in vita loro ti hanno perseguitato. For those who in their lives have persecuted you."

"Why would Luke be praying for stuff like that?" Lee asked.

"You don't even know that Luke wrote these cards," said Adriano. "Trust me, Luke isn't the only member of Opus Dei in Italy, and I'm sure not the only one with that secret decoder ring of his."

"This close to Orvieto?"

"There's Archbishop Arnaud," Lee observed. "Maybe Arnaud stamped them and Luke brought them here for some reason."

Adriano just frowned. Somewhere in town, a telephone rang.

"Here, what about these two. There's just one line on each card, and they don't have the secret decoder ring Opus Dei stamp."

"Eighteen. Per quelle che per i loro occhi troppo licenziosi patiscono. For those who suffer for the licentiousness of their eyes. Hey, honey, someone must have seen how you were looking at Grigori the other day in the garden."

"Nice." Lee smiled, ignoring the bull's-eye. "How about the next one?"

"Twenty. Per quelle che sono castigate per i loro disordinate amori e desideri. For those who are punished for their disorderly love and desires. Ah! One for both of us! Homosexuals in purgatory! I'm *so glad* the Church thinks we can be saved!"

"Dante too," said Lee straight-faced. "The Florentine sodomites he meets in *The Inferno* are quite the nicest sinners he meets along the way."

"Hocus-pocus." Adriano was already moving toward the door. "The whole religion, *all* religion, is one big scam. What *are* you doing?"

Lee had quietly knelt down in front of the purgatory board, picked up the pencil and was filling out a card. After a few seconds, he put down the pencil, folded the card, and slipped it into the slot.

Just then, the wooden door of the church crashed back on its hinges, followed by the feminine sound of hurried and clicking heels ricocheting toward them. A thin beam of moonlight projected the shadow onto their faces seconds before their visitor's arrival.

"I have to go." Clarissa Bernardone was frantically pulling on a coat and gloves and rushing toward them. Her visage was unsmiling, pale, and drawn tight across a face wrinkled in anxiety. All of the evening's earlier cheerful hospitality had been completely banished from her features. "Something...ah...ah, it-a come up. I must-a go. Ciao, ciao. I leav-a key. Bye."

She was halfway out the door of *San Donato* before Lee could toss the question at her.

"What about the bill? What about our breakfast?"

"What?"

She had the look of someone who had just been awakened by the news of a loved one's death. Lee knew the look.

"Bill? No-a worry. Just-a talk to La Donna Volsini when you back in Orvieto. I getta the money from-a her. Someone-a come tomorrow morning to make you breakfast. They-a be-a here by eight o'clock. Ciao." she said, and she was gone.

A few seconds later, he heard her running into *La Torre dei Sigreti,* then out again, then back in as if she'd forgotten something. Within two minutes, Adriano and Lee heard her aging Ape putter into life and surge through the abandoned square and careen toward the bridge leading away from Civita and into Bagnoregio proper.

They were alone.

"What was *that* about?" Lee asked in slack-jawed consternation, crossing himself and getting up from the kneeler in front of the purgatory board.

"I don't know," Adriano said. "Hey, what's that on the sole of your shoe?"

"Did I step in something?" Lee asked, cringing. Not afraid of mice or rats, nonetheless he was squeamish when it came to dog, cat, or pigeon poop.

"Actually, yes." Adriano smiled mysteriously. "That's exactly what you've done. Stepped right into something."

Lee lifted his left foot to see a name, thickly inscribed, in black water-proof ink on the rubber sole of his borrowed boot.

Diacono Andrea Bernardone.

Lee was walking in a dead man's shoes.

CHAPTER XLV

Death Comes Knocking

Saturday, December 21, 2013, 9:03 p.m., the road from Rome

There are bad people in the world. They do bad things. They hurt people. They do not care. They have no fear of death but neither do they have a fear of life. They are. They breathe. They eat. They shit. Some kill for money. Some kill for sexual gratification. Some kill for revenge. Some call it justice.

Such a man was sitting in the back of the bus headed north from Rome this night, the nativity of winter. He had taken the local. There were few people on with him tonight, mostly students or workers headed out of town. No one would remember him. He could sleep at will and wake up fully loaded. Once, when he was in the service in Africa, he had shot a man within seconds of morning consciousness. He had dreamed of it, and on opening his eyes his target was there. That had been gratifying.

He had never been surprised or captured or tricked. He was well paid. He ate well, fucked well, and lived well. He spoke seven languages and was a fan of American cartoons. He read self-help books and Eastern philosophy. Once in a cave, a Sufi wise man had told him, "Hitler went to heaven. When you understand that, you will comprehend the reckless love and unfathomable forgiveness of God."

He had killed the man then, a quick, painless snap of the neck. Take that, Adolf. He didn't like hearing stories about Hitler. Amateur. Coward. Suicide.

Mussolini had come first: *Il Duce del fascismo.* Nay, *Il CREATORE del fascismo.*

The bus hit a pothole in the road, bumping his thoughts to another track, like a misfiring eight-track cassette player. He was proud of his work. His anonymous career had been widely documented but never proven in the pages of *Le Monde*, on the television affiliates of CNN, on the computer screens of Al Jazeera, and on internet sites—banned and reinstituted and rebanned around the planet—of the most degrading war sites imaginable.

The bus screeched to a halt, a deserted and graffiti-mocked stop just outside of the almost deserted town. Across the road, an "Amer---n Bar" sign winked its sporadic neon of lascivious Morse code. Brothel. A Nigerian prostitute, two months ago a teacher in Bengazi, leaned pathetically outside one of the doors. She caught his eye as he stepped from the bus. She smiled. He smiled back.

He would have preferred a boy tonight. After all, diversity was the spice, but, she would do. He walked toward the hotel. He'd need his sleep, but before, why not a bit of diversion. Tomorrow was going to be a big day.

The hooker shifted her stance in anticipation of her late-night client. She twirled a cheap crucifix between her breasts as the man approached. Perfect, the assassin thought, as he grabbed her by the waist and pushed her inside. Anyone wearing a cross deserved to die.

CHAPTER XLVI

The Tower of Secrets

Sunday, December 22, 2013, just after midnight, Civita di Bagnoregio

Adriano watched Clemente yawn, stretch his back, and settle in to observe the crime unfold with a bored but not totally disapproving nonchalance.

"You know this is breaking and entering," he scowled.

"We're not breaking and we've already entered. We're just *looking*. Hold the flashlight higher."

Lee sat at Signora Bernardone's small, tidy desk in the back room-cum-office for *La Torre dei Segriti*, B and B.

"I don't know why you don't just turn on the lights. There's no one else in town," Adriano huffed, surrendered now to his own curiosity despite moral and fearful misgivings.

"This building overlooks the valley. A light could be seen all the way from Lubriano. Plus, maybe Andrea's mother was wrong. Maybe she forgot someone and there are others in town."

"Meow!" Clemente padded in, purring like a furry Vespa-on-paws, and jumped into Adriano's lap.

"See, only thee, me, Clemente, and an army of cats. What are we looking for anyway?"

"I don't know," said Lee. "Something. Anything. Hand me the flashlight."

As Adriano reached for the torch, Clemente jumped to find a more suitable perch, landing smack in the middle of a precariously stacked tower of books that instantly went tumbling onto the floor.

"Jesus Christ!" Adriano roared, his exasperation fully unsheathed. "Now Andrea's mother will *know* we've been snooping!"

"Shh... We can blame it on the cat, and well, that will be true. Nothing broke. It's only an old album full of pictures. Hey, who's this?"

Lee picked up one of the scattered photo pages.

"It's Andrea," said Adriano, taking the page.

"And Grigori." Lee pointed to the photo's second subject.

Andrea and Grigori were seated at a table at some seaside café, the young deacon in shorts and simple black T-shirt, Grigori in a bathing suit and, well, a smile. They were leaning away from each other, but underneath the table, Adriano could see that their feet were touching.

"Well, Andrea's certainly not wearing clericals here," said Adriano, handing back the photo.

"And Grigori's not in uniform."

"Uniform?"

Lee sighed. "Grigori is—*was*, I guess is more correct—a Swiss Guard for the Pope at the Vatican."

"How do you know?"

"You know too. You've seen the picture. Here. I'll show you." Lee whipped out his iPhone and googled. The search came up in the handheld's memory: Swiss Guard Pope Benedict Communion.

"I called up the image right after that day working on the living Nativity when I got a close-up view, and whiff, of Grigori.

"It's that picture from the program at the pope thingy you dragged me to," said Adriano.

"Exactly. That's Grigori, admittedly seven years and a few hundred workouts ago, taking Holy Communion from Pope Benedict."

"Hmmmm. Well, maybe that rumor that Peg told you was true. Andrea and Grigori were lovers. I can see the headlines now. 'Pope's Bodyguard in Gay Love Triangle With Young Priest.' Your Vatican press guy..."

"...Gorgeous George."

"Yeah, even Roman Catholicism's flack-in-chief would have been hard-pressed keeping that one under wraps."

"Maybe he did before the story hit the media."

"You mean, someone killed Andrea to keep this story from going public?" Adriano's eyebrows were raised higher than a Vulcan's.

"No. I mean a story with that headline, or the threat of one, might just be enough to have the Vatican intervene in the ordination of an idealistic young priest from Orvieto. And, that intervention might just be enough to push said priest over the edge. More to the point, to jump over the edge."

Adriano started to speak but stopped. The subject of jumping from heights was one not lightly entered into during their marriage. If broached, Lee would have to initiate the conversation.

Lee picked up another page from the album, and another, and another, all laden with images of Andrea and Grigori together. There were photos at the beach—seemingly from the same day as the first one given their outfits, or in Grigori's case, lack thereof—and in front of the Duomo in Orvieto (this time both of them in jeans and polo shirts). There was a black-and-white triptych of Andrea and Grigori, one of those vertical film strips taken in a coin-operated photo booth. The first two images were goofy and laughing. The third, taken a split-second later, showed Grigori's face turning for what, obviously, would have been a kiss in frame four. As if to confirm the narrative even more completely, there was a photo of them both in the garments of their respective ranks, Grigori in full Swiss Guard attire standing at the entrance to the Vatican, unsmiling, rigid, on duty. Next to him stood Andrea in clericals.

Turning the page, Lee revealed an envelope stuffed to the point of bursting. On its cover was written three words: il purgatorio è la chiave.

"Purgatory is the key," Adriano translated.

The couple looked at each other. The envelope was unsealed. They turned it on its end and watched the contents spill out.

File cards, dozens of file cards, just like the ones from the Church of San Donato next door, spilled onto the desk like entries from a ballot box. Plus, there were two other items, a folded map of the world and a final picture of Andrea and Grigori standing in front of the purgatory prayer board. Lee turned over the photo. There was a handwritten date: *30 Novembre 2012.*

Andrea's birthday. The day he jumped.

Lee was already rising from his chair and headed for the door.

"We're going back to the church, aren't we?" said Adriano. All his hopes of putting a stake through Lee's paranoiac obsession with Andrea were now crushed. The gay *Romeo & Juliet* of Andrea and Grigori was once again a bad film noir plot. He watched with annoyed trepidation as Lee pushed all the cards, the photo, and the map back into the envelope, and stuffed it into the pocket of his jeans.

"Let's go."

The plaza of *San Donato* was now fully lit by moonlight, the intermission scrim of clouds completely retracted in anticipation of the second act with Adriano and Lee, the only actors on stage. Civita di Bagnoregio. Population: two humans, a cat named Clemente, and a supporting chorus of feline falsettos.

They opened the church door.

It is said that cemeteries are the most frightening things at night, but the ancient, moldy, and abandoned interior of *San Donato* ranked right up there. For once, Adriano didn't push back against Lee's dip into the holy water next to the entrance. Frankly, like the punchline to a dirty joke about fallen Irish nuns, he was ready to gargle with it. Opting for a quick splash, he held on to his husband's coattail and tiptoed across the sanctuary toward the purgatory board, wondering as he did why the pretense of quiet. There was no one to wake, except the dead.

Santa Vittoria's freeze-dried visage glowed brothel red in the shimmering reflections of a dozen glass-encased votive candles. Undoubtedly Clarissa, in her enigmatic haste to leave, had forgotten to extinguish them before her exit. Adriano wondered if they posed a fire danger. He'd take the risk. Rats didn't like fire.

In the flickering rose of the candles, everything was as it has been, save one thing.

The box was gone.

CHAPTER XLVII

Time Grows Short

Sunday, December 22, 2013, late evening, Orvieto

For once, the smoke bothered Arnaud. His visitor's cigarette was hand-rolled, and made of strong Egyptian tobacco. It was unfiltered and cloying, like the smell of freshly killed game. The scent of death.

The Archbishop clasped his hands tightly in front of him. He hoped his companion could not see that they were shaking in the darkness.

The man inhaled deeply of his cigarette, then casually dropped it onto the tapestry carpet of the Bishop's office. Briefly, a flare destroyed a fourteenth-century motif before the man stamped it out, in no particular hurry. The Bishop said nothing. He would have to invent a story about an acolyte being clumsy with a candle to explain the damage or move the desk to cover the scar. That could wait. There were other things to be dealt with now.

Finally, the man spoke.

"Your Eminence, the package has not been delivered."

"What do you mean?" Arnaud croaked.

"The girl. She has not arrived as promised."

"Oh."

"And one more thing. The box is missing."

A foul puddle congealed on the floor underneath the desk. The Archbishop had wet himself.

CHAPTER XLVIII

Songs from the Grave

Monday, December 23, 2013, 8:10 am, Orvieto

Kiri Te Kanawa was singing.

"Happy birthday, dear one." Lee turned up the volume on his iPhone and put the portable vocals next to Brian's ashes on the bookcase.

Adriano saluted their friend with a lifted cup of cappuccino. "How old would he have been?"

"Ninety," Lee said, lighting a special birthday candle in front of his best friend's ashes and moving the Padre Pio battery-operated one to the side. Today required wax and wicks. Birthdays *were* special, and especially to Brian—his own, Lee's, Adriano's, the Queen's. Every birthday required a morning of music, generally at an hour guaranteed to awaken the celebrant before he was ready. For the last three years of Brian's life, living in Adriano and Lee's downstairs guest room, birthday preludes included a full-throated and fully volumed recording of opera singer Dame Kiri Te Kanawa singing "Happy Birthday" to Queen Elizabeth II during the opening ceremony of the 2006 Commonwealth Games in Melbourne, Australia. A global audience of 1.5 billion people had tuned in to see Her Majesty receive her due in front of 80,000 spectators. Slightly fewer across San Francisco could hear the Kiwi icon belting it out when Brian turned up his speakers.

"Well, as Brian used to say about the Anglican Church, 'If they do something twice, it's a tradition.'"

"Exactly," Lee agreed, somewhat distractedly. "And just because someone is dead doesn't mean you cancel a tradition. All the more reason, actually, to continue it." Why is it I'm always celebrating the birthdays of people now dead? he thought, but pushed it away. Adriano nodded in agreement and took a sip of his coffee.

Lee stared with Adriano at Brian's makeshift altar in silence, less grief than an excuse not to talk about what had happened in Bagnoregio. After all, that's what traditions were designed for, what religious liturgy was all about. Scripted processions to help people get through the inexplicable. Baptisms. Weddings. Communion. Funerals. All of them connect-the-dot formulae of human interaction to give pattern to the ineffability of life and love and to keep uncontrollable emotions at bay. Exactly what they were both doing this morning.

Yesterday, they had taken the bus to Orvieto from Civita di Bagnoregio in almost complete silence and spoken little since their return. The previous day's dawn had broken cold and rainy, perfect for their mood. Neither relished a soggy schlep home. Lee had lain next to Adriano, side by side, fully dressed where they had collapsed after the previous evening's drama like the couple in *On the Beach*, waiting for the silent invasion of a radioactive breeze. They didn't bother to change or shower, and were up and out the door of *La Torre dei Segriti* before Clarissa Bernardone's breakfast surrogate could arrive. They had left a note of thanks and a saucer of milk for Clemente as they exited like escaping burglars, which is exactly what they were. When they got home, Lee discovered the crumpled envelope of petitions stuffed into the pocket of his jeans. Adriano just shook his head. In the rush to leave *La Torre dei Segreti,* Lee had forgotten that he had it. Of course, while that had been an accidental crime, the real theft of the evening was all too purposeful. The purgatory box from *San Donato*. Supposedly alone in town, they had been side by side with the thief himself. Lee could not shake the thought that someone had watched them go into the church. Had stalked them. Had feared that they had discovered some secret better left undiscovered and then stolen the box before they could return. Adriano, ever the logician, had a simpler explanation: "The priest came at night and took the box away for the night, to pray or something."

Knowing that Adriano was close to one of his epic temper tantrums, Lee didn't extrapolate that San Donato, a town with fewer than a dozen inhabitants, was too small to have a regular priest living in it. And, even if the priest from Bagnoregio wanted to gather the box of petitions for Mass the next morning, they would have heard him driving into town. Or, even walking up the steep, cobblestoned ramp that connected Civita to the town beyond. No, Lee was certain of one thing. Whoever had stolen the box of prayers—or clues, as Lee was now more and more convinced—had seen them enter the church, had watched them rifle through the box, and then when given the opportunity had stolen the evidence before it could be better and more fully contemplated. Whoever that was, he had been hiding in the church all along.

"Maybe it was Clarissa, Andrea's mother," Adriano had reasoned, but even he had backed away quickly from that. Both of them had heard her speed away in her mini three-wheeler, a contraption whose noise and speed precluded any return that would not have been noticed.

Their clothes lay where they had dropped them last night, a pile of discarded garments that might have been a memory of earlier debauches, but not this time.

"So, what happened in Bagnoregio?" Adriano asked.

Lee looked up from where he was quietly shuffling the pile of purgatory cards in front of him on the table. He had awoken before Adriano, and had laid out the petitions like the pieces of a jigsaw puzzle awaiting assemblage. Next to it, the map lay unfolded, the photo of Andrea and Grigori leaned against the sugar. Adriano had most purposefully ignored the display as he prepared their breakfast. Lee noticed his husband's not-noticing and pretended not to notice. He wasn't happy about either.

"I have no fucking idea," Lee spat out with cool and uncharacteristic venom. He wanted to add, don't ask questions you don't want answered, but he stayed silent. Adriano retreated into the kitchen for another cup of coffee.

But, thought Lee, I do know what it's all about. *Andrea.* The photos they had found in the office of *Il Torre Segreti*, Clarissa's weird flight into the night, the strangely tantalizing deck of prayer-ridden cards, and the box stolen right under their noses. They all had one common thread: Deacon Andrea Bernardone and his leap from the cliffs of Orvieto a year ago on his birthday after the Vatican ended his vocation before it got started.

Lee looked across the room to see their clothes, piled next to the boots, lying where he had shrugged them off last night after their trudge back from Bagnoregio. "Diacono A. Bernardone" stared up at him in rubberized accusation. One of the neighbors could be heard moaning through their ceiling, a woman. I guess someone's morning was off to a good start, Lee smirked to himself. He felt numb. Tired from three days of hiking, tired from his brain that could not be shut off, tired and more than a bit frightened from the strange theft of a container of prayer intentions whose bizarre markings and random numberings left him with a foreboding sense of déjà vu.

"We should have told Clarissa Bernardone about what happened in the church, and we should tell her about taking the envelope. Actually, we should never have taken the envelope or even broken into her office," Adriano said, sitting down at the table and offering more coffee to Lee, who motioned away the effort.

"We didn't break in," said Lee, ashamed of himself for the semantics of a lie. It was like Bill Clinton saying "It depends on what the definition of *is* is."

The file cards from *La Torre dei Segriti* were spread out between them, a no-man's-land both tempting and prohibiting conversation. Adriano wasn't going to go there. Not today, not quite yet. He would make Lee make the first move; make him suffer a bit. This was Lee's freak show. Adriano wasn't going to engage. Almost immediately, he felt dirty for thinking such things, but he still pretended that the cards weren't there. He looked over at Lee, who was doing his best not to return the gaze. Although it often drove him crazy, Adriano longed for a bit of his husband's usual caffeinated morning perkiness. It was most decidedly not in evidence today. Lee's demeanor was positively dark.

"Maybe we should report it to the carabiniere," Adriano said, stronger than he had intended.

"Oh right," Lee said with a nasty bite. "Hi, we're a couple of faggots from San Francisco who snuck into a church to make fun of the Catholic voodoo, and then we found some prayer cards with a secret code penned by superstitious wing nuts—"

"I never said Catholics were superstitious wing nuts."

"—and then we snuck into the office of the mother of a boy who killed himself, ransacked her office, and stole an envelope marked 'Purgatory is the key.' Oh yes, then we left our hotel without paying. Isn't that about it?"

"You need some more coffee."

"I need my husband to fucking take me seriously for once in our god-damn life."

The outburst came so quickly that it stunned both of them, Lee hurling the accusation across his husband's face like a slap and Adriano's retort of flinging the teacup across the room. It shattered against the bookcase. A residue of strong Italian coffee bled down Brian's urn and puddled onto the cover of the birthday present book from Magda, *41.43 N; 49.56 W.*

They both said it at once. "I'm sorry," and then dropped to the floor in tears followed by other things.

~

Afterward, they lay in the nest of their wrinkled and muddy hiking clothes from the last four days. Adriano picked up a T-shirt and started to wipe off Brian's urn. Lee found his one sock not caked with mud and did the same to the *Titanic* tome.

"I guess we're both pretty brave," Lee said, caressing his husband's neck and kissing his naked back.

"What do you mean?"

"Brian's advice, remember? 'The first person to apologize is the bravest. The first person to forgive is the strongest. The first person to forget is the happiest.'"

"I'm sorry, honey." Adriano returned his husband's kiss. The floor was now a mountain of clean and dirty clothes, postcoital proof of the power of love after a fight brought on by pent-up stress. "I do take you seriously, I just..."

"I know," Lee said, putting a finger to his partner's lips. "I know. I'm not very good at the last part. Forgetting. I shouldn't have said that. It's just that I know I've become obsessed with Andrea's death, his suicide, and it's brought up a lot of, a lot of..."

"A lot of painful memories."

"Yes." Lee's eyes were brimming pools, threatening to overflow. "You know I don't like to talk about it, but I think about it, about them, all the time."

Lee's silence lingered.

"Your suicide attempt?"

Lee felt blood drain from his face. They had never talked about it. "Yes." Lee turned and faced his husband full-on and grabbed his hands hard—harder than he had ever grabbed anything—anything except the railings of the Golden Gate Bridge. "Yes. I tried to kill myself on my eighteenth birthday. Andrea succeeded on his twenty-ninth. It's just so weirdly seren-dipitous, us being identical in age and my being here in Orvieto, arriving here on his birthday, our birthday. It's been too much. That, and thinking of my parents, of that...that...horrible day."

Lee stopped talking. Adriano just sat. In ten years of marriage, they had never discussed it, Lee's family's death. Of course, Adriano knew. There were passenger lists. Newspaper articles. The internet. Relentless reporters doing stories about victims' families, especially two years ago on the tenth anniversary. Lee never discussed it. Some things, even in marriage, were better off left unsaid. The title and numbers of that day when the world seemed to career out of control hung in the air, no need to be spoken.

9/11.

"My family was on that flight that crashed into the Pentagon." Lee spoke simply, with the words and the emotion of someone for whom any-thing other than simplicity is an obscenity. "I was going to fly down to LA to meet them, and they were going to spend three months with me in Cal-ifornia and then celebrate my birthday before heading home. I graduated early from high school in Richmond, and had been accepted at the Catho-lic Seminary in San Francisco. I was supposed to take my preliminary vows on December first, the day after my eighteenth birthday."

"It was around then that you met Brian?"

"Yes," Lee stated, wiping his eyes. "Brian was at the Pacific Divinity School, Anglican, Episcopal. We met at some interfaith conference that summer. I knew I was called to the priesthood but there was something wrong, I just didn't feel right being ordained Roman Catholic..."

"...being gay."

"Exactly," Lee said. "Yes. I remember, Brian gave the sermon at Grace Cathedral. I'll never forget the opening lines. 'We must reinvent Christianity.' Some of the Catholic priests sitting around me almost plotzed. The Anglicans just looked, well, *smug*."

"I imagine so."

"That's when I decided," Lee said, reaching into the tangle of clothes around them for something approaching wearability. The apartment was suddenly very cold. "I wasn't going to be a priest...not a Catholic priest. I was going to reject Catholicism, convert, and become an Episcopal priest."

"What did Brian say?" Adriano's mouth was ajar. This part he had never heard. And while Lee might have kept a decade of secrets, during the death-rattled weeks leading up to Brian's death, many confessions had been made at the dying deacon's bedside. If Brian had known, he would have shared this with Adriano.

"He never knew." Lee smiled, pulling on a pair of underwear and searching for his pants. "I had made the decision the week before my family arrived. I was going to tell them, and Brian on September eleven. Ta-da."

"Oh."

"Yes," Lee sighed. "Exactly. My family took the train up from Richmond the night before and stayed at a hotel near Dulles Airport in Northern Virginia, just across the Potomac from the Pentagon. They called me from the hotel to tell me good night. That was the last time I ever spoke with them. I was getting up and heading to the airport to fly down to LA to meet them and then take a long drive up the coast when I turned on the TV. They had never been to California. They had never been on a plane before. They were so excited. Especially my grandmother."

"Oh." Adriano started to say more but couldn't find the words.

"Afterward, I was pretty depressed, pretty angry. Brian stayed with me a lot. I drank a lot. He let me. I crashed on his couch a bunch of times, actually, the night before my birthday. Then, that morning, my birthday, I popped awake early and I knew what I had to do. So, I walked to the Golden Gate Bridge."

"And Brian followed you and kept you from jumping."

Lee just nodded.

"I'm glad he did."

Lee looked deep into his lover's eyes as he pulled on his pants. "I am too. I am too."

They sat there on the floor for a while, just holding each other. Outside, the Tower of the Moor chimed eleven. Finally, they got up. The candle next to Brian's ashes started to smoke in punctuating surrender.

"You think I'm crazy?" Lee asked.

"No," Adriano said, pulling Lee toward him. "I don't. I really don't, I just..." His voice trailed away and his eyes grew moist. "It's just that, ever since we got to Orvieto it seems like the ghost of Deacon Andrea is everywhere. And then these cards, prayer cards last touched by a man who threw himself from the cliff, it was like...like, you were trying to tell me that you were getting ready..."

"...to kill myself?" Lee took Adriano's face in his hands. "Is that what you thought?"

Adriano just nodded.

"Don't worry, husband. I have everything in the world to live for. I have you. I promise. Cross my heart and hope *not* to die."

The woman's moaning upstairs grew a bit louder. The couple laughed.

"I guess someone else had the same idea." Adriano laughed, and Lee joined him.

Just then, a scream pierced the plaster between the apartments. The woman screamed again, and not in pleasure. This was the sound of agony, of someone in pain. Adriano and Lee jumped up and headed for the door, Lee thinking as they dashed into the hall, We don't have neighbors.

CHAPTER XLIX

Camorena

Monday, December 23, 2013, 11:45 a.m., Orvieto

Soon, it would be over. For now.

Don Bello sat quietly in the front row of *San Giovanale*, waiting and wondering. Tomorrow, the church would be full of parishioners, lighting candles, making offerings, heading out the ancient portal to the garden below to take part in the annual living Nativity, his favorite event of the year. *Andrea's favorite too.*

He liked thinking about Andrea, and he smiled. *Better than crying.* That is my cross, Don Bello thought, allowing himself a luxurious moment of self-indulgent pity. I must always be smiling. Always be jovial. Always be Christian. Don Bello must never be sad, or unsure, or unprepared. I must be a rock. My congregation depends upon it. My *sanity* depends upon it.

Who am I kidding? He grimaced. My sanity depends upon the myth of my own fortitude.

Well, it had lasted him lo these almost ninety years. It had gotten him through the Depression, and the rise of Mussolini. More to the point, it had gotten him through the *fall* of Mussolini. It had gotten him through Mussolini himself when Il Duce came to Orvieto and ripped down part of a church to build a new barracks for his Fascist recruits. That had been the Dominican monastery where St. Thomas Aquinas had written a special Mass in honor of the Miracle of Bolsena. It had been rumored that the dictator had designs upon the strategic cliff where stood *San Giovanale*, but even he would not stand up against Don Bello. He had been a new priest then, and Mussolini could certainly have found some crime with which to charge the young cleric, something for which to arrest him. But, he did not. Even in his early twenties, Don Bello was formidable.

So, Don Bello had survived the war, the Nazi occupation of Orvieto, and, of course, its liberation in June of 1944.

If only he could liberate himself from his memories. Those were their own war and held their own prisoners, their own concentration camps. And, of course, Orvieto, and the Orvietani, were not innocent. Official histories and seventy-plus years had a way of painting everyone upon this rock as an antifascist freedom fighter, as an enemy of Mussolini, an opponent of Hitler. Prophets who knew what was coming—who would win, who would lose. Who would live, and who would be dragged away to die because they chose the wrong political party, or sometimes, just because they fed young and idealistic rebels in the woods surrounding Orvieto.

The Camorena.

The road leading up the hill from the train station in Scalo bore the name *Via Sette Martiri*. The Street of the Seven Martyrs. The sign on the wall of the building where they were condemned by the local fascist leader of Orvieto bore witness. The names of the seven on the plaque above their graves just outside of Orvieto marked the spot where Don Bello had found them, too late. Holy water and prayers did little to bring back those with a bullet through the brain. Lazarus was a nice story, but nothing with which to comfort the shredded life of a mother, a lover, a wife, a son. The painting in Café Volsini was a daily reminder. As if he, or Velza Volsini, needed art to remember.

Don Bello had pleaded for their lives. The German commandant had argued for mercy. But, officially, Mussolini's second government was the law—officially at least—and the Fascist mayor of Orvieto wanted to make a point. And so, the seven partisans—no, children, most no older than nineteen—were herded into the back of a pickup truck, sitting on their own freshly carved coffins, and driven to the forest of Camorena to be executed.

I should have done something, he thought, but I did not. *I was helpless. Bullshit. I was complicit.* After the execution, he and La Donna Volsini—Velzna then a very young girl—had gone to find the graves. The same young Catholic German officer had driven them to Camorena to find the bodies. Don Bello blessed them. They dug fresh graves, one for each victim, instead of the mass pit rapidly prepared by the Italian Fascists. Velzna fainted.

Five months later, the war was over. Over for Orvieto. The Germans left. The British freed the city, but not without cost. The meticulously groomed British War Cemetery just across the river confirmed the price: 188 marble gravestones. Afterward, of the Fascist Orvietani who had overruled the Germans to kill their own neighbors, many left, but others...

Yes. Orvieto had many secrets, and most of them still hiding in plain sight. Some of them buried in unmarked, unsanctified graves between here and Camorena. Even a priest could not be expected to give Christian burial to a Christian who murdered in the name of Mussolini, couldn't he? Couldn't *he*? After so many years?

Today, the memories came rushing back, and the name, Camorena.

Why? Why today did the incident whose memory still was barely scabbed over in Orvieto after more than seven decades come rushing back? Something had resurrected it, rolled back the stone of his carefully sequestered past to collide with his thoughts this day. His thoughts of Andrea.

Andrea.

Camorena.

He knew why the secret and his secret grief had returned. The photo. He saw it today as if for the first time. The photo from the crinkled newspaper reporting on Andrea's jump from the cliff's last year. He had never really looked closely at it before, at him. *At him.*

But today, he looked. He looked deep into the newsprint and for the first time he saw. He *saw*. He *knew*. He knew how—no, that he had always known, the how. But like a vision from above, for the first time looking at the photo accompanying that painful article, he had truly seen its subject, and he knew something more important than the *how* of last year. He knew *who*, and he knew *why*. Peering at the faded photo in newsprint had driven him deep into his cedar chest, flat on his stomach, pulling the ancient valise from under his bed, stuffed with photos from Orvieto's past. Families and funerals and futilities. Finally, he had found it. The photo of a boy, at the funeral of his father. Carefully, he laid it next to the photo in the paper from last year, and he knew they were the same.

The grieving boy had become a killer of men, of many.

I the Lord your God am a jealous God, visiting the iniquity of the fathers on the children to the third and the fourth generation of those who hate me.

So much for the existence of a loving God. The sins of the father had indeed been visited upon the son, upon many mother's sons.

How many people have died keeping this secret, he thought, and how did I not see it until now?

That whole dreadful winter of 1944 came pouring back into his brain, like slides dropped across his eyes. January 28, 1944, the bombing of the Bridge at Allerona just beyond Orvieto. March 24, 1944, the Ardeatine Massacre in Rome. March 29, 1944, the Camorena.

A trinity of horrors, whose connection had been kept secret until today. Today, when Don Bello made the connection between the faded photo under his bed and the picture in last year's newspaper.

"The sins of the father..."

I will die with these secrets, mine and Orvieto's, and my guilt, Don Bello thought, wrestling himself back to the *present. Enough. Stop the vanity of such thoughts. You are a* priest. Holding the confessions of seventy years worth of sins is not your cross, it's your job. Pull yourself together.

And yet, some sins were difficult to forget. Forgiveness was easy. That was the job of the Almighty. But forgetting? That was the occupation of men. But Don Bello was the earpiece of the Almighty. He was supposed to be able to do both. Forgive *and* forget. The sins of a Nazi colonel? They were forgiven. The sins of a pregnant girl? They were forgiven. The sins of a fallen priest? They were forgiven.

But who would forgive the unforgivable? Who would forgive him? Who would forgive a priest who had refused to give Christian burial to a murderer?

Only God can forgive the sins I have cataloged, mine included. The sins flow over me, like waterfalls from a cliff, a cascade of human misery and desperation relieved by the sign of a cross, a few *Hail Marys*, and the obligatory Act of Contrition. They touch my stony face, weep down and disappear. Ego absolve. I absolve you. I absolve nothing. No one. All I do is prattle and dictate prayers. I'm not a priest. I'm a theological stenographer. I help no one. I couldn't even help Andrea last year. Seventy years ago, I couldn't save seven young boys whose only sin was believing that one day their home, Orvieto, might again be free.

"Don Bello?"

The priest looked up, but too late. The giant had entered silently and thrown himself at the Pastor of San Giovanale before he could stand.

"Help me!" he cried, and Don Bello enfolded the weeping man in his arms. "Help me! They have come for her."

Don Bello rose and pulled his companion up with him. Forgiveness would have to wait.

CHAPTER L

What Child Is This?

Monday, December 23, 2013, 11:45 a.m., Orvieto

The woman's screams led Lee, followed by Adriano, to a doorway one flight up from their own. Locked.

Shrieks punctuated by groans of unmistakable pain echoed through the empty corridor. This time, words accompanied them. "الرجاء مساعدتي!"

"That sounds like Arabic," Adriano said.

"What does it mean?"

"Even I don't speak Arabic. I just know the sound. Whatever it means, she's in trouble. We'll have to break it down." Adriano was already pulling backward, ready to throw himself at the portal.

Lee grabbed his arm.

"What if there's a murderer in there!"

Adriano opened his mouth to say something but nodded instead.

"يا الله، وقف الألم. رجاء!"

"We'll have to risk it," Adriano said. "Let's roll."

Just then, the front door three flights down burst open. Lee looked over the railing to hear two pair of footsteps pounding up the stairs, both taking the steps two at a time. Lee looked at Adriano and mouthed "I love you." There was nowhere to go. Whatever was about to happen would be over in about twenty seconds. They held each other's hands tightly and steeled themselves for conflict as the shadows dashing up the stairs crossed their faces and then materialized into two familiar faces.

"Grigori?"

"Luke!"

Rushing past them without a word, Grigori pulled out a Swiss flag-emblazoned key ring, and with practiced ease slipped one of its members into the lock. Nonetheless, the tumbler wouldn't turn.

"Hurry, Grigori!" the German doctor urged frantically. "It may already be too late!"

"Back off, Doc," Grigori snarled, pushing Luke backward with his substantial shoulder muscles. "I'm doing the best that I can! The lock is stuck."

Suddenly, the door gave way and the quartet tumbled into the darkened apartment.

The young woman was lying on the bed in a pool of blood. The sheets congealed around her legs in a sticky cocoon. The young doctor was beside her instantly, and just as quickly shouting out orders that even the belligerent Grigori obeyed without hesitation.

"Get me as much hot water as you can, and towels. *Schnell!*"

For the next few minutes everything was purposeful chaos. Grigori and Luke tended to their patient as if slipping into previously practiced roles that even their obviously mutual antagonism could not prohibit. Lee and Adriano stood in the background like the lost tourists they were. Adriano tapped his husband on the shoulder and pointed. The wall opposite the bed held a bulletin board overflowing with a cacophony of content held intact by multi-colored push pins. Holy cards, a map of Italy dotted with Post-it notes, and a laminated sheet listing the sins from *San Donato*'s purgatory board in Bagnoregio, 1–90. Beneath it, a small desk groaned beneath an Arabic/Italian dictionary, an aging computer, printer, fax machine, and...

The stolen purgatory box.

"I'm beginning to think we should leave," Adriano whispered to Lee.

"The apartment?"

"No. Orvieto."

Just then, a sliver of light from the back of the apartment shot across the room. Everyone turned to its source. Clemente the cat padded in like a verger leading the principal celebrant.

"Am I too late?" sighed Don Bello, making a mysterious and panting appearance in the doorway to the kitchen. "How is she? How is Maryam? I brought my holy oils."

"She's lost a lot of blood," Luke said, dropping his stethoscope into his pocket. "I can't tell yet, but I think the baby's umbilical cord may be wrapped around its neck and putting pressure on the mother as well." The young doctor had a strange look on his face as he spoke, as if he repeating a diagnosis he had given before.

"I'd forgotten how steep those stairs were, and how low the ceiling," said Don Bello. He leaned on Grigori as he gently descended into an armchair whose frame seemingly matched his own age. Clemente immediately jumped up into his lap and settled in for a nap, a kitty calm in the midst of chaos. "It's been a long time since I used them."

"A year," Grigori stated flatly.

"Quite so." The old cleric smiled with a pained melancholy. "Exactly, a year."

"Don Bello, we need to get her to the hospital," said Luke.

"We can't go out the front door. They could be watching," said Grigori.

"Watching? Who's watching?" asked Adriano in alarm.

"Probably too late for that," Luke said, ignoring Adriano's query. "We could have been seen rushing into the apartment. What about Arnaud?"

"The Archbishop won't bother us tonight," said Don Bello. "It's others I'm worried about."

"ARRRRGGGHH!" Adriano howled, freezing everyone in place.

"Oh, my dear boys, I didn't see you there," said Don Bello, as if Adriano's scream was as normal as breath. "Buon Natale."

"What is going on here and where did you come from?" Adriano pressed, heaving from his outburst.

The room was silent except for Maryam's moans. Luke started to speak but thought the better of it. Grigori opened his mouth, but Don Bello motioned for silence.

"Well?"

"I came from *San Giovanale*," Don Bello said simply, folding his hands. Adriano just stared at the old man.

"Through the basement."

"We're on the third floor," Adriano said dryly.

"Oh, all right." Don Bello surrendered with a slap of his palms to his sides. "I came up through the secret passage."

"The secret passage," said Lee, who was beginning to feel like a game piece in the penultimate move of Clue.

The elderly cleric just shrugged. "Grigori, get me a little something to revive my flagging spirits. I'll need it if we're going to retrace my steps. Can you find us some grappa?"

"Meowwww."

"And some condensed milk for Clemente."

"It's been a while, but I think I remember where the stash is kept," Grigori said blankly.

"Isn't this your apartment?" Lee asked, remembering Grigori's key ring.

It was the priest who answered. "This is the apartment of Deacon Andrea Bernadone."

Lee's mouth opened, and closed.

CHAPTER LI

Black Market Art

Monday, December 23, 2013, 11:45 a.m., Vatican City

A phone rang in the Vatican Museum. The man who answered didn't need caller ID to know who the call came from. How many black market purveyors of ancient Etruscan art had his direct line? Answer: only one. Only *her*.

"Buonoserra."

"Buonoserra, Tua Eminenza. You received the shipment?"

The cardinal curator inhaled deeply. So typical a question from his caller. She knew that he had gotten everything. She also knew that he was getting ready to vest for the midday audience in St. Peter's Basilica and didn't have time for this call, which, of course, he would take. He also knew that she'd gotten what she was waiting for. The exchange was simultaneous.

"Si, Signora. Si. I have everything. And, as usual, it is of the highest quality. Unique. It has been a long time since we did business. I had forgotten the excellence of your work and the exquisite nature of your product."

"You shouldn't have." The voice on the other end of the line obviously wasn't interested in mindless pleasantries. "Save the flattery for grant applications."

"Of course, of course. And, I trust you received your, paym—ah, your *package* as well?"

"Would we be having this cordial conversation now if I hadn't?"

Good point, the Cardinal thought, frowning and chewing on the inside of his cheek. "Is there anything else?" He dared to push his caller as he looked at the clock. He was expected at the Pope's anteroom in less than ten minutes. He didn't want to be late. This was the new pope's first Christmas season and everyone from the previous regime was on ice as thin as a communion wafer. Oiy. If this latest escapade ever became public, he'd be flattened just as surely.

"No, that is all. Good afternoon, Your Eminence."

"Good afternoon. Buon Natale. Merry Christmas."

"Merry Christmas," said La Donna Volsini and hung up the phone.

Christ on a bike. What I don't do for art. He rushed out to meet the Pope. Lucky him. All he had to do was bless people.

CHAPTER LII

Nativity of Truth

Monday, December 23, 2013, 2013, 3 p.m., Orvieto

Lee held his discovery tightly in his right hand and stood in the middle of the last place Deacon Andrea had called home.

The apartment looked like a crime scene.

Maybe it is...or was, Lee thought, fingering the piece of paper he'd discovered in Andrea's desk. The silence was total. For a brief moment, it was just him, here in this place. He felt like a tomb raider. After three weeks of wondering about, obsessing about the young deacon, Lee was now alone in the room Andrea had left before he jumped. He remembered his own trip to the Golden Gate Bridge railing years before and wondered if Andrea had locked the door behind him. Turned on a night light, made the bed, put away the dishes. That's what Lee had done. He closed his eyes against the memory. A sharp bang shook him from his thoughts and he wheeled around to see the trap door as it fell back against the tiled floor. A cloud of dust hung in the air like a mini atomic blast.

"A secret passage." Adriano stated the obvious, pulling himself up from the hole in the kitchen floor.

Lee helped his husband out of the hole and stared back down a steeply sloping corridor cut from Orvieto's ubiquitous tufo—the place from where Don Bello had mysteriously appeared and just as suddenly retreated, followed by Grigori and Dr. Luke gently carrying Maryam to the hospital.

"Where does it lead?" Lee brushed dust off his husband's shoulders.

"I don't know," Adriano said, looking back. "I only walked about thirty feet down and then it splits into two different tunnels."

"Hmmm," was all Lee could manage, looking around the apartment. Maryam's blouse and bloody bed clothes having been tossed aside, Clemente was now curled up at the foot of the bed, seemingly quite at home.

"OK, let's review." Adriano exhaled. "We just stumbled onto a pregnant refugee hiding in a dead man's apartment."

Lee shook his head in the affirmative, putting together the clues in his head.

"Complete with the James Bond-like appearance of a humpy Swiss Guard and a German doctor right out of central casting."

Another nod.

"Oh, and the sudden appearance of Pandora's box, last seen by us before it was mysteriously stolen from a semi-abandoned church in a town with three people."

"Uh-huh," Lee grunted.

"Have I missed anything?"

"Just this." Lee put a neatly folded piece of printer paper into his husband's hand.

"Peg's missing blog post?"

"Bingo. While you've been playing *Beneath the Planet of the Apes* I've been going through Andrea's desk. It was right there."

"Anything useful?"

"Judge for yourself."

Adriano read aloud.

Heresy, Homo-cide, and Homosexuality in a Small Italian Town
30 November, 2012—A Special Report from Lady Peg

Adriano put down the paper. "That's the day that Andrea jumped."
"Yep. The day he got the ax by the Vatican. Keep going."

In an extensive and exclusive interview given to this reporter, Archbishop Jean Claude Arnaud, senior prelate at the Vatican, said that a "cabal of homosexuals" exists at the heart of the Holy See, operating within steps of the Pope himself. In fact, in one of the more shocking revelations, at the epicenter of the carnal conspiracy are perverse and sexually adventurous members of the once pure and hitherto elite Swiss Guard, sworn to protect His Holiness to point of their own death. One of the Guards—a young "male" with ties to Orvieto, Grigori Morgarten—was forced to resign last year following scandalous revelations about his part in a bisexual prostitution ring operating out of the Swiss Guard barracks. Perhaps their new motto should be "Bisexual, as in buy me something and I'll be sexual," and they should be called "The Swish Guard."

"Bitch!" they exclaimed as one.

"I cannot refute the claim that there is a hive of immorality and homosexual influence within the Church," said Arnaud, alternating tears with prayers during our hour-long conversation. These revelations follow the shocking and controversial experiment at Orvieto's storied church of *Sant'Andrea* earlier this month on All Souls Day, a display of radical ecumenicalism presided over by the pin-up girl for American Episcopalianism, "Vicar Vicky." According to Arnaud, the femme fatale Episcopal priestess is beginning to exert a troubling and growing influence over the hitherto bastion of traditional morality, Bishop Gio Sancarlo. It is of some concern to Arnaud, and to hear him explain it, to His Holiness, Pope Benedict XVI.

"Yeah, right," Adriano huffed, looking up from the page. "Ratzinger, the new Nazi pope and Arnaud as Bishop Goebbels."
"Or Emperor Palpatine and Darth Vader," Lee agreed. "Don't stop. It gets better. Or worse."

Adriano continued.

"I have nothing against the Anglican Church per se," said the Archbishop. "However, Roman Catholicism is the One True Faith. More to the point, the American Episcopal Church is a stinking cesspool of immorality and politically correct social experimentation masquerading as a contemporary interpretation of the Holy Gospel. If the Archbishop of Canterbury wants to allow homosexuals, antithetical communist activists, and women onto its altars and into the ranks of its clergy, so be it. It's not my affair. But, neither will I...ah...will His Holiness allow such in His Church. Not while I—we—draw breath."

Arnaud, 64, seemed especially concerned that members of the Pope's personal security detail, the Swiss Guard, had been tainted by the actions of a homo hooker within its ranks, the aforenamed Grigori Morgarten, a 29-year-old native of Fluelen, Switzerland, on Lake Como near Italy's northern border. Perhaps we should call him the "Homo from Como."

"Bitch!" they both repeated.

"Well, whatever Grigori did after he left the Pope's service, he must have come from a good family," Lee said.

"What do you mean?"

"Not just anyone can apply to be a Swiss Guard. Candidates have to be devout, practicing Catholics and of the highest moral virtue."

"Yeah, well," Adriano said with a smirk, "thankfully, Grigori failed that test. Would have been a terrible waste with that body."

"I didn't think you'd noticed." Lee frowned.

"I'm married, not blind," Adriano said.

Lee motioned for him to finish.

After undergoing the most rigorous of physical and military trainings, the Swiss Guards swear an oath to lay down their bodies to defend the life of the Pope and his cardinals. To hear Bishop Arnaud tell it, our working girl/boy toy Grigori did indeed lay down, and with quite a few live bodies.

The Swiss Guard—easily identifiable around the Vatican by their medieval (and according to legend, Michelangelo-designed) uniforms of blue, red, and orange—are popular with tourists. Evidently in the case of G. Morgarten, his popularity was voluntary. Unnamed sources have spoken with this reporter about sordid tales of prostitution, bisexual orgies within the guard barracks, and even the propositioning of a young visiting monsignor. According to the story, verified by witnesses, the prelate was approached by Grigori at a popular Roman café during the guard's off-duty hours, along with a group of other new recruits. When asked if he would be joining them for dinner, Grigori replied, "Yes, and I'm the dessert."

"It's all complete bullshit," Lee said, taking the paper from Adriano and putting it back in Andrea's desk drawer. "This is *not* the first time a sex mess rocked the Vatican. Just a few years ago, there was a huge scandal involving the Swiss Guard. A young soldier shot his married lover, the Swiss Guard's commander no less, turned the gun on the wife, and then knelt and put the trigger in his own mouth. The Vatican was in full press crisis mode. They swept up the three bodies like it was a minor car accident. I've never heard of a story shut down quicker, much less a ménage à trois murder. Since the Vatican is a sovereign state, the Italian police could do nothing. The Vatican Press Office declared the case closed and blamed it on the young guard's mental instability. It was Gorgeous George's first attempt at PR spin. He gives my profession a bad name."

"So, you think Lady Peg is telling the truth about Grigori?"

"About Grigori being a hooker?"

"All of it."

"Nastiness aside, it could explain a lot," said Lee. "Grigori uses his obvious assets to make a few extra bucks while working in Rome, likely with members of the Curia as clients. He gets caught. The Swiss Guard quietly fires him, and he comes to Orvieto to regroup with his friend Andrea, a nice, young priest he met while on duty in Rome." Lee remembered the photo of the two of them, both in official garb.

"Once here, free from the prying eyes of the Vatican, they do what young people do."

"They fall in love."

"Possibly."

"Absolutely," Lee reiterated. "The pictures don't lie."

"Gossipy Lady Peg finds out, writes her blog post. Someone in the Vatican finds out, your PR friend, Gorgeous George, perhaps."

"The Vatican is already awash in scandal. Vatileaks, pedophile priests, gay communion parties..."

"...and they decide to make an example of Andrea."

"And it's all too much for him and he jumps."

"He jumps," said Adriano, squeezing his husband's arm. "It makes sense."

"Hmmm," was all Lee offered, but his lips were quivering like a Cessna warming up for flight. Adriano would have called it his Spidey-sense, and he would have been right. The whole thing was at once too complex, and too simple. Andrea commits suicide, and within days one bishop has voluntarily retreated to a monastery, never to be heard from again, and the one non-Catholic ordinate in Orvieto, Reverend Vicky, hightails it to Rome. Not to mention Andrea's mother, in exile, but not that far away. Bishop Sancarlo. Reverend Vicky. Sofia Bernardone—all fled from Orvieto but still within its orbit. I'd have wanted to get as far away as possible after something like that, Lee thought. And, I did. I fled as far as possible. I went to sea. And the box, what about all those coded prayers?

"What, you think there's more?"

"What?" Adriano's question pulled Lee from his reverie. "Yes, I do." Lee pointed to the hole in the kitchen and then to the purgatory box on Andrea's desk.

"You have a point," Adriano said.

"Andrea jumped," said Lee.

"Or was pushed?"

"Either by a hand or a motivation, I don't know, but yes, in a sense, Andrea was pushed off that cliff by something. Of that, I'm sure. But, I think the reasons are more twisted than his just having been denied the priesthood. There's something else going on here."

"Like what?"

"Like why Archbishop Arnaud gave that interview to Peg."

"Because he's a hateful homophobe and wanted to keep Andrea off the altar," Adriano said, slapping his hands against his thighs. "He wanted to disgrace Andrea totally, and Grigori."

"He could have done that privately. Why speak to a second-rate blogger, and one from Orvieto?"

"Maybe because he thought Andrea would read it, be so embarrassed that he'd resign from the priesthood, and spare the Church the effort."

"No," Lee said, getting up from Andrea's desk. "No. Archbishop Arnaud wanted to embarrass someone, all right, but I don't think it was Andrea. I think Andrea just got caught in the crossfire of something bigger. Something *much* bigger. Oh no!"

Lee looked down to see Clemente padding toward them like a feline way of the cross, bloody paw prints paving the way back to the bedroom where Maryam had been in such agony. "What a mess. Clemente, bad kitty."

"MeoWWW!"

"Ow! He scratched me!"

Clemente was pawing frantically at Lee's leg, finding a strategic spot of exposed flesh between sock and jean.

"He wants something," Adriano observed. "He's being positively doglike."

"He's being positively annoying. Ow! He scratched me again!"

The cat fixed them both with what could only be described as a withering stare, and then turned to retreat through bloody paw prints back to the bedroom.

Lee and Adriano followed to find the cat next to Maryam's discarded blouse, pulling at an errant string at the hem of the garment, unwinding the thread like a lock.

"Look, there's something sewn into the fabric." Lee picked up the blouse and helped the cat pull. A few seconds later, a small leather satchel tied with a cord plopped out on the bed. Lee looked at Adriano aghast.

"How much weirder can this get?" Adriano asked, picking up the tiny purse. "Smells like salt water and fish."

"Well, Maryam was on a ship for a while. Open it," Lee said.

The string undone, two tiny scrolls of parchment rolled on the bed. Clemente purred, as if to say, "OK, my job is done. You have opposable thumbs. Take it away," and lay down on a pillow away from the mess.

"What do they say?" Lee asked.

Adriano unrolled the two pieces of paper, which offered a scribbled revelation like nothing so much as two playing cards from a board game or a tiny representation of the Dead Sea Scrolls.

"What language is that?"

"They're in Arabic." Adriano exhaled. "Except this one line at the bottom of each card in Italian. Il purgatorio è la chiave."

Lee didn't need Adriano to translate—"Purgatory is the key."

It was going to be a long night.

CHAPTER LIII

Bridge of Cries

Monday, December 23, 2013, sunset, Allerona

Death was coming for the Archbishop, but not quite yet.

The assassin exhaled, feeling the carefully concealed tools of his trade press ever so gently against his rigorously trained torso. A stiletto. A German revolver. A silencer. A capsule of Cyanide—not for him—for others who might get in his way. Suicide was for cowards. Not for him. He turned his mind to the job soon at hand.

It would be neat, tidy, and if possible, bloodless. Not that he had anything against blood. Far from it. It was just so hard to sculpt a memorable tableau when the scene was coated in sanguinity. There was always an errant shoe print, or a handprint, or, in this case, a medieval tapestry to be stained. He had a healthy respect for history. After all, he had a lineage to uphold. Madrid. London. New York. Washington. Tripoli. Blood on a massive scale was an easily staged chaos, the theater of mere terrorists. Uncreative. Vulgar. Cheap. Bloodless murder was preferable. So much more challenging to undertake. So much more satisfying and memorable. So much more horrifying in its starkness. To first see a collation of tourists or school children coated in blood, that was one thing. But to discover a body that at first appeared to be alive, and then to find it lifeless, that was a double shock to the discoverer. That was a statement. That was *le grand opus*. That was *art*.

Yes. Arnaud must die, but not quite yet.

After he was sure there was no information left to extract from the Prince of the Church. *After* he had retrieved the box. *After* he had turned Maryam over to her rightful owners. *After* he had retrieved the final two cards from her clothes—the cards her brother was supposed to have delivered to San Donato. Dawud! His disobedience would have to be dealt with. That one, he might let get bloody. Who would mourn another dirty migrant washed up on the shores of Italy or tossed along the road next to some Winnebago brothel? No one. Nevertheless, he'd make it look like an accident. *Pimp killed in a fight with his hooker and a client.* That one always worked well.

He took out one of his expensive Egyptian cigarettes, leaned against the wall underneath the railway bridge. All was quiet, a silent night. Suddenly, the masonry of the oft-destroyed, oft-replaced edifice groaned and shook, a violent rape of the night. Dust fell onto the assassin's face, but he didn't move. He had seen worse than dust under this bridge. Overhead, the night train to Vienna sped by. As quickly as it began, the assault was over. Silence, restored. He was alone with the memorial of World War Two's worst "friendly fire" disaster and his memories, his father's memories.

A train full of prisoners. An aerial bombardment by the Allies meant for Nazis. A lifetime explaining *how*? Then banishment and, finally, a self-made death.

His memories: A parked car. A bullet to the back of a throat. A night spent hugging his father's body until a farmer found him the next day. A week later, he was at the orphanage. Ten years later, he was learning his trade—a killer's skills—in the north of Africa. And now? Now there were other vows to pervert, but only for a little more. Then, this journey would be over.

But, not quite yet. He was in no hurry. His victims would wait through the night. They weren't going anywhere, at least not yet. They would wait for him, just down the road from this tainted spot. He didn't have the key, but no matter. Someone would let him in. Italians were so friendly, especially this time of year.

He inhaled deeply and blew out three perfectly circular smoke rings, an infinity of poison. He watched them hover in front of him, and then float upward toward the train tracks above. He watched them rise from his lips, past the monument to the victims of the WWII tragedy that had killed over six hundred British and American prisoners of war, scores of German guards, and more than a few civilian train operators. Of course, the memorial was only to the Allies. Post-war Italy didn't convene international design competitions to mark the graves of Nazis or Italian workers, oh no. Victors wrote the history books, and American expats funded memorials to fallen fathers, brothers, and heroes whose only courage entailed getting captured and killed. An accidental heroism dredged up for masses and magazines and memorialists.

No one built a monument to my father, the assassin thought with a brief moment of self-reflective bitterness.

No matter. In a few days, his honor will have been restored. He spat onto the ground at the foot of the monument next to the memorial plaque, which read:

On 28 January 1944, while a freight train was transporting British, South African, and American prisoners of war toward prison camps in Germany, the United States Army Air Force bombed the bridge at Allerona just a few miles outside of Orvieto, causing over 600 dead, many never to be identified.

His father had tried to keep the train in Orvieto. The German officials had not listened, especially that arrogant and self-righteous Nazi colonel. Catholic—a Roman Catholic Nazi. They had listened to him and ignored his father, a true Italian. A follower of Mussolini who had restored the Vatican to independence. An Italian. No matter. They had ignored his father. They sent the train on. His father knew. The Americans did not care who was in the train, or if there was a train. The bridge would be bombed.

Fratello che passi, ricorda:
Noi siamo morti qui
Per la tua liberta.

Remember this
All you pass by this place:
We died that you may be free.

28.01.44–28.01.2012

He didn't need a plaque to remember, and nothing could ever make him forget.

His father had no plaque. His father was barely allowed to have a grave. The beloved pastor of Orvieto's San Giovanale wouldn't even bless it, some bullshit about "the soil crying out for justice" and "consecrated earth."

Don Bello.

Yes, more than all the others, Don Bello must die. But only after he had watched, helplessly, as all the others preceded him. *That* was the ultimate gift he would leave behind as his legacy, proof of the perfidy and hypocrisy of that supposedly kind and Christian man, Father Nicola Moldadeschi. Don Bello. Proof of the perfidious faith known as the Holy Roman Catholic Church.

He turned away from the monument under the bridge and its scarred, shrapnel-laced pilasters, its concrete spine sticking up from the river bed, from which summer rains still brought forth the skulls and bones and occasional medals of those who had died here. A tidal pool of sun-bleached putrefaction. Two months later, his father had done his duty again, eking out punishment for seven traitors to the *Patria*. Partisans, the Germans called them. Spineless Nazi. Traitors. His father knew otherwise. Three days after the justified reprisals at the Ardeatine Caves, Orvieto was expected to show its fidelity to the fatherland. The motherland. To Mussolini. And so, his father had done his job, and been cursed for it. And now, every year students trooped to the forest of Camorena to pay tribute to those traitors, martyrs only to a fictional future, fodder for essays about a history that was only half taught.

Enough of this morbid melancholia. The assassin turned away. He had victims waiting for him, including two new ones that he had not yet met, but soon. Two Americans who had stumbled into something they should never have known.

Oh well, it was the Season of Giving.

Merry Christmas.

He turned his steps to the town that had given him life, the town that had raised then destroyed his father. The town that had forgotten *his* name and erased the memory of his father's. In a few days, they'd remember it again. It was just a ten-minute train ride away, but all the trains had passed for tonight. On foot, perhaps two hours, and he knew the way. He had time, all the time in the world. He laughed to himself. It was the people he'd see in a few hours who were now out of time.

The assassin turned his steps for Orvieto.

CHAPTER LIV

Revelation

Monday, December 23, 2013, 11 p.m., Orvieto

"This is some sort of code." Lee spoke with certainty. He had done too many acrostics over the years not to recognize a puzzle when it presented itself.

For the last several hours, Lee had poured through the mysterious card catalogue of heavenly petitions, comparing them to the envelope they had lifted from Clarissa Bernardone's office in *Il Torred dei Segriti*. Using Andrea's Arabic/Italian dictionary, Adriano was laboriously translating the two pages hidden in Maryam's blouse. They didn't even contemplate the serendipity of the dead deacon's reading cache so conveniently at hand. Every now and then, Adriano would check something online using Andrea's computer. Like an abandoned spaceship in one of Adriano's favorite late-night sci-fi films, the Deacon's computer was just as he had left it, including being internet enabled. Their lucky night.

"Look at these," Lee said, scooting a chair next to Adriano. "There are a bunch with these certain phrases repeated over and over."

Adriano read and translated:

(40) Per quelle che confidate nella misericordia di Dio, facilmente peccarono

For those who trusted in God's mercy, easily they sinned

(43) Per quelle che frastornarono gli altri alla devozione
For those who distracted others from devotion
(5) Per quelle alle quali particolarmente sei tenuto
For those of your particular intentions

"So," said Lee, taking back the cards with some pique. "These sentences repeat over and over." He looked at them intently, as if somehow like a message written in lemon juice, the concentration of his eyes would somehow "heat" the paper and reveal the solution. "I've got it." He snapped his fingers. "It's like a trigger word or the amen at the end of a prayer! The phrases substitute for something else. The trick is finding the key, the thing that makes it possible to translate the code."

"You really have been reading too much Dan Brown," said Adriano.

"What about the stamps on the back, huh? What about Opus Dei?" Lee's voice was rising in excitement.

"Maybe it was just the Pastor's way of saying 'done,' kind of a holy checkmark. Opus Dei for 'prayed for' or 'needs two more *Hail Marys*' or 'Sorry, you're a miserable sinner and you're going to hell.'"

"There is no hell," Lee stated flatly. His parents' faces, his grandmother's, popped into his brain. He tried to push it away, but couldn't. "I wish there were a hell, for some crimes, but I don't believe it. Everyone can be forgiven." He was trying hard to believe it now.

"But you believe in God's waiting room," Adriano rolled his eyes. "Hell, no. Purgatory, yes."

"That's the point," Lee said with some urgency. "*No one*, well, not many people talk about purgatory. It's a pretty esoteric concept, even for good Catholics."

"No one says 'Go to purgatory,' as a curse, you mean."

"Exactly," Lee said. "Listen, I've done too many crosswords over the years with Brian Swathmore. He was relentless until he figured something out. The real question is, Whose box is this? Andrea's? His mother's? Someone else? Also, why would a refugee have two scrolls sewn into her blouse? And what do they say?"

"Well," Adriano said with a satisfied look, turning around in the swivel chair. "That I think I can answer."

"You finished the translation."

Adriano nodded and started to read, in Italian first, followed immediately in English.

Per quelle che per la loro incontinenza sono tormentate
For those who are tormented by incontinence
Per quelle che portarono poco rispetto chiesa
For those who do not respect the Church

Per quelle castigate per la loro accidia nelle opere di pieta
For those who are punished for their sloth in doing works
    of mercy
Per quelle dei quistirati e scordati
For those who have died and been forgotten

"It's the text from the purgatory board in Bagnoregio!"

Adriano just nodded and continued.

"Read the other one." Lee's lips were practically on vibrate. They were close to solving it. He knew it. Of course, the "it" was still unidentified.

Per quelle che in questa vita poco amarono Dio
For those in this life who just loved God
Per le anime di quelli che, ti furono nemici
For the souls of your enemies

Per quelle che sono piu care a Maria Santissima
For those most dear to our Lady, Holy Maria
Per le anime di questa famiglia che ancora penanon in purgatorio
For the souls of this family that still languish in purgatory

Lee asked the obvious rhetorical question. "Why would an African refugee have Christian prayers sewn into her clothes, written in Arabic?"

"I have to admit, I thought you were being a little weird about this whole purgatory thing, but this is a little woo-woo," said Adriano. "The prayers are identical to ones we just found in a semi-abandoned church in a town with twelve people. I mean, *exactly* the same words"

"Not exactly. There's one big difference," Lee said, slapping his knee. "I can't believe I didn't see this before. I'll be right back." With a quick kiss to his husband's forehead, Lee was up, out of the apartment, and dashing downstairs before Adriano could respond. Less than two minutes later he was back. "I knew I had seen these before. Look." Lee was holding a book and smiling.

"What does this have to do with the *Titanic*?" Adriano asked, taking Magda's birthday gift.

"Esempio," Lee said in quivering triumph. "Don't you see! Ah. Here it is!" Lee had rifled through the purgatory prayer box and pulled out a card with obvious success. "Read *this*!"

Adriano exhaled but complied.

"ESEMPIO
(41) Per quelle che in questa vita poco amarono Dio
For those in this life who just loved God
(43) Per quelle che frastornarono gli altri alla devozione
For those that distracted others from devotion

(49) Per quelle che perdettero tempo in luchare e ridere
For those who wasted time in mockery and laughter
(56) Per quei padri e quelle madri che non educano i loro figli
For those fathers and mothers who did not educate their children"

"So what?" Adriano asked.
"Look at the title of the book."
Adriano read. *41.43 N; 49.56 W.*
"Those are the coordinates of where the *Titanic* sank, perhaps the most famous and most published coordinates in the last hundred years. There are hundreds, maybe thousands, of books about the *Titanic*."

"So?" Adriano repeated with a sigh that was becoming more than exasperation.

"They're the same numbers on the prayer card. Just read the numbers."

"41.43. 49.56." Adriano looked, mouth open. "You're right!"

"Here, try another one, one of the ones with the Opus Dei symbol on the back."

Adriano found one and pulled it out. "Here, this one. Wait. It looks like it did have an Opus Dei stamp on it, but someone's erased it out. You can just make the original ink from the stamp before it was rubbed away."

"Good enough. Let me feed the coordinates into Andrea's computer. Dictate."

"(48) Per quelle che patiscono per causa della loro orecchie
For those who suffer for because of their ears
(56) Per quei padri e quelle madri che non educano i loro figli
For those fathers and mothers who did not educate their children
(13) Per quelle per le quali il Padre desidera che si preghi accio siano liberate da quelle pene
For those whom the Father wants freed of their pain
(43) Per quelle che frastornarono gli altri alla devozione
For those who bewildered others with devotion"

Lee was typing away. "OK, I think this is it. 48.56 N; 13.43 E. That's smack-dab in the middle of the Danube River in Passau, the border between Germany and Austria." Lee looked up perplexed. "Another coordinate in the middle of a body of water. What about this one?" Lee handed Adriano another card, this one clearly stamped with the symbol on Luke's ring.

Adriano read the card:

"(40) Per quelle che confidate nella misericordia di Dio, facilmente peccarono
For those who trusted in God's mercy, easily they sinned
(71) Per quelle che sono piu vicine a finire i loro tormenti
For those who are closest to ending their torment

(74) Per quelle che aspettano soccorso dai parenti e sono abbandonate
For those who expected help from their families but were abandoned
(1) Per le anime di tuo padre e di tua madre
For the souls of your father and your mother"

"OK. That must be 40.71 N; 74.01 E." Lee was watching Google Earth take its miraculous digital spin of the earth, then home in on its destination. He wondered if this was how US soldiers targeted drones. "Hmmm. That's somewhere near New York harbor off lower Manhattan, actually, I've seen those coordinates before." He quickly picked through the box, looking for another card stamped Opus Dei. His visage suddenly drained of all color. "Read this one," Lee said with a face of blank certainty. "I know these numbers."

Adriano read and translated:

"(38) Per quelle che penano per pigrizia
For those who are in pain because of laziness
(87) Per quelle che sono comparse a quelche persona non hanno avuto soccorso
For those who have cried out for rescue but been denied
(77) Per quelle che invita si raccomandarone a Dio con poco fervore
For those who do not worship God with sufficient fervor
(5) Per quelle alle quali particolarmente sei tenuto
For those of your particular intentions"

"Another shipwreck?" Adriano asked.

"No," said Lee, taking back the card and reciting by rote the numbers he would never forget. "38.87 N; 77.05 W. Not a shipwreck, a plane. Those are the coordinates of the Pentagon. And the one by lower Manhattan. The World Trade Center."

Lee felt faint.

"Oh my God." Adriano squeezed his husband's hand, remembering their conversation earlier today and Lee's revelations about his parents' death. "Are you..."

"I'm fine," Lee said with finality. "Really. Here, try this card. It's one of the last ones with the Opus Dei symbol. Also, it's weird. The first two lines repeat themselves."

Adriano read while Lee took his place at the computer:

"(40) Per quelle che confidate nella misericordia di Dio, facilmente peccarono
(40) Per quelle che confidate nella misericordia di Dio, facilmente peccarono
For those who trusted in God's mercy, easily they sinned
(3) Per le anime di questa famiglia che ancora penanon in purgatorio
For the souls of this family that still languish in purgatory
6) Per quelle che in vita loro ti hanno perseguitato"

"40.40.3.6 coordinates." Lee typed into the computer. "It's in Spain."

"I know where it is," Adriano said with a chill in this voice. "It's Madrid. Atocha. The train station that the terrorists blew up killing over one hundred and fifty people. It was Spain's 9/11."

"Who would put the coordinates of terrorist attacks on prayer cards? And, why?"

"I don't know, but I'm beginning to think we should call the police."

"Or Don Bello," Lee said, turning back to the keyboard. "He seems to be at the center of everything."

"Hmmm. Our very own Don Mateo."

"Who's that?"

"A TV detective on Spanish television. My parents love that show." Quickly, Adriano changed the subject. "Lee, check his favorites."

"What?"

"His favorites. Andrea's history tab on the computer. Here, let me." Adriano pushed his husband aside and started playing the keyboard. Then he leaned back. "Check it out."

Lee leaned over his husband's shoulder and read, search after search after search with the same coordinates they had just found themselves.

"Whatever is going on with these prayer cards, Deacon Andrea was involved somehow."

"Or was figuring out how someone else was involved."

Lee looked at Adriano.

"I'm going to phone Don Bello, or Luke, or someone. I'll be right back. My iPhone is downstairs," Adriano said.

Lee turned back to the computer as his husband ran downstairs for the cavalry. Down in the lobby, distant laughter could be heard and Christmas greetings exchanged as the front door slammed.

"Meow!"

Clemente was rubbing against Lee's legs persistently and looking up at him quizzically. "I know, Clemente. It's strange." Lee leaned down to scratch his companion's back. When he looked back up at the screen, he noticed it—a document on the desktop of Andrea's computer that he hadn't seen before. His whole body went cold. He knew what it was before he opened it. Andrea's suicide note. There staring at him in terse, digital prose, was the proof of Andrea's last act and the clue to what led him to the edge of that cliff.

I wanted to be a priest, and dedicated my whole life to this goal, but it was denied me. I am fragile and I ask for forgiveness.

Lee had seen the words before, read them in the article about Andrea's suicide, but like the purgatory cards now scattered around him like tainted confetti, again it wasn't the words that drew Lee's eyes to the screen. It was the numbers, the date next to the document that indicated when it was created. *Of course! The numbers. The date!*

"Jesus Christ," Lee whispered, hearing footsteps returning. He turned to greet his husband.

"No," the shadow said from the doorway. "Not yet."

CHAPTER LV

Coronation

February 24, 1530 (Julian Calendar), Bologna

Clement was alone—for now.

The Church of San Petronio was blessedly empty, and quiet. But it wouldn't stay that way for long. Already, he could hear the stirrings of the masses on the square outside the basilica.

Ave Caesar! Imperator Invite!

The Pope ground his teeth without giving breath to the name of the person he was about to crown Holy Roman Emperor: *Charles.* As if being dragged kicking and scheming to Bologna wasn't bad enough, today was Charles's thirtieth birthday.

He better not be expecting a cake. Clement harrumphed. *Holy God, in what have I offended Thee? Answer me.* Blasphemous, I know, he thought, to paraphrase the words of our Savior in jest, but really, *Caesar? Oy vey.* What a world when Belgians get empires.

"Gaul is divided into three parts"—Clement remembered the self-congratulatory tone of Julius Caesar's Gallic Wars diary—"one of which the Belgae inhabit, the Aquitani another, those who in their own language are called Celts, in ours Gauls, the third. Of all these, the Belgae are the strongest."

"Well, perhaps not strongest," Clement growled *sub voce,* "but at least the luckiest by birth, and certainly endowed with—what was it the Jews called it? Chutzpah?" Charles V certainly had that, asking for a papal blessing over his crown not quite three years after he had attacked Rome with a legion of lust-filled Lutherans, pillaged the Vatican, tortured and killed thousands of citizens, and forced Christ's Vicar on Earth—namely Clement —into exile. Not to mention the 140 Swiss Guards whose bloodied corpses were left to rot on the steps of St. Peter's after having bought time for his escape to Orvieto.

Orvieto.

Clement sighed. It seemed a lifetime ago, those six months of blessed, forced retreat in which he had connived to save—nay, resurrect—what was left of his papacy.

To whit: Charles was being crowned in *Bologna* not Rome; in San Petronio, not St. Peter's. Charles wasn't happy about it, but Rome still wasn't quite up to an imperial coronation. Not yet three years on from its sacking, the citizens of the Eternal City were in no mood to see money wasted on spectacle. Most of them were still struggling to eat. Clement had returned, briefly, to Rome and his Vatican apartments—what was left of them, covered with pornographic cartoons of Clement and the Medici. Some of them, actually, showed talent but the subject was always the same. Disgrace, disembowelment, and death for Pope Clement VII.

Well, thought Clement, pulling himself together and continuing his stroll through San Petronio, that will come soon enough, but not quite yet. He laughed to himself. *My God.* Cardinal Farnese and the rest of the unholy college were practically ready to bury him last year. He *had* been sick and thought himself that the end was near. But, no such luck. He had survived. They'd have to wait a bit longer for white smoke over the Vatican. He still had a few good years left. Well, *years*, at least. However many cycles of the sun were still left to the last true Medici prince, they likely would not be *good*.

Of course, he wasn't really the last. There was still Alessandro. There was still his son.

The Pope stopped in front of the Chapel of the Magi. Splendid, he thought, admiring the spectacular marble balustrade and the frescoes depicting the Three Kings at the Nativity alongside a representation of the

life of Bologna's patron, San Petronio. There was a nicely executed coronation of the Virgin Mary. Clement frowned. *Typical. Virgins get crowned,
but courtesans do all the work. If sex was so bad, why hadn't God found
another way to keep the species alive?* But, of course, the chapel's namesake
aside, it wasn't the Magi who had artistic pride of place here. It was Lucifer,
a grotesquely magnificent demon surrounded by illustrations from Dante.
In his Satanic mouth, he gobbled a heretic and in a bizarrely hermaphro-
ditic display, squeezed out another through his vagina. Clement shook his
head. His cousin Pope Leo may have been a sodomite, but he had nothing
over the artist Giovanni da Modena when it came to kink. The Pope stood,
strangely compelled by the hellishly intriguing fresco, in all its gorishness,
devouring the damned. Just over his left shoulder, one would-be Satanic
snack was being tenderized with red-hot pitchforks by a demon in waiting.
Lest anyone doubt the sufferer's identity, his name had been quite clearly
painted underneath: Mahomet. Mohammed.

"Is my mother in hell?"

The question clawed its way out deep from where it had long been buried in Clement's brain, stirred to life again by the image of Modena's fresco
of the tortured Moor, a stream of putrid water from beneath the earth,
released as if by earthquake.

"Is my mother in hell?" repeated the young voice.

Clement, then still Cardinal Giulio de Medici, had squirmed visibly
under the query and avoided the questioner's eyes that long-ago day in
Rome during the reign of his cousin, and best friend, Pope Leo X. Finally,
he had looked down at his inquisitor, barely eight years old and precocious
beyond his years. Alessandro. His son. *No, no...must be careful.* His *cousin*,
or as everyone referred to him, his nephew, *nepoti*.

"Of course not, Alessandro. Of course not. Your mother was a good
woman." Yes, he thought, and beautiful too. "A very good woman, indeed.
Why would you think such a thing as that, my Simonett, your mother in
hell?"

The dark-skinned boy pursed his lips and looked down at his feet as
if ashamed. "Cousin Ippolito and Lorenzino said my mother was in hell."

Giulio de Medici had gasped, a mixture of horror and true anger. "How dare they!" the Cardinal had roared, clapping his hands to summon a servant. "Quickly, bring me the young Medici cousins, Ippolito and Lorenzino. Seek them out this instant!"

"NO!" Alessandro had screamed. "No, please Uncle Giulio, no! Please don't say anything to them. They hate me already! They'll *kill* me if they find I've told you! Please!"

And suddenly the young boy was weeping in his uncle's—his father's—arms. Giulio had waved away the servant and sat on the ground holding the boy until his crying gave way to choking sobs. The Cardinal offered his silken sleeve to the boy, who blew his nose upon it with unembarrassed enthusiasm. When he was finally quiet, Clement said to him quietly, "Alessandro. What else did your cousins say to you?"

Clement steeled himself for the next revelation. The cruelty of youth had no prohibitions. If they had teased the boy about his mother, the leap to saying his father was a Cardinal of the Church was not an unexpected vault. *God, what hellions have sprung from the font of the Medici?*

The youth looked up, wet-eyed but composed. "They said my mother was a whore and that's why she died so soon after I was born, as a punishment. And then to make sure everyone knew she was a sinner, He made me *black*, just like Cain in the Bible! And my father"—Clement waited, not breathing—"and that my father died from something called sisyphus! They made it sound horrible!"

Clement inhaled, grateful and ashamed for his gratitude in the same breath. I, he thought, am the only whore here, preserving my career through the lying defense of my cousin, Lorenzo the Duke of Urbino. Yes, better for Alessandro to think that the younger Lorenzo was his father, and that the lovely young orphan, Caterina de Medici, his half-sister. As for cousin Lorenzo dying from "the French disease," syphilis, well, that was harder to avoid than mispronouncing it as the name of the Greek demigod condemned to eternally push a boulder uphill. He'd let sleeping veneralities lie. Children were so easy to convince. They believed that God had been born of a virgin. Spinning stories to the young was so effortless. They could probably be made to believe that San Nicola could appear down chimneys with sacks of toys on his back at Christmas. Lying to children, a necessary and distasteful evil.

"Alessandro," Giulio de Medici had sighed with a loving theatricality. "Your mother died out of happiness because she knew that only in heaven could she find more joy than witnessing the birth of something as beautiful and noble as you. Your color is not a curse. It is a blessing, it is you. It is who you are. God's creation is a diversity of hues and yours is a rich and royal tone. Your cousins are jealous of what they do not understand, and in their jealously, are cruel. Forgive them." Although, Clement had thought, if I could I'd throttle them both right here and now. Then, he added, quietly, forcefully, and truthfully, "And, your mother was one of the kindest, gentlest, and loveliest women ever to put foot to earth."

"You knew her!" Alessandro had brightened. "You knew my mother?"

"Yes," Cardinal Giulio de Medici had said simply, and with a smile he thought that he had forgotten how to conjure, had not conjured since first the luscious chocolate skin and golden heart of Simonetta had entranced him so many years ago on a visit to his cousin's house. "I knew her very well, indeed." Then, before Alessandro could ask again, Clement punctuated an end to the interrogation. "She was no whore. Next to the Blessed Virgin, there could be no better example of purity of heart, kindness, or compassion than your mother." Clement started to respond with what he believed—heretical though it was for a Christian, much less the heir to St. Peter to express—there is no hell. Instead, he punctuated his lie. "No, Alessandro. Your mother is not in hell."

"What was her name?" Alessandro asked.

"Simonetta." Clement smiled again, enjoying the momentary truth of speaking her name. "Your mother's name was Simonetta."

And for all he knew, then, or now standing here as the Vicar of Christ in the Church of San Petronio in Bologna, her name still was Simonetta. The well-trod story of Alessandro's fake patronage left no clues. A dead mother and a dead father. The truth was not so neatly tied up. Alessandro had been born, and Simonetta, like so many Medici mistresses before and yet to come, sent quietly far, far, away.

Certainly not. If she was still alive, Simonetta was not in hell. If so, cruelly a mythology existed. But neither was Clement sure she was in heaven. She had disappeared after their brief affair, paid to be discreet. He had heard that she actually had married. Happily, he hoped. Truly, he did. Her faith in Christ's Church had been greater than his. Better to pretend to being the lover of a minor Medici—and a cruel and faithless one at that—than to admit to having lain in love and conceived with a future Prince of the Church. For her, the Church was supreme. Clement had loved her. She had given birth to their son. They had both lied to preserve his future. Theirs was already so full of lies, a fresco painted daily—quickly, in brushstrokes wide and fanciful—soon to dry into a hardened crust. Beautiful from the outside, but really just rotten eggs and paste at its core.

Clement coughed and turned resolutely from the Dantesque images before him. Yes, and here I am, he thought, Supreme Pontiff of that Supreme Church in which the mother of my son had such faith. In an hour I will lay my hands upon the head of Charles V of Spain, giving him my blessing, and he will acknowledge that as a Catholic Monarch—the Emperor, no less—that all he does is in service to God, through me. This entire charade is about making sure that people know their kings are controlled by and in service to God Almighty.

Bullshit. Clement almost spat. Complete and utter *merde*, as the French would say. He looked around the church in all its gaudy approximation of Rome. Banners, plaster saints, even a replica of the porphyry circle from St. Peter's Basilica on which Charlemagne had been crowned Holy Roman Emperor on Christmas Day 800. Bread and circuses, Clement mused. Bread and circuses. *Charles will pretend to be subservient to me and I will pretend not to be his hostage.*

I have not lost my faith, Clement thought, striding resolutely toward the Chapel of San Abbondio where the coronation was soon to take place. This was to be a sign of Charles V's subservience to the Pope, to Rome, and to God. *My faith has lost itself. It has stumbled a long way from the sands of Palestine and the simple words of a carpenter to the gaudy gold-leaf of our present Mother Church. She is the only whore here.*

"*Is my mother in hell?*"

The Pope again let his mind wander back to that childish conversation of more than ten years past, the only time when he and his son, his Alessandro, had actually been close, physically or emotionally. Over the years, they had drifted apart. No, not drifted. Been pulled apart. Now, behind the scenes, Pope Clement, secretly, did what he could to advance his son's career. Clement had made Alessandro governor of Spoletto, and through the intervening years of papal and imperial intrigue, Alessandro had somehow, genuinely, become close to the Emperor Charles V. Clement heard that they were truly friends. It was Alessandro who had escorted the imperial entourage into Bologna. It was Alessandro who attended him here. It was Alessandro's whose hand had been promised to Charles's daughter, Margaret, a quid pro quo that served both Pope and imperium. It was a match good on paper, but one not soon consummated as Margaret was still all of seven years old. And, if all went well, soon, Charles and his troops—the same troops that had booted Clement and his curia out of Rome almost three years ago—would reestablish the Medici as rulers of Florence, this time, with Alessandro at the head, first Duke of Florence. Eventually, I'll find a home and a husband and appropriate honors for that dear little orphan, my niece Catherine de Medici, Clement thought. Adorable child. *Yes, if all goes well, my complete capitulation to the will of Charles V will serve to make my name synonymous with surrender and defeat. But, perhaps, from my ignominy, the family de Medici will live on, and who knows, perhaps be remembered.*

"Is my mother in hell?"

For not the last time that day, his mind wandered back to that question and the time and place of its asking. Rome, 1519, at the home of Alfonsina Orsini, wife of the late Lorenzo, Medici central. They had all been one, big happy family there. But that didn't last long. Leo had died. Clement had become pope. Charles had looted Rome and once again the Medici had been routed from their native Florence in the name of democracy.

Democracy. Clement ground his teeth. *The worst form of government except everything else that has ever been tried.* Hmmm, I should write that down, thought the Pope, before someone else thinks of it and makes it famous?

"Your Holiness?"

The Pope turned at a quietly familiar voice, made foreign by its echo in the vast cathedral nave.

"Gio! My boy! My *son!*"

The two ran into each other's arms and embraced, the most genuine of hugs.

"What are you doing here?" The Pope held his former Swiss Guard at arm's length to inspect him. Had it really been fewer than three years since this soldier had fled with him to Orvieto following the Sack? They had lost everything, but in their loss, had found each other.

"Am I not a Swiss Guard, Holy Father?" Gio bowed low in supplication. "Where you go, there I am also."

"You're retired." The Pope fixed him with a glare. "You should be with your wife in Orvieto. How are they? How are dear Sofia and her father Moses? You have better priorities than being caught up here in Bologna with all this rabble and obsequious pontificating—forgive me the pun."

Gio laughed. "Ego absolved and yes, my family is fine. Sofia sends her love and also this." The young knight reached into a fitchet on his shirt sand pulled out a small embroidered satchel tied with a leather cord. "Open it."

"Gio." Clement wagged his fingers. "Please. We are past gifts, and you shouldn't have spent your treasure bringing a gift to a Medici, fallen though he may be."

"Oh." Gio smiled coyly. "It is expensive. Proof of my treasure, indeed."

Clement untied the sack and reached in. "Oh, my boy! This is the greatest gift that ever I could receive!"

"I thought you'd be pleased!"

The Pope's smile beamed in the oppressive vault of the church, still awaiting its legion of candles and oil lamps for the coronation. In his hand, he held a most delicate presentation, a tiny fistful of blond baby curls, tied with silk.

"A child! What is...?"

"*His* name is Clemente Giulio. My firstborn is named for you, Holy Father. Giulio de Medici. My friend, the father that I never knew."

"Oh, my boy." And Clement hugged him again, both of them with tears in their eyes. "You have given me and the world a most precious gift."

Their reverie was interrupted by a shaft of sunlight and the muffled, now clearly heard shouts, pouring through a side door thrown open behind them. The Pope and Swiss Guard turned to see the entrant approaching as he let the heavy door slam shut behind them, once again restoring a momentary quietude.

"Your Holiness." The elderly cardinal knelt down and kissed the papal ring. Clement pursed his lips and motioned for the cleric to rise. Gio helped the old man to his feet.

"In what can I serve you, Cardinal Farnese?" the Pope asked with a smile that bespoke an annoyed impatience for his red-robed colleague.

"The Court has been looking for you! It is time to start. The Elector Palatine of the Rhine is in position with the Orb of Empire, the Marquess of Montferrat is carrying the Golden Sceptre, the Duke of Urbino the Sword of State, and the Duke of Savoy the kingly crown. Oh, and the Spanish delegation includes the noted poet Garcilosa de la Vega and his comrade, the youthful and esteemed Duke of Alba. And, of course, Holy Father, Il Moro—I mean, the noble Duke of Penne, Governor of Spoletto. Your nephew, Alessandro de Medici, is in attendance to His Imperial Majesty."

"Thank you. I wasn't aware that I was keeping the Emperor waiting. I thought it was ourselves for whom Charles was waiting."

"Of course, Holiness, of course. Most correct, but you know how these Spaniards are." The elderly man chuckled lightly, quickly swallowing his own joke when Clement did not join him. "I was just checking to see if you needed anything."

"I am fine, Your Eminence," Clement snapped. "Is there anything else?"

The aging Cardinal started to speak, then wet his lips. He did it again, as if not sure of how to start.

"For God's sake, man, speak. You look like a fish gasping for air on the beach. What is it?"

"Well"—Cardinal Farnese resumed his prattle—"there is the manner of the anointing, the application of the holy oils to the forehead of the emperor Charles. By tradition, it is done prior to the actual blessing and coronation by the Pope, usually by a senior member of the curia." His voice trailed off.

Clement's ironic smile went as flat as a squashed slug. "I see. Well, Your Eminence, since you were raised to the red by the Spanish Borgia Pope, Alexander the Sixth, perhaps *you* would do us the honor of anointing His Majesty."

"Thank you, Your Holiness! You are most—"

"Leave us." Clement interrupted Farnesse mid-genuflection, and pulled the ring from his grasp before his lips could brush it. "Go tell His Majesty that I will be with them shortly to start the procession." With a wave of his hand, Clement dismissed the cleric, who backed out with a surprising speed and dexterity. As the door opened again, the cries of "Imperio! Imperio!" and "Espana! Espana!" wafted in.

"God, I loathe that man." Clement rolled his eyes. "He can barely wait for me to die so he can become pope."

"Your Holiness," Gio gasped. "He's ten years older than you! Besides, you have many years left to live, to serve."

"Hmmm," Clement grunted. "We'll see about that, but mark my word. Cardinal Farnese has been waiting to swing the keys of Peter ever since that hideous Alexander the Sixth made him a cardinal, at age twenty-five no less! And all because he was the brother of Borgia's lover, Julia Farnese. Christ on a stick. And they say we Medici are corrupt."

"Holiness!" The young Swiss Guard guffawed, joined in chuckles by the Pontiff.

"Walk with me a bit. I'm not quite ready to let in the hoards of the Emperor's adoring public."

"Yes, Your Holiness."

The pair walked on in silence for a bit, circling around the still-empty cathedral. Finally, they stopped in front of the Magi Chapel with its huge and grotesque rendering of hell and the torture of Mohammed.

"We will never have peace in the world as long as religions hate each other," Clement sighed, staring up at Modena's gory masterwork. One day, he thought, that painting will cause problems. *Mark my word.* "Jews, Muslims, Christians, all children of The Book and each so convinced that only they understand it. I am pope, and I don't understand it."

"You understand it better than most, and you have encouraged scholarship and cooperation between religions," the young Swiss Guard prodded. "Even now, our friend Cardinal Egidio of Vitero is at work on *Schechina*, the great comparison between the Judaic Cablla and Christian mysticism. Hassan de Wazzan continues his travels, and his writings, always with an eye towards healing the rift between Islam and Christianity. Even my dear Sofia continues her education, reading about the man called Buddha and the ancient Vedic texts from the Hindu faith. All of this because you, Holy Father, the Bishop of Rome, have said it is good. You have set aside the resources of the Vatican to study and preserve such religious and spiritual study."

Clement smiled and gently stroked Gio's cheek. "Thank you for that, my son. But, none of it is enough. If I had a papacy of fifty years, I couldn't undo the grotesque and glorious corruption that is Mother Church. I wanted to make our Church stronger as a way to unite all men, but I have failed. King Henry threatens to start his own Church of England because I won't grant him a divorce. Luther's reformation has poisoned northern Europe against me. Three Christian kings now vie to rip apart the Papal States, and with it the last barrier against complete anarchy throughout Europe. No, I have produced nothing of worth in this world. Nothing."

"You have produced a son." The young Swiss Guard spoke quietly.

"Yes." The Pope smiled. "My son, Alessandro. A son in secret, for even he does not know I am his father. It is better that way. Better not to be tainted with the sins and failures of a father like me."

"I would be proud if you had been my father."

"Gio." Clement pulled the young man to his breast. "You, truly, are the son I never had. If I am remembered for anything in this world, I hope it is that I was blessed enough to have known, and loved, a boy, a man, as noble as you."

"I love you, Holy Father. No, just father."

"Thank you, my son." Then, pulling himself together, the Pope took Gio's arm. "Let us go out to greet His Imperial Majesty, King of Spain and the New World, Holy Roman Emperor, Charles the Fifth. Now, he has it all, the richest man in the world, the richest man in history."

"There are some things even Charles will never have," Gio said slyly. "Some things of history that are reserved only for the future, for your legacy, Pope Clement the Seventh."

The Pope stopped and pulled Gio around to face him. "Moses has done it, hasn't he?"

The young Swiss Guard just shrugged. "Who am I to say, Your Holiness? I am just a young mercenary sent to protect Christ's Vicar on Earth and all that He deems important. All that he says must be preserved."

"The Etruscan Statues of Metrodorus! They are safely hidden in Orvieto?"

"Upon this Rock, Your Holiness. Upon this Rock."

CHAPTER LVI

Purgatory

Tuesday, December 24, 2013, Christmas Eve, 2 a.m., Orvieto

I t was a cold day in hell.

In his dream, Adriano was at the ocean, on a high promontory facing an endless sea of hypnotic waves and an elusive horizon unmarred by clouds. The gentle drone of the surf lapping against the rocks lulled him to the edge. There below, Lee waved back from the water, smiling, just before a massive shark took him in its jaws and bit him in half.

Lee!

Adriano cried out his husband's name, but only in his mind. No noise came from his lips and his throat was dry and itching. His nose was full of strange smells that he did not recognize, save one. Frankincense, like the candles at San Giovanale. His last memory was of bending down to pick up his phone before a soft leather glove slipped over his nose and mouth and a black bag smelling of that mythic gift to the Baby Jesus descended over his head. Then he drifted into unconsciousness.

He awoke with a start. He could tell without attempt at movement that his hands and feet were bound, tightly. The numbness from lack of blood to his extremities was proof enough. His head, however, he could move. At first, he thought that the sickly- sweet mask was still over his face, but then he realized that his eyes were open. Slowly, his sight adjusted to the darkness. Like a lifting mist, his prison revealed itself, dank, dark, wet, and empty. Every second allowed him to make out its outline. A drip of water echoed in the chamber. With no competition for sound, it ricocheted like a bullet against the walls. He was sitting in a chair, wooden it seemed from the creaking it gave beneath his squirms, but the floor was metal, a hollow, vibrating thud confirming its composition. To his left and right was an iron railing and beyond, a circular stairway of stone ascending into nothingness. He twisted his neck, with no little discomfort, to look around. A dim and moss-covered emergency light next to the floor cast a hazy glow. Just underneath, he could barely make something out: a torn ticket stub inscribed "Pozzo San Patrizio." He was at the bottom of St. Patrick's Well.

Today was a holiday. The well would be closed for Christmas. No one would know where he was.

A gentle squeak grabbed his attention. In the corner, he could just make out its source. A rat.

The thought crossed his brain like a ticker tape. No emotion, just information. *This is how I die, alone, to be eaten by rats.*

"Lee!" he cried out. This time his vocal chords responded and echoed upward against the pitiless stone. As the reverberation died, Adriano hoped as much as feared an answer. *Please be all right. Please don't be here. Please be safe.*

"He is not here, yet."

A single match flamed in the darkness, briefly illuminating the speaker's face.

Adriano recognized it from the photo Lee had shown him. Cardinal Giorgio Maltoni of the Vatican Press Office.

"What have you done to my husband?"

The assassin laughed softly. "My goodness, such political correctness. Don't you know there is no such thing as gay marriage in Italy? Actually, in most of the world?" Maltoni chuckled again and took a drag. In the intervening seconds he closed the space between his shadowy perch and Adriano's chair. He drew close to his captive's face and exhaled thick, sickly-sweet Egyptian tobacco. Expensive. It lingered like a toxic halo around Adriano's head, dizzying him with its smell and that of something else—something even sweeter, nauseatingly so. Cinnamon.

"Fuck you." Adriano spit into his face.

Maltoni laughed again, the spittle dripping from his nose. He licked it off.

Adriano turned away and wretched.

"What did you expect?" Adriano's torturer was quite jovial. "A slap? Doing the unexpected is so much more terrifying, don't you think?"

Adriano said nothing. *I am seconds away from death. Lee, I love you.*

"Please, please don't hurt Lee," Adriano finally got out. "Please. I beg you."

The assassin carefully extinguished his cigarette in a small puddle of water and then dropped the butt carefully into a sealed plastic bag and stuffed it into his pants pocket. He's getting rid of clues, Adriano thought. The Cardinal wrinkled his face as if littering was distasteful to him.

"There's no need to beg," the perverse cleric said matter-of-factly. "Your beloved will be here shortly. I'm waiting for him myself."

At just that moment, the creak of a rusty hinge echoed from above, cascading down the circular cavern punctuated by a flashlight beam.

"You see. Right on time," said the murderer, as calmly as if announcing an approaching train. "We're down here," he said, speaking upward to the shimmering beam. "Take your time. It's a long walk down, 175 feet and 248 steps to be exact. Don't slip." The Vatican spokesman seemed to be enjoying himself.

For the next ten minutes, everything was silence, except for the echoing steps edging ever closer to the bottom of the well. Two sets of footfalls. One, certainly was Lee, he thought. But he hoped not. *At least one of us needs to live through this.* The other, figured Adriano, was Maltoni's accomplice. Finally, the beam of an electric torch pierced the darkness and Lee was pushed from the descending staircase by an unseen arm. He fell at Adriano's feet, hands bound behind him. Then Archbishop Arnaud emerged from the shadows.

"What a touching tableau. A gay Pietà," the Cardinal hissed, lighting another cigarette. "Now we can begin, and end, this tiresome distraction. I do hate loose ends."

"You killed Deacon Andrea," Adriano said, a question asked and answered in one breath. "And now you're going to kill us."

"No." It was Lee, in a voice of absolute calm. The voice of the first time that Adriano had heard Lee say I love you. The voice of certitude. "He could have killed us back at the apartment. He needs us. All of us. He brought us here to find out what we know."

Maltoni smiled as he took a drag, flaring the cigarette like a candle. He slowly walked over to the Bishop. Then, with a cruel suddenness ground the cigarette into Arnaud's right eye.

Arnaud's screams echoed against the damp stones as he slumped to the floor clutching his disfigured face. The Cardinal waited until the howls became a whimper, then spoke directly to Lee, who was kneeling next to Arnaud. "The next one is for your dear Adriano."

"What do you want to know?"

"Very good, Lee, very good. Graceful acknowledgment of defeat is the mark of a true gentleman." Maltoni grabbed Lee by the ropes and pulled him to his feet.

"Lee, don't!" Adriano begged. "It doesn't matter what you tell him, there's no way he's not going to kill us in the end."

"But not before he gets his answer," Lee said, looking straight at the criminal. "He answers to someone else. He's just an errand boy."

This time, Maltoni's hand stopped short of a slap, centimeters from Lee's cheek. Lee didn't wince as the murderous face pressed in close to his.

"I am my own boss," he growled, re-exerting self-control. "I answer to no one. They think they control me, but without me, without my information, they are nothing. All of them. And yes, tonight, they want a very important piece of information. The information that was hidden in the garment of that migrant piece of shit named Maryam. The final move in a game that started with—"

"—with September eleventh," Lee said simply. "You killed my family."

"Lee." Adriano struggled against his bindings to move toward his husband. "No, don't."

"Did I, hmmm?" Maltoni stated simply. "Well, if they died that day, then yes I suppose I did have a hand in it. The Lord, after all, does work in mysterious ways."

"And you call yourself a cardinal," Lee spat out.

At this, Maltoni laughed loud and long. When he stopped, the only sound was the muffled cries of the wounded Bishop Arnaud huddling on the floor. "Yes, I am, indeed, a cardinal. His Eminence Giorgio Maltoni. Prince of the Church. Mouthpiece of the Vicar of Christ. It is quite an exalted position, and no one dares question me, *even the Pope.*"

Maltoni leaned in quite close to Lee with these last words.

Adriano winced.

"What made you turn against the Church?" Lee asked, fear pushed aside by genuine curiosity.

"*Turn* against the Church?" Maltoni scowled and turned away for a second. "I was never *with* the Church. Pathetic relic, but useful as pathetic relics go. I have never loved God, or the Church. I spent years getting ready for this mission. Decades working my way up to the level of cardinal. God, the hypocrisy of it all. The right prayers and the more than occasional blackmailing of a member of the curia. They all have secrets, and they all feel so guilty about them. Before you know, I am seated at the right hand of the Bishop of Rome."

"Why?" Lee continued.

Maltoni was upon him in a second, an inch from his face. "You should have asked your friend Don Bello."

"You've been following us."

"Well, more to the point, having you followed, yes," the murderer acknowledged almost politely. "Precisely. If you hadn't been so curious, you could have spent a lovely sabbatical here in Orvieto and returned to your life in San Francisco in a few weeks. Just another spoiled American enamored of the dulce vita."

"Dawud, the CD peddler," Adriano answered suddenly figuring it out. "Dawud followed us and reported back to Bishop Arnaud."

"I didn't know," the Bishop whimpered from the damp stones at their feet. "I didn't know about the rest."

"True enough," the assassin sighed, looking down at Arnaud. "You were a handy and malleable tool for passing on information whose importance you feigned to ignore, and all the while pretending to be a servant of Christ helping poor migrants leave a troubled land and a heretical belief for conversion to the one true faith of Mother Church. You and God deserve each other."

"Dawud and Maryam," Adriano gasped. "And others! You were helping traffic migrants into Italy."

"Migrants, some of whom carried encoded messages sewn into their clothes that got translated into coordinates courtesy of the purgatory board at San Donato in Bagnoregio," Lee said. "Some, you supposedly sent to work in area businesses or churches, but most ended up as prostitutes along the backroads of Umbria."

"I didn't know." Arnaud was weeping now, tears mingled with blood from his now-destroyed eye.

"Bravo." Maltoni chuckled. "I didn't think I'd enjoy this so much." He lit another cigarette and motioned for Lee to continue. "Please, go on."

"Arnaud would be notified when a shipload of trafficked migrants would arrive and be told how to recognize the ones with the coded message. Then, Dawud would translate the message from Arabic and give it to Arnaud, who would write it out as a prayer for the purgatory board, stamped with the seal of Opus Dei to distinguish it from the other ordinary prayers. For a terrorist to pick up later during a tourist visit to Bagnoregio."

"Very good." Maltoni inhaled. "Very good. You've figured it out exactly."

"But not this time." Adriano spoke up, suddenly understanding the last few hours. "This time, Dawud didn't turn over the message. The messenger was his sister. He knew that once her usefulness as a courier was done, she'd be enslaved as a prostitute, or worse. So, he hid his sister and stole the prayer box as an extra precaution. Which means..."

"Which means"—Lee finished the sentence—"that you don't know what was on the code sewn into Maryam's blouse. More importantly, you don't understand the meaning of the code, the coordinates for another spectacular terrorist attack."

The assassin's applause reverberated against the ancient walls of St. Patrick's Well. "Brilliant, truly brilliant. You are correct. And now, please, I would like to know what the message said, and what are the coordinates for the next attack."

The Bishop pulled himself up from the floor. "Fear!" Bishop Arnaud said. "You're afraid. They're on their way to kill you! The men on the phone! They know you haven't found Maryam yet, or had time to decode the message."

"Which means there's a terrorist cell en route to Bagnoregio to get their attack plans," Adriano said. "But the prayer box is missing, so they're coming here to Orvieto."

Lee suddenly found himself pinned against the wall, the back of his skull held hard against the cold, mossy stones by Maltoni's grip. "Yes," the Cardinal-turned-killer hissed. "Except, they are already here, somewhere in town, looking for me now, looking for Maryam, looking for that clue. I want it now. I *need* it now."

"Or they will find you and kill you," Lee said quietly. "Either way, all of us are dead. I won't tell you."

"So be it," the assassin spit, as he pulled a revolver from his pocket and cocked it against Adriano's head. He maintained his grip on Lee. "I was the cause of your family's death, but you will be the cause of your husband's."

In the darkness, the sudden explosion of sound and light momentarily robbed Adriano of sight and hearing. He screamed for Lee, could see nothing but thick smoke. A few seconds later, his ringing ears calmed down and he heard...

"Adriano!"

"Lee!"

All was chaos as four men in tactical gear descended from above on rappel wires and harnesses. They quickly threw Adriano and Lee to the ground for protection and untied their ropes. Adriano realized it wasn't a gunshot that had stunned them. It was concussion bombs. Someone, somehow, had found them, sent in the cavalry, and rescued them. However, in the melee, the assassin and the Bishop had escaped.

"Are you OK?" one of the soldiers asked.

Adriano shook his head. He couldn't believe it.

"Grigori!" Lee acknowledged the name of their rescuer.

"We've got to get you out of here," Grigori said. "Let's go! They can't escape. There's only one way out. But we have to beat them to the top."

The Swiss Guard hooked both Lee and Adriano up to grappling wires and motioned upward with his thumb, sending both of them flying upward like they were on an all-too-real and all-too-frightening carnival ride.

Two, Adriano thought as he flew upward through the stone cylinder. There were two ways out of St. Patrick's Well. Two ramps constructed like a double helix. There was no way of knowing into which one the assassin had fled.

"Doesn't matter," said another soldier as if reading Adriano's mind as the couple was helped over the lip of the well and through the open glass ceiling that usually protected the historic site from rain. Beside them, a black, unmarked van stood next to the tourist entrance. Next to it was an equally ebony limousine with consular license plates. In the back seat, Adriano could just make out the dull glow of a cell phone in a white-gloved hand.

"We've got men coming down each staircase now," Grigori said, hauling himself over the ledge, having just followed them up. "This will all be over soon. We have a team and a negotiator heading down now."

A single gunshot echoed through the well.

Adriano, Lee, and their military rescuers all looked down to see Maltoni standing in one of the well's seventy semicircular windows lining the ramp. In front of him, the loaded revolver pressed against her skull, was Reverend Vicky Lewis, the negotiator. Dear God, Adriano thought. They're all in on this. A wounded guard lay bleeding nearby. At their feet, on the edge of the ledge abutting the precipice, was Archbishop Arnaud.

"Pull back, *now*, or I'll kill her," Maltoni shouted. "The Bishop too. Do the Swiss Guard special forces want the death of two ordained on their hands, including a *woman?*" Even now, he laughed. "Let me pass, or they both die here."

"No!" Arnaud screamed, and from his bloody crouch he pushed against Maltoni's legs, sending him tumbling into the abyss as the gun went off, narrowly missing Reverend Vicky's head. Adriano cried out despite himself. He waited for the thud of the body hitting the cistern floor a hundred feet below.

The sound never came.

"Jean Claude! Hang on!"

In the hazy smoke now lit by portable military torches, the final tableau was played out in front of them all.

"Jean Claude, don't let go!" Vicky was kneeling on the sill of the masonry window, legs braced against the stone for support, desperately clutching Arnaud's hands in hers. Below, the assassin clung to the Bishop's feet in a precarious dangle.

"Don't shoot!" someone shouted from above. "You might hit the lady priest, or the Bishop!"

"Vicky," the Bishop's gentle whisper cut through the horror. "I'm sorry. I'm so sorry, for everything. Ignosce me, sacerdos."

With tears in her eyes, she spoke. "Episcopus Jeanne Claude Arnaud, in nominee Dei, ego te absolve."

Bishop Arnaud let go, sending himself and Maltoni plunging to the bottom of the well.

For several seconds, all was silence and darkness. Suddenly, a single beam of light pierced the gloom and a flurry of hands were pushing Adriano and Lee toward the van.

"Wait!" a familiar voice called from the back of the parked limousine. The door swung open, and a cell phone light shone down on a pair of insanely long legs in red stilettos stepping out of the car. Lee and Adriano cried out as one.

"Magda!"

CHAPTER LVII

Repeat Performance

Tuesday, December 24, 2013, Christmas Eve, 7:29 a.m., Orvieto

He stood on the cliff and prayed.

Useless, he thought, to turn my thoughts to God.

Behind him, the lights of Orvieto reflected in a million icy crystals.

Below, the road was deserted. He wondered who would find him. Someone would, of course, and for that he was sorry. What a horrible thing to see, to discover. The body of a reprobate, crushed against the rock. And yet, this man had sought forgiveness. This man would see the face of God. But, yesterday had been his final sunrise.

The dawn this morning should be beautiful, and he smiled. He had often come here to sit near the altar and wait for the dawn. Even now, its rays were reaching out to warm the city across a quilt of virginal frost. He had seen it before, prisms of color in the ice. Like a miracle it had seemed to him as a child.

For the body now lying at the foot of the cliff below San Giovanale, there would be no more. No more dawns, no more rainbows, no more miracles.

"Don Bello?"

The elderly priest turned to face them.

"You're needed at the hospital, Don Bello."

The old man nodded. "He has died."

"No," the Reverend Vicky Lewis said quietly, coming forward from the group and gently laying her hand on his shoulder. "He lives."

Don Bello started to weep uncontrollably and fell to his knees.

"Nicolo, caro." La Donna Volsini knelt beside him in the damp grass overlooking the Rupe. "Nicolo. It is done."

"But is it enough?" Don Bello wailed amid his tears, pushing his old friend until she fell backward onto the grassy knoll. Her grandson, Marco, bent to help her up but did not admonish the priest. For a moment, they all just sat in dewy silence, spokes of a broken wheel splayed around the Pastor of Orvieto's oldest church, Vicky Lewis, La Donna Volsini, Marco, and Grigori. Finally, his weeping stopped and he crawled toward the only person with more years upon this Rock—more memories—than he. "Finally, Velzna. Is it enough? *Now,* is it enough?"

Velzna Volsini merely nodded, but did not cry. Her oldest friend knew that her tears had emptied themselves decades before. Don Bello knew that she had forgotten how—no, forbidden herself, to cry. "No, Reverend Father. It will never be enough. But it is done. It is done. And I...I am done."

With that, she held out her hand to Don Bello. Marco on one side and Grigori on the other, the two oldest Orvietani were helped to their feet. As they rose, Vicky stepped forward and silently made the sign of the cross on each of their heads. Then, without another word, together, the pentagon of conspirators walked up the muddy ramp from the garden of San Giovanale and made their way to Orvieto's tiny hospital in the shadow of the Duomo.

Behind them, at the foot of the cliff, at the door of the tiny *Ciesa del Crocifisso del Tufo*, at the spot sanctified by Floriano, at the spot where lay Andrea a year ago, was a new body. The mangled corpse of Cardinal Giorgio Maltoni. But not for long. A small cadre of men dressed as EMTs completed the final act of the passion play.

The sun rose on Christmas Eve.

CHAPTER LVIII

All the News that Fits...

Wednesday, December 25, 2013, Christmas Day, Vatican City

25 December, 2013 (AKI Newswire)—It is with great sadness this morning that the Holy See has announced the death His Eminence Cardinal Giorgio Maltoni following a car crash near Orvieto in the predawn hours of Christmas Day. Also seriously injured in the accident, including the blinding of his right eye, but expected to survive, was the Most Reverend Jean Claude Arnaud, Archbishop of Orvieto–Todi. Maltoni, who had traveled to Orvieto to spend Christmas Eve with his longtime friend and colleague, was driving back to Rome along with Arnaud to be together for the St. Peter's Christmas Day Mass. His car hit a patch of ice, lost control, and went over a small embankment in the remote countryside outside Orvieto.

Maltoni, 57, head of the Vatican Press Office and a close advisor to Pope Emeritus Benedict XVI, will be buried within Vatican City in the Teutonic Cemetery, in the shadow of St Peter's Basilica. The cemetery is normally reserved for German-speaking clergy and members of German religious foundations in Rome, and its proximity to St Peter's means that burial plots are highly prized. The funeral mass will be private.

During Archbishop Arnaud's recuperation, the Reverend Father Nicolo Monaldeschi, known to his parishioners as "Don Bello," will substitute for the Archbishop at Orvieto's Christmas Week celebrations.

In unrelated news, three non-Italian men, suspected of being involved in a North African human trafficking ring and believed to also have been part of a recently uncovered terrorist cell operating near Gallipoli, were arrested at a security checkpoint near Civita di Bagnoregio. They are being held without bail in a Roman jail awaiting charges.

CHAPTER LIX

Deus Ex Magda

Wednesday, December 25, 2013, 11 a.m., Orvieto hospital

"Open it."

Magda stood at the foot of, and exactly equidistant between, the matching hospital beds into which Adriano and Lee had been coerced—nay forced—following their ordeal. Dr. Luke was quite insistent, especially for Adriano, who was still sloughing off the system-depressant drugs pumped into him by the late Cardinal Maltoni. Lee, although he had not been drugged, nevertheless had cracked two ribs during the rapid and athletic ascent by rappel wire while pressed against Grigori's chest. Swiss Guard to the rescue. It had almost been worth the pain, Lee thought with wicked enjoyment.

"Go ahead, *open it,*" Magda commanded in her usual tone, but said with a smile. "It is Christmas, after all."

The couple looked at each other and shrugged—"Ouch"—an effort that caused Lee no little discomfort. They then set about opening the elaborately wrapped packages on their laps. Only Magda could coordinate a SWAT team and a holiday party, not to mention a runway-ready ensemble, as witnessed by the immaculate forest-green skirt, blazer, and ubiquitous heels in which she now presented herself. Her hair was upswept and pinned a la Carlotta from *Vertigo.* A Hermes scarf with jingle bells capped it all off in an expensive bit of whimsy. Ho ho ho.

"Magda! I love it!" Adriano practically squealed.

"I thought it was rather perfect," she winked, leaning over Adriano for a thank-you kiss. In his lap, was a book titled *Goddamn God: How Religion Is Destroying Mankind.* "I didn't know exactly how apt it would be given the circumstances of the last week."

"Magda." Lee spoke up. "Why and how did you—"

"Open *your* present, Lee," Magda interrupted. "Questions after."

"Ouch!" As Lee tore into the paper, he again pulled against his damaged torso.

"Here, let me," said Magda, leaning over to assist. "Only you could manage to get injured while getting rescued," she said with a smile.

Wow, Lee thought. I wish I had my iPhone to record this. I've never seen her this proactively perky.

"You need to get better. I need you back in San Francisco. You can't stay on vacation forever!"

In a second, the wrapping had been undone and there on Lee's blanket was something that only Magda could have produced, a book on the *Titanic* that Lee didn't own—indeed, an event worth noting.

"*Conspiracy on Ice: Who Really Sank the Titanic, and Why,*" Lee read. "Wow. I can't wait. A conspiracy theory about an iceberg. Now that's a new one."

Magda laughed, and pulled up a chair between her two friends and sat down, those impossibly long legs crossed in front of her. "Yes, well, again, I bought the books before the events of this past week. I imagine by now you've both had quite enough of conspiracies, theories, and facts. Oh, Adriano, I have something else for you."

"Oh boy, oh boy, oh boy." He rubbed his hands in anticipation.

Magda handed over a simple envelope, postmarked Madrid.

"What is this?" Adriano said coldly.

"It's a letter. Open it."

Lee started to speak, but Magda shushed him. "Don't thank me. All I did was pick up your mail while you were traveling. I saw the postmark and thought maybe it would be something important."

Adriano slit open the envelope with his fingernail, unfolded the one-page letter, and read silently. At the end of the sheet, he turned it over and inhaled, then turned with tears in his eyes toward Magda and Lee. "It's from my parents. They want to see me—to see *us*, Lee. They said they're sorry, ashamed, and want to know if I can ever forgive them."

For a few minutes there was nothing to say. Adriano cried, something Lee had only seen once in ten years. Magda offered her Hermes scarf, and Adriano blew his nose. Finally, composed, he pulled himself up, and simply said, "Thank you, Magda."

"Well, I guess next year, we'll go to Spain," said Lee. "Olé!"

Adriano just rolled his eyes. "Yes, we'll go. Both of us." He returned the dampened scarf. "Magda, what the hell is going on, and why and how are you here?"

Lee waited, but rather than bite his head off—Magda always did have a soft spot for Adriano—she breathed in, folded her Prada-gloved hands across her lap, and started.

"Two days ago, I got a call," she said, not ready to be interrupted until she was quite done. "For some time, the Italian authorities and the US Department of Homeland Security have been tracking reports of connections between radical terrorists and the Roman Catholic Church. Without going into too much detail, last year, it was believed that the linchpin to how terrorists were getting their assignments lay within the Vatican itself."

"Gorgeous George. Cardinal Maltoni," Lee interjected.

"Yes," Magda answered curtly. "I was getting there. The Italian authorities, working closely with Homeland Security, Interpol, the State Department, various friendly governments—"

Wow, Lee thought, that phrase, "friendly governments," hides a multitude of sins.

"—and others," Magda continued, with a glare to Lee, as if she could read his mind. "All have been working quite tightly and quite in secret to prove the connection to the Holy See."

"But they didn't yet have direct knowledge of Cardinal Maltoni?" Again, it was Adriano who dove into the breech.

"Exactly," Magda answered, with a wisp of a smile. "Until last year."

339

"Deacon Andrea somehow figured it out." This time, it was Lee who spoke. Fools rush in.

"Again, exactly right," Magda said, but not unkindly. "And, we know what happened to Deacon Andrea."

"Maltoni killed him, or had him killed."

"For that, you'll need to ask your friend, Don Bello," Magda said with an inscrutable pursing of her perfectly tinted jungle-red lips.

"So..." Lee took a deep breath, a careful inhale calculated to guard against his painful ribs and a claw swipe from Magda in equal measure. "You're a spy."

For the first time in memory, Magda let out a peel of laughter, no, a snort, something between a fornicating pig and a mucus-clearing tissue attack. It was as ugly and amusing a juxtaposition to Magda's carefully coiffed elegance and beauty as could possibly be imagined. After a few seconds, she composed herself, dabbed her nose on a Hermes jingle and said, "I work for the Mayor of the City and County of San Francisco."

Adriano's mouth opened. Lee's followed.

"Close your mouths," Magda said, rewrapping her scarf. "And never ask me that question again."

They both nodded.

At painful risk, Lee ventured on. "You said you got a call. From whom?"

Just then, the door swung open and Dr. Luke walked in.

"How are my patients this morning? Ah, good morning, M—"

"Good morning, son," Magda said. She stood up and offered her cheek to Luke.

"Luke, I am your mother" flashed through Lee's brain like an upside down film track. Magda as Darth Vader and Luke clinging to the Cloud City railing like a *Star Wars* fan parody. Adriano giggled.

"Yes," Magda said with the most genuine smile either Lee or Adriano had ever seen. "Luke is my son. Luca, you've done quite well for yourself. I'll be flying home through Cologne to see Papa before he heads off to visit some old friend from the war. Shall I deliver your greetings?"

"Well, thank you, Mother." He kissed her lightly on the cheek and was then once again all German efficiency. "That would be lovely."

Lee looked on in rapt, if baffled, attention at the reality show playing out in front of them. Luke fumbled with his stethoscope and then bent to check first Lee's and then Adriano's vitals while Magda continued.

"Two days ago, Luca called me. He said that somehow you two had stumbled into the whole scenario and he was worried. He thought maybe I could be of help should things get dicey. So, I called Paulo, that handsome Italian ambassador—you remember, Lee, from the Consular Corps reception a few years ago in San Francisco."

Lee just nodded.

"I told him I needed some help. So, he sent a plane and here I am."

"Wow," Adriano said, mouth once again agape. "Just wow."

"It pays to have connections," Magda said without irony. "And family. Of course." She pinned Lee with a withering stare he knew well. "Little did I know you'd start playing detective and stumble into all of this when I recommended Orvieto for your sabbatical. Most people on vacation mind their own business. Events of the past year aside, normally, Orvieto is quite a quiet town."

"Well," Luke said with an awkward cough as he repocketed his stethoscope. "You're both coming along nicely. I'd like to keep you here for at least another night, but then I see no reason why you both can't go back home to your apartment. Mother." Luke bowed quite formally, as did Magda.

"Luca."

"I'll be back later. I have several other patients to attend to."

"Dawud's sister!" Adriano suddenly spoke up. "How is she? How is the baby?"

"Maryam?" Luca's demeanor transformed, for a second looking more like a proud father than a physician. "I'm delighted to say mother and daughter are doing fine. It was touch and go there for a bit, and I had to deliver the baby by Cesarean, but they are both in good health and resting comfortably. Thank God that procedure was complete before Grigori and his unit burst in here with you two and his body count."

"Grigori saved our lives," Adriano stated simply.

"Yes," Luca said with a grudging twitch of his lip. "Grigori has many talents, and admittedly he was quite helpful here in the emergency room.

His Swiss Guard emergency training was extremely useful, and appreciated, since I had no nurse and, obviously, we couldn't call for assistance to the hospital outside of town. As I think my mother has made obvious, the last few days have required an unusual discretion. This tiny facility hasn't been this busy, I am quite sure, since the fighting when Orvieto was liberated and the war—"

"Luca! Well!" Magda snapped, interrupting her son. "Enough of all this. They need rest, not a World War Two history lesson." She turned back to the couple. "Lee, Adriano, now you know. And, of course, all of this must never leave Orvieto. What you have found out, and anything you might find out," she added cryptically, "must stay here, upon this Rock."

"State secrets and a smattering of out-and-out untruths," Lee said, having read on his iPhone the AKI wire reports about Maltoni's death and the cover story of Arnaud's injuries. Being online was a disconcerting experience indeed, since he was able to peruse the news, but the ability to post, write an email, or otherwise send outgoing communications had been quite blocked. Ditto for Adriano. They had been discussing this very "Great Fire Wall of Orvieto" when Magda had come in bearing gifts.

"Public relations," said Magda, "not lies. Lee, I thought by now you'd understand the difference, and the important distinction therein. Luca, I'll see you later for dinner, then I have to fly."

With a final buss and a gentle hug, mother and son parted. Magda resumed her seated post.

"Magda," said Adriano. "What happens now? Certainly, Bishop Arnaud will be arrested for his part in all of this. And, you really don't think that Maltoni's crimes and death can be kept secret, do you?"

With that, the hospital door opened again and an elderly figure dressed all in white stepped in. Outside, several young- and fierce-looking military guards, including Grigori, could be seen standing at rigid attention. The old man walked in slowly and deliberately. Magda immediately dropped to her knees.

"Your Holiness!"

CHAPTER LX

Befana

Monday, January 6, 2014, sunset, Orvieto

As he mounted his broomstick, the truth was clear. Don Bello made for a singularly ugly woman.

"Befana! Befana!"

A hundred feet below the tower of *Sant'Andrea*, scores of children and their families crammed into the Piazza della Repubblica and screamed in fanatical anticipation. Soon candy, like manna, would rain from the skies. From his perch next to Don Bello, Adriano could just make out Lee, standing stiffly bandaged, flanked by La Donna Volsini and Marco in the crowd scanning upward. Even from this distance, Adriano could translate the trio's faces: I've got a bad feeling about this, he thought.

"Befana! Befana!"

"Are you sure you're up for this?" Adriano asked, helping the old man up onto the medieval ramparts.

"Of course, dear boy," Don Bello said, smiling and touching up his rouge. "I am La Vecciarella, the Good Witch Epifania. I've been performing this particular Christmas miracle for decades, now give me a push."

With that, Don Bello stepped into the air, and flew.

～

Later, having exited the Italian fire brigade's extendable cherry picker that had provided his miraculous flight, makeup removed, broomstick stowed for another annum, and returned to clericals, Don Bello was again in his usual drag: Pastor of *San Giovanale*.

"That was fun." He chuckled.

Lee removed an errant eyelash from his face.

Don Bello chuckled. "I look forward to it every year."

"So, explain the tradition to me," Lee said, always one for a new historical anecdote.

"According to legend," said Don Bello. "when the Magi, the Three Kings, saw the star in the East and were headed to find Baby Jesus, they stopped along the road one night for food and shelter. An old woman took them in."

"The Befana," said Lee.

"Yes," said Don Bello. "That night, the Three Kings regaled their hostess with the prophecy of Jesus and the reason for their journey. They encouraged her to join them on their quest, but she declined. She was too busy, she had to finish her sweeping."

"Hence the broom," Adriano said.

"Exactly. Later, when the story of Jesus was revealed to the world, she regretted her choice deeply, and went in search of the young Messiah, but never found him. So, for the rest of her life, and into eternity, she devoted herself to giving candy and presents to children on Epiphany, January sixth, today, the day the Magi found Our Lord."

"And, in Spain," said Adriano, "the tradition is similar. It isn't Santa Claus who brings gifts. It is Los Tres Reyes, the Three Kings, Gaspar, Melchior, and Balthasar, and not on Christmas Eve. That's the day Jesus was born. Spanish children get their gifts today, the day that the Magi arrived at the manger with gold, frankincense, and myrrh."

"Hmm," Lee said with a teasing grin. "Not a bad Bible story from an apostate."

"I'ya remember the first-a time I saw Befana fly when I was-a leetle, I was-a so excited," said Marco, hugging tight La Donna Volsini as they made their way slowly through the sea of people in front of *Sant'Andrea*, all heading to *San Giovanale* for the final event of the Christmas season, the living Nativity and the arrival of the Three Wise Men. "You remember, Nonna?"

"I remember everything." The old woman pouted. "I am eternal."

Everyone laughed, including La Donna Volsini, but Lee noticed for the first time how old she looked, how old she truly was. In the twelve days since the secret drama of St. Patrick's Well, she had visited Adriano and Lee every day, first in the hospital and later at home—although how she managed the sixty steps to their apartment was still a mystery to him—and always bearing food and good cheer. Today, however, she moved like the nonagenarian that she was. Today, Velzna Volsini looked every bit her age and then some.

"You're tired and need a rest." Don Bello wagged a finger at his friend. "It's been a difficult week."

"A difficult year," Adriano interjected.

"Si, molto." Marco nodded in agreement, giving Adriano a squeeze on his arm. "Especially for mi nonna."

"Well, tomorrow, the holidays will officially be over, and we can all take a well-deserved rest. Especially you, dear Velzna."

"I'm not dead yet," La Donna Volsini said, brushing away the suddenly enfolding arms and protestations pressing in around her. "I've got more energy than all of you put together, and I still have plenty of work to do. And let me a-tell you, it's a good-a thing I did no see that *man*." She punctuated this last with a mortar-like spit bomb to the pavement.

"The Pope, you mean," Adriano said.

"Benedict, yes." La Donna Volsini pulled herself up. "Him. Pope Emeritus. Papa Horrificus he should be called. It is because of him that Andrea is not with us today. It is because of him that Andrea jumped from the rock."

No one said anything for a few minutes. Finally, Lee interjected. "Yes, he said as much when he came to visit."

"Go on, my son," Don Bello said gently. "What did he say. We've all been waiting to hear."

Lee looked to Adriano as if seeking permission. Adriano merely nodded.

"He apologized," Lee said simply.

"And he cried," Adriano said. And then, as if surprising himself, he added, "I felt sorry for him, actually. He was so pathetic. A broken man."

"I'd like to break him," La Donna Volsini interjected. "Che disgrazia. The only papa who ever did anything good for-a Orvieto was the last pope to visit here, Clemente Settimo, Guilio de Medici, at least he left us—"

"Now, now, carissima," said Don Bello, uncharacteristically interrupting his old friend. "Don't upset yourself, and besides, even you don't remember the Medici."

"I remember enough," said the old woman, glaring at Don Bello. "Certo, you are a' right. There was another pope who visited Orvieto after Clemente. Papa Paolo il Sesto."

"That's right," Don Bello nodded, touching a finger to his lips. "He flew here by helicopter in 1964 from *Castel Gandolfo* for the seven hundredth anniversary of the Miracle of Bolsena. Landed right next to the Duomo. I think it was the first time the Holy Father ever flew."

"And he didn't have a broom," Adriano said, as they all laughed.

"What did he *say!*" It was Marco who brought the conversation back to the obvious. "Pope Benedict. What did he say to you?"

Lee took a deep breath and continued. "First, he sent Magda and Luke out of the room. Then, he sat down between our beds, reached out both of his hands, to hold one of ours in each, and he confessed to being responsible for Andrea's death."

La Donna's lips quivered slightly, but she uttered no sound.

"Yes." Adriano picked up the thread. "He said that Archbishop Arnaud had come to him with rumors about Andrea and Grigori having an affair. There had already been a lot of gay gossip and scandal last year around the Vatican, and for Benedict, this was too much. He ordered Cardinal Maltoni to send a fax to Bishop Sancarlo here in Orvieto, relieving Andrea of his upcoming ordination. He knew nothing about Maltoni's involvement in the terrorist ring."

"And," Lee jumped in, "as you know, Maltoni had been kind of Benedict's right hand in the Curia. He trusted him implicitly."

"'I was blind, and did not see,' were his exact words," Adriano said. "He repeated it twice. Then, he said, 'Because of my blindness, I condemned a man to death. More horribly, because of my blindness, I committed a soul to eternal damnation."'

"That's what seemed to bother him the most," Lee said, squeezing his husband's hand. "Andrea's death broke his heart. But knowing that he had pushed Andrea to suicide, a mortal sin, broke his life. It's the real reason he resigned from the papacy."

"Did he offer you his blessing?" Don Bello asked quietly.

"No," Adriano said with a wry, sad smile. "Although, of course, Lee asked."

"He refused to bless us," Lee said. "He said he was not worthy. Instead, he asked us to bless, and forgive, him."

"Mamma mia," was all Marco could say. "Nonna, you're crying!"

And, indeed, she was.

For the first time since the end of the war in 1944 when she had helped a young Don Bello and a German colonel bury the bodies of the seven martyrs of the Camorena, including one very special to her indeed, La Donna Volsini cried. She wept all the way to *San Giovanale*.

CHAPTER LXI

Resurrection

Monday, January 6, 2014, sunset, Convento dei Cappuccini

His cell was cold. Outside, an evening fog wrapped around the tower in a misty vise.

He wasn't going anywhere. Hadn't gone anywhere, for over a year. He'd likely die here, alone with his thoughts. Better that way. He didn't want to see anyone, and he was sure there was no one interested in seeing him. Well, at least one person who didn't want to see him, or hear from him.

He had sanctioned enough perversity in her life, in their lives. His was a voluntary purgatory, but a living penance nonetheless. Only the living can know that death is not a punishment.

With nothing else to do, he prayed, playing out his sentence on the map of his mind:

(48) Per quelle che patiscono per causa della loro orecchie
For those who suffer for because of their ears
(56) Per quei padri e quelle madri che non educano i loro figli
For those fathers and mothers who did not educate their children
(13) Per quelle per le quali il Padre desidera che si preghi accio siano liberate da quelle pene
For those whom The Father wants freed of their pain
(43) Per quelle che frastornarono gli altri alla devozione
For those who bewildered others with devotion

Guilty as charged, my Lord God.

As he had done for a year, the priest looked out his window and stared toward the cliff.

Across the valley, he could see the flickering flames, the campfires and celebrations in the garden of *San Giovanale* for the Epiphany and Living Nativity.

The Magi were arriving: Gaspar, Melchior....

"Balthasar," the man said to himself. "I could not give her the one gift she truly wanted. Instead, I killed the gift I never should have brought."

It was time.

Slowly, but very deliberately, he arose from his cot and stepped outside of his cell. A young monk was passing by.

"Brother," he said. "I need you to drive me somewhere."

"Of course, Reverend Bishop. Where?"

"Orvieto."

CHAPTER LXII

The Holy Family

Wednesday, January 8, 2014, dusk, Orvieto, the Garden of San Giovanale

The mood at the manger was quite festive.

Several hundred people bundled up against the cold at Orvieto's western edge, darkness having driven away what little warmth had remained of the day, replaced now with campfires, torches, mulled wine, and bruschetta toasted over coals and slathered with olive oil. Plus, a plethora of local artists, artisans, and artfully costumed locals in Biblical dress. At the center, under Grigori's carefully hung electric star, was the manger main stage, with Joseph, Mary, and Baby Jesus.

"It's Maryam!" Adriano was the first to notice, pushing through the crowd and pointing. Lee followed behind, carefully maneuvering his bandaged torso. "She's playing, well, her namesake, Mary!"

"And, as usual, the newest baby in the parish playing the Son of God," said Don Bello with obvious pride. "I think our young Dr. Luke makes quite a good St. Joseph as well, don't you?"

In truth, it was a touching tableau, and one whose diversity seemed quite apropos given the revelations and ramifications of the last two weeks. Lee looked around at the jostling crowd, young, old, straight, gay, rich, poor, pagan, pure, princess, and prostitutes, the usual gathering for the end of the holidays, all, of course, encouraged by bread, circuses, and healthy doses of cheap red wine.

"He looks quite pleased with himself, and with his company," Adriano noted, seeing the broad smile on Luke's face and a visage whose focus was laser-like on Maryam. "He can't take his eyes off of the Virgin Mary."

"She is lovely, isn't she?" Don Bello giggled. "I think, indeed, perhaps our sad young doctor may yet find love and human companionship. He was in love with a lovely young girl from Orvieto. They got married. She got pregnant, but there were complications. She died in childbirth, the baby too. Luke blamed himself and was quite despondent. For weeks, Andrea didn't leave his side. Frankly, I think our Andrea kept him from doing harm to himself. He pulled him back from the brink. For someone with such a proud connection to Orvieto, our Luca has had quite a sad young life."

"What do you mean?" Perhaps now, Lee thought, we'll find out the whole story about Magda, et al. "What proud connection to Orvieto?"

"Luke and his mother are Orvieto royalty," Don Bello pronounced simply. "Magda's father was the German officer who saved Orvieto during the war. Quite simply, he's the reason we're here. Obviously, Magda was born quite a few years later, after her father returned to Germany. Where is Magda anyway?"

"She flew back to San Francisco a few days ago," said Adriano. "As usual, duty called."

"Well," said Don Bello, "she has always been something of a mystery, but nonetheless, no matter where she is, she will always be an Orvietani."

"How did Luke end up here?" Lee asked.

"Evidently Luke was the product of a brief and not terribly successful marriage between Magda and a young Italian diplomat," said Don Bello. "It was a short marriage, but a shorter divorce. *Annulment*, rather. Magda didn't leave anything to chance."

"Not a surprise," said Adriano sotto voce.

"As a baby, he went to live with his grandfather in Cologne, Germany."

"The German officer who spared Orvieto from bombing?" Lee interjected.

"Quite right."

"And you," said Adriano, with a sudden epiphany, "were the young priest who communicated with Magda's father, the German commandant, in Latin and coordinated Orvieto becoming an open city with the British officer."

"Reverend Vicky's father," Lee said, filling in the blanks.

"Nihil habeo quod defendam. Et loquens iustitiam adnuntians recta," said Don Bello with a slight bow. "You speak the truth. I have no defense."

"I got it," said Lee. "My seminary studies were worth something."

"It's quite obvious they were worth a good deal."

"Why didn't you tell us this before, or why didn't Magda?" asked Adriano. "Why all the mystery?"

"My dear boy," said the old priest with a painfully patient nod of his head. "Orvieto has not survived for three thousand years by easily giving up its secrets."

Adriano and Lee both crossed their arms and just stared.

"All right," Don Bello said with an annoyed frown. "Come into the church. I'll pour us a drink and answer all your questions. Well, most of your questions. Ye gods, after what you've been through, I guess you deserve a few more answers, but keep track of the time. I don't want to miss the entrance of the Three Kings."

~

"And then?" Lee turned from contemplating the eleventh-century frescoes in *San Giovanale* to face Don Bello. They were sitting around an ancient wooden table in the sacristy, sipping vin santo from spare chalices. Over the last forty-five minutes, Don Bello had laid it all out. The human sex trafficking network that was coordinated by Cardinal Maltoni. The cooperation with first Bishop Sancarlo and later Archbishop Arnaud in passing along coded prayer cards for the Church of *San Donato* at Civita di Bagnoregio. Deacon Andrea having realized the significance of the cards, and more to the point, the significance of the numbers on the prayer cards: coordinates for terrorist attacks—the ones with the Opus Dei symbol stamped on the back. And unmarked cards being the coordinates for where African girls and women were dropped off to be picked up as sex slaves for their Italian mafia masters. The final tightening of the noose on Christmas Eve by Grigori and his special forces and Maltoni's expertly obfuscated death—now, according to official Vatican new sources, an early morning car crash—and finally the capture of three would-be terrorists who had been in search of the final clue hidden in Maryam's blouse. The events at St. Patrick's Well? They never happened.

"And then, you showed up," said Don Bello. "We certainly didn't expect you two to become involved. Magda was *quite* upset when she found out somehow you two had gotten mixed up in our little undercover drama."

"I bet," said Adriano. "Magda is quite formidable when pissed off."

"Si," exhaled Don Bello. "Molto."

"Blame it on my love of crosswords," said Lee.

"Blame it on Lady Peg's big mouth," said Don Bello with a bite. "Malicious, gossip-spreading witch. Mea culpa." He crossed himself.

"I don't get it," said Adriano. "Why was she so hateful to Grigori, and so fawning towards Archbishop Arnaud?"

"Dear boy. For a sophisticated urbanite, you can be quite naïve. Lady Peg was, *is* in love with Arnaud."

"And Arnaud didn't reciprocate," said Adriano.

"Because he was celibate?" asked Lee.

Don Bello guffawed and errant holy wine dribbled down his chin. He mopped it up with his cassock. "Let us just say Arnaud did not return her affections. That is all I will say about that. My secrets alone are for me to reveal. Other's secrets...they are for others to reveal...or not."

"And what about Arnaud?" asked Lee, suddenly confronted with the memory of watching the Archbishop's left eye gored out in St. Patrick's Well by Maltoni's cigarette. "Why is he still here? Why isn't he in jail?"

"My dear boy," said Don Bello, "Archbishop Arnaud was how we captured Maltoni."

"I thought he was in league with Gorgeous George," said Adriano.

"Well, yes, and no," equivocated Don Bello. "When he worked at the Vatican, he was quite literally Cardinal Maltoni's right hand. Not only officially according to curatorial rank, but by virtue of their association."

"Opus Dei," Adriano stated.

"Cherto," said Don Bello. "To accept Opus Dei is to squeeze out all other Christian associations, and to my mind, there is nothing Christian about Opus Dei. Maltoni demanded obedience. When Andrea jumped, it was too much for poor Giovanni, Bishop Sancarlo. He retired to a monastery and Maltoni put Arnaud in his place. But, what Maltoni didn't know was that Arnaud was working with those of us here in Orvieto and the Italian special forces."

"Arnaud was a double agent?" Adriano gasped. "A spy?"

Don Bello chuckled. "Well, I wouldn't go that far. Let's just say, we convinced him to cooperate with us. It was actually quite dangerous and stressful for him."

"He was Snape from *Harry Potter*," said Adriano with a slight laugh and a snap of his fingers. "Too bad not to be good."

"Who is *we*?" Lee asked.

"Well, the Orvietani, of course," said Don Bello. "Me, La Donna Volsini, Luke, Marco, Grigori, and Reverend Vicky. Arnaud, Vicky, and Bishop Sancarlo, Gio, have been friends for years."

"How can three people so different stay friends?" Lee asked.

"Dear Lee," said Don Bello with a kind but nonetheless ruthlessly curled lip. "That is the stupidest question you have ever asked. People don't need to agree with each other to be friends, or sometimes even *like* each other. They just have to *love* each other and love God. They each had a vocation, and each had a different path to that vocation. Of course, Andrea's death caused quite a rift among that little trio. They met in Rome a number of years ago when they were each beginning their vocation, during an ecumenical conference. They even had a nickname for themselves."

"The Magi," said Lee with sudden clarity.

"Quite right," said Don Bello. "How did you know that?"

"The photo on Reverend Vicky's bureau in St. Paul's Outside the Walls in Rome," said Lee. "I saw it when we had dinner. It was inscribed 'Magi,' and a date—"

"Yes, I know the photo very well," interrupted Don Bello. "I took that photo. I was their spiritual guide, as you might say during the conference. Each of them brought unique gifts to the Church..."

"...hence the Magi," finished Lee.

"Exactly." Don Bello nodded, smiling at the memory. "Gio with his radical compassion, Arnaud with his unshakable faith in the institutional church, and Vicky with her irrepressible and intellectually superior curiosity."

"Vicky was the ringleader?"

"Interesting choice of words, Adriano," contemplated Don Bello. "Let's say she was the center of the wheel around which spun the Magi's spokes. She was subversive, in a sense, the most like Jesus of the three. She was the fearlessly doubtful...a modern-day feminist Martin Luther. She challenged Gio and Arnaud in ways that neither had ever been challenged."

"Some *women* see things as they are and say why. I dream things that never were and say why not," said Lee, repeating the placard paraphrasing Bobby Kennedy's eulogy from Reverend Vicky's salon.

"She wanted to be a priest," said Adriano with a snap of his fingers. "A Roman Catholic priest."

"...which, of course, is quite impossible," Don Bello interjected again, more aggressively than before. "More wine?"

"Is it?" It was Lee who asked the question, pinning Don Bello with a stare and then pulling out one of the prayer cards he had saved from Bagnoregio. He placed it gently in front of the old man.

(48) Per quelle che patiscono per causa della loro orecchie
For those who suffer because of their ears
(56) Per quei padri e quelle madri che non educano i loro figli
For those fathers and mothers who did not educate their children
(13) Per quelle per le quali il Padre desidera che si preghi accio siano
liberate da quelle pene
For those whom the Father wants freed of their pain
(43) Per quelle che frastornarono gli altri alla devozione
For those who bewildered others with devotion

Don Bello started to speak, mouth opening like a carp sucking for food at the top of a pond, but said nothing. He sighed, a defeated man, but one seemingly grateful for the defeat. "What do you want me to say?"

"These coordinates, 48.56 N; 13.43 E, are in the middle of the Danube River in Passau, the border between Germany and Austria. The site of the Danube Seven."

"The Danube Seven?" Adriano asked.

Don Bello just stared ahead, silently.

"The Danube Seven were seven Catholic women who wanted to be priests," Lee explained. "The Church strictly forbids the ordination of women anywhere in any country on earth. So, in 2002 the Danube Seven did it smack-dab in the middle of the Danube River, international waters, no-man's—or I guess Vicky would say, no-*women's*—land between two countries. Actually, over the years, since then, there have been others."

"OK, I'm a bad Catholic, but it takes a bishop to consecrate priests," Adriano slipped in. "And, the Vatican, at least unless I've missed something, hasn't agreed to the ordination of women, and certainly would excommunicate any rogue bishop who performed such a ceremony."

"Don Bello?" Lee prodded with a smile.

"Quite right." Don Bello spoke simply and without emotion. "Any bishop, duly consecrated and so ordained is in direct line of apostolic succession and thus considered valid by the Roman Catholic Church. And, any such bishop, should his identity become known, would be instantly removed from fellowship from the Church."

"But, to your point, as a duly consecrated bishop, his ordination of the women, spiritually and theologically speaking, would be valid, yes?" Lee continued. "The women, spiritually, would be priests. And Arnaud and Sancarlo were already bishops in 2002."

The pastor of *San Giovanale* said nothing.

"So, who was it," Adriano pushed. "Arnaud or Gio? Who ordained Vicky?" Then, answering his own question he said, "Wait. That's easy. Arnaud is Opus Dei. He'd *never* ordain a woman!"

Don Bello just sat in silence. Finally, quite quietly, but with a force hitherto unwitnessed by the couple, he spoke. "I have been a priest for over seventy years. In all that time, I have never once broken the seal of the confessional and I don't intend to start now. Having said that, there are some things that are best not known, or, rather, confirmed. Bishop Sancarlo, Bishop Arnaud, and Reverend Lewis are people of God, flawed, imperfect, humans, doing their best. I have too many sins on my own conscience to judge others for their choices. And, if I may be so bold, dear Adriano, I would not assume too much by one's titles or official pronouncements. In my experience, most evil is done in full view, and good, in private, even in secret." He poured them some more wine.

For a while, nothing more was said, then Lee ventured into territory whose map he had been quietly contemplating since they were in the hospital. "Magda said to ask you about Maltoni."

Don Bello sighed and leaned back in his chair. "I have lived a long life. Too long. But I now realize that my life has become my penance. All of this is my fault. Maltoni turned against God, the Church, against everything, because of me, because of the war."

"World War Two?" Adriano queried. "I don't understand."

"During the last year of the war, Orvieto was under German occupation," Don Bello explained.

"Yes, under Magda's father," said Lee.

"An *accidental* Nazi if you wish."

"A Nazi is a Nazi," hissed Adriano.

"I'm not defending him," Don Bello said grimly. "I am merely relating history."

"Go on," said Lee.

"Officially, of course, the government was Mussolini's fascist regime. The local fascist leader was Cardinal Maltoni's father, a man as troubled and conflicted as became his son. In the last few months of the war, things were going quite badly for the Germans, and, of course, for those Italians who still supported them."

"The fascists loyal to Mussolini," said Adriano.

Don Bello nodded. "Yes. The Allies had landed in Sicily and later Anzio as they moved up the Italian peninsula. The fighting was brutal, especially around Monte Cassino. Your friend, the gay bishop, Brian Swathmore, the one whose ashes you carry, he fought at Cassino, as I recall you telling me."

"Yes," Lee said. "He always said it was horrific."

"All war is horrific," said Don Bello gruffly. "There are no heroes in war. Only victims. Only those who die, those who survive, and those who wish they had died."

He took another sip of wine, quite a healthy one.

"Go on," Lee prodded gently.

"A few months before the liberation of Orvieto, the Allies were bombing the area nonstop, trying to knock out the military airport nearby, and even more importantly, the train line between Orvieto Scalo heading north. The bridge at Allerona was bombed repeatedly, but never quite destroyed until January twenty-eight, 1944."

"You remember the exact date?" It was Adriano who spoke.

"Dear boy," said Don Bello, smiling with wet and weary eyes. "I remember it every day at waking and every night before sleep. That, and other dates besides. Yes, that date is one that no one around Orvieto will ever forget. That morning, a trainload of Allied prisoners of war was stopped at the Orvieto train station. I went down to visit them. Offer Communion, a friendly word...doing the useless but expected machinations of a man of God." Don Bello uttered this last with more than a bit of bile. "Maltoni's father, ostensibly the official leader of Orvieto, ordered us to stop. He saw no reason to give 'aid and comfort to enemies of Il Duce and enemies of the Reich,' as he put it. He was trying very hard to impress the German high command."

"Magda's father?" Lee said.

"Yes. Exactly. The Bridge at Allerona would be bombed again that night, and Madga's father thought it would be inhuman to risk sending the train over until the danger had passed. The senior Maltoni was furious at having his authority impugned. So, later that afternoon, he went back to the station, and told the Italian conductor to go ahead, that plans had been changed."

"He lied," Adriano stately simply.

Don Bello just nodded. "More to the point, he ordered the train to stop on the bridge."

"As a human shield!" Lee said, suddenly understanding. "He thought if the Allies saw a train on the bridge that they would not bomb it."

"Or perhaps," Adriano said, "He wanted it to be bombed. If he was trying to show himself as the strongman, not being afraid to kill a trainload of prisoners just might do it."

"Yes, perhaps, I don't know," said Don Bello angrily. "Who knows what his true motivations were? But I do know this. Around dusk, the train left the station. It stopped on the bridge. It was bombed that night. More than six hundred people were killed, mainly Allied prisoners of war, but also a number of German soldiers escorting the train. It was horrible. I went to help bury the bodies...well, what was left of the bodies. Bones, uniforms, shoes...many things...washed up on the river bank for years. There's a memorial there now, under the bridge. The new bridge. The one that night was completely obliterated. Only part of the stone base remains."

"What did the Nazis do to Maltoni?" asked Lee.

"Nothing." Don Bello threw up his hands. "Nothing. Officially, he was the power in the town. Plus, the Germans had bigger problems on their hands. The Allies were quickly advancing up the peninsula."

"But why should any of this turn Maltoni's son into a terrorist?"

"Two months after the bombing at Allerona," Don Bello continued, "there was an ambush attack by a group of Italian partisans on a Nazi brigade in Rome. Thirty-three Germans were killed. Hitler was outraged and ordered a reprisal to take place immediately. In less than twenty-four hours, three hundred thirty-five civilians, Jews, and Roman passers-by were rounded up, herded into the Ardeatine caves on the outskirts of Rome, and killed, each one with a bullet to the back of the head. Each five new victims were forced to kneel over the five preceding bodies. March twenty-four, 1944. It's a date that every post-war Italian school child learns. The corpses were found a few months later. They're still entombed there. It's one of Italy's most sacred sites."

"Ten to one," Adriano gasped.

"Yes. Tit for tat times ten, plus five," Don Bello shook his head.

"Plus five?" Lee interjected.

"In the confusion and haste to round up enough 'guilty' people to meet Hitler's demands, five extras were arrested and taken to the caves. One of the Germans started to release them, but the Nazi in charge of keeping the list had them shot. Otherwise, they would go back into the city and reveal the massacre. He actually survived the war. Erich Priebke was his name. He escaped to Argentina and lived there for over fifty years until a television reporter, of all things, found him. He admitted to everything. Said he was 'just following orders.' He was deported to Rome, put on trial, convicted, and found guilty."

"And executed, I hope," said Adriano with force.

"No," Don Bello said, with a strange glint in this eye. "Found guilty, yes, but sentenced to life, what remained of it. He was even older than me." At this, Don Bello polished off his wine and held out the chalice for a refill. Lee complied. "He died this past October under house arrest in Rome, of natural causes. He was one hundred years old."

"I remember reading something about that," Lee said. "There was a controversy about where he was to be buried."

"Correct. Huge riots, pro- and anti-fascist, broke out. Unbelievable, that there are still 'pro' fascists," Don Bello said, slamming down his cup so hard that Lee and Adriano shrank back. "He wanted to be buried in Argentina, next to his wife. Argentina refused. The German town where he was born refused, afraid it would become a pilgrimage spot for neo-Nazis. The Vatican forbade any church in Rome from receiving his body. It was unprecedented, denying burial like that."

"So, what happened to him?"

"No one knows," said Don Bello, this time with a wry smile. "He was buried secretly. His final resting place is a mystery."

"Like Osama bin Laden's," said Lee. Adriano squeezed his hand.

"Very similar," said the priest. "Although even the Americans were careful to give bin Laden a Muslim service, albeit a brief one aboard ship before his body was sent into the ocean."

"But what about Maltoni's father?" It was Lee who guided them back to the subject at hand.

"Ah, yes. Maltoni. As I have described, the last few months of World War Two were unspeakable on every front in Italy. On earth. Here in

Orvieto, the Nazi hold on power was slipping. More to the point, the official fascist government led by Maltoni was becoming untenable. The people despised the Germans but knew one day that they would leave. The local fascist Italians who still supported Mussolini, like Maltoni, well, they were not trusted by their German overlords, nor by the local citizens. A few days after the Ardeatine massacre in Rome, seven local boys, local partisans, were captured by the local fascisti. They were put on trial, by Maltoni, and sentenced to death. The trial was in the same building where you've been staying. There's a plaque by the door. The German colonel, Magda's father, tried to intervene, but Maltoni insisted."

"Again, he needed to prove that he was as tough as a Nazi," Adriano interjected.

"Precisely," Don Bello agreed. "Also, these seven partisans, children, were mainly communist, anti-Catholic, and Maltoni was rabidly pro-Church. He saw Mussolini as the savior of the Christianity. All the usual insanity. 'Remember,' he could often be heard spouting around town, 'it was Benito Mussolini, Il Duce, who finally ended the imprisonment of the Pope in Vatican City. It was Il Duce who signed the Lateran Accords and restored the power of the Holy See.' So, he had the seven martyrs shot. One of them was La Donna Volsini's young beau."

"Dear God," said Lee, remembering the painting in Café Volsini.

"Dear God, indeed," said Don Bello. "The Almighty was not much in evidence during the last few months of Orvieto's occupation. Maltoni had the martyrs driven away in a truck, sitting on their own coffins, and shot them all, personally, in the little hamlet of Camorena, just down the road from here. A few months later, in June, Orvieto was liberated. And you know the rest."

"And what became of Maltoni's father?" Adriano asked.

"That is the reason his son hates me...hated me," Don Bello said. "It is the reason all of this has happened. The reason that Andrea is no longer with us. The reason that, for me, purgatory would be too kind a relief. I am destined for hell."

Adriano and Lee said nothing.

Finally, Don Bello composed himself and continued.

"After the war, Maltoni left. Where, I don't know, but he left. If he hadn't, the locals, Velzna Volsini and others, would have lynched him or thrown him from the rock. Then, ten years later, he returned, and took up residence in his old house, the house where the seven martyrs were sentenced to death. With a wife and a young son."

"The future Cardinal Maltoni," Lee said.

Don Bello just nodded. "They were shunned. No one would speak to him. His house had the windows broken. His wife and the boy were relentlessly assaulted. Finally, it became too much. One night, he drove to the bridge at Allerona with his son, took out a gun, and blew out his brains."

"Young Maltoni saw his father commit suicide, in front of him?"

Don Bello nodded again. "Afterwards, a young farmer found the boy and brought him back to Orvieto. His mother went mad with grief and threw herself from the cliffs near Porta Romana. Dead, of course. She's buried in the cemetery outside of town."

"Next to her husband, the fascist," said Lee.

"No," said Don Bello quite simply. "No. Some of the local townspeople dragged Maltoni's body back to town, demanding vengeance for the seven martyrs ten years before. When I tried to bless the body and give it a Christian burial, they revolted, especially La Donna Volsini. In the end, to my shame, I relented. I refused to bless him or give him a Christian burial. I don't know what happened to Cardinal Maltoni's father. The mob dragged away his body. I have no idea where they buried him, or not."

"What about his son?" Lee asked.

"Young Maltoni was sent to an orphanage. From there, he disappeared. Later, I found out he had become a mercenary and then, somehow, found his way into the arms of Mother Church, clearly a perversion of vows. Only from the inside could he destroy the edifice of Christ, or so he thought. He never forgave me for refusing to bury his father. He never forgave the Church. He never forgave Orvieto. I fear the death of thousands of people can be laid at my feet, including the loss of dear Andrea. Without my sins, Andrea would not have jumped."

"Don Bello," said Adriano. "As you know, I am no fan of the Church, but you are not responsible for the sins of Cardinal Maltoni..."

"...or for the death of my parents and grandmother on 9/11," said Lee, laying his hand on the old man's knee. "Cardinal Maltoni made his own decisions, for whatever twisted logic he could use to justify it. But now he is dead, and if there is hell, he is in it."

"No, my son," said Don Bello with silent tears running down his face, wrinkles now rivers of salt. "No, Cardinal Maltoni might this day be in heaven."

"Don Bello!" Adriano recoiled. "How can you say that?"

"Cardinal Maltoni didn't die instantly in St. Patrick's Well. He lived long enough to confess his sins at the hospital, and for me to absolve him."

"How could you," said Lee with a look of horror on his face. "How, how could—"

"How could I not!" roared Don Bello. "I ignored my vows once by not sanctifying the grave of Maltoni's father. I was not going to damn another soul because of my pride, my *weakness*. My job, the *Church's* job, is not to forgive. That is up to God. My job, my vocation, *my life*, is to bring people back to God."

"I don't know if I understand that," said Lee, too stunned for tears. "Even the Vatican refused to bury Erich Priebke, and yet you gave absolution to the man responsible for September eleventh?"

"For the attacks in Madrid," said Adriano, just looking away.

"I don't know if I can ever forgive the people who killed my family, so many families," said Lee. "I don't understand. I will never understand. I will *not* understand!"

"I know," said Don Bello, gently stroking Lee's head. "Unfortunately, nothing I can do, or anyone can do, can bring them back. Forgiveness is the heaviest burden of life in general, and the thorniest cross for a priest of the Church."

Lee pulled away from Don Bello's touch and turned on him fiercely. "Then it was good that I never became a priest. I could never forgive such evil." He could never forgive someone who had killed his parents. Who had killed his grandmother. Suddenly, he remembered how she used to wash in her huge kitchen sink in the country. No, if that was what was required of a priest, truly, he was not up to it. Who could be?

"I am sorry," was all Don Bello said. "I am so very, very sorry."

"I know you are," said Lee, looking deep into Don Bello's eyes and squeezing tight his hands. "I know. I know."

The three men sat, crying, and holding one another in their tears.

Suddenly, the door to the sacristy swung open and Marco strode in, complete with caftan, crown, and gold cup filled with myrrh.

"Welcome, my Lord Balthasar of Arabia," said Don Bello with waving hands of saalam, all of them grateful for Marco's tension-slicing entrance. Lee and Adriano pulled themselves up and joined the priest in faux enthusiasm. "I assume the trio is complete? Their majesties Gaspar of India and Melchior of Persia await outside on their steads, yes?"

"Si, Don Bello. Ciao, Adriano. Ciao, Lee," said Marco, kissing them all in turn. "But there are three other visitors here that want to see you. Three other wise *men*."

Marco stepped aside to reveal the Magi: Reverend Vicky, Archbishop Arnaud, eye patch in place, and someone who Adriano and Lee had never before met, someone who had not set foot in Orvieto for over a year. Lee looked deep into the kindly eyes of the man in front of him, and before Don Bello spoke his name, Lee knew who he was.

"Bishop Sancarlo. Welcome home."

CHAPTER LXIII

Upon This Rock

Wednesday, January 8, 2014, 12:00 noon, Rome

The last few days of their sojourn in Orvieto were surreal for Adriano and Lee. As if a terrorist cell coordinated out of the Vatican Press Office, being kidnapped by an unhinged cardinal, and breaking open a sex trafficking ring with clues hidden on a medieval purgatory prayer board, not to mention the revelation of barely scabbed fascist-era wounds, a Nazi war criminal, rogue bishops, and forbidden Catholic women priests ordained on water were not enough, what was truly strange about their ultimate week in Orvieto was how all of the preceding had suddenly receded into the background as if nothing had happened. La Donna Volsini provided Lee with a fresh cannoli and a folded crossword puzzle every day (although she did smile more). Marco would sneak Adriano cigarettes and Lee would pretend not to notice. The Tower of the Moor rang out the hours. The sun set over *San Giovanale* and rose over the Duomo. Clemente the cat ruled over all, although Lee thought he detected an even greater sense of feline superiority. The only subtle nod to the capture and death of the greatest mass murderer since WWII was at St. Patrick's Well, where a handwritten sign was hastily hung: "Chiuso per pulizia."

"Well, of course," Adriano had observed two nights ago as they were getting ready for a farewell dinner at the home of La Donna Volsini following the Living Nativity. "Everyone we know in Orvieto was in on the plot, and they ain't talking."

Their last evening in Orvieto had been quite jovial, in a strained sort of way. La Donna Volsini had cooked every Umbrian specialty in her repertoire, ably assisted by her grandson Marco. The youngest Orvietani, newborn Luca—"named for the man who saved our lives," according to his mother, Maryam—had pride of place in a bassinette in the corner, doted over by everyone, especially his namesake. It was pretty obvious that Maryam and her German savior were fast becoming an item. Hmmmm, Lee thought, would that make Magda a grandmother? He shuddered at the potential conversation: *I'm not going to die in that ditch.*

Don Bello sat quietly in the corner, stroking Clemente the cat and chatting with Dawud. Grigori and Clarissa Bernardone, Andrea's mother, seemed lost in thought, a melancholy pair, obviously with their thoughts on the absent Andrea. They left together, earlier than the rest, but not unusually so. Reverend Vicky, Bishop Sancarlo, and Arnaud were not in attendance, evidently having gone on a retreat somewhere north to contemplate the events of the last year and rekindle their friendship. The dinner was heavy on pasta but light on painful topics.

"Clearly Lady Peg has been kept in the dark," said Lee. "I'm quite sure she wasn't invited, and no one is granting interviews to her."

In point of fact, Lady Peg had made herself scarce since Three Kings Day. She had walked, no, rather *slalomed* into the garden at *San Giovanale* in an even-for-her over-the-top ensemble, including a hat decked with holly and reindeer motif. She looked like a sleigh ready for flight.

"She left pretty quick," Adriano had said and laughed. "As soon as she saw the reunited Holy Trinity—or should I say, the Magi—of Vicar Vicky, Bishop Sancarlo, and her beloved Archbishop Arnaud standing at the manger, she knew the gig was up. All of her bitchy and pithy blog posts would certainly come back to haunt her."

"Don Bello told me she had decamped to Sicily for a bit," said Lee. "She had seen Arnaud's eye patch and wanted the full 411 and to write about his convalescence. I gather that Don Bello finally told her what he really felt, and she hightailed it to the slopes of Etna."

The morning after the dinner, they awoke early, leaving their bags just inside the door for pickup later. Marco would drive them to the train station. As they exited, they were met outside by an escort.

"Clemente," Lee crooned, reaching down to pick up the cat in a hug. The furry-eyebrowed feline gave a look making clear such intentions were unwelcome. However, he did tag along.

"OK," said Lee. "There's one last thing to do."

"Actually, two things," Adriano reminded, and off they went, including Clemente.

First, they walked to the British War Cemetery, a pristine quadrangle of perfectly manicured grass with 188 gravestones from the delayed battle of Orvieto manipulated by the fathers of Magda and Reverend Vicky.

"Truly, life is stranger than fiction," Adriano said.

"If he hadn't been wounded at Monte Cassino, Brian might have ended up here," Lee said.

"In a way, he did," said Adriano. "He did."

Afterward, their final stop in Orvieto was obvious. The grave of Andrea Bernadone. It took them a while to find it, but, as usual, Clemente did the honors.

"There's something strange about that cat," said Lee, as Clemente lay down at the foot of a marble wall of shining funerary drawers. It was on the third and top tier:

Diacono Andrea Bernadone
30 Novembre 1983–30 Novembre 2012
Figlio di Dio
Amato da Orvieto

"Child of God," said Lee, no translation needed.

"Beloved of Orvieto," Adriano added.

A vase of fresh flowers stood on the small ledge in front of the crypt, next to a long-burning votive candle. On the face of the tomb, a photo of Andrea's smiling face. It was a well- and oft-tended grave.

"It's the picture we found in Bagnoregio," said Adriano.

"Yes," said Lee. "He looks happy. In that photo, I think he was."

Now, having said their goodbyes, and tearful ones at that, Adriano and Lee found themselves in Rome for two all-expenses-paid nights at the Exedra, a ridiculously lavish hotel not far—but otherwise quite a world away—from the Hotel Byron.

"Oh, shoot," Lee teased. "Poor Cedric will be *devaste* not to see you again."

"I kinda like that you're jealous," Adriano said, pinching his husband's butt as they sat sipping midmorning martinis on the Exedra's pricey piazza, all courtesy of the Italian Ambassador's Office.

"Which means, of course," said Lee, polishing off his drink, "courtesy of Magda."

"Are there strings in any country she can't pull?"

"Probably not," And they raised their glasses to Magda.

"We're just down the street from St. Paul's Outside the Walls," said Adriano. "Should we stop in and say goodbye to Vicky?"

"She's not there, remember? Evidently, she, Bishop Sancarlo, and Arnaud are on some sort of spiritual getaway," said Lee, popping an olive into his mouth. "Poor one-eyed Arnaud. It's a miracle he didn't die in St. Patrick's Well."

"Maltoni's body beneath him helped break the fall. Of course, he's quite blind in one eye."

Lee shuddered at the memory of Maltoni's cigarette piercing Arnaud's face and the threat, unrealized, that Adriano would be next.

"Actually," Adriano continued, "he probably wasn't looking forward to a meal cooked by La Donna Volsini. Likely afraid that she was going to poison him again."

"Not poison," Lee corrected. "Remember, Marco told us all about it. She just wanted to pay him back a little for all the hurt he had caused in years past."

"Even if for the last year, secretly, he had been on their covert team."

"Exactly," nodded Lee. "Don Bello may have absolved Cardinal Maltoni of his crimes, but La Donna...."

"A Volsini never forgets."

"Hmmm," Lee muttered to himself, as his lips started to twitch, a sure sign of his brain at work. To his mind, everything had been wrapped up just a bit too tightly for comfort. And, there was the one final question he wanted to ask. However, now, there was no one around to receive the query.

"Scusa, Signori." An impeccably dressed and persistently perky Italian steward presented himself at their table, a gold-embossed envelope on a silver tray at the ready. "This has just been hand-delivered for you. I am to wait for a reply."

Adriano reached for the envelope, took one glance, then whistled. "I think you should open this," he said, passing it to his husband.

The gilt-embossed stationary was impossible to mistake, the Latin inscription unique to one person on earth.

"Miserando atque eligendo," Lee read, translating from the Latin. "Choose mercy." Carefully opening the document, Lee silently read, then turned to the messenger. "We accept." Then to a nonplussed Adriano he said, "Upon this rock."

~

The Swiss Guard standing at languid parade rest at St. Anne's Gate wasn't quite up to the pulchritudinous standards set by Grigori, but not by much.

"Damn," Lee whispered as they waited for admittance to the normally off-limits sections of the Vatican crypt. As a parting gift, Magda had arranged for a private tour of St. Peter's Tomb, something most decidedly *not* on the regular tourist rota. "Where do they recruit these guys?"

"Swiss gyms," Adriano smirked, eyeing the pouty Teutonic hunk stationed at the most prestigious of Vatican City's private entrances. "They all look like they should be shooting a Bel Ami video."

"Knowing Grigori, it's entirely possible," Lee said, wondering what had become of their studly rescuer. Don Bello had said something about maneuvers with a special private security firm that recruited former Switzers and members of the Italian armed forces, but had been rather vague—intentionally, Lee thought—about his specific whereabouts.

"Bitte! Folge mi!" A member of the Pope's elite guard, equally hard-bodied and purposefully petulant, presented himself, saluted his posted comrade, and motioned for Adriano and Lee to follow.

Even Lee had understood that command.

Then, switching into heavily accented English. "From here on, there is no talking, and no photos. *Verstanden?*"

"*Jawohl,*" Adriano answered for them both with a naughty grin. "We understand."

It *was* a Bel Ami movie, Lee thought, giggling inwardly. This was the intro before the good stuff. A few minutes later, and after more than a few marbled turns and stony descents, they stopped before a simple but impregnable steel door. Their Swiss German escort knocked firmly on the metal portal, six sharp evenly spaced raps on the frame and three staccato taps on the door itself.

With a slight hiss of escaping air and the squeak of long-closed hinges, the gate to the Vatican underworld swung open, pushed by a white cas-socked arm. The guard snapped to attention.

"Welcome, my children," the old man said in smiling, albeit halting, English before switching to his native Spanish. "Hola, mis hijos. Bien-venido al Vaticano."

To Lee's disbelief, Adriano beat him to a ring-kissing genuflection.

"Pope Francis!"

~

Jorge Mario Bergoglio, now the 266th Bishop of Rome (give or take a few) led Adriano and Lee deep into the bowels of the Vatican necropolis. They were quite alone, the Swiss Guard having saluted rigidly and left them at the door. For about ten minutes, they walked in silence. I mean, please, Lee thought, how does one make small talk with the Pontifus Maximus in the St. Peter's basement?

"Thank you for coming," Pope Francis finally said, grinning, looking over his shoulder. He led them deeper into the crypt, with every step the path growing skinnier and the ceiling growing shorter. "I understand that I have much to thank you for." He giggled slightly.

"I, ah, we..." Lee started to answer.

Pope Francis stopped and turned to the couple, coquettishly putting his fingers to his lips. "Shhhh. Now is not the time to talk. God gave you two ears and one mouth, so he meant for you to listen twice as much as he meant for you to talk, sí?" He turned to Adriano and smiled. "Es un placer conocerte, ambos. Y, muy agradable hablar en mi lengua materna. Estos italianos, ¿qué puedo decir, bárbaros, no?"

Adriano laughed out loud, his voice echoing off the thousand-year-old stones. "Sí, sí, Santo Padre, sí."

"What did he say," Lee whispered as the Supreme Head of the Roman Catholic Church turned back to continue his guided tour.

"He said it was nice to meet us and to speak his native tongue, Spanish, and that the Italians are barbarians."

"Is-a true," the Pope said over his shoulder in heavily accented English. "Contrary to popular belief, I am not infallible, but I do have very good hearing for an old man. Ah, here we are."

The strange trinity had reached their destination, a blank stone wall with a small window.

"Take a look," said the Pope with a smile. "Here. Here is what you have saved. Not many people get this close."

Adriano and Lee squeezed past, unable to avoid touching in such tight quarters the world's last true absolute monarch, and peered in.

"Super hanc petram ædificabo Ecclesiam meam," said Lee in a whisper.

"Et portae inferi non praevalebunt adversus eam," Pope Francisco answered back, also in Latin, and then translated immediately, "Upon this rock I shall build my church."

"And the gates of hell shall not prevail against it," replied Lee.

"The bones of Peter," gasped Adriano.

"Si, claro," said the Pope, once more slipping into Spanish. "Well, as close as we can ascertain. Of course, nothing is certain. But teams of archaeologists have assured us of the probability. The age of the bones is correct. The legendary placement under the high altar of St. Peter's, although, that's several basilicas ago. It all matches. Personally, I believe it, but it's not important what I believe. What's important is what it represents."

"The Church," said Adriano, without irony.

"No, mi hijo." The Pope wagged his finger at Adriano. "Not the Church. The *idea* on which the Church was founded. *Love.* Love and the continuity of love. The bones," the Pope shrugged, "I find them interesting in an academic sort of way. But the message of the bones, and the one who gave authority to these bones, that is the reason for my life, my vocation."

"These were the final coordinates sewn into Maryam's blouse," Lee said with sudden illumination. "Maltoni was going to plant a bomb at the heart of St. Peter's. Here, next to the bones of Peter."

"Sí, that is what I've been told," said the Pope with a sad sigh. "And, evidently his connections had secured, how do you say, a dirty bomb. Very strong, but also full of radioactive waste, taken from the illegal dumps in Southern Italy managed by the mafia."

"He wanted to bring down St. Peter's Basillica," said Lee.

"He wanted to do much more than that," added Adriano, again without any edge. He turned to Pope Francis. "He wanted to bring down the *Church.* He wanted to start a holy war. Imagine the outcry if the Vatican had been destroyed and Rome rendered radioactive by terrorists with ties, no matter how peripheral, to the Muslim world."

"Yes." Pope Francis shrugged in sad resignation. "Had that happened, I could only pray that I, too, would be dead under the rubble. The Sack of Rome would have been but a Renaissance footnote to such horrors. It is enough that I must live with the shame of a young deacon throwing himself from the cliffs of Orvieto because the Pope, albeit a different one," he added with a sly smile, "deemed him unworthy. It is more than enough that a cardinal of the Church, no matter how perverted, has been responsible for the death of thousands. It is too much for any man, but I am not any man, I am pope. And so, I must live with the lies forced upon me"

Lee looked directly into the eyes of Pope Francis. The Vicar of Christ. God's representative on earth and, once upon a time, the man to whom he would have sworn eternal fidelity. But, now, Lee saw just a man. A man overcome by the acts of other men—and by his own.

"The lies you choose to tell," Lee said not breaking his gaze.

"Yes, if you like." The Pope nodded wearily, and he looked to Adriano.

"So then, the truth about Maltoni will never be known," said Adriano with a sad shake of his head.

"No," said the Pope with pursed lips. "No. The secret stays here. Upon this rock. My new head of the Vatican Press Office, better than most, understands the need for this story to be buried as surely as are these bones."

"Archbishop Arnaud," said Lee in revelation.

"Sí, certo," said the Pope, switching briefly to Italian. "Who better? In Arnaud's mind, he has many sins for which to repent. Handling public relations for the creaking edifice of a medieval monarchy will not be the easiest client in the world. It is a fitting penance. Take a final look. It's not good to spend too much time down here in the land of the dead. Our place is outside, in the air, with the living. There are too many people focused on the dead."

A few minutes later they were once more at the steel door leading to St. Peter's Square. Again, silence gripped the trio. There were so many questions to ask. So many things to say, but neither Adriano nor Lee could find the words. Finally, opening his mouth for a request, Lee was cut off by the Pope.

"My sons. It is said that there are only two prayers to offer to God. 'Please' and 'thank you.' So now with little more that I can do, I offer them both in your honor." And with that Pope Francis laid his hands on their heads. "Divine Mystery of the Cosmos, thank you for the life and love of these two men and please protect them and their love. May it flourish and feed others with their curiosity, their kindness, and their talents. What God has brought together, let no one pull asunder."

Adriano and Lee looked at each other, mouths agape, and then at the Pope.

"Who am I to judge?" Pope Francis smiled, turned, and walked back into the crypt.

CHAPTER LXIV

Ashes to Ashes

Friday, January 10, 2014, 11:11a.m., Cliffs of Moher, Ireland

Adriano and Lee stood on the cliffs and prayed.

Lee reached in his pocket, gripping the rolled-up paper tightly against the stiff breeze blowing in from the Irish Sea, and began to read.

In Memory of Bishop Brian Swathmore, December 23, 1937–January 10, 2013.

"The most I can do for my friend is simply to be his friend."

Those were the words of Henry David Thoreau, written in the front of a journal that Brian gifted me with before I went to work at sea, after he pulled me back from the cliff, after he saved my life, after he prevented my suicide.

Brian was courageous. Complex. Compassionate, but often capricious and sometimes honest to the point of near brutality. The five scariest words in the English language were Brian saying "Dear, we need to talk." He loved giving sermons: from the pulpit and also from his living room couch. But above all, Brian was generous, loving, and loyal.

His wit was sharp, often self-deprecating, and sometimes completely inappropriate. When a mutual friend was cremated a few years back, Brian whispered to me in the midst of the crematorium, "Be careful when they shove me into the fire. You'll be advised to stand far back." Indeed, Brian loved his martinis, Cheetos, and crosswords. "My indulgences," he called them. He was horrible at charades but repeatedly brought down the house with his memorable interpretation of Stephen Sondheim's "I'm Still Here" from Follies. His stories were delicious, his cooking not so much, although he did master an exquisite coq au vin and his British trifle—well, it was nothing with which to trifle. He loved disco dancing, cruising aboard ship, and lighthouses. But, most of all, he loved his family and friends. He loved me. He loved Adriano. He loved us."

Adriano squeezed his husband's hand and wiped away a tear.

Brian, Bishop Swathmore, was out as a gay man long before it was wise or safe to do so. He brought that integrity into his church, and all are better for it. Brian lost a generation of friends to AIDS and cared for the generation that survives. Because of Brian, thousands of people each year visit the AIDS Interfaith Chapel at San Francisco's Grace Cathedral. The chapel was his idea, and I helped him paint its walls. Three times he walked the Camino de Santiago, the legendary pilgrimage in Spain, and twice biked from San Francisco to Los Angeles as part of the AIDS/LifeCycle. He blessed Adriano and me from his hospice bed before we did the same ride in his honor. I'm convinced it is the reason we didn't have one flat tire in the entire 545 miles.

Brian greatly admired Somerset Maugham's The Razor's Edge, especially the film into which it was made. It chronicles the life of a WW I veteran who returns, shattered, by what he has seen in the trenches and devotes the rest of his life to seeking a higher truth. Brian, too, spent his time in the trenches, fighting AIDS discrimination, homophobia, and injustice. There's a quote near the beginning of the film that, I believe, honors Brian as well.

"The man I am writing about is not famous. It may be that he never will be. It may be that when his life at last comes to an end he will leave no more trace of his sojourn on earth than a stone thrown into a river leaves on the surface of the water. But it may be that the way of life that he has chosen for himself and the peculiar strength and sweetness of his character may have an ever-growing influence over his fellow men so that, long after his death perhaps, it may be realized that there lived in this age a very remarkable creature."

With that, Adriano opened the small box containing the mortal remains of Bishop Brian Swathmore. Without their having to reach in, Lee and Adriano watched as the Irish winds pulled the ashes heavenward, scattering them over the waves below.

~

Afterward, the couple walked along the cliff holding hands. A few people gawked. Another gay couple smiled. Adriano and Lee didn't notice any of it. They just walked. Like a miracle, or a special event planned by Magda, the skies over Moher, notoriously prone to fog and frigid rains, had cleared during their private remembrance for Brian. But now, Ireland's more classic weather returned with a fury, obliterating the sun and sending hordes of tourists scurrying for cover toward the cave-like Cliffs of Moher information center and museum.

"Over here!" Lee said, pulling his sodden sweatshirt hoodie over his head and motioning toward a small stone structure at the entrance to the cliffs. "This is closer."

The pair ran down a short gravel path, horizontal sleet as escort, trying to avoid slipping in their dash for the rough-hewn stone building with a sign over the entrance that read "Meditation Room." Behind them in the soaking mist, two other people were also running for the same shelter.

Lee turned the handle and walked in.

The building was small, and semicircular but quite cozy and relaxing, clearly its architectural intent, like a glorified confessional or artisan-constructed doctor's examination room. There was just enough room for maybe four people, although two was more appropriate. A photomural of native grass curved along the wall to the right of the door, punctuated by a polished wood bench that extended the length of the interior. Above the seat a quote was inscribed, peeking out from among the foliage:

"I have found life an enjoyable, enchanting, active, and sometime terrifying experience, and I've enjoyed it completely. A lament in one ear, maybe, but always a song in the other."—Seán O'Casey

At the end of the room a simple fountain filled with smooth pebbles provided the only sound, a gentle, seducing melody designed to soothe. On the wall opposite, there was a circular sign featuring black and white letters on a background of mossy green:

Worried? Lonely? Under Stress? Suicidal?
Samaritans are here.
24-hour helpline
1 850 60 90 90
www.samaritans.ie
jo@samaritans.org
Confidential emotional support.

Behind them, the door pushed open again, letting in a frigid blast from the coast. Adriano and Lee turned to greet their fellow refugees.

"Grigori!" Adriano exclaimed, as the Swiss Guard entered, clearly startled, and made an attempt to flee, an attempt blocked by his companion.

Grigori's friend pulled down his rain-soaked hood and stepped fully into the room. Lee recognized him immediately.

"Deacon Andrea."

The dead man smiled.

CHAPTER LXV

Absolution

Friday, January 10, 2014, 2:00 p.m., Liscannor Village, Ireland

It was a rowdy crowd at the Pope's Own Pub.

"What *is* that they're watching?" Lee had to yell to be heard above the constant din of screams at the television screen, where a squadron of humpy young men were chasing each other down a muddy field.

"I think it's soccer or Gaellic football," said Adriano, likewise raising his voice to be heard as equal parts groan and cheer arose from the packed crowed squeezed into the tiny bar. Evidently, someone scored.

A bell behind the bar rang out as the red-faced barman yelled.

"Drinks on the house for Mayo, but not for ye Dublin scum!"

More groans and cheers erupted, followed by the occasional flung handful of peanuts and matchboxes toward the bartender. He dodged all projectiles with a laugh as everyone returned to the game.

With Grigori in the lead, followed by the resurrected Andrea, the quartet pushed through the bar toward a blessedly open area Lee could just spy over Grigori's substantial shoulders near the back of the pub. From what he could see on the television, Lee thought the Swiss Guard would have been quite at home on the field. As they forced their way through the scrum, Lee couldn't help but notice Andrea's limp while he walked, a kind of right-foot-forward, left-foot-shuffling-behind sort of maneuver.

Suddenly, like Charlton Heston parting the drainage ditch on a Hollywood backlot, they popped out of the melee into a small semi-private room, somewhat shielded from the competitive dissonance in front by a curtain and half wall crowded with sports trophies. Five people were squeezed into a large, leatherette booth, two elderly men that Adriano and Lee did not recognize and three middle-age clerics that they did.

"So, you have found us. Life is, indeed, stranger than fiction. Or the Bible," said Reverend Vicky Lewis, standing up in greeting. Her smile was genuine if somewhat wan. Next to her, Archbishop Arnaud and Bishop Gio Sancarlo nodded in guilty politeness. "I'd like you to meet my father, and an old friend of his."

The two former enemies—Vicky's father, the British officer who had postponed the battle of Orvieto at the end of WWII, and Magda's father, and Luca's grandfather, the German colonel who conspired with Don Bello to save *Il Duomo*—tipped their respective hats with broad smiles.

"How do you do?"

"Eine freude, sie zu treffen."

"I need a drink," Grigori grunted truculently. He waved his right hand in the universal symbol for "another round," and getting affirmative nods from the quintet, turned to secure alcoholic sustenance.

"I'll help," said Andrea with a perky grin. Except for the two old men, he seemed the only person perfectly comfortable, even happy, about this strange, surreal reunion, arranged via text and cell phone call from the Cliffs of Moher meditation room.

"No, it's crowded," said Grigori protectively. "Your leg!"

Andrea gave him a look, the sort that both Adriano and Lee instantly recognized as the "Don't patronize me, dear" glance of couplehood. Grigori just shrugged in surrender and put his hand on Andrea's shoulder as they navigated back into the packed saloon. A few seconds later, they were swallowed in an Irish sea of revelers.

Vicky smiled. "Please, sit down."

It was Archbishop Arnaud then who spoke. "Nothing we're about to say is ever to leave this room, understood?"

It was Adriano who answered back. "Your *Eminence*," he snarled with a smile. "We'll be the ones to decide that, unless you'd like to fake another auto accident for us as well."

"Now, now," said Bishop Sancarlo. "Please, none of that. No threats, and no secrets! There have been far too many of those. Arnaud, you may be the new head of the Vatican Press Office, but you're not on duty here." Then, turning to Adriano and Lee, he said, "When Grigori called us from the Cliffs, we decided it was time for a full confession..."

"...but only to *you* two," said Arnaud with so much force that his eye patch slipped. Lee caught a glimpse of the red and scarred flesh beneath before Arnaud pushed it back into place.

"Jean Claude," Vicky interjected, "we *agreed*. All of us."

"Yes," said Gio. "And, we have no choice. It's what Andrea wants, and whatever he wants is the only thing *now* that matters."

"Excuse me," said Vicky's father, pulling himself up by his cane. "We have heard this story before and it is a bit much for those of us raised in more genteel times. It was a pleasure to meet you. Wagner?" he said, motioning at Magda's father. "Let's let the young people talk." With that, the two remarkably spry nonagenarians stood up, tipped their hats again, and walked farther back into the building toward a private office whose doorway was bedecked with Irish, English, Italian, and German flags.

"Auf wiedersehen," said the retired Wermacht colonel. "I am glad you got to visit my beloved Orvieto and my grandson, Luca. It has been a long time since I have seen it, but I think, maybe Victor and I will go back soon, one more time. I'd like to see it again, before I die."

"Your daughter has been incredibly good to us," said Lee.

"Magda? Yes." The old man shrugged. "She is a good, if mysterious, girl. So many secrets. So many secrets. Goodbye."

With that, the elderly pair retreated.

"This is your father's bar," said Adriano, remembering their conversation at St. Paul's in Rome.

"Yes," answered Vicky. "It is. After last year, it seemed the perfect place for Andrea."

"And Magda's father?" Lee queried.

"He likes Irish whiskey."

"Enough chitchat," huffed Arnaud, clearly the least enthusiastic member of the gathering. "Let's get it over with. I don't like talking about it, and I certainly don't want to rehash all of this in front of Andrea and *him*."

"His name is Grigori," said Vicky with some pique. "You may have never wanted to know it before, but you cannot escape it now and you certainly had chances to learn it before."

"Tell us what happened," said Adriano. "Everything."

The trinity of collars exchanged looks, at a loss how to begin.

"If I may," said Lee, looking at Vicky's pectoral cross with complete clarity. "I think I have a hypothesis."

"Go ahead," growled Arnaud. "It's easier to confirm and deny than speak."

Gio and Vicky motioned to Lee to continue.

"You are Andrea's mother, and you, Bishop Sancarlo are his father."

Adriano gasped.

"Yes," said Vicky. "That is the truth."

"And you," Lee said, turning to a visibly consternated Arnaud, "were the bishop who secretly ordained Vicky as a Catholic priest as part of the Danube Seven."

Arnaud simply nodded.

"How did you know?" It was Bishop Sancarlo who asked the question.

"The photo in Vicky's dining room at St. Paul's Rectory in Rome," said Lee. "The date, 1.3.83. For the longest time I thought it said January third, 1983.'"

"Of course." Adriano snapped his fingers. "Not in Europe. I can't believe I didn't see that myself. In Europe, the first number is the day, not the *month*."

"I searched online for religious conferences in Rome for January 1983 but couldn't find anything," said Lee.

"But you did find one for March." Vicky smiled, first at Lee, and then at both Arnaud and Sancarlo. "Remember?"

The two men merely looked down. Arnaud shook slightly. Sancarlo's eyes were moist.

"I did the math," Lee continued. "Nine months from March first, 1983, was the day Andrea was born. Me too, actually."

"Andrea has always been punctual, even in birth," sighed Vicky. "Yes, a few months after the conference, I realized that I was pregnant. I *wanted* the baby, but I knew that it would spell the end of Gio's career. So, I called an old friend for help. La Donna Volsini. She took me to Civita Bagnoregio, then even more abandoned than it is now. It was the perfect place to wait out my pregnancy."

"And you gave the baby to Clarissa Bernadone to raise as her own."

"Yes," said Vicky. "Actually, that was the idea of Velzna Volsini and Don Bello. Clarissa's husband had been killed by the mafia. She was almost mad with grief. She and her husband never had a chance to have a child of their own."

"So, she adopted Andrea," said Adriano.

"There was no 'adoption.'" Vicky shrugged. "The less paperwork the better. I gave birth and left Bagnoregio. Andrea stayed and Clarissa raised him there."

"I didn't know," said Sancarlo, looking up, his cheeks now coursing with silent tears. "I didn't know until that day in Orvieto when Andrea got the letter from the Vatican putting a halt to his ordination. All that time, I knew Andrea, trained him as a priest, and didn't know that he was my own son."

"And that..." said Archbishop Arnaud, looking up with an almost preternatural calm. Lee thought, it's the voice of a man speaking his last confession before the noose descends around his neck, the voice of complete, unmagnified truth. Arnaud continued, "...was among the worst of my sins. I am the one who found out that Andrea was the child of my two beloveds, Vicky and Gio."

"The blood test," said Adriano. "The blood drive on All Souls Day that Andrea arranged for the migrants. Luke was the doctor. He figured it out."

"Yes," confessed Arnaud. "He told me. But the fault is not Luca's. The sin is mine. The sin of obsession and anger and jealousy. Luke confessed to me a few years ago after the death of his wife, and his unborn child, a death for which he unfairly blamed himself. He was looking for order in his life... direction."

"And you and Opus Dei provided it," finished Adriano.

Arnaud simply shrugged. "Luca came to me with what he had discovered, never knowing that I was friends, family," he said, reaching out with both hands to squeeze those of Vicky and Gio. "After so many years, and so many risks—"

"—secretly ordaining Reverend Vicky and the Danube Seven," interjected Lee.

"Yes," said Arnaud. "I loved Vicky, and I-I..." Arnaud broke down and could not continue.

"And you loved me, Jean Claude." Gio finished for him. "My dear, troubled, conflicted friend. It was a triple seduction." Gio turned to Adriano and Lee. "At that conference in Rome we were full of love. Love for God, and love for each other. We didn't know how to express it and expressed it in ways that have brought us here."

"I was deeply attracted to both of you," Arnaud finally managed, "but knew I could have neither Vicky nor Gio, and clumsily tried with both."

"Jean Claude," said Vicky with patience, "our sleeping together was not your fault. It was no one's fault. We wanted to."

"Yes," said Bishop Sancarlo. "We acted as adults and we have paid the price."

"I knew that I could never give either, Gio nor Vicky, the love that my body wanted to offer them. So, I retreated. I gave Vicky, secretly, the one thing she most wanted."

"The Catholic priesthood," Lee offered.

Arnaud nodded. "Yes. Then, I realized that the Church would never forgive me, so I threw myself into the arms of Opus Dei, a penance of absolute servitude and nonquestioning obedience. When I found out that Andrea was their child, all the old jealousies and fears came back. I wanted to hurt them. Hurt them both."

"So, you managed to do the one thing that would cause the most pain to them both. Deny the priesthood to Andrea."

"Yes," said Arnaud. "I went to Pope Benedict with stories of a gay affair between Andrea..."

"...and Grigori," said Lee. "You set them up."

Arnaud nodded.

"But how did you know about their affair?" Adriano asked.

"From Grigori," said Lee. "You were one of Grigori's clients."

Adriano gasped again.

"Yes," said Arnaud in an even cadence. "I compounded my sins through lust and coercion. Grigori and I would meet in secret."

"At the Hotel Britannia," said Lee. "I saw you once sneaking out, the day we went to visit Vicky. Actually, I smelled you. The cinnamon cologne. Grigori always reeked of it."

"That was our meeting spot," Arnaud admitted. "But the day in question, we had stopped our carnal activities. We were meeting there to plan Andrea's escape."

"An escape that Grigori blackmailed you into helping with because he had photos of you and him together."

"Yes," said Arnaud. "All true. Before I knew about Andrea being the child of Gio and Vicky, Grigori and I would meet regularly. Over time, we actually became quite friendly. My, ah, *needs*, were quite simple to meet. Actually, I just liked looking at Grigori's naked body."

"Perfectly understandable," Adriano added quietly. "Sorry, continue."

"At some point, he told me that he had met someone and fallen in love."

"With Andrea," Lee said.

"Yes," said Arnaud. "He was quite conflicted. As you see, Grigori and I share the same desires."

"You're both bisexual," Adriano summed up.

"Yes," said Arnaud. "When I found out about Andrea's parentage, I made up a story about him and Grigori. That, too, was a lie."

"What do you mean?" said Adriano. "You just said that Grigori confessed to you about his affair with Andrea."

"His *love* for Andrea," Arnaud corrected. "There was no affair. Andrea was faithful to his vows. Coming vows. He and Grigori never touched each other, although Grigori certainly wanted to. I remember Grigori once told me, the last time we were together actually, that Andrea was the only person ever to love him just for him, and not for his body. Before Andrea, that was all anyone saw of interest in Grigori. His form."

Lee started to add, "perfectly understandable," but thought the better of it. This wasn't the time for witticisms. Indeed, it was a time for wisdom, world-weary wisdom from the wounded Arnaud. He almost felt sorry for him. Actually, he did. If anyone would live with an eternal penance from all this, it would be the Archbishop.

"I couldn't have Vicky. I couldn't have Gio. I couldn't have Grigori, not really, so I decided to hurt them all through the one person they all loved. Andrea. Then, to make sure everyone knew, I gave an interview to Lady Peg. I knew she had unholy thoughts about me, and I used her too. I used her to spread malice about Andrea and Grigori."

"That's fucked up," said Adriano. "Excuse me, sorry."

"You are correct," said Arnaud, flashing a smile.

It was the first genuine smile Lee had ever seen cross his face.

Arnaud went on. "It was... It *is,* indeed 'fucked up,' as am I."

"Was," Gio said. "Was. You have confessed all and been absolved."

"What a crock of *shit*!" This time Adriano offered no apology. "I'm sorry, there is no forgiveness for such a thing. Christ. Is everyone in the Church this screwed up?"

"A great many of us, yes," said Sancarlo sadly. "A great many of us, indeed."

"Does Andrea know?" Adriano asked.

"Yes," said Vicky. "That is why he jumped."

"Jumped? I thought that must have been faked too," said Adriano.

"No, that was my sin." Everyone looked up to see Andrea standing next to the table, a pint in each hand.

"You've never sinned a day in your life," said Grigori, putting down a tray with five glasses, and taking the two that Andrea was holding and placing them on the table. "Every one of us, Arnaud, Bishop Sancarlo, Vicky, me included, has reason to suffer, to be punished. Everyone except you."

"No, my darling Grigori," said Andrea, again, with that beatific smile. "I have to thank you all, for without you, I would not have found my life's purpose, my true calling."

"What happened that night, Andrea?" said Lee. "Tell us."

Andrea began. "I remember, I had just come back from visiting my mother in Bagnoregio."

"Clarissa," said Adriano.

"My *mother*," Andrea added with emphasis, but not unkindly. Vicky stared straight ahead. "As usual, I went to the purgatory board in the Church of *San Donato*. I'd gone there my entire life and the cards were like old friends to me. But, over the last year, I had noticed more and more strange combinations of prayers. I even mentioned it to Grigori."

"He became a wee bit obsessed with it," Grigori added, but not unkindly.

"I understand that," said Adriano with a glance at Lee.

"Also, at strange hours I would notice strangers coming to the church to pray, and always at the purgatory board," said Andrea. "I never questioned them—what business was it of mine?—although they didn't appear to be Catholic, or knowledgeable about how to pray in church. Every few weeks, men would come and walk right to the purgatory board. Also, about this time, Bishop Sancarlo was passing along pray petitions from the Vatican. That was a strange request, but again, I thought nothing of it."

"I didn't know why Maltoni was sending the petitions," said Sancarlo. "But I thought it might have something to do with his childhood."

"You knew about Maltoni's connection to Orvieto?" Adriano asked.

"Yes," Sancarlo said. "One day, he told him about the death of his father, and how it tortured him. He said that the pray cards were for him. Prayers to release his father from purgatory."

"He lied," said Vicky. "He lied and made you an unwitting accomplice in setting up terrorist attacks and brothels for migrants. You are *not* to blame!"

"May I continue?" asked Andrea.

Again, Lee thought, with a directness and certainty that in others might be mistaken for arrogance or anger, but in him, seemed merely *correct*.

"As I was saying, I would take the cards that Bishop Sancarlo would give me, and I was observing an ever-increasing number of men visiting the purgatory board. I thought it was odd but couldn't quite put my finger on it. It was like the crossword puzzles that La Donna Volsini would leave for me to do. A clue whose answer was right in front of me but just beyond reach."

I know the feeling, Lee thought. But he said nothing so as not to interrupt Andrea.

"That was November thirtieth, my birthday and my feast day. My mother was coming to Orvieto that night for Mass at *Sant'Andrea*. Reverend Vicky, Bishop Sancarlo, and I all were all going to be on the altar together. When I got back to Orvieto, there was a fax from the Vatican. I was to be denied the priesthood."

At this, Andrea stopped for a second, and took a sip of beer. Out in the bar, a howl arose. *Goal.*

"Go, Mayo," Andrea said raising his glass. Everyone else just sat, transfixed. "Becoming a priest was the most important thing in my life. It *was* my life. I was filled with love of God and knew that was the only way to express such love, through service to God as one of his priests. When I got the fax, I was crushed. I immediately ran over to the Bishop's residence. Sancarlo was outraged but said not to worry. He said he would take care of it. I tried not to worry, but I was overcome with fear and anxiety. I couldn't think straight. I walked around Orvieto in a daze. Finally, I had an idea. Perhaps, if I couldn't become a Catholic priest, perhaps I could become an Anglican priest. So, I went to see Reverend Vicky."

"You didn't know that she had secretly been ordained a Roman Catholic priest," said Adriano.

"No one knew," said Vicky, her voice squeaking in anguish. "No one except me and Jean Claude. When Andrea showed up at my door, it was already getting dark. He was in a state of spiritual anguish. I called the one person I thought might be able to help."

"She called me," said Archbishop Arnaud. "I was expecting the call. I was *relishing* the call. She asked me if there was anything that could be done, and I told her that I was the one who had convinced Pope Benedict to intervene and prohibit Andrea's ordination. Then, I told her why."

"He told me he had found out that Andrea was my son, and Gio's."

"I still didn't know," said Bishop Sancarlo. "Once Andrea left me after getting the fax, I did the only thing I knew how to do. I prayed."

"Not very effective this time, dear Gio," added Vicky with more than a touch of malice. "At any rate, I suddenly knew that everything would come out. It would be the end of my ministry as an Anglican, the end of Gio's career. And if I tried to turn the tables on Jean Claude, that, too, would backfire. All the other secret women priests would be destroyed. It was a double bind no matter how I approached it. Finally, I made my decision."

Everyone waited. It was Andrea who picked up the slack.

Lee shifted in his chair. *Once more in emotionless control.*

"We laid it before God. We said Mass." At this, he laughed slightly. "I have to admit, it was a very strange Mass. I was angry, confused, hurt, fearful. And, I could tell that both Vicky and Bishop Sancarlo were distracted as well. But I thought it was only because they were worried about what I had told them. After Mass, they told me."

"*Vicky* told *both* of us," Sancarlo interjected. "That was the first time I knew the truth..."

"...that Andrea was your son," said Lee.

"And that Arnaud was behind it," added Adriano.

"No." Grigori spoke up for the first time. "No. That was me." He squeezed Andrea's hand but couldn't bring himself to look in his eyes. "I, ah, I..."

"That's all right, Grigori. I'll tell them."

Lee blinked. Again, Andrea's smile cut through the miasma surrounding the table like a fog-piercing beam.

"After Mass, Vicky told both Bishop Sancarlo and me the truth. I was their son and that Archbishop Arnaud was using that information as a way to hurt them. I was devastated, and so I called Grigori in Rome and told him what I knew and that's when he confessed about his relationship with Arnaud."

"I just blurted it out," Grigori moaned. "I had given Arnaud the ammunition he needed to destroy Andrea." He couldn't help but glare at Arnaud as he said it.

"That was the last straw," said Andrea simply, like someone reciting a recipe. "I felt like Jesus betrayed by Judas. With a kiss. I went back to my apartment and put on my robes, the ones that my mother had made for my ordination the coming week. I don't remember much of anything else, until I was standing on the cliff at *San Giovanale*. I waited. I knew that Grigori would come. I had told him to meet me at *San Giovanale* so we could talk. It was a lie. I was so angry. I wanted him to see me jump."

"I borrowed a friend's motorcycle and rocketed up to Orvieto," said Grigori. "I made it in forty minutes. I drove right to the garden at *San Giovanale* and saw Andrea on the cliff. I screamed, 'Don't!' but he ignored me. He jumped."

Andrea took a deep breath, smiled again, and took a drink of his beer. For a while, no one said anything.

"But you didn't die," said Lee. "Why?"

"Like Floriano, I lived," said Andrea. "I *lived!* It all happened so quickly, and in an instant. Like the near-death experiences you hear about on TV. As soon as I was airborne, I understood everything. The meaning of the purgatory cards, the meaning of the numbers. Coordinates. The strange men coming into the church. Also, I understood why Arnaud and Vicky and Bishop Sancarlo and Grigori all had done what they had done. They did the *best they could* but they didn't do it to hurt me. I was filled for the first second of my jump with an incredible clarity, and then, with an incredible grief, for I realized that I had committed a mortal sin."

"Suicide," Lee said simply.

"No." Andrea took Lee's hands in his own. "Not the giving up of my own life. That is the secondary sin. I had given up on *God*. I had given up on *me*. I had abandoned hope. And, in that moment, I was filled with an incredible sadness and then in a second moment of incredible clarity. I saw my true calling."

"To be a priest," Adriano said.

"No." Andrea smiled. "I realized in that instant that I needed no ordination by a church or a bishop or a religion. *No one* needs that. I was ordained the moment that I found hope in that fall. My calling is now to help other people to not lose hope, to keep them from falling from or jumping from these cliffs. All cliffs. My great grandfather, Vicky's grandfather, jumped from the Cliffs of Moher in despair after the First World War. Maltoni's father killed himself with a gun beneath the bridge at Allerona. His mother threw herself from the walls of Orvieto. Luca almost did. I did jump, and somehow miraculously lived. My life now is devoted to keeping others from such despair."

"But *why* didn't you die?" asked Adriano. "What kept you alive?"

"My vestments," said Andrea with a chuckle. "The ordination gown my mother had made me. Evidently, halfway down the cliff, they caught on the branch of an olive tree growing out of the rock. It stopped my fall for a few seconds. Then, it ripped and I fell again, hitting the small roof over the *Chiesa de Crucefisso*."

"Yes," said Adriano. "We saw the broken tiles."

"And the broken tree branch," added Lee.

"Then, I fell to ground. I was pretty beaten up, and, as you can see, I have a limp that will be with me always. Grigori found me, got me to the hospital. Luke saved my life. I was unconscious for about ten hours."

"But the body," Adriano interjected. "The news reports mentioned a body on the Rupe."

"The morgue." Lee snapped his fingers. "You substituted the body of the vagrant mentioned in the newspaper."

Grigori nodded grimly, and Lee noticed a look of displeasure on Andrea's face. "Yes. Luke and I lugged the body through the back streets, dressed it one of Andrea's cassocks, and then threw it from the cliffs at *San Giovanale*. It was good enough to fool the carbiniere."

"And, of course," Adriano added, "Luke was the one doing any autopsy, so it was a fairly easy deception."

"Vile," Andrea said, shaking his head. "Vile. So many people have been disgraced and degraded because of my weakness. My vanity."

"That's why you buried him from the Duomo," Lee said, looking at Bishop Sancarlo. "It wasn't because of your love for Andrea. It was because Andrea insisted."

"Yes," Andrea said. "His mortal remains deserved the highest honor Orvieto could afford him."

"So, that is who is buried in your grave?"

Andrea started to speak, but just nodded in confirmation.

"What happened next?" Adriano kept them moving along.

"When I woke up, everyone was there." He motioned around the table. "Also, Don Bello, Marco, La Donna Volsini, and my mother. Everyone, except Archbishop Arnaud, of course."

"I was not yet part of the conspiracy," Arnaud added quietly.

"I told them what I had figured out about the coordinates from the purgatory board, and they conspired to save me."

"Save you? But you were already saved," said Adriano.

"No," said Grigori. "Saved from Maltoni. As soon as Andrea revealed what he had realized about the purgatory cards, I knew the key had to be Maltoni. Especially after Bishop Sancarlo told us about Maltoni's seeding the box with prayers, supposedly, for his father. We knew then that the only way to catch Maltoni, and prove our suspicions, was to lay a trap."

"So, I had to stay 'dead,'" said Andrea. "Grigori used his connections with the military to smuggle me out of Italy, and he convinced Archbishop Arnaud to convince the Vatican to replace Bishop Sancarlo."

"I was, and still am, filled with guilt about the sins that led me to betray Andrea and Vicky and Gio," said Arnaud. "Whatever years I have left will be devoted to doing penance."

"Of course, Your Eminence," Grigori added with an unctuous bow. "That's what did it. Not the folder of photos I had of us naked in your Vatican apartments."

"Yes, well." Arnaud lapsed into silence.

"Wow." Adriano shook his head. "Just *wow*."

"Andrea," Lee prodded. "What now? When do you go back to Orvieto? Maltoni is dead. The terrorist ring has been revealed. You can return now with your family."

"Return?" Andrea looked genuinely puzzled. "I can never return to Orvieto. If I did, this entire operation would be revealed. More to the point, my work, my life, is here now. When I jumped from that rock, I found freedom. Tonight, this dinner, is my goodbye to most all that I was, and *where* I was. In Orvieto, I am dead. My family here"—he motioned around the table—"and my mother in Bagnoregio, sometimes, they can come to visit me here but only in secret. But my vocation now is here."

"Alone?" said Adriano. "Why are you punishing yourself?"

"Not alone," said Andrea. "Grigori and I will live here together."

At that, the Swiss Guard leaned over for a kiss, one that indicated a clear end to celibacy.

"There is no sin in sexuality," said Reverend Vicky, wiping a tear from her eye. She handed a handkerchief to Arnaud and Sancarlo as well. "Sadly, our generation has learned that too late."

Sancarlo blew his nose while Arnaud dabbed beneath his eye patch.

"Andrea," Lee said, "I have one final question."

"Please."

"This entire, *escapade...*"

"...conspiracy," Grigori offered.

"Yes, OK, right," Lee said. "Things like this don't happen for free. Who paid for all of this? Where did you get the money?"

"Ah, well," said Andrea, for the first time squirming in caginess. "That is a question for La Donna Volsini. Grigori, would you like to field that one?"

"Let us just say that the Family Volsini have been benefactors of the Orvietani for many, many years."

"Many," Bishop Sancarlo added from the sidelines, with approving nods from Reverend Vicky and Archbishop Arnaud.

"Volsini philanthropy is restoring the frescoes in *San Giovanale*, providing help and homes to the many migrants and refugees coming to Italy's shore," Grigori enumerated on his fingers. "And yes, it helped fund Andrea's recovery, escape, and new life."

"But with what?" Adriano pushed. "That's a lot of biscotti to sell from the floor of Café Volsini?"

Andrea just smiled. "Dear friends. To find the source of Orvieto's riches, look not on the floor. Look beneath. Always, the treasure of Orvieto is not only upon that rock, but far below, and far older, even, than Velzna Volsini, although not older than her family or their creations."

Like a mechanical fortune teller at a county fair, the penny dropped into Lee's brain and his mouth popped open in a soundless epiphany. The mythical Etruscan statues of Metrodorus were no myth. They were a bank, La Banca di Volsini.

CHAPTER LXVI

Death of a Pope

September 25, 1534 (Julian Calendar), Rome

I *am dying.*
Clement opened his eyes for the last time and looked around his Vatican apartments. Oh well, he thought, at least I won't have time to screw up anything else.

It was a hot, sultry afternoon in Rome. The distant rumblings of a thunderstorm promised cool relief, and perhaps a little drama, somewhere to the north. Somewhere near—

Orvieto. He turned his head as another crack echoed through the stuffy room, closer this time. Not thunder—the Pope frowned—merely the muttering of cardinals praying in the incense-heavy air. Clement raised his right hand and thirty Princes of the Church fell to their knees crossing themselves. Christ, Clement thought, I'm not blessing you. I just want a drink. He gestured again, with effort. Soon, his hands would beckon no more. No more commands. No more genuflections. No more bulls.

"Yes, Holiness? What may I get you?"

Cardinal Farnese was at his side with remarkable speed for a man his age, over ten years senior to Clement, but not surprising as he was in the first row of clerics gathered at the papal deathbed. *Patience, Farnese. Patience.* He would be dead soon, and Farnese would pick up this cross. God knows, Clement thought, you've manipulated hard enough—and waited long enough—for it. If I liked you more, I'd give you advice. But, you wouldn't take it anyway. No one ever wanted advice from a Medici. Only money.

"Water? No wine? Please, Your Eminence, some wine...sweet, something sweet."

The Cardinal bowed and backed away, motioning for someone at the door. Out of the corner of his eye, Clement could see a form dashing into the passageway. *Don't hurry*, he thought. *I can wait for a drink. I'm in no hurry...well, I'm in no hurry, but death is.*

The heavens sounded again, closer this time, with a punctuation of light against the stained glass windows overlooking the construction site that was the Basilica of San Pietro. *Well, I guess I won't live to see that done. At the speed Michelangelo is taking, that's a few popes down the road. Ah, Michelangelo, my dear childhood friend. Buonarroti Simoni was a pain in the fresco but he was undisputedly a genius.*

Just three days ago, the artist had visited the dying pontiff for the last time. "Micky," Clement had said, using his private nickname. "I have one last commission for you. The wall above the altar in the Chapel Sistina. Finish it. God knows, you're the only one who could and should."

Michelangelo kissed the papal ring, tears in his eyes, and answered quickly. "Si, Santo Padre. Whatever you want."

"Resurrection," Clement had said forcefully. "Paint me a Resurrection. And don't let that fraud Farnese change anything. Don't look so shocked. Of course, he'll be the next pope. He's dying for me to die so he can swing the Keys of Peter like an immense sack of holy testicles. God, if his sister hadn't been the Borgia pope's lover, he'd have stayed what he truly is, a mediocre bookkeeper. Knowing him, he'll want something pedantic and hoary, like the last judgment. We have enough condemnation in this world, enough judgment. The resurrection is one of the only hopeful stories in that book of lies called the Bible. Make it so." And with that the Pope had been consumed with a fit of coughing.

"Yes, Giulio," Michelangelo had said, also using the Medici's youthful sobriquet after the coughing subsided. "It shall be done."

That had been three days ago, a triduum of waiting for the inevitable. More like three years, Clement thought with a sigh. Death has been stalking me since the Sack. Pity that wasn't the case. That would have made me a martyr. Instead, I'm slowly being consumed from the inside. I'm sure someone will say I've been poisoned after I die. Papal murders always make for a good story. But, no such luck. I'm just worn out and burning away from the swampish fevers of Rome.

The thunder sounded again—or perhaps it was episcopal praying. He couldn't tell. *Oy, why can't a pope just die in peace?*

Clement was not afraid of dying, but he was annoyed. So many things unfinished. So many things done and undone. Clement pursed his dry, thirsty lips. For a while, he thought things were going to be all right. He managed to get that poor orphan Caterina de Medici married to the son of the King of France. Holy Roman Rat Charles V wasn't happy about that, but, well, too bad. He had threatened to call a Church Council—undoubtedly one that would have removed Clement from Peter's Throne—but had retreated. Predictable. He knew which side his empire was buttered on. *Papal blessing, don't forget, papal blessing.* Hard to get rid of Christ's Vicar on Earth when he'd just declared you the descendant of Charlemagne. And, of course, now the Emperor had a new best friend, Alessandro di Medici, Duke of Florence. How strange, thought Clement, more perplexed than sad. *My son has become the tool of the man who destroyed his father. Oh well, God does have a sense of humor.*

The thunder rolled again, the lightning closer. The Palatine shuddered. The gods were angry, or more likely, beating a celebratory tattoo for the death of the man who had lost Rome, the man who had lost the Church. *A drumroll, please, for the death of the bastard, Giulio de Medici, Pope Clement Septimo.*

"Your Holiness, I am here."

The last true Medici looked up from his sweat-stained pillow and smiled.

"Gio! My son!"

The Pope reached up to hug the Swiss Guard who had become more son than his own. His arms fell back on the pillow, unable to make the short, embracing journey from shoulder to neck.

"I am here, Holy Father."

"Father," Clement managed to croak. The time was now close. "Only father, my son. Call me father."

A tear flowed from the young man's eye onto his quivering lips. Gio licked it quickly away and bit the inside of his cheek to keep his grief in check. My God, Clement thought, at least there is one person on earth who will miss me. One person on earth who loves me.

"Leave us," Clement motioned with difficulty at the cardinals lurking by the door. "I want to be alone with my Switzer."

"But, Holiness. What if you need something?" Farnese scrambled toward the Pontiff's side.

"*Roma locuta. Causa finita est!*" Clement roared, for a brief, final moment still the Pope, still Il Medici. "The only thing I need now is a peaceful death, and I won't have that with *you* around. Be gone from my presence. Don't worry, you won't have to wait long. I want to be alone with Gio. I want to be alone with my son."

The cardinals exchanged glances, but all bowed and retreated into the antechamber, executing their final orders from the progeny of Peter. When the door had closed, Gio sat down on the bed next to his friend.

"I love you," they both said simultaneously, and Gio lifted his friend's face a few inches off the pillow for a drink. "Here, a taste of something sweet. It's from Orvieto, the first vintage from our vineyard. I call it Dolce Clementine."

Clement sipped from the chalice with effort. "How nice, my last drink on earth is from the place on earth I love most. Orvieto."

"Orvieto."

The pair sat for a while not saying anything, their silence saying more than any words could convey. Suddenly, Clement stirred.

"Giovanni. The Statues of Metrodorus, they are safe?"

"Yes," Giovanni said. "They are safe and hidden. Sofia and her father and I have made certain of that. A cat couldn't find them."

"Don't be so sure." Clement grimaced. Even the muscles of his face were failing him. "Cats are the smartest of creatures. If Plato and the Egyptians are correct, and we return after death, I want to come back as a cat."

"Such heresy from Christ's representative on earth." Gio smiled with wet eyes, bending down to kiss Clement on the forehead. "Mother Church doesn't believe in reincarnation."

"Well, I don't believe in Mother Church. I only believe in the here and now. And love, and family. Those Etruscan statues are your future. Keep them safe. Promise me. Never have such treasures been seen by the world. I was a terrible pope, but we Medici do know art. Promise me—they are well hidden?"

"Yes, my dearest friend. What the Romans couldn't find will remain a mystery to everyone except my family—your family. If anyone searches for five hundred years, they will never find them, unless they are meant to."

"My family," Clement said, his last syllables now approaching. "Thank you for that."

"I brought you a gift," the Swiss Guard said, reaching into his pocket and unwrapping a tiny leather satchel. "The jeweler Cellini gave it to me. Here."

The Pope took a small medallion into his hands and looked at the exquisite craftsmanship in gold.

"*Ut populus bibat*," Clement read in Latin.

"Yes," Gio said, no longer trying to hide the tears that flowed down his face. "'So the people may drink.' It's a tribute to the work you did in Orvieto, the wells, the fountains, the aqueduct. You brought water...life... back to Orvieto. You were the resurrection of the Rock."

Clement turned the medal over in his hands, noting as he did so that there no longer was any feeling in them. Cold. Hot. Sharp or smooth. He could feel nothing of the medal in his grasp and could barely even see it. His gaze was cloudy now, but not from the miasma of candle smoke that hung around him. His senses were shutting down. He strained to make out the image: Moses striking the rock with his staff, from which water then gushed forth.

"Thank you," Clement said, squeezing Gio's hand. The Swiss Guard squeezed back, but Clement felt nothing. Death was crawling up his body like water devouring a sinking ship. He hadn't felt his feet in days. Soon, his spirit would exit through his head, and the cardinals would wield a silver hammer and tap his brow to make sure he was truly dead. Silly, Clement thought, but of course, I won't feel it.

A huge crack of thunder shook the Vatican, instantaneous with lighting and a cascade of raindrops so huge, they echoed off the tiles overhead like marbles. The storm had arrived. Soon, it would pass, but now, it was here, directly overhead.

"Open the windows," the Pope commanded. "I want to see the storm. I want to feel the breeze."

Gio did so, and immediately a mighty blast of wind blew in, extinguishing all the candles and throwing a mighty wave of horizontal rain upon the bed where Clement lay dying.

Heaven, Clement thought. A final baptism from the sky. The water felt good upon his face, like a kiss. *Simonetta!* Suddenly, he could see her. The beautiful woman who had been his only love. And cousin Gio, raunchy, heretical, homo-fabulous, and beloved, the man who became Pope Leo X. Then, Alessandro, a beautiful black babe in his mother's arms. Lorenzo Magnifico. Moses de Blanis. Egidio, his old friend, and Hassan de Wazzan, the wise child of Islam. Sofia, and her son, his namesake, Clement. The Pope saw him too, even though he had never seen the boy, now three years old, pulling at his mother's smock. How was that possible? But, he saw them. Clement saw them all, and more. He saw it all. His life. Their lives. *Life.* He *saw* it, and as his last breath worked its way up his torso through his throat and into his nostrils, he grasped, tightly, the hands of the best friend he had ever known. And, he felt it. If there was a God, he was granting him one last, blessed tactile communion on earth.

"Giovanni?"

"Yes, my father?"

"Give them my love, my son. Give all of them all of my love."

"Who, Giulio? Who?"

With his last breath, he answered, "Orvieto."

Epilogue

Wednesday, January 22, 2014, in-flight, Dublin to San Francisco

Lee looked over at his husband, comfortably encased in his Aer Lingus first class pod, the final arrangement per Magda's international connections. He wouldn't be surprised if the pilot was in her Rolodex...or little black book.

"Do you think we'll come back?"

"To Orvieto?"

Lee nodded.

"Who knows?" Adriano shrugged, eyeing the "Fasten Seat Belt" sign for its indication of freedom. He'd consumed too much good Irish whiskey at Dublin's swanky VIP lounge, and Lee knew that his bladder must be painfully itching for relief. "We certainly have friends there now."

"Well, co-conspirators at least."

Adriano grunted. "We'll *definitely* go back to Ireland. Grigori and Andrea made us promise."

"Yes," Lee said, remembering the last two weeks with the burgeoning young couple playing tour guides for them. An extended Irish double date. With Grigori at the wheel and Andrea as navigator, the foursome had circumnavigated the Emerald Isle from Cork in the South to the Giant's Causeway in the north.

"Remember, you'll always have a home here," Andrea had told them.

"Yes," said Grigori. "Think of us as your gay Irish welcome wagon."

"Your *secret* gay Irish welcome wagon, not in the closet, just incognito."

"They make a cute couple," Adriano said, catapulting up as the light overhead blipped out. "But not as cute as us. I'll be right back. My eyeballs are swimming."

Lee reached up for a kiss and got it as Adriano stepped over him. Certainly not as cute as you, Lee thought. *My husband has got quite a nice bum.*

Settling back in his seat, with San Francisco ten hours away, he'd have plenty of time to process the past two months. It hadn't exactly been the most relaxing of sabbaticals, but it certainly had been unique. He thought about their small apartment back in San Francisco. Two months of mail. The inevitable "How was Orvieto?" questioning and "Did you do anything interesting?" Lee almost laughed out loud. What would Brian have said?

"Be careful what you wish for."

Next trip, actually, clearly would be Spain. Since the first icebreaking message that Adriano had received in Orvieto from his parents, a steady stream of calls, texts, emails, and postcards had ensued. Whatever bridges had been burned over the years were quickly being rebuilt.

"We can't wait to meet Lee," Adriano's parents had cooed over the phone (Adriano translated).

"Yo tambien. Gracias," Lee had managed, reading from his iPhone-enabled Google Translate. *Christ, and I just learned how to find the bathroom in Italian.* Of course, besides familial bonds and tentative Iberian PFLAG intentions, Spain *did* have gay marriage. *We'll see how long, or if, the good old US of A ever catches up.*

"Look who I found!"

Lee glanced up as his husband returned, perky steward in tow with a tray of nibbles and a bottle of <u>Vieux Clicquot</u> on ice.

"Cedric!"

"Ta-da!" The flirty former Hotel Byron front desk man giggled with arms akimbo, putting down their treats. "Compliments of *me*. I'm in training! Now, I can travel for free to San Francisco! We can finally get together for that drink!"

"Great." Lee smiled despite himself, noticing Cedric looking at Adriano like a popsicle on an August day in Texas. "Thanks for the drinks."

"De nada." He curtsied as he offered newspapers and magazines. "Enjoy!"

As he sashayed off, Lee and Adriano looked at each other and laughed.

"Small world," Lee said.

"Small *gay* world," Adriano said, flipping open the *New York Times*. "I love you, Pooh."

"I love you too," Lee said, reaching over for another kiss. Hmmm....a champagne kiss. Tasty. It would be good to be home, home and *truly* alone. "What's new in all the news that's fit to print?"

"Not too much. Nothing to compete with breaking up an international terrorist and sex trafficking ring run from the Vatican, but there is this comedic bit of news."

"What?"

"Donald Trump says he may run for president in 2016."

Lee almost spewed forth expensive sparkling wine and reached for the paper. "A reality show president? I can't see that happening."

"Or Magda having to work with him."

"Well, stranger things have happened," Lee said, squeezing his husband's arm. "And they've happened to *us*."

"But if it does," Adriano said laughing. "We have somewhere to escape to."

"Spain?"

"Orvieto."

A Note from the Author

In 2014, I started writing *Upon this Rock*, an idea that came to me, literally, within hours of my first moments in Orvieto. Over the next five years, my husband Alfredo and I visited numerous times. I finished the book sitting at Orvieto's Capitano del Popolo two years ago this month. To us, Orvieto is very much home—no different than where we live in California or when we visit our family in Spain. Both Italy and Spain suffered much during the early days of COVID-19, as now have we all. The spirits of both those countries, and their people, run through this book. Having *Upon This Rock* published during this most difficult global year is something that demands an acknowledgment to both those countries, to all who have suffered and died, and also to those who are "keeping on keeping on," ready for whatever comes next.

—David Eugene Perry, 26 July 2020

About the Author

Photo by Alfredo Casuso

David Eugene Perry is the founder and CEO of the public relations firm David Perry & Associates, Inc. For ten years, he was the host/producer of *10 Percent TV*, which he created, and which was the longest running LGBTQ TV show in California history. He has written for such publications as *The Advocate*, the *San Francisco Examiner*, *Omni*, *The Desert Sun*, and *The Utne Reader*, and hosts the online interview show *Ahoy!* He and his husband, Alfredo Casuso, live in Palm Springs, and take frequent trips to San Francisco, and when possible, Orvieto and Spain.

Readers are invited to contact David in the following ways:
news@davidperry.com
www.facebook.com/UponThisRockOrvieto
twitter.com/UponBy
Instagram @uponthisrockorvieto

CPSIA information can be obtained
at www.ICGtesting.com
Printed in the USA
JSHW040846230820
7319JS00004BA/4

9 780941 936064